Blind to the Bones

A Cooper & Fry Mystery

STEPHEN BOOTH

WITNESS
IMPULSE

An Imprint of HarperCollinsPublishers

This book was originally published in 2003 by Collins Crime, an Imprint of HarperCollins Publishers Ltd.

EPub Edition JANUARY 2014 ISBN: 9780062301994

Print Edition ISBN: 9780062350459

10 9 8 7 6 5 4 3 2

For Tom Jefferson

I'm grateful to John and Von Morley, and members of Black Pig, for their help during the writing of this book. Although the Border Rats are fictional, the Border tradition exists in many parts of Britain.

Chapter One

_____

FRIDAY

AS SOON AS he opened the door, he could hear the screaming. It ripped through the damp air and shrieked in the yews. It echoed from the gravestones and died against the walls. It was like the sound of an animal, dying in pain. Yet this sound was human.

With every breath he took, Derek Alton seemed to draw the noise into his own lungs with the air, until something like an answering scream came from deep inside him. The asthmatic wheeze of his inflamed air passages was so high pitched that his ears couldn't locate its direction, but identified it as a noise that came from the air around him. The pain in his upper chest told him where that noise came from.

And Alton knew where the screaming came from, too.

With shaking fingers, he brushed some of the dust from his sleeve. The exertion had made his collar stick to the back of his neck, and a few strands of hair had fallen over his forehead, where they lay like barbed wire on his skin. He rubbed at a fresh scratch on his knuckles, but managed only to smear a streak of blood across the back of his hand. He could taste dust in his mouth, too – old dust, the debris of years, stirred into the air by a random act of violence.

The screaming reminded Alton of the shriek of agony he had once heard from a rat, when a terrier had flushed it from its nest in a barn and its back had been broken under a farmer's spade. The dying rat had squealed with its last strength, as its legs kicked and its pale claws clutched and uncoiled in the dry earth.

Now he waited, expecting to hear other noises. At first, there was only the stirring of the breeze in the yews and the drip of rainwater from the ivy on the church walls. But gradually he began to distinguish something else – a rhythmic thudding. It reverberated inside a room some distance away, well beyond the first houses on the road into Withens. It was like a ritual drumbeat, folding over on itself and creating multiple layers of sound. He shivered as he recognized the undertones of menace, which spoke of imminent death.

Then there was a burst of laughter somewhere in the village, followed by the slam of a door. A female voice shouted something that Alton couldn't make out. It was just one sentence, half a dozen words, and then the voice had gone. Further away, a ewe called to its lambs on the slopes of Withens Moor, where the hefted flocks still roamed their territories on the heather and peat bog. Alton had seen Withens Moor. He had seen Black Hill and Hey Moss, too. And he knew the moors themselves were dying.

Death had been on Derek Alton's mind all day. He had awoken with a jolt in the early hours of the morning, panicking that he might have disturbed Caroline with one of his bad dreams. But as soon as he opened his eyes and stared at the faint light on the bedroom curtains, he realized that his mind had been banging back and forth like a pendulum, swinging between the distant dualities of darkness and light, winter and spring, death and renewal. He might have been thinking of the end of winter and the first invasion of spring. But, mostly, he was sure he had been thinking of death.

Alton heard footsteps approaching through the aisle of the church. There were no carpets in St Asaph's, and his visitor was wearing heavy work boots that thumped on the stone flags.

He turned back towards the nave and squinted at the figure moving slowly out of the light to stand beside him. Once they were standing close together, the porch of the church seemed far too small.

Neil Granger was wearing a black leather jacket of the kind that Alton thought of as motorcyclist's gear, though he knew Neil didn't have a motorbike, only the old Volkswagen Beetle he used for getting to and from his job at the Lancashire Chemicals factory in Glossop. He looked very tired.

'You might as well go, Neil,' said Alton. 'You can't do any more here tonight.'

Neil had sweat running from his temples into the black smudges on his cheeks. He wiped a hand down the side of his face, spreading the smudges even more. But he looked at Alton with concern when he heard his wheezing.

'Are you sure you're all right?'

'I'm fine,' said Alton. 'I just needed some fresh air. And we ought not to do any more until the police have been to take a look.'

'Don't hold your breath, then. They might get here next Easter.'

'I know, I know. But all the same ...'

'You want to do things by the rules.'

Alton sighed. 'I wish there *were* still rules for this kind of thing.'

'You like rules, don't you? It goes with the job, I suppose.'

'Well, there *are* the Ten Commandments.' But Alton smiled to show that he knew it was a joke.

'In Withens?' said Neil.

'Yes, even in Withens.'

'I think you'll find they've broken all the tablets of stone.'

A few feet away, a blackbird scuttled into the under-growth over the horizontal gravestones that lay like fallen monoliths in front of the church. The blackbirds were always the last to go to their roosts in the dusk. They hopped jerkily across the graves in the half-light and rustled hopefully among the dead leaves, searching for insects and larvae. It was enough to make some people nervous of entering the church at this time of night. Even the blackbird had its duality. It was a creature of darkness, as much as of light.

Neil flapped the lapels of his jacket to fan his face. Alton could smell his sweat, and he felt a surge of affection and gratitude towards the young man for taking the trouble to stop by and help. Not many people would have done that. Not in Withens.

'I appreciate what you've done, Neil,' he said.

But instead of acknowledging Alton's thanks, Neil turned his face away, staring out into the churchyard.

'Vicar,' he said, 'I'm sorry.'

'What for?' said Alton, surprised.

Neil waved a hand vaguely towards the village. 'Well, all this. It's not what you expected, is it? Not what you deserve really, I suppose.'

'I don't know what you mean, Neil.'

Neil laughed, then coughed as the dust got into his throat. Alton caught the glitter of the rings in his ear and the sheen of his black hair. He wanted to put his hand round the young man's shoulder and tell him it was all right. Whatever Neil was apologizing for, it was perfectly all right. But he hesitated, worrying that the gesture might be misinterpreted, then cursing himself for being so cautious. He ought to be able to give forgiveness, if that was what Neil Granger needed. But by the time the reactions had run through his brain, the moment had passed, and it was too late.

In any case, Neil immediately seemed to have forgotten what he had been saying, and his mood changed again.

'Well, like I said, we'll tackle the churchyard this weekend.'

'Yes,' said Alton. 'We'll do that.'

'I was hoping Philip would help us, but he's being mardy about it.'

'Your brother is busy these days. I understand.'

'Some new business he's got involved in. I don't know what he's up to any more. But we'll get it sorted between the two of us, eh? Remember, Vicar – death and renewal, winter and spring –'

'The darkness and the light.'

'That's it. Time for a bit of light on the subject, I reckon.'

Neil turned to look at the vicar then, but Alton could barely see his eyes. They, too, were dark, and they were at the wrong angle to catch the light leaking into the porch from the nave. Alton couldn't tell what expression was on Neil's face. But a strange thought ran through his mind. If he had been able to read Neil's eyes at that moment, he might not have seen any expression at all – only a reflection of the gravestones outside in the churchyard.

'I've got to be up early in the morning, anyway,' said Neil.

Alton nodded. 'Do you remember, the year before last –?'

But Neil held up a hand before Alton could finish his question.

'I don't even want to think about it,' he said. 'Two years ago, Emma should have been there.'

'Of course. I'm sorry.'

'It's all right. I suppose it seems a long time ago now, for most people. I don't expect everybody to remember.'

'But I do remember,' said Alton. 'And there are her parents, of course.'

'Oh, her parents remember,' said Neil.

Because of the failing light, Alton could see little beyond the wall of the churchyard now, except the street-lights in Withens. He was sure it wasn't Caroline's voice he had heard in the village earlier. Perhaps it had been Fran Oxley, or even Lorraine, or one of the other members of the Oxley family.

But it definitely wasn't Caroline – she would never laugh like that, or shout so loudly in public. At this moment, Caroline would be walking past the Old Rectory, averting her eyes from the house and garden until she could turn into the crescent and reach their bungalow.

Somewhere in the darkness beyond the streetlights was Waterloo Terrace, where the Oxleys lived. Alton could picture the eight brick cottages, tightly packed like a row of soldiers, standing shoulder to shoulder against the larger stone buildings that clustered around them.

Derek Alton and Neil Granger stood in the church porch a few moments longer, listening to the noises from the village. The screaming faded, then grew louder again.

'Does that sound like a rat to you?' said Neil.

'Yes, it does.'

Neil nodded. 'OK, then.'

He rubbed at his face as he began to walk away down the flagged path. His clothes rustled like the sound of the blackbird in the dead leaves. Alton lifted his head for a second to look towards the village. And when he turned back, he found that Neil had already disappeared into the darkness beyond the yew trees.

Later, Derek Alton would have a lot to regret. He would be sorry that he hadn't watched Neil Granger leave, and hadn't observed the moment when the young man passed out of his sight. Perhaps he could have called Neil back and said something that might have changed his mind. But he hadn't. Alton had been too distracted by the noise coming from the village, and too absorbed in his own concerns. He would feel guilty for that, too.

But most of all, Derek Alton would regret not saying goodbye.

THERE WERE TEN more dead bodies to collect that night. Others had probably died underground, or had been trapped deep in the spaces between the stone arches and the hillside behind them. But Sandy Norton wasn't satisfied.

'We're going to have to put more poison down,' he said. 'The buggers are breeding like, well –'

'Rats?'

'Yeah.'

Norton shone his torch into the mouth of the middle portal. It was one of the nineteenth-century tunnels, the old westbound line, which wasn't used for anything these days. The railway track had long since been ripped up, and the tunnel abandoned. The arched walls glistened with water, and a small stream ran into a stone conduit near his feet. Just beyond the limit of his torch beam, there were shadowy, scurrying movements on the dirt floor.

'It makes you wonder what they find to eat,' said his mate, Jeff Cade, as he took off his rubber gloves and put them away in a pocket of his overalls. 'I mean, aren't they supposed to live near people? You're never more than six feet away from a rat, and all that? But there are no houses around here any more.'

Norton laughed. 'That's no problem. Look up there, where the old station and platforms used to be. You see that car park and the picnic area, right? Well, that's like a drive-in McDonald's as far as these little buggers are concerned. Just think – there's all the food that people leave on the grass when they've been having their picnics, and all the bits of sandwiches and chocolate bars, and God knows what, that they chuck out of their car windows. There's thousands of people coming past here, especially at the weekend, ever since they turned the old railway line into a footpath.'

'It's called the Longdendale Trail. I know.'

'And then there's the road up there – the A628. Have you ever seen how much stuff lorry drivers bung out of their cabs? You can't walk along the roadside up there without getting splattered with lumps of flying pork pie and pasties. It's disgusting. Particularly when they have tomato sauce. I hate tomato sauce. But it means there's waste food lying all along the roadside. Not to mention the cafés in the lay-bys. The bins are overflowing with rubbish up there sometimes.'

'I suppose you're right.'

'No, there might not be people living here any more. But the whole world comes by to feed the rats in Longdendale.'

'It's a good job they can't get to the cables in the other tunnel. They can gnaw their way through anything, given time, can rats.'

'We need some more poison, anyway,' said Norton.

A few yards away, in the old eastbound tunnel, a pair of four hundred thousand volt cables ran through a concrete trough. The cables entered the tunnel three miles away at Dunford Bridge, carrying a section of the National Grid between Yorkshire and Manchester. As they emerged again at Woodhead, they ran past a relay room, then up into a series of giant pylons that marched down the valley towards Manchester. The abandoned Woodhead tunnels had saved the moors from being covered in pylons for those three miles.

Sandy Norton had often admired the quality of the stonework in the tunnel arches, which had survived in good condition for more than a hundred and fifty years. But their present use was one the navvies who built the tunnels couldn't have imagined as they hacked their way through the hill with their pickaxes and gunpowder.

In fact, those navvies wouldn't even have been able to imagine the newer two-track tunnel to the south, which had been cut in the 1950s and accommodated the country's first electrified rail line. That tunnel was empty, too, now. Apart from the little battery-powered locomotive that ran on the maintenance track in the National Grid cableway, the last trains had run through the Woodhead tunnels over twenty years ago.

Norton and Cade were packing up to leave the site when a car slowed and stopped on the road overhead. They heard it pull on to the bare concrete pad where a house had once stood above the tunnel entrances, but which was now no more than a pull-in for a good view down the valley. After a few moments, the car started up again and drove off.

'That was an old Volkswagen Beetle,' said Norton.

'How do you know that?'

'I recognize the sound of the engine. It's distinctive – air-cooled, you know. I used to have a Beetle myself years ago, when I was a lad.'

'Have we finished with these rats, then?'

'For now,' said Norton. He turned off his torch. 'You know, I wouldn't like to walk through this tunnel in the dark.'

Cade shuddered. 'Me neither. Three miles in the dark? No thanks. It'd be bad enough, even without the rats.'

He turned back towards their van. But Norton didn't follow him immediately. He was looking up at the stones over the arch of the tunnel mouth. He'd once been told that the navvies who built the old tunnels had been very superstitious men. They were convinced that their tunnelling had disturbed something deep in the hill, which had been the cause of all the disasters that happened to them – the tragedies that had earned Woodhead the nickname 'Railwaymen's Graveyard'. Norton had heard that when the navvies had finished tunnelling, their final act had been to carve faces at each of the tunnel entrances to control the evil spirits. But if the carvings were still there, they were so worn now that he couldn't make them out.

Sandy Norton shrugged. He didn't know about evil spirits. But the faces hadn't done much to control the rats.

Finally, he locked the steel gate that prevented unauthorized access to the middle tunnel. All three tunnels had their own gates. Without them, rail enthusiasts and others who were even less welcome would always be trying to get into the tunnels. Some of those folk would want to walk all three miles to the other end, just to prove they could do it. They wouldn't be bothered by the rats. They wouldn't take any notice of the risk from the high-voltage power cables. They wouldn't even be deterred by the National Grid's yellow-and-black signs on the gates. The meaning of the signs was clear enough, with their symbol of a black lightning bolt cutting through a body. It was clear even without their message, which read: 'Danger of Death'.

WHENEVER THE PHONE rang in the Old Rectory, Sarah Renshaw stopped what she was doing and looked at the nearest clock. It would be important to have the exact time, when the moment came.

She was in the sitting room, where the mahogany wall clock said five minutes past ten. Sarah checked her watch, and adjusted the minute hand slightly so that it read the same. She didn't want there to be any confusion. All the times were important – the time Emma had last been seen, the time her train had left Wolverhampton, the time she should have arrived home. And the exact minute they got news that she had been found would be vital. Sarah felt comforted by the recording of the minutes. It was more than a ritual. Time was important.

Howard had gone to answer the phone, so Sarah waited. In the middle of their big oak Jacobean sideboard, a candle was burning. The wick was already halfway down, and the melted wax was pooling in the brass holder. There were plenty more candles in one of the drawers, and Sarah wanted to light a new one right away to mark the moment, as if the act itself would make a difference. But she hugged her hands under her armpits and restrained herself as she listened to Howard speaking in the next room. She would be able to tell by the tone of his voice.

Sarah looked at the clock again. Six minutes past ten. For a moment, she panicked. Which would be most important – the exact time the phone had rung, or the moment she had got the news? Which would she celebrate, in the years to come?

'Howard?' she called. 'Howard?'

But he didn't respond, and Sarah quickly calmed again. Howard's voice was subdued. If the call had been about Emma, she would have known it by now. The news would have communicated itself to her through the wall. Sarah had often thought that the call, when it came, wouldn't produce any normal-sounding ring on their phone, but would announce itself like a fanfare. She vaguely imagined a line of liveried trumpeters like those who appeared with the Queen at state occasions. Her ears already rang to the sound they made.

And certainly there would be the sensations – the tingling and the little quivers of pleasure that she experienced whenever she felt that Emma was close by. When the call came, she expected a jolt like a great charge of electricity, like the entire four hundred thousand volts from the cables that ran through the hillside two hundred feet below their house.

Yes, when the phone call came, she would know. Sarah would have no need to listen to the sound of Howard's voice, or to hear what the person at the other end of the line was saying. The fanfare would sound, and the electricity would surge through her body, stinging her hands and burning the skin of her face. And the mahogany wall clock would stop of its own accord at the exact moment, at the precise second and micro second, and it would never start again. Sarah would know.

Howard came into the sitting room, instantly dominating it with his bulk. He was wearing a thick, white Arran sweater that made her want to wrap her arms round him and bury her face in the wool. But he shook his head briefly, and averted his eyes.

Sarah had been standing at the bookcase near the door. She ran her hand along some of the spines, and touched a folded and dog-eared piece of paper that had been used to mark a page in *Twentieth-Century Design*. She tried to breathe in the scent of the books, but the familiar smells of paper and ink seemed fainter tonight. *Subjects and Symbols in Art* had a small stain on the cover that had almost faded now because Sarah had touched it too often. She took out *Art Deco Graphics* and a David Hockney book, and put them back the other way round.

Many of the books were inscribed in Emma's own handwriting on the title page. She had only put her name and the date, but the inscriptions seemed to offer a sort of continuity, a narrative reflecting a particular period in Emma's life.

These were the books Emma had once handled and read, which meant that the words on their pages must have entered her mind and become part of her. Sarah was able to pick up a book that Emma had once opened, and read the words that Emma had studied.

Sarah Renshaw often found herself spending time rearranging the books. Perhaps by shuffling the dates on the books, she could change the order of events in Emma's life. If she had read *this* book before *that* one, might things have been different? Would Emma have been at home now, complaining that her mum was messing up the order of her books?

Sarah wiped a tear from her eye. She caught herself just before she spoke aloud, and dropped her voice to a whisper, so that Howard wouldn't hear her.

'I'll help you put them back exactly how you want them, dear. We'll do it together.'

Sarah turned away from the bookcase and took down a calendar from the top of the TV set. She crossed off another day, neatly deleting it with two short, sharp strokes of a black marker pen.

It was Day 743. Emma Renshaw had been missing for over two years.

NOW THE LAUGHTER in the village had subsided, or the woman making the noise had moved out of earshot. Derek Alton stood in his church porch and listened to the sound of Neil Granger's car engine as it moved slowly out of Withens. It climbed the road away from the village and began to cross the miles of bare moorland towards the valley of Longdendale.

Finally, even the sound of the engine disappeared behind the hill. The blackbirds settled into the yew trees, Alton's breathing returned to normal. And as it grew dark, Withens became almost entirely silent. Except for the screaming.

Chapter Two

SATURDAY

WITH A HEAVE of his shoulders, a police officer in body
armour swung the battering ram. The door split at the first
impact. He swung a few more times, and the thump of
steel hitting wood wrecked the stillness of the early morning. A burglar alarm began to shriek as the lock shattered,
and the officer gave the door a kick with his boot.

Standing in the damp bracken at the edge of the road,
Detective Constable Ben Cooper watched officers wearing Kevlar vests burst into the house as their team leader
began to shout instructions. The door had given way a
bit too easily, he thought. Maybe the householder should
have spent more money on security, and less on the plate
glass and patios.

'Well, they give the impression of people with nothing
to hide,' he said. 'But God knows what all that glass does
to their heating bill.'

Cooper could feel a fine rain in the air, like feathers touching his face. Sunlight and showers were passing across the hills so quickly that it was almost dizzying. Though he was standing still, he seemed to be moving from darkness into light and back again, as the clouds obscured the sun, showered him with rain and were blown westwards by the wind. The raindrops hardly had a chance to dry on his waxed coat before the next bank of clouds reached him.

For some reason, PC Tracy Udall was wearing her body armour, too. No doubt it was a sensible precaution, but it looked a bit odd when the most dangerous thing in sight was a patch of stinging nettles. Besides, she seemed to Cooper like a candidate for a breast reduction operation to make the vest fit properly.

For the moment, PC Udall had left her yellow waterproof jacket in the car. But the banks of darker clouds rapidly moving towards them from the east suggested that she might regret moving too far away from the car without it.

'If we're right about their source of income, they won't be worrying about sharing a bit of it with Powergen,' she said.

He wiped the rain off his binoculars so that he could study the house more carefully. It had been a farmhouse at one time, but part of the side wall had been taken out and replaced with floor-to-ceiling glass, which must let more light in than had ever been seen by several generations of Derbyshire hill-farming families. There was new glass at the back too, and dormer windows had been built into the stone-tiled roof.

The room he could see through the glass had a floor made from patterned blocks of light-coloured wood, where once there would surely have been stone flags. There was a glimpse of light from another window way down at the far end. That could only mean that an internal wall had been removed to create one large room running right through to the back of the house. An estate agent would probably call it an open-plan living space.

As they had descended into the valley, the police team had been careful not to disturb the dawn with the lights of their beacons and the wail of their sirens. But now the time for discretion had passed. On the way to the raid, one of the task force officers had joked that they'd need to get inside the house quickly to be out of the rain. Kevlar fibres were known to deteriorate if they got wet. Also if they were exposed to direct sunlight. That was why police officers in body armour never went out in sunlight, or so they said. But at least it provided a lot more protection than if you had left it hanging in your locker at the station.

A few hundred yards beyond the target house was another cluster of roofs, including a number of old farm buildings, one of which had been converted into a double garage. But there was also a four-wheel-drive vehicle standing on the brick-paved driveway – a Toyota or a Mitsubishi, he couldn't quite be sure from this distance. As he watched, a large, shaggy-haired dog wandered into sight, sniffed at the vehicle's front near-side tyre, looked over its shoulder guiltily, and slunk off towards the back of the house. There was a paddock at the side of the driveway, newly fenced and containing a Shetland pony, a Jacob sheep and two Muscovy ducks.

'What about the neighbours?' said Cooper.

'Well, the house actually belongs to an architect,' said Udall. 'Apparently, he's employed by the Cooperative Society, and he designs grocery shops and crematoria for a living.'

Udall had an air of briskness that Cooper liked. In the car on the way from Glossop section station, she told him that she'd been in the force ten years. She was a single mother, and had joined up after her youngest child was old enough to attend nursery school. When she had been on the wrong shifts – which she usually was, she said – her mother had collected the children from school. Now her son was thirteen, and she was starting to get worried about him.

'Grocery shops and crematoria?'

'Or, as Sergeant Boyce puts it, "rashers to ashes". He's a scream.'

'Every team needs a comedian.'

'But the architect is working abroad. Somewhere in the Gulf States, I think. So he leased the house for a couple of years. The present occupier also has an address in South Manchester, where his neighbours say he's a motor dealer.'

One of those brief, unnerving silences had developed down at the house. The officers waiting outside checked their earpieces. These moments never lasted long, but they were worse than any amount of overexcited shouting over the airwaves.

Cooper looked at the unused farm buildings and thought of his brother Matt, struggling more than ever now to support his family on the income from Bridge End Farm. Revenue from livestock farming had plummeted, and not just because of the aftermath of the foot-and-mouth outbreak. Farmers like Matt lived on a knife edge, wondering when the bank would pull the plug on their overdraft. There were some advantages to a regular salary from Derbyshire Constabulary, after all.

'What about the barn conversion?'

'Holiday lets,' said Udall. 'It's divided into two studio apartments, with a shared patio round the back. No doubt they provide a useful bit of extra income, in case the crematorium market dries up.'

'Not much chance of that. There's no shortage of people to burn. And nowhere to bury them these days, either.'

'No, the graveyards are really in demand. People are dying to get in them.'

'Is that one of Sergeant Boyce's, too?'

Udall flushed a little, but said nothing. She tugged at the bottom edge of her vest to pull it down over her hips, where her duty belt was heavily hung with baton, handcuffs, CS spray, and a series of leather pouches that Cooper had forgotten the use for. In fact, he didn't think they even had all those things to wear in the days when he was in uniform. Changes happened fast in the police service, and six years away from a uniform was long enough to get out of touch.

Tracy Udall had dark hair pulled back almost painfully tightly into a short ponytail that protruded from her white trilby-style hat. Cooper had presumed from what she'd told him that the father of her child hadn't been around from the word go. Now she must be only a couple of years on the other side of thirty. Unfortunately, Sergeant Jimmy Boyce was married, with four kids of his own.

Cooper knew he could probably learn a lot from PC Udall and her colleagues – the day-to-day, on the ground stuff about policing that had started to pass him by after six years at a CID desk in Edendale. It was his chief superintendent at E Division who had first uttered the words 'lateral development' when he had failed to get promoted to the detective sergeant's job he had hoped for. Lateral development meant a move to a different speciality without the benefit of promotion, but it came with the suggestion that wider experience might count favourably towards future advancement. On the other hand, his mother might have said it was just a case of 'always jam tomorrow'.

Yet, suddenly, here he was on a secondment to the Rural Crime Team – playing an advisory role to Sergeant Boyce's pro-active squad of uniformed officers. These were people who knew the problems of the Peak District's villages. They had gained their knowledge from years as community constables, liaising with the local people and listening to their troubles. Those troubles often involved a catalogue of burglaries, petty thefts, vandalism and car crimes that were committed with impunity, to all intents and purposes. Prioritization was the buzz word these days, and property crime was low priority. Members of the public in some areas could consider themselves lucky if they got any police response at all, except for the offer of a crime number for their insurance claim and a sympathetic letter from Victim Support.

Cooper was glad to help, if he could. But while he stood with PC Tracy Udall on this roadside in the Longdendale valley, he couldn't help wondering if this was the first step on the path of his lateral development. Was Sergeant Boyce tipped to move onwards and upwards after the initial success of his team? Did a uniformed sergeant's job await some lucky detective constable in a few months' time? He wondered what Detective Sergeant Diane Fry would make of that, as his immediate supervisor. But it didn't take much effort to imagine the smile on her face. She would be glad to be rid of him, he was sure of it.

Now Cooper was standing in sunlight, and he found he was sweating under his waxed coat. It was one of those spring days when you didn't know what to wear when you went out in the morning. Whatever you chose, you knew you were going to get wet, or too warm. Probably both. There was nothing predictable about the weather in the Peak District at any time of the year, no matter how long you lived there. Outdoors, you were forever taking off layers of clothing and putting them back on again, as you passed from sweaty uphill slog to the biting wind of an exposed plateau. In April, you never knew from one moment to the next what sort of weather was going to hit you. A squall, a gale, a deluge of hailstones, or a warm burst of sun – you could get it all within an hour.

Down in the converted farmhouse, the suspects roused from their beds would be getting ready for a trip. With a bit of luck, they wouldn't be seeing much sunlight for a while.

'An isolated farmhouse is an ideal base for an illegal operation. And God knows, there are plenty of those between here and Edendale,' said Udall.

'Too many,' said Cooper.

'And they make great drugs factories particularly. It's taking diversification a bit far, if you ask me. Definitely too far. If they can't make a living at farming, they should stick to opening tea rooms and doing bed and breakfast.'

'But there's more money in drugs. And you don't have to deal with tourists.'

'The neighbours are going to get a shock,' said Udall. 'You can see they've got no security to speak of. There are no walls and no gates, and the lights are mostly to show off the garden and the fish pond. And the Afghan doesn't look as though it would put up much of a fight.'

'People are used to thinking that they don't need to set up fortifications around their homes in this area.'

'Ah, but the architect isn't from this area. He lived in Sheffield until two years ago. He ought to know better.'

'It's the scenery,' said Cooper. 'It gives people a false sense of sanity.'

If Cooper were to be honest with himself, his short spell with the E Division Rural Crime Team was already starting to feel like a breath of fresh air. Winter in Edendale had been long and hard, and full of other complications. Diane Fry, for one.

And then he had chosen to move out of Bridge End Farm for the first time in his life. He had left home at almost thirty years old, and now he had all the business of looking after himself, and the unexpected implications of having property, even though his flat in Edendale was only rented. He had his own territory now, and that made life look different. That, and his looming thirtieth birthday, made a lot of things look different. It was as if he had suddenly been lifted out of his old, familiar rut and pointed in a different direction, so that he wasn't quite sure who or what he was any more. In fact, he was a bit like the former farmhouse down there – designed for a different purpose entirely.

'Besides, houses like this need security these days. Almost every house of any size in Longdendale has been targeted by thieves during the last eighteen months or so,' said Udall. 'Some of them have been hit more than once. If the thieves don't get in the first time, they do a recce and come back later.'

'Professionals, then?'

'No doubt about it.'

'Local? Or the travelling variety?'

'Well, we definitely think they're using somewhere on our patch to store the stuff they've nicked. Another isolated farmhouse, probably.'

'What items are they going for?'

'This lot go for antiques: clocks, porcelain – anything small that looks as though it might be worth a bit of money. There's a huge market for that kind of thing. It's likely they're collecting enough for a vanload, then shipping it off to the States or somewhere in Europe. Easy money, all right.'

The Shetland pony was deliberately bullying the two Muscovy ducks, nudging them around the paddock until they began to flap their wings and quack angrily.

'Did the architect design the alterations himself?' said Cooper.

'I believe so. But he seems to have designed them for looks, rather than with security in mind, doesn't he?'

'You're right. He really should have known better. Here they come.'

The task force officers were escorting two men out of the target house. Each man had his hands cuffed behind his back and an officer gripping his elbow. They looked as though they had dressed hastily in whatever had come to hand first. Much as Cooper had done himself, in fact. But these two would have the chance to put their feet up for a while in a warm, dry cell when they reached the section station at Glossop.

Cooper turned the binoculars westwards, looking for more signs of civilization in the bare Dark Peak landscape of peat moors and heather. His attention was caught by a small, tree-lined valley and the glimpse of a church tower.

'What's over there?' he said.

'That? Oh, that's Withens.'

Cooper could hardly see the village itself. It seemed to be lying in the bottom of a hollow, slipped casually into a narrow cleft in the moors. There were trees above the village on the lower slopes, through which the roofs of houses were barely visible. But the valley was so narrow that it looked as though the two facing slopes were only waiting for the right moment to slide back together and crush the village completely, and all its inhabitants with it.

'Withens,' said Cooper, trying the sound of the name in his mouth as he might taste an unfamiliar morsel of food, not sure whether it was going to be bitter or sweet, soft on the teeth or difficult to chew.

Above the village was a moorland plateau, a gloomy blend of dark khakis and greens, with no sign of the purple flowers of the heather that would bring colour in the summer. Much of the landscape up there would be quagmire – a wet morass of peat bog that shifted underfoot, sucking at the soles of boots and clinging to trousers. Across the valley, Bleaklow Mountain stood right on the watershed of England, and attracted sixty inches of rain a year to its wastes of haggs and groughs.

'I thought we'd go down to the village and take a look when we've finished here,' said Udall. 'You might be interested to see it. Withens has its own problems. As it happens, the local vicar reported a break-in yesterday.'

'Fine.'

Cooper noticed a pair of black shapes in the distance, circling over the moor. He turned the binoculars towards them, grateful for any sign of life in the landscape.

But this wasn't the sort of life he welcomed. They were carrion crows. Though he couldn't see what had attracted them, he guessed they probably had their eye on a weak lamb. Sometimes, before shearing, their prey might be an adult sheep that had rolled over and couldn't get up again because of the weight of the unshorn fleece on its back. But in the spring it was the sickliest lambs that the crows were looking for as they flapped and circled over the moors. Just now, their diet would consist mostly of young grouse and the eggs of other birds. But a weak lamb was a great bonus. Its carcass would last them for days.

If they'd found a lamb up there, then they would land in a little while and perch on a handy rock as they waited patiently for it to weaken enough to be helpless. Then they would begin to work on its eyes, picking at the white flesh as if they were delicacies that had to be eaten fresh. And once the lamb was blind, the crows could eat the rest of it at their leisure, while it died.

Cooper lowered the binoculars and looked up at the dark bulk of the hills beyond Withens.

'Tracy, have you noticed the smoke?' he said.

Udall followed his gaze. 'Hell!'

Black clouds were billowing across a wide stretch of the moor, with an occasional flicker of flame visible behind them. The seat of the fire looked as though it might be just below the horizon. PC Udall went off to her car to use the radio, but was back in a couple of minutes.

'Moorland fire. They think it was started by some kids on a school outing from Manchester. The fire service are turning out all the crews they can muster, but it's right on the summit above Crowden, so it's pretty inaccessible. The poor bloody firefighters will have to do the last half-mile on foot with their equipment. They're also saying they might have to mobilize the helicopter to bomb it with water from the reservoirs.'

'Beyond our remit, anyway,' said Cooper.

'Thank God.'

A gust of wind blew along the road and another shower spattered their faces. But there was too little rain to help the firefighters.

'I think they're ready for us down there,' said Udall.

'OK.'

Cooper took one last look at the moors above Withens. The smoke was spreading in the wind rolling low over the heather. But in front of it, blacker even than the smoke, the two carrion crows were still circling.

EVEN BEFORE THE sun had risen on Withens Moor, Neil Granger had known he wasn't alone. He had been standing with his back to one of the air shafts above the old railway tunnels, facing east towards the approaching dawn. There was nothing but air between his face and the black ridge of Gallows Moss, where the light would soon begin to creep up among the tors.

Every sound from the surrounding valleys had reached his ears – a bird splashing out of the water on one of the reservoirs in Longdendale, the growl of an engine on the A628. Even the slightest movement of the wind stirred the coarse grass, like fingers groping for his presence in the darkness. The air was so clean that he could taste the first vapour rising from the dew on the heather, like the tang of cold metal in his mouth. But in a few minutes, the dawn would take away the darkness and the dew.

At first, the sounds he heard nearby could have been the shifting of small pieces of stone on the slope behind him. The scree was loose, and the changing temperature could easily make the stones move against each other. But gradually Neil became aware that someone had walked up to the air shaft behind him. Now, he thought, they were probably resting on the other side of the high, circular wall.

'Well, I'd given up on you,' said Neil. 'I was starting to think no one was coming.'

His voice dropped into the valley, carried away on the wind. There was no response from the darkness, and he smiled.

'It's a bit of a steep climb, isn't it? It creased me up completely.'

He expected to hear someone gasping for breath. But there was nothing – only the darkness and the distant sounds from the valley.

'I'm so unfit after the winter that, by the time I got to the top, I thought I was having a heart attack.'

He paused, but still there was nothing.

'I thought I was going to die up here, and nobody would know. If I'd died and you hadn't come, then no one would have found me for days.'

Neil glanced at Gallows Moss. A pale wash of colour was starting to touch the clouds. He raised his voice a little, as if the appearance of the light had revealed something that he hadn't suspected until now.

'Are you all right?' he said. 'Do you want a hand?'

Neil waited in the silence, no longer facing east, but looking back over his shoulder into the west. Away from the light and towards the darkness. Something was different. The wind no longer felt refreshingly cool, but was cold enough to make him shiver. The sensations against his face weren't like gentle fingers, but sharp claws scratching his skin. The air didn't taste of the dew, but of an unnamed fear. Neil wondered if he would ever hear the first bird calling at the sight of the rising sun. It had been only the darkness that had made him feel safe, after all. And in a moment, the dawn would take away the darkness.

'Yes, I thought I was going to die up here,' he said.

The first blow that hit him was so unexpected – like the world falling in, like a ton of stone toppling on to him from the air shaft, or a train bursting out of the ground from the old railway tunnel.

Neil went down, instantly unconscious, crashing on to the stones with a thud and crunch of bone. Part of his scalp had peeled away, and the bone underneath had shattered, ripping the membrane that covered the brain. Within a few moments, his cerebrospinal fluid was leaking from the tear on to the stones – stones that were already covered in blood that was spreading from his scalp wound. Blood had matted his hair and trickled in small rivulets down his face and neck, forming an interconnecting web like the meandering channels that drained the peat moor on which he lay. But the blood could find nowhere on his skin to settle and dry. So it continued to trickle across the greasy surface until it touched the stones and ran into the ground.

Where the fluid was leaking from his brain, infection would soon enter. But it would be too late to matter. Part of his brain tissue had been bruised by the impact, and now a small haematoma was forming deep among the tangled pathways and ganglia. The haematoma would be fatal.

But Neil might still have survived, if he had received urgent attention in a hospital emergency room. A neurosurgeon could have ordered a CT scan, operated to remove the haematoma, then sutured the membrane and carefully picked out the remaining bone fragments. With immediate surgery and a course of antibiotics against the infection, Neil might have lived.

But Neil Granger was destined never to reach a hospital, or a neurosurgeon. As his life oozed away into the peat, there was one person who waited for him to die. But there was no one to call an ambulance. Neil would never recover from the unconsciousness that followed the first blow to his head, or the coma that the second produced. He would never know what happened after he was left alone, and never feel the fear of what would happen to his body after death.

Nothing moved around the air shaft except the steam that trickled out of its mouth and drifted down the valley – and, a little while later, the two black shapes that circled over Withens Moor.

Chapter Three

DS DIANE FRY knew all about fear. Some people were excited by it, and liked to play with the taste and smell of it, teasing their senses to the limit. But others were destroyed by its poison, eaten away by a senseless, insidious acid that seeped into their brains before they could fight it.

It wasn't always possible to know what made you afraid. A therapist had once told her that fear conditioning could be created by a single episode, because that was the way nature had designed the human brain. It was an evolutionary advantage, a mechanism to prevent you from returning to a dangerous situation. Once frightened, forever cautious. And that was why just one sound, a single movement or a smell, could trigger the train of memory that stimulated fear. The sound of a footstep on a creaking floorboard, the sliding pattern of shadows as a door opened in the darkness, the soapy smell of shaving foam that made her nauseous even now.

The evidence bag that Diane Fry was holding contained none of those things. It contained only a grubby and stained mobile phone. So why did she feel as though the process had begun that would send her sliding down a long, dark tunnel towards the source of her fear?

'Do the parents know about this yet, sir?' she said.

Detective Inspector Paul Hitchens was also nothing to be afraid of, as far as Fry was concerned. He was capable enough, but had a disrespectful attitude towards his senior officers that wasn't going to get him any further in the promotion game. It was a tendency he didn't seem able to control, any more than Fry could control the dark shadow that had flapped and squirmed somewhere in her mind when she had picked up the bag.

'No, Diane,' said Hitchens. 'In fact, we need to be a bit cautious about that. We'll have to consider how much information we give them.'

'Why?'

'Mr and Mrs Renshaw are, how shall I put it … a bit difficult to talk to.'

Fry didn't feel in the least surprised. Since she had transferred to Derbyshire Constabulary from the West Midlands, she had found most people in the Peak District difficult to talk to – including her colleagues in E Division. Not only did they find her accent strange and exotic, but they also seemed to be living in a different world entirely, a world where the city streets she had known before just didn't exist.

'I'd like to see exactly where the phone was discovered,' she said.

'Of course. The contact details are all there. It was found by members of a rambling club doing a spring clean on an overgrown footpath near Chapel-en-le-Frith. The phone was one of hundreds of bits of rubbish they picked up. If it hadn't been wrapped up tight in a plastic carrier bag, there might not have been anything recognizable left to be found.'

Despite its condition, the mobile phone had still contained its SIM card when it was found. It had been traced via the network operators, Vodafone, to the ownership of Miss Emma Renshaw, the Old Rectory, Main Street, Withens.

Fry opened the file that Hitchens had given her. As soon as she saw the first photograph, she thought she knew what had triggered the fear. Emma Renshaw was standing in a garden, wearing a white sweater with leaping dolphins across the chest. Her hair was fair and straight, hanging almost to her shoulders, and she looked happy, but shy, and a little nervous too.

The second photograph was slightly more recent. A note said it had been taken while Emma was on a study trip in Italy. Not Venice or Florence, or even Rome – the places where everyone was supposed to go to look at art. She was in Milan, visiting contemporary design houses. But the weather had been warm and sunny in Milan. The photo showed her standing in front of a café with another girl, of Asian appearance. Emma's hair was pulled back, revealing good cheekbones and delicate ears, which made her look more vulnerable, despite the increased confidence in her smile. She was wearing a sleeveless T-shirt, and the skin of her arms and neck was bare and pink.

'Emma Renshaw disappeared just over two years ago,' said Hitchens. 'She was a student in Birmingham, where she attended the University of Central England's School of Art and Design. She was last seen by the young people she shared a house with in Bearwood, about three miles from the art school. Bearwood is in the area called the Black Country.'

'Yes, I know,' said Fry.

'Oh, of course you do.'

Fry could see the information from her personnel file gradually being dredged up into her DI's mind. The expression on his face changed as he remembered the awful details, became embarrassed for a moment, then resumed his professional manner.

'You're from the Black Country yourself, aren't you, Diane?'

'Yes, sir. That's where I'm from.'

The Black Country was the name given to the urban sprawl west of the city of Birmingham. Old industrial towns like Wolverhampton, West Bromwich, Dudley, Sandwell and Walsall were in the Black Country. And many smaller communities, too – like Warley, where Fry had lived with her foster parents, a string of housing estates tucked between Birmingham and the M5 motorway. Right next door to Bearwood.

'Anyway, the house the young people shared is in Darlaston Road, Bearwood. Emma's housemates say they left her in the house getting ready to travel home by train to Derbyshire for the Easter holidays. At least, that's what Emma told them she was doing, and they had no reason to doubt her.'

'The housemates being Alex Dearden, Debbie Stark and Neil Granger,' said Fry, consulting the file.

'They were all old friends, it seems. The two young men grew up in the same village as Emma, in Withens. Debbie Stark is from Mottram, a few miles away, but she was Emma's best friend at high school.'

West Midlands Police had sent copies of all their files to Derbyshire – there were reports of interviews conducted with Dearden, Stark and Granger, and with several others among Emma Renshaw's friends, neighbours, and classmates and teachers at the art school. Fry noted that the officer assigned to the missing person case had been based at the local Operational Command Unit headquarters in Smethwick – a place she knew well.

In fact, Fry could picture Darlaston Road, Bearwood, but wasn't sure at which end of the road she would find 360B, the address Emma Renshaw had shared. Bearwood possessed most of the local shops for the Warley area. She had been there many times.

'I'm not clear on Emma's last-known movements,' she said. 'Who was individually the last to see her? Or did the young people leave the house together?'

'Neil Granger was the last to leave, by a matter of some minutes. He was on his way to work, but had overslept. He said he had been drinking the night before.'

'Did Granger arrive at work on time?'

'A few minutes late,' said Hitchens. 'He had a car, which he drove into Birmingham. He claimed the traffic was heavy that morning, and it delayed him even more. The foreman at the site said it was unusual for Granger to be late for work, and he was normally very reliable. So he believed what Granger said, and didn't think anything of it. He said he had a lot more to worry about with his other employees.'

Emma had been nineteen when she disappeared, and the guidelines said that immediate enquiries should be made in the case of a missing female under twenty-one. They were considered vulnerable, and, if they went missing, statistically more likely to have been the victim of a crime.

So the police officer in Smethwick who had taken the case had followed the proper procedures. Mostly. He had enquired whether Emma had done anything similar previously, and had checked the information her parents had given him against the missing person files. He had confirmed that Emma wasn't involved in current criminal proceedings, in case she had left home to avoid prosecution for something her parents didn't know about. He had collected all the identifying details. He had recorded her full name, age, address and description, along with the two photographs provided by the Renshaws.

'But if Emma was going home by train, how was she planning to get to the railway station?' said Fry.

'By taxi – or so she told her housemates. West Midlands were unable to trace any taxi driver who picked her up from the house at Darlaston Road, or anywhere nearby. Nor was there a booking for that area where the passenger failed to appear. But I suppose she might have hailed a cab in the street.'

'It's unlikely, in that neighbourhood.'

Hitchens nodded. 'But West Midlands checked that, too.'

'I wonder why Neil Granger didn't offer to give her a lift to the station, if he had a car?'

'He said it was because he was already late for work, and he was afraid of getting in trouble. And Emma assured him she didn't need a lift.'

'So he said.'

Fry turned back to the reports. Enquiries had been made at several pubs and clubs that Emma had been known to visit. Friends and classmates had been spoken to. The university had no indication that Emma had been having problems with her work, or emotional or financial difficulties, or had any intention of leaving the course. There was a note on the bottom of the officer's report that the parents of the missing person had agreed to any publicity.

It looked fairly comprehensive, at first glance. There was certainly a shortage of leads for West Midlands to have followed up, but all the usual enquiries had been gone through. No one had been able to suggest any reason why Emma should have decided to disappear, or anything she might have been worried about. No one had any idea where she might have gone – except back home to Withens.

'So we need to talk to all the housemates again,' said Hitchens. 'Alex Dearden lives and works here, in Edendale. Neil Granger moved out of Withens, too, but not very far – he's a few miles further down the Longdendale valley, in Tintwistle. Debbie Stark, I'm afraid, is still in the West Midlands. She got herself a job there after she graduated.'

'Well, they could have scattered a lot further than that,' said Fry. 'So we should think ourselves lucky.'

But to Fry's critical eye, the West Midlands reports had something missing. There seemed to be no air of urgency to them. Enquiries had taken place over a long period – several weeks, in fact. It was as if the officer assigned the case had been fitting it in between other jobs, when it was most convenient. And there was no mention of assistance being brought in from the local CID. No detective's name was appended to any of the enquiry reports.

It didn't really surprise her. In a huge metropolitan area, thousands of people were reported missing every year. Some priority was supposed to be given to women under twenty-one, but how many of those were there? And how many children and young people, too? The children were the biggest priority of all when it came to missing persons. Given a CID team already stretched to the limit by multiple murder cases, violent crime and drug problems, burglaries and car theft, how much attention could Emma Renshaw have expected, when there was no evidence that a crime had been committed?

Fry had been in that situation herself. She had worked in one of those CID offices. She guessed the officer had tried his best. But in the end, his sense of relief almost rose off the page as he concluded that the facts pointed towards Emma Renshaw having left the West Midlands, just as she had been supposed to do. He had passed the problem back to Derbyshire.

Fry shook her head, not sure whether she was puzzled, or whether she was trying to shake off the feeling that had been creeping up on her ever since she had taken the evidence bag in her hands.

'You know, it's all too vague, sir,' she said. 'It seems to me that none of Emma Renshaw's housemates was bothered enough about her to make quite sure that Emma could get to the station all right on her own. They *think* she was getting a taxi, but they don't know when, or where or how, or what taxi firm was coming to pick her up. And no one actually saw her leave the house.'

Hitchens shrugged. 'Well, that's the way it is, Diane. You know it happens all the time. People just disappear through the cracks.'

She nodded. Hitchens was right, of course. Throughout the country, teenagers went missing all the time, and were never seen again. But Emma Renshaw had last been seen in Bearwood, in the Black Country, no more than a mile or two from her own childhood home. That made a difference.

'And we have to consider the other possibility ...' said Hitchens.

'Sir?'

'The possibility that Emma Renshaw may have lied to everyone – her parents, her friends and her housemates. She may never have intended coming home at all.'

'Of course.'

Fry looked at the railway timetable attached to the reports. Emma had been due to catch a train from Birmingham New Street station a few minutes before eleven o'clock on the morning of Thursday, 12 April. Virgin Trains should have taken her to Manchester Piccadilly, where she would have had a quarter of an hour to change platforms and transfer to a local train. She had been expected to arrive at Glossop station at twenty past one, and her parents, Howard and Sarah Renshaw, had been waiting to collect her. But Emma hadn't got off the train. The Renshaws had tried to call her mobile phone, but had got only the message service. So they had waited for the next train from Manchester. And the next.

The schedule filled Fry with a sense of despair. No wonder the West Midlands officer had been glad to get the case off his desk. If Emma Renshaw had left the house in Darlaston Road as planned, there were two possibilities. Either she had disappeared in Birmingham, and had never made it to the train at all. Or she had vanished when she changed trains in Manchester.

Fry was looking at the names of two of the largest metropolitan areas in Britain, cities where a girl of nineteen could melt away so easily. A change of identity, and her family would never see her again, if she didn't want them to. Fry knew that all too well.

On the other hand, the evidence bag that she was holding contained a Motorola Talkabout with a bright blue inlay over the keys – a phone which Vodafone said had belonged to Emma Renshaw. Without a group of ramblers deciding it was time for a spring clean, the phone might have lain undiscovered for ever. If one of those ramblers hadn't been the mum of a teenager whose mobile phone had been stolen by muggers, it would have been sent to the council tip with the rest of the rubbish. And if it hadn't been for the police officer at Chapel-en-le-Frith who had taken the time and trouble to trace the owner of the phone, no one would ever have thought of submitting it for forensic examination.

But that's what they had done, and the result was in Fry's hands. Down the right side of the phone, the blue inlay was streaked with the dried residue of a dark brown liquid that had glued up the keys and trickled into the little hole where the lead for the re-charger should fit. According to the label on the bag, the stains had been confirmed as human blood.

Fry knew that she might be looking at the last remaining biological traces of Emma Renshaw. Her fingers might almost be touching the pathetic remnant of Emma's life, a desiccated dribble of her DNA.

And that was what opened up the tunnel of fear that she had already begun to slide down.

DC GAVIN MURFIN had sandy hair and a pink face, and he always seemed to have dabs of tomato sauce on his lower lip. He was well past forty, yet he took no notice of any nagging about the condition of his heart. He had experience, though, and that was worth gold these days. Even Diane Fry had to admit it.

Fry found DC Murfin at his desk in the CID room, answering the phone with one hand and eating from a paper bag in the other. She waited impatiently until he put the phone down.

'And I'll complain to the Chief Constable about *you* too, madam,' he said to the empty air. Then he looked up and grinned at Fry. 'We're not providing the high quality of customer service the lady expects for her Council Tax.'

'I hope you were polite, Gavin,' said Fry.

'Polite? I charmed her so much that she's coming round straight away to have sex with me.'

But Fry wasn't in the mood for Murfin's brand of humour.

'Gavin, what are you doing at the moment?'

'Eh?'

'Nothing much, by the look of it.'

'I'm just having a minute, like.'

'Well, your minute's up. There are crimes to be detected.'

'I've already detected one this year, Diane.'

'Well, it's time to get your average up. Let's see if we can make it one point five.'

Murfin sighed. 'I'll just finish this sarnie.'

Fry looked at his sandwich more closely. 'Gavin, is that what I think it is?'

'Bacon and sausage.' Murfin licked a bit of the grease off his fingers, then wiped the rest of it on a forensics report.

'There's half an inch of fat on that bacon, Gavin. Have you never heard of cholesterol?'

'Yes, of course I have. Me and the wife went there for two weeks' holiday last summer.'

Fry breathed in slowly, suppressing an urge to begin screaming. She knew it came from the fear, not from anger at Murfin. It was something she would have to deal with later.

'Get the jokes out of your system now, Gavin,' she said. 'We've got a couple called Renshaw coming in.'

Murfin gave a muffled groan from behind a mouthful of sausage. 'You're kidding! Not Emma Renshaw's parents?'

'Do you remember the case?'

'*Everyone* remembers it. What have they been doing now?'

'Who?'

'The Renshaws, of course.'

'Why should they have been doing anything?'

'Well, they're regulars. Ask Traffic.'

'Gavin, I don't know what you're talking about.'

'Then you ought to pull some of the files on the Renshaws before you talk to them. It might reduce the shock, like.'

Murfin answered the phone and pulled a face at Fry.

'Too late. They're here already.'

'Bring them up then, Gavin. No, hold on a minute. Come here.'

Murfin stopped at Fry's desk on his way out of the CID room. She opened a drawer and pulled a Kleenex tissue out of a box. She carefully wiped the tomato sauce off his chin, screwed up the tissue and threw it in the bin.

'OK. Now you look a bit less like an overweight vampire. You won't scare the Renshaws so much.'

'You're kidding. It's *me* you ought to be worrying about, Diane. Those two are scarier than any vampire. They're like something straight out of *Night of the Living Dead*.'

'You're watching the wrong videos again, Gavin. Try something a bit more sensitive.'

'I don't do sensitive,' said Murfin, as he went to meet the Renshaws.

Fry sat down, took another breath and looked across the room. Opposite Gavin Murfin's chaotic, paper-strewn desk was another that looked empty, almost abandoned. It had been cleared by its occupant before a secondment to the Rural Crime Team. The sight of the empty desk made Fry wonder if there would come a time when there was nowhere she could go for support when she needed it.

Chapter Four

By FULL LIGHT, black-headed gulls had been drifting up from the reservoirs in the valley, scavenging for the previous night's roadkill.

Every day, on his way into Edendale from Bridge End Farm, Ben Cooper had got used to seeing the squashed and bloodied remains of the wildlife slaughtered by traffic during the hours of darkness. Dead foxes and badgers, rabbits and pheasants, hedgehogs and stoats littered the roadway and the verges. Some of the corpses looked quite fresh until they were flattened into the tarmac by the rush of vehicles. Then their skins burst and their intestines were spread on the road, and it was impossible to tell what species they had belonged to.

It was a pretty hard lesson for the wildlife to learn. The road was part of their territory at night, attracting them because the tarmacked surface retained heat longer than the surrounding landscape. By dawn, though, the road had become a different world entirely, when it was occupied by thundering juggernauts and hurtling cars. As a battle for territory, it was the most unequal of struggles, and the fate of the victims was inevitable and predictable.

Nature never accepted defeat, though. She might lose a battle, but never the war. The gulls and the crows, and a thousand smaller scavengers, made sure the corpses didn't go to waste. Cooper had always thought it would be a good idea to have nature on your side, rather than against you.

'And there it is,' said PC Tracy Udall. 'Way down there is Withens.'

She passed Cooper the binoculars.

'Not very scenic, is it?' he said.

Udall shrugged. 'It's just Withens,' she said.

The vantage point they had found was a lay-by on an unnamed minor road off the A628 – the only place, according to PC Udall, where Withens could be seen without actually being in it.

By 6.30 in the morning, the A628 was already busy with a constant stream of lorries and cars. But, apart from the traffic, there seemed to be no signs of human life for miles along the route through the Longdendale valley. Close to where they had turned off, there had been a pull-in on the left at the top of the hill, with an orange emergency phone provided for stranded motorists. But that was about it for civilization. As if to make the point, a sign by the roadside said: 'Sheep for seven miles'.

To the north, above Withens, Cooper could see one of the stone air shafts for the old railway tunnels standing on a rise in a fold of the hills. Around the shaft, Withens Moor seemed to be suffering badly from erosion. Where the last layer of peat had been worn away, the bedrock was bare. Ice and rain might loosen the rock eventually, so that it slipped and crashed down on to the houses in the valley or closed the road, as had happened at Castleton.

'You're right, it's not very scenic,' said Udall. 'It's certainly not what the tourist brochures want. There doesn't seem to be any colour, for a start.'

Cooper sighed. Back home at Bridge End Farm, in the limestone country of the White Peak, the banks of dazzling yellow gorse were in flower now. Many of the fields were a mass of white daisies or golden dandelions, and the umbrellas of wild garlic plants were spreading along the roadside verges, with the pale blue stars of forget-me-nots underfoot.

The warm, damp weather conditions of early spring had caused an explosion of plant growth and animal activity, with the landscape changing by the day. The swallows were nesting, the first cuckoo calling. And just now, there were swathes of bluebells in the broadleaf woods of the Eden Valley. The bluebells had to flower and seed before the tree canopy cast shade over the woodland floor, so every year they had a race against time to reproduce and survive. In this weather, even their colour would be changing – blue when the sky was overcast, and purple in sunlight.

But here was Withens, where the only colour visible was provided by the red canisters of propane gas against the outside walls of some of the houses. So there was no mains gas supply here. Probably it had been one of the last places to get electricity, too, despite the fact that the National Grid power cables ran right through the hillside. As for solar power – in Withens it would have been a joke in poor taste. The lie of the land meant that the sun would rise behind one hill to the south east and disappear behind another to the south west, without touching Withens. No wonder the gardens he could glimpse through the trees had yet to show signs of colour.

'So what's the situation here?' said Cooper.

'Well, some of the homes have been suffering from the same problems we're getting elsewhere – recurrent burglaries, often with associated criminal damage. Particularly the more isolated homes, which are less overlooked. There's one just past the village itself, which has been a particular target. Also the church, I'm afraid.'

'Oh yes. You said the vicar had reported a break-in.'

Cooper could see the tower of the church above the trees. It seemed to stand a little away from the village, on the near side of the river. It was a short, square tower, in the Norman style, but nothing like so old as that. There were genuine Saxon and Norman towers in Derbyshire, but this wasn't one of them. He estimated its date as the middle of the nineteenth century.

Cooper turned his attention back to Withens.

'You said *some* of the homes have been targeted. So presumably others haven't. Is there any pattern there?'

Udall hesitated. 'Possibly.'

'What do you mean?'

'There's a problem family in the village, by the name of Oxley. Dad is the type who makes his living in a way you can't quite pin down. There's an extended family and loads of kids, most of them known to us – not to mention Social Services. There's one little lad who got himself excluded from his primary school for anti-social behaviour. You might have seen something about him in the newspapers. They couldn't identify him, of course, but they started to call him the "Tiny Terror".'

'It does ring a bell,' said Cooper.

'I'll show you when we can get down into the village,' she said. 'That would be the best way.'

This bit of the county was hardly accessible from anywhere else in Derbyshire. It was much easier to get to it from Sheffield on the Yorkshire side, or even from Hyde on the Manchester side. But in the 1970s, someone in an office in London had ruled that it should be in Derbyshire, so that was the way it was. Which county you lived in could make a difference of several thousand pounds to the value of your house.

Cooper looked down at the village once more, feeling that there was something he hadn't paid proper attention to. Just below the bridge near the church, the river widened into a pool where a few willows were still bare now, but would surely add a bit of greenery later in the summer. Here, the bank was full of nettles and rosebay willowherb. But there was something strange about the pool.

He focused PC Udall's binoculars on the water. But in fact, he could barely see the water, because the pool was half-full of large, flat objects. They seemed to be rectangular wooden boards of various sizes, floating on the surface, but tied to trees on the edge of the water. He could make out some lengths of blue nylon rope dipping in and out of the water. The boards looked as though they might have been there for some time, because there was duckweed clinging to them, and green mould growing in patches on many of the panels. Cooper could see no purpose for the boards at all. They weren't the usual sort of fly-tipped rubbish, either.

'That's strange,' he said.

But Udall just shrugged. 'Well, this *is* Withens,' she said.

THE FIRST BUILDING they saw by the side of the road in Withens had long since collapsed. Its walls were tumbled and its timbers blackened, as if there had been a fire a long time ago. Maybe several fires. Now, grass was growing over the stones, and it looked well beyond conversion into a holiday home. Next to the ruins was a fallen oak tree covered in thick moss, which clung to the dead bark in pale green shrouds. Where the main bough of the tree had hit the ground, it had begun to rot back slowly into the earth.

Nearby, a burnt-out car stood on the grass verge. It was something about the size of a Ford Fiesta, with its tyres gone, its windows shattered, and its paintwork scorched down to the metal. But removal of abandoned cars was a problem for the local council.

The village itself was no more than a scatter of stone houses, a pub, a church, a phone box, and a few run-down farms. The farms still had yards that opened directly on to the main street, the way it had been in most Peak District villages at one time, until the demand for residential development drove up the price of land. Then the farmers had moved out of the villages that had originally grown up around them, and the old farmyards and dairies had been swept away, to be replaced by desirable residences in attractive rural settings.

It hadn't happened in Withens. Perhaps nobody had found the village desirable enough. If the farms went out of business here – as looked more than likely from their condition – then their barns and dairies would probably remain rotting for decades before the demand for new housing reached Withens. For now, the presence of the farmyards meant that the main street was well plastered with mud that had dropped from tractor tyres and been churned by the feet of passing cattle.

On the face of the opposite hill, the air shafts looked from a distance like those Second World War gun emplacements known as 'pill boxes'. They were round and squat, built to survive – though in this case, they had been intended to survive the weather that a century of Dark Peak winters could throw at them, rather than bombardment from the German navy.

Just past the Quiet Shepherd pub, a car park and picnic area had been created. There was a bus stop in the entrance to the car park. As Cooper parked his Toyota next to Udall's liveried Vauxhall Astra, a little red, white and blue Yorkshire Traction bus turned in from the road. Along the side of the bus was an advert for a local firm of solicitors. After making a circuit of the car park, it drove out again. There were no passengers on board, and no one waiting at the stop.

'No problem kids hanging around at the moment,' said Cooper.

'You're joking,' said Udall. 'On a Saturday? It's much too early. Come back in the evening, and it'll be different.'

'You've got two children, haven't you, Tracy?'

'A boy and a girl. But they'd damn well better be in their rooms with their PlayStations in the evening, not hanging around on the street.'

'Or doing their homework?'

'Well ... I don't expect them to be Einsteins.'

Then Cooper noticed something he hadn't expected. From the centre of the village, looking towards the north east, he could see a wind farm. Three rows of tall, white turbines stood on a prominent summit, in a location where they would best catch the Pennine winds. Their vast arms turned slowly in the wind, and their blades glinted as they caught a bit of sun from a break in the clouds. They looked like the advance armies of the twenty-first century, marching over the hill towards Withens.

PHILIP GRANGER WEAVED his way between lines of vehicles that had slowed to a crawl on the A628 in Tintwistle. Cars were backed up from the turning to Hadfield, and motorists were getting frustrated. Three long back limousines parked half on the pavement outside the church while they waited for a wedding weren't helping very much, either.

Further on towards the motorway it would be even worse, with lorries jamming the lights on the A57 and traffic at a standstill right the way through Hollingworth and Mottram. It was always like this. And it always would be, unless someone got around to building a bypass. That's what Neil always said.

Philip found a gap between two cars that was just wide enough for him to reach the kerb and drew his motorbike on to the pavement in front of his brother's house. He gave the engine a quick rev before he switched it off, then kicked down the stand and propped his bike against the brick wall. The machine was an old Triumph that had been carefully restored once, though not by him. The roar of its engine was deep and loud, and people who knew him were usually in no doubt that he had arrived somewhere.

He stared back at the car drivers on the road as he took his time unfastening his helmet, locking it into a box mounted over the back wheel of the bike and fastening a chain through the front spokes. You couldn't be too careful in these parts.

By now, Neil would normally have recognized the sound of the Triumph and left the front door off the latch for his older brother to get into the house. But when Philip walked up the short path he found the door still locked. He rapped the knocker a couple of times, and rang the bell, but got no answer. He knocked again, waited a minute, then backed down the path to look up at the bedroom window, where the curtains were still closed.

Philip glanced at the windows of the houses on either side. Sure enough, the woman on the right was peering at him through her curtains. She didn't like him, or his motorbike. But Neil said she didn't like anybody very much. She hated cars and their drivers even more than she hated bikers.

So Philip gave the woman a little wave, gestured at his brother's bedroom, shrugged and grinned. She stared back at him without a smile.

He fumbled in the pockets of his leathers for some keys. Neil had given him a key to the house when Philip had first helped him move to Tintwistle from Withens. The front door opened straight away with the Yale key, which meant it wasn't bolted on the inside. Philip couldn't remember whether Neil used a bolt when he was in the house or not.

In the hallway, with the front door still open, Philip shouted up the stairs.

'Neil! It's me!'

He waited a moment.

'Neil! Are you awake?'

There was no answer. Philip went up the stairs, his motorcycle boots thumping on the steps. The walls of the houses in this terrace weren't very thick, and the woman next door would probably be waiting outside to complain about the noise he was making, but he didn't care.

He could see there was no one in the bedroom, though the bed had been slept in. He checked the other rooms and went back downstairs, where he opened and closed all the doors, just to make sure. Finally, he went out into the little back garden and looked at the patch of ground behind the houses where Neil normally kept his car. The VW wasn't there.

Philip looked at the house next door again, and caught a glimpse of the neighbour watching him. He decided to knock and ask her if she knew where Neil was. But when he did, she shook her head at him from behind a security chain.

Slowly, he went back through Neil's house and stood for a few moments in the sitting room to take one last look round. Everything seemed as it should be. There was nothing out of place, as far as he could see. But Philip picked up a small brass box on the mantelpiece and looked at the ornate pattern beaten into its lid before putting it down again, a couple of inches to the left. He cocked his head and examined it until he was satisfied.

Then Philip locked his brother's front door and dug his phone out of an inside pocket. He dialled Neil's mobile, but it rang without being answered. The second person he called was the Reverend Derek Alton.

IN ST ASAPH'S Church a few minutes later, Derek Alton found his eyes drawn towards the east window and its stained-glass representation of St Asaph, the obscure Celtic saint to whom his church was dedicated. The saint was depicted carrying hot coals in his cloak without setting fire to himself or his clothes – an act that had provided enough evidence of his saintliness for those who decided these things. It was almost the only thing known about his history.

The picture had been created from hundreds of tiny fragments of glass – some green, like fresh grass, or blue like the sky, or red like fire. In the morning, they glowed in the sun from the east. But Alton could see that the bottom half of St Asaph was darker than the rest of him. No light passed through the glass below the red glow of the burning coals held in a fold of his cloak. The saint looked as though he had been cut off at the waist. Alton knew that the effect was caused by the rampant ivy that covered the east wall and was now spreading over the windows. Its spring leaves were a virulent green where they lay against the stonework, and its tendrils were grasping and eager, seeking new holds in the lead that held the pieces of coloured glass together.

When Alton looked closely at the saint's waist area, he could see the triangular shapes of the young ivy leaves clearly. They were like little green tongues licking at St Asaph's robes. They were growing day by day now, creeping towards the sun, slowly eating up the picture. Already, the saint's legs had been swallowed by the relentless force of nature.

If nothing was done to curb the ivy, the lead would crumble and the glass would be pulled apart, piece by piece. One day, it would take only one loud noise to shatter the entire window, and St Asaph would drop into the east aisle.

'Catching flies, Vicar?'

Alton felt a guilty flush rising under his collar. A tall young man stood in the aisle near the west door. He was dressed in jeans and a blue sweater, and his blond hair had recently been cut and gelled.

'Oh, it's you, Scott.'

'Thank goodness it's only me, eh? It's a good job I'm not the chuffin' bishop. He'd whip your frock off and give your dog collar back to the dog before you could say "Heil Mary".'

'Hail Mary,' said Alton.

'Yeah, right.'

He watched Scott Oxley move towards him up the narrow aisle, slapping his hand on each pew and rubbing his palm over the carved wooden ends.

'Did you want something, Scott?'

'No.'

Scott let him wait for a minute, looking around the church with a smile.

'Have you heard from Neil today, Vicar?' said Scott.

'No, I haven't. And he said he'd be here to help me work on the churchyard.'

'Good old Neil.'

Scott walked up to the oak pulpit and smoothed the pulpit cloth with his hand. Alton wished he wouldn't touch anything, but he held his peace.

'I phoned Philip and he called at Neil's house, but he's not at home. Do you know where Neil is, Scott?'

'No idea.'

Scott walked back down the aisle of the church, slapping the ends of the pews again as he went. Alton listened to Scott go out into the porch. He needed to make sure that the young man had left. He knew that the big oak outer door would close with a painfully loud slam, as it always did.

A thud shook the church as Scott Oxley slammed the door. Layers of dust danced on the window ledges. But the stained-glass picture of St Asaph didn't shatter. It wasn't the time. Not yet.

Chapter Five

SARAH RENSHAW LOOKED as though she hadn't combed her hair that morning. She had a perm several weeks old, but it was springing out in all the wrong directions, like a burst mattress. Her plaid skirt was covered in dog hairs, and her shoes had dried mud clinging to the edges of the soles.

Also, her eyes were bright and her face looked unnaturally flushed. In a younger person, Diane Fry would have suspected alcohol or substance abuse. With a woman of Mrs Renshaw's age, her first thought was the menopause. Hot flushes and irrational behaviour – that's what the menopause offered.

Fry shuddered a little as she experienced one of those moments when the future poked its unpleasant face into her mind and leered at her.

Gavin Murfin had been chattering cheerfully to the Renshaws as he brought them upstairs. Fry had been able to hear him all the way along the corridor, telling them little jokes about the difficulties of getting good detectives these days. As they came nearer, Murfin had been explaining that after he had done twelve years in CID, his reward would be that he'd get sent back on the beat, because twelve years was the maximum tenure for a detective constable.

'Of course, they don't call it being on the beat any more,' he said. 'They call it "core policing". That's because everyone says "Cor blimey, not this bloody lark again."'

Murfin had ushered the Renshaws in and pulled a face at Fry over their shoulders. She realized he had simply been filling the silence with words to avoid having the Renshaws talk to him. It was quite clear that Sarah and Howard Renshaw were more than happy to discuss their daughter. But it felt so odd that they talked about her in the present tense. It clashed with the conviction that Fry was already forming in her own mind.

'Emma had phoned us just the day before, to say she'd be home on the Thursday afternoon,' said Mrs Renshaw. 'She's always very good about phoning us.'

'Yes.'

'But she never arrived. We thought she'd changed her mind, or that something had come up in Birmingham. We couldn't get through to her on her mobile, because it was switched off. So we rang the house where she lives during the term, and the girl she shares with told us she'd gone home for Easter. But she hadn't gone home. She never arrived.'

'No.'

'We rang the police in Birmingham, but they weren't interested,' said Mrs Renshaw.

'It was Smethwick,' said her husband. 'The local station.'

Howard Renshaw was a big man, well padded, like a businessman who had eaten too many lunches. His hair was a little too long for the image, but at least he combed it away from his bald patch rather than trying to hide it. He looked neater than his wife, as if he took more care over his appearance. But he sat back in his chair, slightly behind Sarah, to let her take centre stage.

'Anyway, they weren't interested,' said Sarah. 'They said she was an adult, and it was up to her what she did. Unless we had evidence that a crime had been committed, there was nothing they could do.'

'I don't think that's quite right,' said Fry. 'She was a young woman under the age of twenty-one. Enquiries are always made in those circumstances.'

Mrs Renshaw shook her head briefly, as if bothered by a small fly. 'So we went to the house ourselves. Number 360B, Darlaston Road, Bearwood. We had to get the landlord to open Emma's room, because all the tenants have their own individual keys. One of Emma's bags was gone, and some clothes she must have packed to bring home with her.'

'What about personal items? A purse? Car keys?'

'She had a couple of shoulder bags, and those little rucksack things, so I couldn't tell which she was planning to carry with her. But her purse wasn't there with her credit cards, or her keys.'

'She has a car, but she decided not to take it to the West Midlands with her,' said Howard. 'The car's still in our garage. It's an Audi.'

'It's only two years old,' said Sarah.

'But if she had her purse, some money, her credit cards –'

'We know. The police said she could have gone away somewhere, if she had money with her.'

'I'm afraid it happens all the time, Mrs Renshaw. In a city full of students, the police will have a lot of similar cases to deal with every year.'

'Emma's at the Birmingham School of Art and Design,' said Sarah, as if that were somehow different from being just a student. 'She's studying for a BA in Fine Art. She's particularly interested in Marketing Design. In fact, she should have had a placement last year, but she's missed it now. It's going to be very difficult for her to catch up.'

'Emma's very talented, you know,' said Howard. 'You must see some of her work. We have all kinds of things in the house. Some of them are pieces we brought back home from her room at Bearwood – work she'd done during term time.'

'She wouldn't want those to be lost,' said Sarah. 'There are some pieces that she hasn't finished yet.'

Not finished yet? Diane Fry looked hard at the couple. Hope was one thing – but did the Renshaws genuinely believe their daughter would turn up tomorrow, or the day after, to finish her latest design project or take her Audi for a run?

She watched Sarah Renshaw turn towards her husband. They exchanged a meaningful glance and a little private smile, as if there were no one else in the room.

'We made our own posters,' said Howard. 'My brother had them done for us at his office. "Have you seen this girl?" they said. We put them up in newsagents and at the students union, and at all the places she went to in Birmingham and the Black Country. Some of them weren't the nicest of places, you know – bars and clubs, not the sort of establishment we would go in normally, or expect Emma to, either. But she's a student, and they live a different life. We understand that.'

'She's an art student, of course,' said Sarah. 'They're allowed to be a little Bohemian, aren't they?'

'But no one had seen her?'

'No.'

'Mr and Mrs Renshaw, you know that the West Midlands police did make some enquiries at the time.'

'Oh, yes? But what sort of enquiries? We expected them to be going door to door, doing fingertip searches. Helicopters with thermal cameras. All the things we see on the TV news when other people's children go missing. They didn't do any of that. We kept complaining. We spoke to an inspector several times. We went to the local newspapers to expose the shortcomings of the police. But it didn't do us any good. They just thought we were a nuisance.'

'For children, some of those things would be done. But Emma was nineteen. And, as I say ...'

'... it happens all the time. Yes, we know. Hundreds of young people go missing every year, and nearly all of them turn up again unharmed. We've been told that. But none of those are our daughter.'

'I realize it must have been very difficult for you. A difficult thing to live with.'

'Difficult? Do you know, we panic if we ever get separated in a crowd, or if it ever feels as though we've lost each other. Until it's happened to you, it's impossible to understand that sense of suddenly losing a person that belongs to you. It's like being cut off from something you were part of. It's the sort of fear that can take a hold on you completely, on your entire life. I don't think we'll ever lose that feeling, either of us. Not until we find Emma.'

'What sort of mood had Emma seemed to be in up to that point?'

'Mood? Well, her usual sort of mood, I suppose.'

'We all know there are a lot of pressures on young people at university,' said Fry. 'Sometimes it's very difficult for them, being away from home, and worrying about being short of money, as well as having all the exams and things. I wondered if you thought she might have been worried or depressed about anything?'

'Nothing in particular. Not that you could put your finger on.'

'I see. But being away from home, being short of money, doing exams ... You're right, it is a lot for them to cope with. Sometimes an emotional complication can be the last straw.'

The Renshaws looked at her in slight puzzlement.

'A boyfriend,' said Fry. 'I wonder if she had a problem with a boyfriend?'

'We don't know.'

'Perhaps there was somebody she was due to meet that night, that Thursday. Something could have happened to upset her. She could have had an argument with a boyfriend. Don't her housemates know who she might have been seeing?'

Mrs Renshaw shook her head. 'Her friends say there was nobody special – just a group of college friends. Both male and female, we gather. They used to meet up for a drink at a local pub, or go into Birmingham for the evening, that kind of thing. Unless Emma had a headache and didn't feel like going out.'

'Did she suffer from headaches a lot?'

'Now and then. She said it was stress. She found some of the assignments and exams a bit stressful.'

'Did she ever see a doctor about her headaches?'

'Not so far as we know.'

'Or about the stress?'

'We don't think so.'

'Stress can be a difficult thing to cope with, for young people living away from home. It isn't a good idea to bottle it up.'

Even as she said it, Fry knew it was a particularly useless piece of advice. Not bottling it up involved having someone you could talk to about things like that. She couldn't follow the advice herself, and wouldn't have appreciated being given it. But the Renshaws took it well.

'She wouldn't talk to us about it much, but there was another girl in the house, Debbie. They were very friendly.'

'How many people shared this house?'

'Four.'

'So the other two were boys?'

'Yes.'

'Were you happy with that arrangement?'

'We trust Emma,' said Sarah. 'Besides, we know Alex Dearden. He's a nice boy – we had no worries on that score.'

Fry waited for one of them to say the same about Neil Granger, but they didn't. Instead, the Renshaws glanced at each other again, passing some hidden message.

'I understand Emma knew both of the boys from an early age,' said Fry.

'They both lived in Withens as children, so they went to the same school.'

'So both Alex Dearden and Neil Granger were old friends of Emma's. You knew them both well, and you were happy for your daughter to be sharing a house with them.'

'We know them both,' said Howard.

'A set-up like that could be enough to cause stress in itself, in some circumstances.'

'I don't think Emma found it a problem. She is a very well-balanced girl.'

'Apart from the stress she suffered because of the work and the exams.'

'Yes.'

Mr Renshaw had been listening to his wife carefully. Now he looked at Fry. 'She isn't the sort of girl to kill herself,' he said. 'We're quite sure of that.'

'Oh, quite sure,' agreed his wife.

'Thank you.' Fry sighed. She had noticed that every time she slipped up and used the past tense in referring to Emma, one of the Renshaws corrected her gently.

'You realize there's no reason why she shouldn't come back,' said Sarah.

'It's been over two years now, Mrs Renshaw.'

'But there's no reason why she shouldn't come back.'

Howard Renshaw leaned forward with a smile, trying to look like a helpful intermediary, ready to calm the situation and smooth over the sudden tension.

'There are plenty of young people who go missing for long periods of time,' he said helpfully.

'Yes, I know, Mr Renshaw,' said Fry.

'And many of them turn up again, safe and sound – sometimes after several years.'

'Yes.'

'And you know perfectly well that the police enquiries at the time found no evidence of a crime.'

'No,' said Fry.

But Howard Renshaw was sharp enough to catch her hesitation.

'At least, that's what they told us,' he said, suddenly fixing her with an accusing stare.

'There's some new evidence,' said Fry.

'Evidence?'

'I'm afraid Emma's mobile phone has been found.'

'Where?' said Howard immediately.

'In woodland a little way outside Chapel-en-le-Frith.'

'Can you tell us exactly?'

'I'd rather not at the moment, sir. Obviously, we want to examine the area thoroughly before we come to any conclusions.'

Sarah Renshaw was smiling. 'Well, that explains why we were never able to contact her, if she had lost her mobile phone. I suppose it was stolen.'

'Well, it's possible,' said Fry. 'But there could be other interpretations. We're keeping our options open.'

'What are you saying?'

Fry could hear the rising note in Sarah Renshaw's voice, and she began to feel uneasy. She was aware of Gavin Murfin shuffling on his chair next to her, as if he wanted to get up and leave the room.

'I'm not trying to upset you, Mrs Renshaw. It's just that we're going to have to look at the circumstances again, and –'

'And *what*?'

Sarah Renshaw was getting flushed. Fry desperately cast around for something to calm her down. She looked at Mr Renshaw, hoping for his placatory intermediary act right now. It didn't come. But Sarah calmed herself with her own thoughts.

'I lit a candle the night she didn't come home,' she said. 'There's been a candle burning for her ever since.'

Fry nodded, not knowing what to say, and decided to say nothing.

'I need to make some initial enquiries,' she said, 'but then I'd like to come and see you at home, if that's all right. Perhaps tomorrow.'

'Tomorrow afternoon,' said Sarah. 'That would be fine.'

'Will you be talking to Emma's friends again?' asked Howard.

'Yes. I plan to start with Alex Dearden and Neil Granger.'

'Alex is a nice young man,' said Sarah. 'I hope that he and Emma might get together some day.'

The Renshaws looked at the clock, and then at their watches.

'We have to go,' said Howard.

'We're going to wait for Emma at the underpass,' said Sarah.

Fry stared at her. 'Sorry?'

Sarah smiled and patted Fry's sleeve as she stood up. 'Don't worry about it,' she said. 'We've been getting *guidance.*'

As soon as the Renshaws had left, Diane Fry got Gavin Murfin to pull out the files on them. Murfin had been right – it would have been helpful if she'd been warned beforehand. But everyone else in E Division seemed to know the whole story, so maybe they had assumed that she knew it as well. It was just one of those little break-downs in communication that made life so frustrating sometimes. Probably everyone but DI Hitchens had also forgotten that she was herself from Warley, near to where Emma Renshaw had last been seen. Fry had spoken to very few people here in Edendale about her past. One too many, perhaps. But very few.

She supposed that Howard and Sarah Renshaw had been normal people once. Until that night two years ago, they had been a nice, middle-aged, middle-class couple living in their detached house in Withens. They probably had a barbecue patio and a holiday caravan at Abersoch, as well as a daughter studying for a degree in Fine Art in Birmingham.

There were a few little facts about them that Fry was able to glean from the files. Apparently, Howard had already been thinking of taking early retirement from his job as director of a major construction company in Sheffield. Maybe he had been wondering every morning whether his bald patch had grown too big to bother combing his hair over it any more. As for Sarah, she had been due to start a year as president of the local Women's Institute. Probably she had been busy planning a series of events for her presidency, and calculating how much money she could spend on a wardrobe of new clothes.

One thing was for sure. Both of them had been looking forward to their daughter returning home from university for the Easter holidays, and they had invited their friends and neighbours Michael and Gail Dearden for dinner the following night to admire Emma's achievements.

Now, though, the Renshaws had both become a little strange. Fry had seen for herself that they were a bit too inclined to those sudden stares and meaningful glances, to raised voices and flushes of colour, and to odd bursts of excitement, followed by dejection and tears.

But the files also recorded the fact that they had become a downright nuisance over the past twenty-four months, bombarding the police with theories and suggestions, pleas and demands, letters and phone calls, and dozens of personal visits to any officer whose name they could get hold of. They had repeatedly reported second-hand sightings of young women who vaguely resembled their daughter. Most worryingly, they had been picked up by traffic patrols several times after they had been found standing in the road, harassing motorists, asking questions that people didn't like being asked. Twice the Renshaws had been brought in to be given words of advice.

And now they talked about getting guidance. It had turned out they meant guidance from some so-called psychic they'd been consulting, who was advising them where to look for Emma, and which roadsides to stand on at what time, in the hope of some miraculous encounter. Fry grimaced at the thought of the person who was taking advantage of the couple, ruthlessly exploiting their belief.

She supposed that the Renshaws were still a nice, middle-aged, middle-class couple with the house and a caravan. The difference was they no longer had a daughter. Yet they seemed to be living in a sort of alternate reality, where Emma was not only still alive, but perhaps simply planning to catch a later train from Birmingham. Two years later.

DIANE FRY LEFT the files open on her desk and walked to the window. From the upper floor of E Division's West Street headquarters she could see part of the stand at the football ground and the roofs of houses running down-hill towards Edendale town centre. Everything looked strangely clean and gleaming out there. But that was only because the slates of the roofs were still wet from the morning's showers, and the dampness was reflecting the faintest vestige of sunlight penetrating the grey cloud cover. A bit of light could be so deceptive.

Fry shuddered, but not at the view from her window. There was one question in her mind. Could fear be avoided by simply ignoring the reality? Perhaps it depended on whether you were ever forced to accept what that reality was. Howard and Sarah Renshaw seemed to be going to great lengths to avoid the reality that their daughter was likely to be dead. Fry might have to be the one who forced them to face it.

Yet who was *she* to talk about facing reality? For years, she'd been perfecting her own techniques for doing just the opposite – burying the fear. Her own reality included a sister she hadn't seen for fifteen years, ever since Angie had walked out of their foster home in the Black Coun-try as a teenager, and the violent rape that had led her to transfer from the West Midlands to Derbyshire. And there were events in her more distant childhood that she didn't even want to guess at. It was hard to pinpoint which of them caused the fear.

According to the therapist she had talked to, phobic behaviour was caused by fear conditioning, the need to avoid the triggers that had caused the fear in the first place. But it could be overcome by experiencing the triggers in a safe context – the process of cognitive behavioural therapy, a treatment for part of the brain the therapist called the medulla. He said new memories had to be created which would over-ride the fear. Extinction memories. A new life to replace the old one.

Fry had begun to imagine this process as being like painting a new picture over a previously used canvas. As a child and a young teenager, she had liked to draw. It had been something she could do alone, absorbing herself in her pictures in her room at Warley. But sometimes a finished pencil drawing had bothered her, and she had rubbed it out with an eraser. That had never seemed enough, though, so she would draw over it again, trying to create a happier picture on paper that was already grubby and smeared with charcoal from the old one.

Then a boyfriend had taken her into Birmingham City Art Gallery one wet Brum afternoon, to try to raise her cultural standards. There had been a special exhibition on, and it was there she had seen one of the visions of Hell painted by Breughel the Younger. There had been a lot of other stuff, too, but it had been the Breughel that impressed her. She had kept the memory of it for much longer than she had kept the boyfriend. He had lasted only a few weeks. But the vision of Hell was still with her twelve years later.

Now Fry imagined her fear as one of those Breughel visions, all demons and flames. With the therapist's help, she had learned to cover her mental painting with a pastoral landscape rendered in gentle colours – brown and white cows grazing in a wildflower meadow, a cottage with clematis growing by the door, a cat relaxing in the sun on a window ledge. And always in her picture there was a young girl. She stood right in the middle foreground, clutching a wicker basket in her bare arms, smiling as she scattered grain for the hens around her feet.

The picture had stayed intact for a while. The cows had never seemed to run out of grass in their pasture, the sun always shone on the cat. And the girl had never aged, so that her skin had remained pink and fresh, and unbroken. Just like the photograph of Emma Renshaw.

But Fry's picture didn't have the advantage of photographic permanence. It had been done with cheap paints. After a year or two, the colours had worn thin. They were scoured away by the rubbing of her hands, by her constant touching and stroking to make sure the picture was still intact. When she had handled her picture too often, the Breughel showed through again. That was when she had to go back for help, to prevent the faces of the tormented souls emerging once more from the red petals of the poppies, to convince herself that the hooves in the grass were those of cattle and not goat-footed demons. She needed reassurance to make her see the leaves of the clematis instead of the flames leaping from the pit. She needed help to see the innocence of the girl, not the scaly claws of the birds at her feet.

Each time she had to lay the paint on thicker, layer upon layer of it, with a bigger and bigger brush and in brighter and brighter colours. Finally, the picture had become so garish that she could no longer see anything but what lay underneath. She saw only blood in the poppies, and mould in the grass. She saw the bones under the skin of the girl.

Chapter Six

BEN COOPER AND Tracy Udall found the Reverend Derek Alton in his churchyard. He'd taken a bit of finding, because he was almost invisible among the weeds and overgrown shrubs. Alton was wearing wellingtons and corduroy trousers, and he was clutching a scythe in gloved hands. Thistle burrs and bramble thorns had stuck to his trousers. Now and then, he took a half-hearted swipe at the weeds, flattening them, but not cutting through them. In between swipes, he paused and stared gloomily at the plants.

'I think your scythe needs sharpening,' said Cooper.

Alton looked up and wiped his forehead with the back of one of his gloves. 'Yes, I know. But the sharpening stone has gone missing.'

'In fact, don't you think that the job would be a lot easier with a decent brush cutter? You could hire a four-stroke model, so that you wouldn't have to trail an extension lead all the way out here.'

Alton looked at the scythe dubiously, then down at his feet. Cooper saw that there was a gaping slash in the rubber across the toes of one of the vicar's wellington boots. Perhaps a petrol-driven brush cutter wasn't such a good idea after all – not if he could nearly take his toes off with a blunt hand scythe.

The church was small and stone-built. But it was a dark stone, almost black, unlike the golden sandstone or the almost white limestone that had been used in other areas. Maybe it hadn't always been black, but had been stained by soot from the steam trains that had travelled on the railway lines below ground here.

PC Udall went to take a look at the vestry, where Mr Alton had reported the break-in.

'Is it your turn on the rota for tidying up the churchyard then, Mr Alton?' said Cooper.

'Rota?' Alton laughed. 'I *am* the rota.'

'Oh?'

'Other churches have rotas. My other church, All Saints in Hey Bridge – *that* has a churchyard rota. The graves are tended wonderfully, and the parishioners don't expect the vicar to lift a finger, let alone wield a scythe. Here in Withens, though … Well, they're too busy to spare the time, I suppose.'

'Who are your churchwardens here?'

'Michael Dearden and Marion Oxley.'

'I've heard of the Oxleys.'

'Good for you.'

'But who's Mr Dearden?'

'Shepley Head Lodge. It's out past the village, that way.'

'Right.'

'They're both very worthy people, but they have their own concerns, you see.'

'Of course.'

'The trouble is, when we get the first bit of sunshine in the spring, this is what happens.'

Cooper looked around at the undergrowth. There were gravestones somewhere in there, but it was difficult to be sure. Mats of rough grass had grown over the plots, and brambles and ivy had attached themselves to the stones, so that few of the inscriptions were decipherable. He realized he was standing on what had once been a flagged path, but the grass and dandelions had forced their way through between the flags and covered them. Burgeoning nature was out of control here, and it was spreading nearer and nearer to the church itself.

'So you have no help at all?' said Cooper.

'A young man called Neil Granger is going to help me. At least, he said he was going to. He said he had one of those things you mentioned, a brush cutter, and some other tools. But he hasn't turned up. I don't suppose he could be bothered in the end.' Alton sighed. 'He's always seemed a very genuine young man, but there we are. It's the way of the world these days. Young people think nothing of letting others down.'

'I don't think that's true,' said Cooper.

Alton suddenly looked at him again, and smiled. 'Good heavens, a policeman who doesn't have a cynical view of humanity. Let me tell the curators of the folk museum in Glossop about you – they might want to preserve you for posterity.'

'Young people always get a bad press. But I don't think they're any worse than they used to be, on the whole. We should put in a bit more effort, take an interest in what they're doing, instead of writing them off.'

'You make me feel positively ashamed,' said Alton. 'It should be part of my pastoral duties to draw the best out of the young people in my parish, not denigrate them. I'll do my best to emulate your attitude.'

If it had been anyone else he was talking to, Cooper might have thought they were taking the mickey out of him. If it had been Diane Fry speaking the same words, they would have meant something quite different. But, strangely, the Reverend Alton seemed sincere.

'Take an interest in them – that's what you should do,' said Cooper.

'I will. Thank you.'

Cooper felt sure he was being patronizing. It was ridiculous to find himself lecturing a clergyman on showing an interest in his parishioners. But the vicar genuinely didn't seem to mind. Probably he had received far blunter advice from his parishioners.

'PC Udall tells me there have been some problems in the village with the children of the Oxley family.'

'I've had to complain to their father a few times,' said Alton. 'They do tend to gather in the churchyard in the evenings – particularly at the back here, because it's completely secluded and no one can see what they're up to.'

'And what *are* they up to?'

'I shudder to think sometimes. I regularly pick up beer cans, and that kind of thing. They cause a bit of damage, and there's some graffiti. It's just a nuisance, really.'

'But you find their father co-operative?'

'Lucas? He listens. And so does Marion, of course. But I'm not sure how much control they have over some of the children.'

'How many children are there?'

'Oh,' said Alton vaguely. He looked at the fingers of his gloves, as if he needed something to count on, but couldn't find enough fingers. 'There are so many of them down at Waterloo Terrace. Lucas has at least three sons – Scott is the eldest, and then there's Ryan and Jake. And possibly Sean. Then there are a couple of married daughters. Well, one is married, but I don't think Fran has ever bothered. And Lorraine and Stacey are the younger girls. But there are some cousins around, too, like Neil. He's a Granger, but I think he's Lucas Oxley's nephew. It's hard to keep track, you know – especially if you see them all in a group. Very often, I can't sort out which is which, except for little Jake, of course.'

'Jake – is he the one they call the Tiny Terror?'

'Yes, poor boy. Now, I think Jake pays more attention to his grandfather than to his parents. That's old Mr Oxley. It's quite surprising, really, since Jake is only nine years old, and Eric must be about eighty. But perhaps Jake is going to take after his grandfather one day. We can but hope. Eric was a hard worker in his day, by all accounts.'

Cooper was having as much difficulty as Alton in counting the number of Oxleys. He had Lucas and

Marion placed as the parents, but he'd already lost track of the number of children. Was it seven or eight? There were Scott, Ryan and Jake, but did Sean count? And how many cousins were there? Did the married daughters have children of their own? It was confusing enough, but now there was an older generation to take into account.

'Is old Mr Oxley a member of your congregation here at St Asaph's?' he asked.

'Sadly not.'

'I'm surprised. I felt sure he would be. At his age, he would have been raised in the expectation that he would go to church every Sunday. Unless he's a nonconformist, of course. There are a lot of Methodists in these parts.'

'Wash your mouth out,' said Alton, and smiled down at his scythe.

'*Is* he a Methodist?' asked Cooper.

'I wouldn't know,' said the vicar. 'I haven't had the chance to ask him. Eric Oxley hasn't spoken a word to me since I arrived in the village. Though I've passed him on the road several times and spoken to him, he's never acknowledged me, never spoken to me at all.'

'Not a word?' said Cooper.

'Not a word.'

'Mr Alton, do you think the Oxley youngsters were responsible for breaking into your vestry?'

Alton sighed. 'I really don't know. They're obvious suspects. But it's a bit beyond what they normally get up to. They've never got inside the church before. There's some quite serious damage to the doors and the furniture.

And, of course, there are several items missing. They've never stolen things before.'

'Some silver plate, I understand?'

'Yes. Oh, they were nothing much, but they were the only things we have of any value at St Asaph's. They were a gift from one of the founders, back in the 1850s.'

'It's quite possible we might be able to get them back.'

'It's kind of you to give me some hope.'

'Not at all.'

'If it turns out that it *was* the Oxley youngsters, what I really hope is that someone will find a way of halting their slide into criminality before it's too late. The boys are getting older. Scott is quite a young man now, and so is one of his cousins. Glen, I think they call him. They're not a good example for the younger ones. Sooner or later, something more serious is going to happen, and then an innocent person might get hurt. I wouldn't want that to happen.'

'I understand.'

Cooper looked at the flourishing undergrowth all around them in the churchyard. There ought to be flower borders under the church walls on either side of the porch, but instead the soil was hidden under elder saplings and clumps of ladies' bedstraw. Later in the year, there would be a good crop of blackberries from the brambles covering the vestry. And it wasn't even the beginning of May. At this rate, the church would have vanished completely by July.

Alton followed his gaze, and sighed again.

'Are the words "losing battle" hovering on your lips?' he said.

'Something like that,' said Cooper. 'Or is it "Fight the good fight with all thy might"?'

Alton intoned: '"Lay hold on life, and it shall be; Thy joy and crown eternally."' He swung the scythe as he sang, and Cooper warily took a pace back. He saw that Alton had unintentionally beheaded a clump of dandelions. Their yellow petals fell at Cooper's feet, like tiny shards of spring sun.

The vicar seemed to see the petals, too. 'Fight the good fight,' he said. 'The darkness and the *light*.'

WHILE PC UDALL went to call in to see if the suspects were ready for interviewing, Ben Cooper tried to identify Waterloo Terrace, where the Oxley family lived.

There weren't many places to choose from. Apart from the church, the pub, and the farms, there were a few detached homes and a little crescent of bungalows. But beyond the car park and below the road, Cooper could see a roofline and a series of brick chimney pots, just visible behind a thick screen of sycamores and chestnut trees. He began to wander towards it, intending only to take a look at the place.

Without the presence of any troublesome youngsters, Withens seemed eerily silent. There was no traffic on the road through the village, and it was protected from the noise of the A628 by the black humps of the peat moors in between. Cooper could hear only two sounds. One was the harsh cacophony of calls from a flock of rooks somewhere in the trees below the road. The other was the equally harsh, but higher-pitched, voice of a petrol-driven chainsaw.

To get to the houses that he could see, he had to pass the entrance to one of the farms. He paused at the farm gate and looked down through a jumble of buildings. Near the gate was an ancient stone barn with narrow, unglazed windows like arrow slits. Further from the road, the buildings were more recent, and a tractor was parked in the space between them. Cooper found he was looking downhill through a tunnel of buildings to a spectacular view of heather-covered slopes in the distance. The dark mass of Bleaklow lay directly across the valley.

He moved on a few yards, sticking to the grass verge because there were no pavements and the edges of the road were starting to crumble. There were streams of small stones at the roadside that had been swept down by the water running off the hills. Here and there, scraps of black plastic from torn silage bags lay like tattered oil slicks on the verges.

In Withens, water seemed to run wherever it chose. At this moment, it was running directly into the entrance to Waterloo Terrace. Because the terrace was on the downhill side of the road, the water was draining towards it in large quantities. And it had been doing so for some time, judging by the holes scoured in the surface of the track leading down to the terrace. Cooper had to step over vast, muddy puddles to reach the safety of drier ground.

In the wide entrance, there were gate posts, but no gate hung between them. Ceramic drainage pipes had been stacked in neat, geometric shapes nearby, so perhaps someone was thinking of putting proper drainage in one day. Horseshoes had been turned upside down and nailed to the gate posts – they were ready to catch luck or trap the Devil, whichever folklore you chose to believe.

There was nothing about Waterloo Terrace that resembled the romantic idea of a holiday cottage in the Peak District. There were no mullioned windows, no rose-filled front gardens, no honeysuckle growing on the walls. The eight houses were built of black brick that had weathered badly. It had become discoloured and was beginning to crumble at the exposed edges. Between each pair of houses, Cooper could see the arched mouth of a narrow passageway that ran towards the back of the terrace. The passages were completely enclosed and must run underneath the front bedrooms.

He stood where he could see into one of the passageways, and he could make out no light at the end of the brick tunnel. The passage seemed to turn a sharp corner at the far end, maybe providing access to a back yard, and all he could see was a blank wall. The builders hadn't thought to install lights in these passages, either.

There was a sudden crack like a gunshot in the air above the rooftops. But it was only a couple of wood pigeons taking off, their wings clapping loudly as they accelerated and performed a circuit of the houses.

Waterloo Terrace puzzled Cooper. It stuck out like a sore thumb in this area, where all the buildings were built in the traditional style, from local stone. Gritstone was so plentiful on the hills all around here that it was difficult to imagine why anyone should have decided to use brick. And black brick at that.

In front of the row of houses there was a long stretch of garden that had been converted to growing vegetables at some time. But the effort had been abandoned, and weeds had been allowed to take over where the earth had been disturbed. There were a few sickly cabbages gradually being smothered by thistles and couch grass. Cooper wasn't surprised by that. Withens was surely one of those places where the wind was strong enough to blow cabbages clean out of the ground – and not just during the winter, either.

Only in one part of the garden had the weeds been held at bay – and that was because black plastic sheeting had been laid over the earth. It was held down by stones and a variety of rusted metal objects that looked as though they had been lying around somewhere waiting for a useful purpose to be found for them. The plastic had torn in a few places, and strips of it flapped lazily in the breeze. The soil under there would be warm and weed-free, and full of worms and insects. But would anything actually be growing?

Across the track from the terrace stood a row of brick privies, with bright blue doors and sloping roofs of stone tiles overgrown with grass and moss. The iron hinges of the doors had been replaced several times, leaving their marks in the paintwork. And now the old privies were padlocked and unused.

Cooper walked on a bit further. The track felt gritty underfoot. The water running down it towards the road had washed away whatever surface had been there originally, leaving a wide channel between banks of grass splashed with dirty water. The wheel ruts of some heavy vehicle had worn through the remaining layer of grit in places to expose the hardcore underneath. Some of it was broken black bricks – presumably what was left over after Waterloo Terrace had been built, or perhaps the remains of some other buildings that had been demolished.

The rookery he had heard was in the chestnuts beyond the track. The birds were setting up a noisy accompaniment to his progress along the front gates of the terrace gardens. The overgrown gardens looked damper than they should have been, even after the morning's showers. In fact, they looked impossibly wet – the peaty soil was waterlogged and washed away in places. No wonder the cabbages weren't flourishing. Rice might have been a better crop to plant here. Presumably the water cascading off the hillsides ran straight through the gardens, too.

Cooper must have been tired, or lulled into inattention by the silence. He had lost awareness of his surroundings, and was taken completely by surprise when he heard the voice.

'Don't come any further, or you'll regret it.'

Chapter Seven

DIANE FRY AND Gavin Murfin had arrived outside a modern office building made of steel, concrete blocks and aluminium cladding. It stood in the middle of a business park on the southern outskirts of Edendale, constructed on what had once been the flood plain of the River Eden.

'This is it,' said Murfin. 'Eden Valley Software Solutions. Have you seen all that smoked glass and fancy furniture? It looks like a brothel.'

'You must know some high-class brothels in Edendale,' said Fry.

'OK. A hairdresser's, then.'

As Murfin got out of the car, Fry glanced suspiciously at a paper bag he had left on the ledge over the fascia.

'What's in the bag, Gavin?' she said.

'Don't worry. It's for later,' he said.

'Much later, I hope.'

Fry had taken her Peugeot to be valeted only two days before, and it was largely because she could no longer stand the debris left by Gavin Murfin when he had been a passenger. There had been crumbs and sticky traces of all kinds ground into her carpet and upholstery. In fact, the man at the valeting company had asked her how many children she had. He had imagined her to be a mum who got lumbered with a car full of whining toddlers on the nursery school run every day. It had been embarrassing, and it was Murfin's fault.

As soon as they announced themselves at Eden Valley Software Solutions, Alex Dearden emerged from a corridor to meet them in the reception area. He was wearing black jeans and a black T-shirt with a designer logo on it that was so small Fry would have had to rest her nose on his left nipple to read it. Dearden's face was slim and fine-boned, but his looks were spoiled by two little pouches at the sides of his mouth, which made him look a bit like an angry hamster. His beard might have disguised the effect, except that current fashion dictated he could only have a goatee.

'You have to sign in and get ID badges,' said Dearden. 'Sorry about that. Security, you know.'

'That's quite all right, sir,' said Fry. 'We're lucky that you're open at all on a Saturday.'

'Oh, it's seven days a week for some of us here at the moment.'

When they had signed in, Dearden went to a solid-looking door and stood with his back carefully turned towards them as he keyed numbers into a keypad. The door clicked, and he pulled it open. A burst of noise came down the corridor – voices talking and laughing, someone shouting, a printer humming.

'It's just like going into our custody suite back at the station,' said Murfin. 'I guess they don't want *your* inmates escaping and running amok on the streets either?'

Dearden laughed politely. 'Actually, we're thinking of switching over to fingerprint-recognition technology,' he said. 'Much more secure. Code numbers are too easy to get hold of.'

'Absolutely. We can't fault you for your security measures.'

'You have to be careful,' said Dearden. 'There's a lot of crime about.'

'Have you ever had any problem with break-ins here?'

'Actually, no. We had a bit of vandalism a while ago. Somebody broke the window in the front of reception. We've had reinforced glass put in since then. They scrawled graffiti on the outside wall, too. Something about Manchester United FC, all spelled wrong.'

'That doesn't sound like Edendale's gang of notorious computer software thieves, anyway.'

Dearden stopped. 'My God, who are *they*?'

'Just joking,' said Fry. But she saw that Dearden wasn't amused.

'There's an awful lot of money tied up in what we're developing here,' he said. 'Unbelievable amounts of money. There's no way of calculating how much.'

'I'm sorry, sir.'

'You don't appreciate what we're developing here. It's really ground-breaking stuff. If we roll some of these programs out for all platforms –'

'There's no need to explain,' said Fry. 'That wasn't what we came about.'

But Dearden wanted to explain. Or at least, he wanted to talk about a subject that had nothing to do with a visit by the police.

'We've actually used top consultant psychologists in the development of this concept,' said Dearden. 'That's how serious we are about it.'

'Mmm.'

Dearden had led them down the corridor and into a small conference room, where there was a long table, a flipchart on a stand, and a projection screen against the end wall. It looked like a million other meeting rooms that Fry had been in for briefings and training sessions. She looked around for an overhead projector to go with the screen. But of course presentations here would be done in PowerPoint from someone's laptop.

To her surprise, Alex Dearden sat at the head of the table as if he were about to chair a meeting. Fry had expected to be facing him across the table. This way suited her, though. It meant she and Murfin could be on either side of him. Dearden couldn't concentrate on both of them at once.

'It's about Emma Renshaw,' said Fry, taking a chair.

'Emma? But that's a long time ago,' said Dearden. 'It was all dealt with a long time ago.'

'It wasn't exactly dealt with, sir. Emma has never been found.'

'Of course, I know that. And it's been very distressing for all of us who knew her.'

'Yes, sir.'

'But, I mean, I told the police everything I knew at the time, which wasn't very much. It was all gone through over and over, though it didn't do any good. Tragic though it is for her family, I think there comes a point when we have to put these things behind us and move on, don't you?'

Fry stared at him. She had to remind herself how old Alex Dearden was. Twenty-two, according to his file. But he sounded like someone thirty years older. He sounded like a respectable middle-aged citizen irritated at being pestered over something that had happened long ago in his past, when he had been a different person entirely.

'You knew Emma from a very young age, I believe,' said Fry.

'For ever. We lived in the same village. In Withens. Do you know it at all?'

'I haven't been there yet.'

'Well, when you see it, you'll understand. There's nothing to the place. Children of around the same age couldn't help but know each other. We went to the same junior school, in Tintwistle. And later on, to the same secondary school, too. But our parents were on friendly terms anyway, so we were thrown together a lot.'

'And after school, you even ended up going to the same university.'

'No,' said Dearden. 'You have that wrong. I went to Birmingham University. Emma was at UCE, where she attended the art school. That's the University of Central England. It's a former polytechnic.'

'Right.' Fry looked at Alex Dearden and saw the little superior smile. He thought he had the better of her now, and was feeling more relaxed.

'But our universities were close enough that we thought it might be a good idea to pitch in together and rent a house,' he said. 'It beats being thrown in with a load of strangers. You don't know who you're going to have to live with for three or four years when you do that. It's madness. At least I knew Emma wouldn't be too much trouble. And our parents thought it was a good idea, too. They put the money up front for the deposit, of course.'

'Of course,' said Fry. She had never been to university herself, and had never had any parents either willing or able to put the money up to rent a house for her. But she nodded and smiled to encourage him.

'And your other housemates – one was Neil Granger.'

'Ah, well, he's a bit of an odd character, is Neil.'

'Odd?'

'Well, don't get me wrong. He's OK really. But he didn't mix with us so much back in Withens, you know, because he was one of the Oxleys.'

'I'm sorry? Could you explain?'

Dearden shifted on his seat and his smile faded. He glanced at Gavin Murfin, unnerved by the silent one, as they always were.

'You'll have to find out about the Oxleys,' said Dearden. 'They're a bit of a rough lot, always in trouble. We never normally had anything to do with them. Actually, I thought you would know of them already – they've all got criminal records, of course.'

He looked at Murfin again, who stared back at him blankly, in the way that only Murfin could. Holding his gaze, Murfin began to work his jaws a bit, as if he were chewing gum. But Fry knew that he hated gum. He said it was like going out with a prick-teaser – it promised to be food, but never was.

She looked down at the notes she'd brought. 'I think I have heard the name Oxley, now you mention it,' she said.

Dearden looked relieved. He was on safe ground again, talking to people who were on the same wavelength. He was uncomfortable about his attitude to the Oxleys, and he didn't like having to justify himself. Fry filed away that piece of information for future reference.

'Neil Granger is some kind of cousin of the Oxleys,' said Dearden. 'There's Neil and his brother Philip, and they were brought up with the Oxleys. But he's a decent enough bloke, Neil. When you're talking to him, you can forget he's an Oxley.'

'He was at the same school with you and Emma? In the same class?'

'Yes.'

'And which university did *he* go to? Birmingham or Central England?' She shuffled her papers. 'I'm afraid I don't seem to have that information, either.'

Fry looked at Alex Dearden with a hopeful expression, and was pleased to see the complacent smile was back.

'Neither,' he said. 'Neil wasn't at uni.'

'But he shared this house with you in, where was it, Bearwood? Why did he go all that way to share a house? I don't understand.'

'It was a bit of a coincidence, really. At first, when we went down there, it was just the three of us – me, Emma and her friend Debbie, who was on the same course. The two girls were big pals, you know, and they went everywhere together. But there was a fourth bedroom in the house, and after a while we started to think we'd have to try to find someone else to share. To be honest, the rent was a bit of a struggle for the three of us. You don't appreciate what expenses you're going to have, you know – books and all that. Emma and Debbie had a lot of equipment to buy for their course work.'

'And there would be socializing, I suppose?' said Fry.

Dearden looked at her suspiciously. 'Why do you suppose that?'

'Well – student life. There's a lot of socializing, isn't there? Or so I'm told.'

'A bit. But if you have any sense, you don't go mad. Not if you want to get through your course with good grades, which we all did.'

'I see. But life was proving a bit expensive, all the same?'

'Yes. Things we hadn't budgeted for – Council Tax, electricity, the phone bill. You know.'

'Yes, I do know.'

'Anyway, it was around then that Neil got in touch. He said he had a job to go to in Birmingham. It was a two-year contract on a development project on the inner ring road, as I remember. Neil wanted to know if we'd let him rent the other room in the house. Our parents weren't too happy, but we talked about it between us, and we decided to go for it.'

'Because he was somebody you knew, rather than a stranger?'

Dearden hesitated. 'Well, the thing that really swung it was the salary he was earning. He was getting good money on this contract, and the rest of us were just students living on loans. So we thought he'd be useful.'

Fry wanted to do something to remove that smile now, but she needed to keep Alex Dearden on her side. Out of the corner of her eye, she noticed Murfin chewing more quickly, as if he had found something with an unpleasant taste in his mouth that he wanted to spit out.

'Mr Dearden,' said Fry, 'did it ever occur to you that Neil Granger might have a particular reason for wanting to rent the room in your house?'

'It was just convenience, I think. It can be quite hard to find reasonable rented accommodation, especially in a city with so many students.'

'No, what I meant was – do you think he might have had an *additional* reason? A personal reason.'

Dearden still looked puzzled.

'An interest in Emma Renshaw, perhaps?'

He raised his eyebrows then. 'Good heavens. Neil? No, I think you're wrong.'

He didn't quite say 'again', but he might as well have done.

'Thank you, sir. In that case, can you tell me about any boyfriends that Emma had during the time she was in the West Midlands? I'm sure she must have had some, despite what you said about the lack of socializing.'

Dearden shook his head. 'There were a few boys Emma and Debbie talked about sometimes. I didn't take any notice, really. When the two girls went out, they always seemed to go together. So I'm afraid I don't know if there were any particular boys involved in their lives. Well, all right, I expect there were. But I'm sure Neil wasn't one of them, Sergeant.'

'Did Neil have his own friends while he was working in Birmingham?'

'Yes, I expect so. Some of his workmates from the development project, I imagine.'

'You don't seem too sure.'

'I didn't ask him. I was busy. I was working hard for my degree. It wasn't my concern where Neil Granger went in the evenings.'

'Or Emma either?'

'Well, no.'

'Despite the fact that she'd been a friend of yours since you were very young?'

'I don't see what that has to do with it.'

'I just thought you might have shown a bit more interest in what she was doing. A bit more concern for who she might have been getting involved with.'

'Emma was OK,' said Dearden confidently. 'She was sensible enough.'

'OK? A large city can be a dangerous place for a young woman away from home for the first time. There are all kinds of people she might have come into contact with.'

'In Bearwood? The place was just boring, if you ask me. Not dangerous at all.'

'But Mr Dearden,' said Fry, 'your friend Emma Renshaw never came home from Bearwood.'

Dearden stopped smiling and started to fidget in his chair. 'I went through all this before, two years ago,' he said. 'I had the police on to me, and I had her parents after me about it constantly. I don't know why Emma didn't come home. I don't know where she went.'

'Are Emma's parents still in touch with you?'

He laughed. 'Every bloody week. One day, I'm going to take out an injunction against them for harassment. I mean it. I know they're upset about Emma disappearing, and all that. But if you ask me, it's turned their minds completely. They're absolutely unreasonable.'

'In what way, sir?'

'Well, Mrs Renshaw phones me every single week to ask if I've seen Emma. And every time I talk to her, it's as if she can't remember having phoned me last week with the same question. And the week before, and the week before that. Every call she makes, it's as if she thinks she's asking me for the first time.'

Dearden leaned forward towards Fry. She could almost make out the designer logo on his T-shirt, but not quite.

'And I know she's going to keep phoning and phoning me,' he said, 'until I give her the answer she wants, which I can't do. There isn't even any point in changing my number at home, because she would only start phoning me here. And that would be a nightmare.'

'It must be very difficult for her,' said Fry.

'What about me? It's difficult for me, too. Isn't there anything you could do about it? Couldn't you have a word with her? It's getting to be a real nuisance.'

'OK, I'll mention it, sir.'

Dearden sighed. 'Yeah. A fat lot of good it will do.'

'And Neil Granger?'

'Neil *again*? What about him?'

'Are you still in contact with him?'

'Not really.'

'When did you speak to him last?'

Dearden shrugged. 'It'd be a few months ago. I was visiting my parents, and I called in the Quiet Shepherd in Withens for a quick drink on the way back. Neil was in there, with some of his relations. The Oxleys, you know. So we didn't say much to each other. It was just "hi". There was no conversation.'

'And neither of you mentioned Emma, I suppose?'

'No,' said Dearden. 'Neither of us mentioned Emma.'

'This software you're developing …' said Fry.

'It's highly confidential at the moment.'

'Can you give me a clue?'

'Well, imagine this. The human brain can run routines and recurrent actions, just like a computer does. But occasionally, you get minor damage to the frontal lobes of the brain, which is the system governing attention. Then actions can still be triggered automatically, but out of sequence, or can't be stopped. The psychologists say it's the penalty we pay for being able to automatize our actions.'

Fry looked at Murfin, warning him not to laugh. She hoped that Alex Dearden wasn't actually a robot but could be stopped at the appropriate moment.

'It's a bit like having a dodgy auto-pilot,' he said. 'For the psychologists, it helps them to understand human fallibility. From our point of view, it helps us to design the technology to allow for human error. It's why computer programs won't let you close a document without deciding whether you want to save it or not,' he said. 'But we're going to take that concept a whole lot further. A whole lot further. I really can't tell you any more than that.'

'Or you'd have to kill me?' said Fry.

'Sorry?'

'Never mind.'

WHEN THEY GOT out of Eden Valley Software Solutions, Gavin Murfin stopped in the car park and pretended to spit out the imaginary gum he'd been chewing. He trod it into the tarmac and ground the toe of his shoe on it until he was satisfied.

'Feel better now?' said Fry.

'Not until I get a piece of that pie inside me.'

'Not in my car, you don't, Gavin.'

'I'll be careful of the crumbs, honest.'

'Do you *know* how much it cost me to get this car valeted?'

'Look, I'll not even take it out of the bag.'

'*No.*'

Murfin's face crumpled, and he sighed deeply. 'Where to next, then?'

'We need to speak to Neil Granger, but I tried to phone him, and he's not at home.'

'Does that mean we call it a day then?'

'Yes. Until tomorrow.'

'Tomorrow? It's Sunday tomorrow, Diane.'

'A good day for a drive to Withens, then.'

Murfin sniffed. 'There's *no* good day for a drive to Withens.'

BEN COOPER HAD his hand on the gate, and had been about to lift the latch. But he stopped at the sound of the voice. A man stood near the end house of Waterloo Terrace, watching Cooper carefully. He had been standing quite still, so that Cooper, who had been more interested in the state of the gardens, hadn't even noticed him. The man was wearing a dark suit and a white shirt, but no tie, and his suit trousers were tucked into black wellington boots. Cooper guessed him to be in his fifties. He had a balding head and some strands of sandy hair that stood up at his temples and moved in the breeze. But his hair was the only thing about him that moved. Even his eyes were quite still, fixed firmly on Cooper. His hands were hanging by his sides, and he carried no weapon of any kind, yet still managed to convey a clear threat.

Cooper felt slightly nervous as he reached for his warrant card, worried that the movement might be taken the wrong way. Maybe he was becoming paranoid, but he had begun to feel that there were other pairs of eyes watching him, too, from somewhere.

'Detective Constable Cooper, Edendale Police,' he said. 'Who am I speaking to?'

The man didn't reply. His expression shifted subtly from suspicion to contempt, as if a detective ought to know whose house he was visiting.

'Are you Mr Oxley?' said Cooper.

'What do you want?'

Cooper realized that he would have to read the answers in the man's eyes. This was almost certainly Mr Oxley. Lucas, presumably. The father of Scott, Ryan, Jake and maybe of Sean.

'If you're Mr Lucas Oxley, I'd like to talk to you.'

'Don't come any further, I said.'

Cooper had automatically begun to lift the latch of the gate again, assuming that once he had made verbal contact, he would be allowed to enter. But he was wrong.

'What I have to ask you, sir, might not be something you want everyone to hear. Not something you'd want to shout out to your neighbours.'

'That's perfectly all right. I've no intention of shouting.'

'I need to ask you –'

'You don't *need* anything. Not from me.'

Cooper was sure he could see movement through one of the downstairs windows of the second house, number two. The curtains were open, but the interior was too dark to be sure if there was anyone there, without staring too hard.

'You *are* Mr Oxley, aren't you?' said Cooper.

'Happen I am.'

'I've just been to the church, where there's been a break-in.'

To Cooper's surprise, Oxley simply turned on his heel and walked away down the passage between the two end houses. The strands of hair bounced around his ears for a moment until he had disappeared into the shadows.

Cooper opened the gate and took a few steps after him.

'Mr Oxley!' he called.

Then he stopped. Something had made the back of his neck prickle uneasily. He stood where he was, a couple of yards along the path from the gate, and he looked at the house. There were certainly faces peering through the windows. Two, three or four of them. He could see their eyes watching his movements. They were like a family glued to a television screen, waiting for the next exciting moment, another car chase or a fight scene. They didn't look worried, or frightened. They looked expectant.

Yet now that Lucas Oxley had disappeared, there was almost complete silence in the front gardens of Waterloo Terrace. Almost, but not quite. Cooper's ears caught a faint click, then a strange skittering noise approaching from the far end of the ginnel.

At the last moment, Cooper turned and ran for the gate. He knew he didn't have time to open it, so he dived at the wall and vaulted it just as a huge, shaggy-haired Alsatian burst from the arched entrance of the ginnel and hurtled down the path towards him.

Cooper stood gasping in the roadway on the other side of the wall, ready to run for his car. But nothing happened. The dog was utterly silent. It hadn't barked once, or even let out a snarl. It had made no sound as it went for him, except for the skittering of its claws on the concrete of the ginnel. But it seemed to have halted the moment Cooper was on the other side of the gate, and therefore out of its territory.

Cooper looked up at the house, expecting to see satisfied expressions on the faces behind the window. But they weren't satisfied yet. They were still expectant.

Then a dark shape flashed across Cooper's field of vision, and a set of sharp white teeth clashed together a few inches from his face. He caught a brief glimpse of a wildly rolling eye as the Alsatian threw itself into the air and lunged its head above the gate in its desperation to sink its fangs into him. He stepped back, sweating. If he had leaned over the gate to see where the dog was, several inches of skin would have been missing from his face by now.

But it was the silence of the dog that was the most terrifying. It was the silence of an animal trained to attack and injure, rather than simply to frighten.

'Mr Oxley!' he called. 'I'm a police officer. This isn't an acceptable way to behave, you know.'

Silence. And now even the faces had disappeared, satisfied at last. Perhaps this was the favourite form of entertainment in Waterloo Terrace.

Cooper took a few deep breaths and moved several paces back from the gate. He wondered what his next move should be. He had a strong feeling that he'd made a stupid tactical mistake. He hadn't been thinking about what he was doing, or why. As a result, he'd put his own safety at risk.

It wasn't something he should admit to, if he could avoid it. He was aware that there had been incidents in the recent past that had already put that question mark over his actions, in some people's minds. DS Diane Fry would take pleasure in marking it down in his personnel record, he was sure.

Follow procedure, he had been told. But sometimes it was hard. One day, he was going to fail to follow procedure, and that would be the end.

'ARE YOU OK, Ben?' PC Udall was looking at him from the road, a slightly puzzled expression on her face. Cooper became aware that he probably didn't look too good. He had been up since well before dawn, and had dressed in his most casual clothes for the raid, which was already a couple of hours ago. He probably hadn't looked too good to Lucas Oxley, either. It was his own fault that he had nearly lost some skin to Mr Oxley's dog.

'Yes, I'm fine.'

'I thought we'd lost you.'

'You nearly did just then. Are we ready to go?'

'Ready when you are.'

AS HE WAVED Tracy Udall off from the car park, Ben Cooper poked around for a CD to play on the way back to Edendale in his Toyota. He found a recent Levellers album and was pleased by the title, *Green Blade Rising*.

On the way out of the village, he noticed two men with a tractor and a length of rope near the pool in the river. Another man was standing in the water in PVC waders. He was already pretty well covered in duckweed as he struggled to attach the rope to one of the boards that floated on the surface of the pool.

'Strange,' said Cooper to himself. And he tapped his fingers to the Levellers as he drove out of Withens.

Chapter Eight

INSTEAD OF GOING back into the wrecked vestry before he left the church that night, Derek Alton turned across the front of the altar and stood for a moment on the patch of stone flags that was always cold. The sunlight from the windows never reached this spot during the day. This was where Alton believed he could feel the presence of the Spirit in the cool air that surrounded him. It was a real, tangible presence. It touched his face with a kind of intimacy and cooled his skin like fresh spring water. It gave him a shiver of pleasure at the awareness of something clean and wonderful beyond the reality of Withens. A few moments of silent contemplation normally helped to calm his anxieties. But tonight it didn't seem to be working.

Derek Alton had his car parked by the churchyard gate. It was a creaking old Escort – all that he could afford, since Anglican clergymen were employed by God, and God didn't pay wages. The old rectory was right behind the church, but the incumbent at St Asaph's no longer had use of it, because it was too big and too expensive for the diocese to maintain. Instead, he and Caroline had been given a bungalow on the new street above the village. And the bungalow was small – too small for the large family that Caroline wanted.

As he passed through the churchyard towards the gate, Alton automatically checked for new litter or damage. Recently, Foster's lager seemed to have been a favourite among the youths who came here in the evening. He could spot the blue cans easily in the brambles and bracken. They had invariably been emptied, then crushed in the middle. Alton pictured one of the Oxley boys casually showing off his adolescent strength to his friends as he smoked another cigarette, rolled another joint, or sniffed another Evo-Stik from a crisp packet. Well, he really had no idea what the youngsters did in the churchyard at night, and he didn't care to speculate too much.

The lager cans always joined the dead flowers and plastic plant pots in a black bin by the side of the church porch. But the bin hadn't been emptied for weeks, and now its lid lay uselessly on the ground, unable to contain the overflowing debris. Alton wondered what the bottom of the bin was like. What was hatching and pupating down there in the foetid darkness? What white, squirming things would be munching their way through the rotting detritus? Now that the weather was warming up, he would soon find out, if the bin weren't emptied. One morning, he would be battling his way through clouds of mosquitoes and swarms of bluebottles to reach the church door.

He caught a flash of incongruous colour in the darkness near the church wall. But it wasn't a Foster's lager can. At some time, a small cloth gnome with a red cap, blue jacket and white beard had been left on the memorial stone for a former churchwarden. Another Oxley, of course.

As he unlocked his car, Alton looked up towards the village. There were streetlamps in Withens – ten of them. He knew the exact number because he'd counted them during the first week after his arrival. They had seemed then to be a symbol that civilization had actually reached the village, and he had clutched at their presence for comfort against the impression communicated by the dark stone houses and gloomy hillsides. But now, as he looked towards the village from the church door, he was struck again by a simple fact about the streetlamps. They lit the road, but not the houses. Their cold, orange glare cast the homes beyond them into even darker shadows.

Even if there had been lighting on their street, he wouldn't have been able to see the new bungalows from here. In fact, all he could see of Withens were the ten streetlamps on the road, the windows of the Quiet Shepherd, and the outline of the pub's roof.

But Alton also saw a group of dark figures moving up the road towards the lights of the village. They were passing from one streetlamp to another, and they looked a little unsteady – whether from tiredness or alcohol, or both, he couldn't tell. He presumed they were the

Oxleys – Lucas, Scott, Ryan and a couple of their cousins. Not to mention old Eric Oxley himself. The Border Rats were out tonight.

DIANE FRY STARED straight ahead through her windscreen at the Sheffield streets, not wanting even to look at the man beside her in the car. She had let him stand by her passenger window for a few moments before she pressed the button to release the central locking. It wasn't that she had any doubts who he was – his brown overcoat and sparse ginger hair were recognizable even through the rain streaking her car windows. It was just that there was always a little voice at the back of her brain that kept nagging at her when she was doing something stupid. There had been a short, internal battle before she had subdued the voice sufficiently to let him in.

Now that he was inside the car, all her senses were prickling at his presence, and her muscles were tensed for danger. Yet he had shown no sign of being a threat to her. Fry knew she had to take control of the situation to keep it that way.

'What name is she going under?' she said.

She could hear the man breathing. He wasn't someone who answered questions too quickly – a habit he had probably learned the hard way.

'Not the one you know,' he said.

Fry was unduly conscious of his masculine bulk as he slumped in the seat next to her, with his right elbow and leg positioned too close, intruding a little too far into her personal space. The interior of a car was too confined for her ever to feel differently. And it didn't matter who it was in the passenger seat – one of her DCs, Gavin Murfin or Ben Cooper – it was always the same. She had thought for a while of telling Murfin he'd have to ride in the back seat. But she knew he would have liked it, because he could pretend he was a passenger in a taxi, and she was his chauffeur. And God knew what damage it would do to her back seat. During the winter, there had been fungi growing from the carpet in the front, where Murfin had scattered his constant supply of junk food.

'No, I didn't think it would be the name I know,' she said. 'That's why I'm asking you.'

He didn't reply, and Fry knew that he was smirking, even without turning her head to look at him. She tried to remember whether she had any air freshener in her glove compartment. She would need to use it once he had left, to take away the memory of him.

'I need a name,' she said. 'And I need an address.'

She could hear him fumbling around in his pockets, then realized that he had taken out a packet of cigarettes. She heard a click and saw the tiny flame reflected in the glass of the windscreen.

'If you light that up in my car, I'll shove it down your throat,' she said.

The man laughed, but let the flame die.

'What are you doing here on your own?' he said. 'Where's your partner? Aren't you supposed to work in pairs? I mean, it can be a bit dangerous, can't it? Especially for a female.'

'Not for me.'

'No?'

'No.'

'Well, I believe you, love. Thousands wouldn't.'

'I couldn't give a damn what you believe. I'm not here to discuss your powers of perception, or even whether you're able to see what's in front of your face. But if you push me, you'll find out.'

'All right, all right. Keep your hair on.'

Fry turned away to stare out of the driver's side window, as if she might be able to forget that he was there if she couldn't see him out of the corner of her eye. But she was still aware of him through the small noises of his movements, the sound of his breathing, his male smell, and the sulphurous whiff of the match he had struck. She knew there were drops of rain glistening on his scalp among the freckles and the tufts of ginger hair, and she was aware of the dark, wet patches on the shoulders of his coat. And with two of them sitting in a stationary car, the interior was getting too warm from their body heat and the glass was starting to steam up. She wound down the window a couple of inches.

They were parked in a street between the dark, blank walls of crumbling factories. But straight ahead, she could see traffic lights and a busier road that was well lit, with cars passing constantly, and a row of terraced houses with flickering TV screens visible through their curtains and shadows passing in front of lamps in upstairs windows. One of the factories must have a night shift. She could hear the rumble of machinery from somewhere nearby.

'A name?' she said impatiently.

'She's living with a bloke called Akerman. Johnny Akerman. Not many folks will mess with him. He's well known around those parts.'

'Which parts?'

'Eh?'

'I need an address.'

'I can't tell you that, love.'

'Look, don't waste my time.'

'I can't do it.'

'Can't, or won't?'

She felt him turning towards her in his seat. His knee touched the gear stick. A fold of his coat fell over the handbrake towards her, and she instinctively flicked it away. He was holding out his hands in a gesture of appeal, and his face was a pale smear that she was much too aware of. He was willing her to meet his eyes, but she couldn't.

'It's not worth it,' he said. 'It could get me a hell of a lot of bother. I mean, it's not as if there's anything in it for *me*, is there?'

'Oh yes,' said Fry. 'You're going to feel a whole lot better, after you tell me.'

'I don't think so, darling.'

Fry pressed the button to close the central locking and reached out to start the ignition.

'Hey, what are you doing?' he said.

'I think we should go for a little ride.'

'No way. I'm getting out.'

'I suggest you put your seat belt on,' said Fry. 'It's not safe without, you know.'

'For God's sake –'

She pulled out from the kerb and drove towards the lights at the end of the road.

'This is the compromise,' she said. 'And it's entirely for your benefit. You say you can't give me the address for this Akerman. OK. I accept that. So what we do instead is, we go for a little drive.'

'Where to?'

'You decide,' she said. 'You give me directions.'

She could practically hear him working it out. He was wondering what the best way was to get out of this madwoman's car.

'Right, left or straight on at the lights?' she said.

He was silent so long that she had almost reached the lights, and she was beginning to think that he wouldn't go along with it. But he was, after all, a man who didn't answer questions too quickly.

'If I were you, I'd go left,' he said. 'It's the scenic route.'

They drove for a few minutes. Fry's passenger hardly spoke, but gave her directions by holding up a hand at junctions to indicate left or right. She guessed he was thinking that he would honestly be able to say that he had never told her anything.

'Stop here,' he said.

'Is this it?'

'I get out here.'

They were in a street of Victorian terraces, with little flights of steps to their front doors and drawn curtains. Fry pulled up in front of a row of shops, mostly boarded up, but for an Asian greengrocer's where the lights were still on.

'Is this it?' she said again.

'Yes,' he snapped. 'The red door. But if you're going to try to get in there, you're crazier than I thought.'

'Thanks for the concern. It's touching.'

He got out, slammed the door and in a moment had vanished into the darkness, walking quickly in the shadow of the deserted shop fronts.

Fry had no intention of going into the house. She was prepared to wait for as long as necessary.

IN THE END, it took two hours. When the woman finally appeared, Fry got out of the car and walked towards her along the pavement, pulling up the collar of her black coat and tucking her chin into her red scarf. She stared at the woman openly, trying to see the girl she was looking for in the way that the woman walked, the angle she held her head, or the look in her eyes.

Fry didn't stop or speak to the woman. She walked on past her, and continued to the end of the block, where she came to a halt on the kerb and stared blankly at the corner of an empty florist's shop. For a few seconds, she had been walking along an entirely different street in another city, in a different time. She had been a younger Diane Fry, the one who had looked into every face she passed, expecting to see someone else. But trying to see ghosts never worked. It hadn't then, and it didn't work now.

As Fry listened to the woman's footsteps fade away behind her, a door opened and closed, a car sounded its horn on the corner and drove away with a screech of tyres, and she realized that she had forgotten where she was.

But, worst of all, she had forgotten why she had been trying to see someone who wasn't there.

SOMEHOW, BEN COOPER had found himself in a room whose walls were covered in white tiles, many of them crazed into patterns of tiny cracks that had absorbed dirt over the years. The only light came from two tiny windows over the doors on to the street, and even the windows were covered in steel mesh and spiders' webs. In front of the doors stood a white Land Rover with its bonnet propped open. There was an overwhelming smell of old sump oil inside the stuffy space.

Cooper took a step down into the garage, then stopped. He knew he was in the wrong place. The day had been going badly already, and this was getting worse. He must have been too tired or distracted to be concentrating properly, otherwise he would never have ended up here.

And what a place to be. The tiles made the garage look the way public toilets had done once, before vandalism had made local councils adopt a more cost-effective approach. Bare breeze-block and polished aluminium were the style these days.

But it was the smell that made Cooper's hands begin to itch. They immediately felt as though they were covered in grease, and his fingernails were scraped and ragged, and full of black dirt. The pathways in his brain had been stimulated by the oily smell, prompted into recalling the many times he had peered and poked inside the engine compartment of a similar Land Rover, or sometimes a David Brown tractor. He could feel the cold metal under his fingers, which were always numb, because it always seemed to be winter. And he could feel the old blue overalls that he had worn, with the sleeves rolled up over his wrists because they were a couple of sizes too big for him.

Most often, the young Ben had been completely ignorant of what he was supposed to be doing inside the engine. But he had been enjoying the feeling of a shared moment, whether it had been with his older brother Matt, or his uncle John. Or even, rarely, his father. Joe Cooper had not been quite so tolerant of inexperienced help, and would snatch a spanner from his son's hand the second he looked likely to turn it the wrong way. There was a curious kind of bonding that took place over a set of dirty spark plugs or a blocked fuel jet. The words alone, as they came into his mind, made Cooper smile with something like nostalgia.

Following a trace of light, he walked to the back of the garage and found himself in a workshop behind it. Two men were in there, drinking tea from mugs. One of them wore overalls, and the other was in uniform, with a yellow jacket and the peaked cap of a traffic officer on a bench next to him. They both looked up at Cooper in amazement. The traffic officer twitched, and spilled some of his tea on his uniform trousers.

'Can we help?' said the one in overalls.

'I've just come from a meeting upstairs and I think I must have taken a wrong turn,' said Cooper. 'Can you show me the way out?'

'CID, are you?'

'Yes.'

'Thought so.'

'I'm DC Cooper, from Edendale.'

The expression on the traffic officer's face changed, and Cooper knew what he was going to say.

'I'm Dave Ludlam,' he said. 'I knew your dad.'

'A lot of people did.'

'I served with him for a while, when I was a young bobby. He was a good sergeant, Joe Cooper. Tough, but fair.'

Ludlam put his mug down as if preparing for a long conversation. 'I bet you're really proud of him,' he said.

'Yes, of course. Look –'

'It was a tragedy, what happened. A tragedy.'

Cooper bit his lip. He wanted always to look as though he was proud of his father. But it made it hard to let people know that he really, really didn't want to talk about what happened. Not any more. There had to be a time when he could get on with his life without someone thrusting the fact of his father's death in his face all the time and waiting for him to react.

'Would you like some tea?' said the overalled mechanic. 'The kettle's not long boiled.'

'No, thanks. I have to get back to Edendale.'

'Can't you stop and talk for a bit? We're just taking a few minutes' break, that's all.'

'It's a bit of a drive from Glossop.'

'Be careful on the roads, then,' said PC Ludlam. 'Don't go speeding or anything daft like that – or I'll be after you. At least, I will once Metal Mickey here gets the bloody motor fixed. Until then, you can do what the hell you like, of course. And so can every other bugger in E Division.'

'If you could show me the way out,' said Cooper.

'Are you sure you won't have some tea?'

'Sorry, I'm in a rush.'

'Ah,' said the traffic officer. 'You're working with Jimmy Boyce's lot. Rural Crime Team. That was the meeting upstairs, wasn't it?'

'Yes.'

It had been a long day. Cooper had been up well before dawn to get from Edendale to Glossop and meet the team for the raid at the suspected drugs factory in the isolated Longdendale farmhouse. After his visit to Withens with PC Udall, there had been a series of interviews to do back at Glossop section station, and then a final debriefing meeting with the Rural Crime Team. Now, he was starting to feel dizzy with tiredness. He had eaten at some time during the day, but couldn't quite work out how many hours ago that was.

Cooper turned back towards the garage, only to find that PC Udall had followed him out of the meeting and was standing watching him.

'I noticed you'd gone the wrong way,' she said. 'It's a bit of a rabbit warren, I'm afraid.'

'Don't tell anybody I couldn't find my way out of the station.'

Udall smiled. 'I'll show you the way. You wouldn't want to be in here all night.'

'No, it's kind of scary.'

'Yes, it's all the white tiles that do it. We call this the morgue.'

LATER THAT NIGHT, two firefighters found they'd taken the wrong path as they were making their way down the hillside from Withens Moor. They were both tired and smelled strongly of smoke. Their personal water carriers felt heavy, but at least they weren't full of water now. They had just finished a late shift damping down the hot spots that still flared among hundreds of hectares of scorched peat moor.

The two men were sweating heavily inside their suits and helmets, and cursing the distance they had to walk to get to the four-wheel-drive Land Rover that would ferry them back to their station. Crews from all over North Derbyshire had been on the moor all day, as well as a dozen Peak Park rangers and a team of gamekeepers employed by the landowners. But because of the location, even Land Rovers had only been able to ferry the men to within a mile and a half of the spreading fire and the clouds of smoke rising high above the hills. From there, they had to walk with their equipment, knowing that there was no possibility of pumping water up to the summit.

'There's the air shaft, Sub,' said Leading Firefighter Beardsley.

Sub Officer Whittingham stopped and peered into the darkness. 'It's the wrong one,' he said. 'The next air shaft beyond it is where we meet the track.'

'You sure?'

'Well, if not, where's the Land Rover?'

'Right.'

As they approached the nearest air shaft, Beardsley asked if they could stop for a rest.

'I'm knackered,' he said. 'This gear is killing me.'

'Just for a minute, then.'

Beardsley eased off his water carrier and flexed his shoulders with a groan.

'You'd think they'd have mobilized the helicopter,' he said.

'We're cheaper,' said Whittingham. 'Besides, it's no good for damping down.'

Though a helicopter had been on standby at Barton Airport, ready to scoop water from the Longdendale reservoirs and bomb the blaze, it had not been called on. Now it was no longer needed. Because moorland fires could burn underground for many months, firefighters had to dig deep into the peat to deal with hot spots.

'Hold on, what's that?' said Beardsley.

Whittingham peered into the darkness. 'I think you mean "who".'

Someone was lying alongside the air shaft, stretched out on the ground with his head turned to the side, as if sleeping.

'It's some hiker,' said Whittingham. 'This is access land up here. They camp anywhere.'

'You all right, mate?' called Beardsley.

'He's asleep.'

'I doubt it. He hasn't got a sleeping bag or anything.'

'That doesn't stop 'em.'

'Hey up, mate. Wake up.'

For some reason, neither of the firefighters wanted to go near the sleeping man. They stood back from him, as if afraid to intrude on his privacy or to make too much noise with their boots and flame-proof overalls.

'You don't think he was caught in the fire, do you?' said Beardsley.

'Why?'

'I don't know. He doesn't look well to me. We should get the paramedics out.'

'Hang on. Let's just check.'

Whittingham laid his equipment on the heather. He bent down to the prone figure and took him by the shoulder to shake him. He got no response.

'Paramedics, Sub?' said Beardsley.

'It's a bit late for that, I think. He's dead.'

'No? Oh God, has this buggered up our rest time?'

'Have you got some light there?'

Beardsley shone a torch on the figure. 'Hey, that's blood,' he said.

'Yes, I know that, Beardsley. Shine it on his face, will you?'

The torch beam moved, but failed to pick up a reflection where they would have expected white skin.

'Bloody hell,' said Beardsley. 'What happened to his eyes? I can't even see them for the blood. And his face is black. Has he been burned by the fire?'

Whittingham leaned a bit closer and took off his right glove. Avoiding the pools of blood where the eyes should have been, he touched a finger gently to the face of the dead man.

'No,' he said. 'I think he did that to himself.'

Chapter Nine

Sunday

SUNDAY MORNINGS HAD become a battleground for Ben Cooper. It was like going over the top in the trenches every time they opened the doors. In the minutes of waiting, he could see the whites of the eyes of the people alongside him, and feel their tension rising. Five minutes to ten, and there was still no sign of anyone on the other side of the glass.

The first time he went to do his weekly shop at Somerfield's supermarket on Sunday morning, he thought he would be the only customer. But he was far from being alone in wanting to shop at that time. There had been a small crowd waiting outside the doors.

After his first few visits, Cooper realized he was seeing exactly the same faces each week. There was the man with the denim jeans so baggy they surely must never have fit him, and the old woman with a knitted hat pulled tight over an explosion of white curls. And then there was the little man with the walking stick and bent legs, who moved slower than everyone else and needed a shopping trolley to keep him upright and mobile.

Soon, members of this group had started saying 'hello' to him when he arrived, as if he'd been accepted into some sort of club. Each of them had their own little rituals once they got inside the store. Some browsed among the fresh vegetables, or rushed to be first in the queue at the delicatessen counter. Some headed straight for the cat food, or did a preliminary circuit to spot the 'Buy One, Get One Free' offers. Occasionally, they would pass each other in the aisles and complain that something had been moved again. There was always a small traffic jam by the cabinets where the frozen meals for one were kept.

When an assistant manager finally appeared and unlocked the doors, Cooper stood back to let most of the Sunday-morning crowd grab their trolleys and get in before him. The little man with the stick reached the doors last, as always. Cooper was just about to follow him, when his mobile phone rang. He pulled it from his belt and checked the number on the display. It was one he didn't recognize. Work though, probably.

For some reason, the idea that the office was calling him on his rest day irritated him more than it ever had before. Previously, it had never seemed to matter. But now, the interruption of his Sunday-morning routine was different. It could upset his entire week. Sunday was for shopping, cleaning the flat or doing some ironing, a quick lunch, then an afternoon with the papers and TV before visiting his mother. Then he would finish off with an evening in the pub, where the usual crowd would be expecting him, and his usual drink would be on the counter almost before he got through the door. Even within three months, the routine had developed a reassuring predictability.

Cooper let the phone ring a couple more times as he pushed a trolley into the first aisle: fresh fruit and vegetables. In a second, the answering service would cut in, and he could pretend that he had been unavailable. Then someone else would have to take on whatever job it was they wanted him for. He wouldn't even know what it had been until Monday morning. He wouldn't know whether it had been something trivial, or the most exciting case of his life.

'Oh, well,' he sighed, as he caught the call before the next ring.

'Hello, Ben. It's Tracy Udall.'

Cooper had a moment's difficulty in putting a face to the name. But then a picture of PC Udall in her body armour seemed to materialize in front of him, among the piles of carrots and parsnips.

'Morning, Tracy. What can I do for you?'

'I thought I'd mention that I'm on duty tomorrow, and I'll be going up to Withens again in the morning.'

'Yes?'

'I'm going to talk to the Oxleys. Or try to.'

'Good luck, then.'

'I'll be setting off from Glossop section station about ten o'clock.'

'I'm working tomorrow myself,' said Cooper, trying to puzzle out what Udall was talking about. He had only been on loan for the day of the raid. There was more than enough work to be done in CID at Edendale, even on a Monday morning.

'Fine,' said Udall cheerfully. 'See you around.' And she rang off.

Cooper shook his head as he put his phone away. But it wasn't worth worrying over. He had fruit and vegetables to think about.

He began to fill a plastic bag with apples. Just up the aisle, the man with the stick was poking a finger at some enormous oranges that looked as though they'd been pumped up with steroids. The old man liked to trail round the aisles with Cooper whenever possible, so that he could talk to him. This morning, he was deliberately lingering in the fruit section to allow Cooper to catch up. The man with the stick never bought oranges. He was a tinned peaches and pineapple chunks man.

Then Cooper's phone rang again.

'What now?'

He couldn't let it ring for long this time. He saw that the number was one of the direct lines into E Division headquarters at West Street.

'Ah, Cooper. I didn't think you were going to answer.'

'No, sir,' said Cooper, recognizing DI Paul Hitchens' voice immediately. 'I mean, yes. I just had a bit of difficulty because my hands weren't free.'

'You're not driving, are you?'

'No, sir.' Cooper tucked the phone between his shoulder and ear as he pushed his trolley past the apples and drew up to the dairy cabinets. He heard Hitchens take a breath.

'Look, I'm sorry to bother you on your rest day, but something has come up, which you need to know about before you come on duty in the morning.'

'A case, sir? Have we got an incident?'

'Well, not exactly. We're loaning you out again.'

'Sorry?'

'The Rural Crime Team were very pleased with you yesterday. They've asked if they can have you for a while longer. Apparently, they have some more enquiries coming to a conclusion.'

'Oh, but sir –'

'The RCT are flavour of the month at the moment, you know. Rural crime has a high profile, so it's getting priority treatment at higher levels. You know what I mean.'

'So you're agreeing to an abstraction, sir?'

'For a while, Cooper. We'll see you back here before long, no doubt. You'll have all this rural crime cleared up in no time. I've got every confidence in you.'

Cooper picked up a milk carton and stared at it blankly. The confidence of your senior officers was good. But Hitchens sounded a little too confident for Cooper's liking.

'How long will it be for?'

'Well … I don't know exactly. Not at the moment. But we'll see how it goes.' He paused. 'Nothing to worry about, Ben,' he said. 'DS Fry will be keeping in touch.'

'Is everybody happy with this, sir?'

'Yes, of course,' said Hitchens. 'Everybody's happy.'

DIANE FRY SAT stony-faced, trying not to show how the news was affecting her. Inside, she felt as though her heart had dropped suddenly into her stomach. For a moment, the clematis flickered into flames, and the cat turned yellow eyes towards her as a shadow fell across its window.

'Well, it goes without saying that I'm not happy,' she said.

'We all have to bear the brunt of abstractions,' said DI Hitchens. 'We benefit from them too, when we need them. You have to look at it from a management point of view, Diane.'

'I can't see the sense of this one.'

'The Rural Crime Team say they have some major ongoing enquiries that are coming to a head. They requested assistance, and they've got it. End of story.'

'I'm not happy, sir. We're already understaffed, as you know.'

'Of course. But what's new?'

'And the abstraction is in effect from when?'

'Yesterday.'

'Damn.'

For a while, Fry had wanted rid of Ben Cooper. She had even seen him as a threat. But that seemed a long time ago now. Instead, she was feeling aggrieved at the idea that she was going to lose him. Maybe more than aggrieved.

'How were the Renshaws, by the way?' said Hitchens.

'Difficult. I don't think they're ever going to accept the possibility that their daughter is dead. They're living in a fantasy world, in which they expect Emma to turn up home at any moment. That makes it very hard to talk to them.'

'Mrs Renshaw has gone a bit nutty, I'm afraid. And she doesn't realize it. We call it the Daft Old Biddy syndrome around here. DOBs, they are. Daft Old Biddies and Daft Old Blokes. We get plenty of them phoning the station. The control-room staff are like saints.'

'I could use a few saints,' said Fry. 'All I have is Gavin Murfin.'

THE MAN WITH the walking stick recognized a sympathetic listener when he saw one. He had news of crimes to pass on to Ben Cooper every week, even though he could have no idea that Cooper was a police officer. Most of his stories were culled from the newspapers, and were therefore inaccurate. But, occasionally, he had one of his own from the Edendale neighbourhood of Southwoods, where he lived.

'Do you know, some of the old girls up my way won't open their doors to anybody now, except Meals on Wheels,' he said as Cooper tried to squeeze past him by the dairy products. 'They're too frightened, see. They had another lot of those blokes round the other day, who pretend to want to check your gas supply for leaks. So some old dear lets them, because she's worried about being gassed during the night, or her bungalow blowing up. Then one bloke keeps her talking, while the other goes through the house and pinches her purse and stuff.'

'Distraction burglaries,' said Cooper.

'It's disgusting. It's always the old folk they go for, you know.'

'Yes, I know.'

'It's because they think we're all stupid. Mind you, some of those old dears *are* stupid.'

'They target anybody who's vulnerable,' said Cooper.

'I'm not vulnerable. They have to show me identification if they want to get in my house. And I phone the council or whatever to check they're who they say they are. They don't like it, some of them, but I make them wait.'

'That's very sensible.'

'And if I ever see one of them make a wrong move, I'll clobber him with my stick.'

'That's not so sensible.'

'Why not?'

'Well, first of all, you might get seriously hurt if they hit you back.'

'I don't care.'

'And you might find yourself on a charge of assault, if you use unreasonable force.'

'I don't care about that either.'

'If you have any suspicions, the best thing to do is to call the police.'

'Bollocks. What would they do? They don't turn up until long after the buggers have gone, and then all they want to do is give you a number to claim on your insurance.'

Cooper's mobile phone rang for a third time when he was in the frozen food section, jostling with his fellow shoppers for the pick of the items from the refrigerated cabinets.

'Oh, for pity's sake,' he said.

A woman standing nearby, with her trolley nudging his, gave him a funny look. He had noticed her before. He always seemed to encounter her in the frozen food aisles, where their trolleys had a regular rendezvous.

He answered the phone, and heard another familiar voice.

'Oh, it's you, Diane.'

The woman with the trolley chose that moment to lean past him towards the frozen Chinese meals for one.

'Sorry,' said Cooper as he moved out of the way.

'Ben, is someone there with you?' said Fry.

'Oh – just someone wanting to get into the freezer.'

'To what?'

The woman was waving a packet at him. Spicy noodles.

'I find these very good when you live on your own,' she said, and smiled.

'Oh, thanks.'

Fry's voice was as chilly as the air rising from the lid of the freezer cabinet.

'What's she doing now, Ben? Offering you an ice cube?'

'Some noodles.'

'You're at the supermarket, aren't you?'

'Yes.'

'You always do your shopping at the supermarket on Sunday morning, don't you, Ben?'

'Yes.'

'I always knew you were a man of routine, at heart. I bet you buy exactly the same things every week and speak to exactly the same people. Am I right?'

'Maybe.'

Cooper decided to keep moving as he listened to Fry. He passed the vinegar and the lemon juice, and headed for the household goods section. He needed some disinfectant in case one of the cats made a mess in the conservatory.

'Have you finished analysing me?' he said.

'I'm told you've been requested by the Rural Crime Team again.'

'I've just heard myself.'

'Have you asked for a transfer to the RCT?'

'What makes you think that, Diane?'

'Well, they're expanding their operations. They asked for you. I thought maybe you'd been talking to someone.'

'No, it wasn't like that.'

'But you're the obvious person for them, aren't you, Ben? You're the one with the right background. And you know the issues. I reckon somebody with a bit of influence has put a marker on you.'

'I didn't apply for a transfer. Look, Diane, I'm kind of busy, so if there was nothing urgent –'

'So you're not planning to abandon your friends in CID, then?'

Cooper thought that probably hadn't come out the way Fry had meant it. But he was sure she wouldn't be surprised when he hesitated.

'OK, it had crossed my mind,' he said.

'You know you should talk to me about these things, Ben. I am your immediate supervisor.'

'I'm sorry.'

'Or am I the reason you want to leave?' said Fry.

'No, Diane.'

'I'd understand, if you told me that was the situation.'

'I said "no".'

Cooper started to fidget. The woman with the trolley was watching him with a quizzical look. He gave her an apologetic smile and moved a bit further away.

'OK,' said Fry. 'So long as we've got that clear.'

'Right.'

'In that case, Ben, you can talk to me about your plans,' she said. 'We'll make an appointment some time, and we'll discuss it fully. I might have some suggestions about your future career.'

Cooper was silent with amazement.

'That's the way it's done in a properly managed department,' she said.

'If you say so, Diane.'

He could hear Fry breathing and rustling some papers. He almost pressed the button to end the conversation, but sensed there was something else she wanted to talk about. Perhaps, even, the real reason for her call.

'I expect you remember the Emma Renshaw case, Ben?'

'The missing student?' he said. 'It was about two years ago.'

'That's right. What was the general opinion at the time? Did everyone think she was dead?'

'Heck, I don't know. There was no reason for her to run away from home, as I recollect.'

'No, none that could be found.'

'Why are you asking?'

'Her mobile phone has been found, so we have a new line of enquiry. But most of the background I have is stuff inherited from West Midlands, which makes life a bit difficult.'

'You also inherit Mr and Mrs Renshaw then,' said Cooper. 'I don't envy you.'

'Right. How come everybody knows about the Renshaws, except me? Isn't it practice to keep your colleagues informed around here? Or does everyone think it's a big joke?'

'It isn't my fault, Diane,' protested Cooper.

Fry was silent for a moment. Cooper found it frustrating talking to her on the phone. He needed to be able to see her face, to try to read what he could from her expression. There was something so taut and thinly stretched about her these days, a tension that was emphasized by her narrow shoulders and lean cheekbones, and the way she had cut her hair even shorter. It meant he always found himself looking for what Fry was thinking in her eyes, rather than listening to her words.

'I suppose Monday's out for a meeting?' she said. 'You'll be too busy with the Rural Crime Team.'

'Sorry.'

'We'll make it some other time, then. Oh, and Ben? I'd take your lady friend up on that offer, if I were you.'

Cooper put his phone away and looked over his shoulder. The woman with the trolley winked at him.

THE CAR PARK in front of the supermarket was full of the sound of smashing glass as couples in estate cars queued up to unload a week's worth of wine and beer bottles into the recycling bins. Cooper wondered if this routine had replaced Sunday-morning church worship – a few minutes spent in Somerfield's car park helping to save the planet instead of sitting in a draughty church trying to save their own souls.

The man with the stick had been lurking, ready to take up his conversation where it had left off. Unfortunately, Cooper had completely forgotten what he had been talking about.

'I've got their numbers you know.'

'Sorry?' said Cooper.

'The burglars. The thieves. I've taken their car registration numbers.'

'I'm sure the officers investigating have found that very useful.'

'No. They won't even look at them.'

'Oh.'

Cooper was starting to come to the conclusion that he had inadvertently become attached to a DOB – a Daft Old Bloke.

'There was even a burglary the other side of the estate – at the big property, Southwoods Grange. It belongs to the National Trust, that does. The burglars got away with antiques worth a fortune. And they must have come right past my house to get there. But you can't tell the police anything. They haven't time to listen to the likes of me.'

'I'm sure they've taken note,' he said. 'They probably have a lot of other lines of enquiry to follow.'

'You sound like one of them top detectives, when they go on TV to explain why they haven't caught a murderer or found some missing kid. They always say they have too many lines of enquiry. You're not a top detective, are you?'

'No,' said Cooper.

'I didn't think you could be. I suppose you just watch too much telly, like me.'

'You're probably right.'

'Anyway, it's bollocks. They don't have any lines of enquiry at all. They don't have a bloody clue, if you ask 'em. Not a bloody clue. And when I offer to help them, they don't want to know. What do we pay our police for, I ask you?'

'Not much.'

'But I bet you, if I accidentally forgot to do my trousers up in the street again, they'd be down on me like a ton of bricks.'

Cooper began to edge away towards his car, manoeuvring his trolley so that the wheels moved sideways. The man with the stick followed him.

'Where do you live?' he said.

'Oh, miles away.'

'I thought you must do. You know nothing about Edendale at all.'

AFTER BEN COOPER had got his shopping home and unloaded, there was time for a glance at the Sunday paper. For some reason, he always picked up the *Telegraph*, though he knew he would never get around to reading all the sections – even if he had any interest in buying a historic property in Suffolk or worrying about a fall in the FTSE 100 index.

Later, the next stage in his Sunday routine was a visit to the Old School Nursing Home, where his mother was currently living, in remission from the schizophrenia that had forced her family to accept they couldn't look after her in her old home at Bridge End Farm any longer. Cooper looked at his phone, tempted to switch it off for the rest of the day. But he decided against it.

An hour later, he was sitting with his mother in the lounge at the Old School, trying to analyse the smells that were partly masked by disinfectant. It was then that he got the fourth call of the day.

Chapter Ten

SCENES OF CRIME officer Liz Petty shook her head. She was crouching in long grass next to a path that ran between trees at the edge of a field.

'I've taken samples from everything in the surrounding area,' she said. 'But there are no signs of disturbance, and I can't see anything that looks like blood. Of course, it depends on the timescale. If it was here a long time, the rain would have washed most traces away by now. But the lab might be able to find something.'

'Don't worry. I'm not hopeful,' said Diane Fry.

Beyond the trees, a new crop was showing bright and green in the field. Fry had no idea what the crop might be. She was only glad that the field didn't contain livestock – she didn't get on with livestock.

She looked towards some distant farm buildings surrounded by a series of limestone walls. The road behind her was narrow, and ran between two more walls. It was no more than a byway that wandered between rural lanes, and she had seen no buildings since she'd turned off from the last village, just outside Chapel-en-le-Frith. She tried to call up a picture of Emma in this place, but she failed. She couldn't imagine any reason why Emma Renshaw should have been here.

'No, it doesn't make sense.'

'More likely somebody stopped at the roadside and chucked the phone over the wall,' said Petty.

'Almost certainly.'

'Are you all right, Diane?'

Fry looked at the SOCO in surprise. She had worked with Liz Petty a number of times, and saw her often around West Street. They had exchanged small talk at crime scenes, and recently had found themselves having a drink together in a corner of the room at the leaving party for their division's old DCI, Stewart Tailby. But surely only friends asked you if you were all right in that tone of voice.

'Yes, I'm fine,' she said.

'I just thought you seemed a bit down today.'

'Down?'

'Fed up. I don't want to intrude, but if you ever wanted to have a chat, you know, we could go out for a drink some time.'

Fry tried to remember what they might have talked about at Mr Tailby's party. Had she given the impression she wanted to be friendly? Surely she hadn't told Liz Petty anything about her private life?

'Well, thanks for the offer,' she said.

'That's OK, Diane. Just let me know.' Petty stood up and stretched her legs, rustling in her white protective suit. 'Anyway, I'm about to pack up here. There's a suspicious death up in Longdendale they need some assistance with.'

'Yes, I know,' said Fry. 'I heard.'

'You're not going to be working on it?'

'Apparently, not. I have enough to contend with at the moment.'

Petty clambered over the wall and began to put away her equipment in her van. 'It probably won't be anything interesting anyway,' she said.

Fry looked at the grass where Emma Renshaw's mobile phone had been found, and thought of Emma's parents, perhaps waiting even now for their daughter to come home.

'Probably not,' she said. 'But at least it might be something in the real world.'

THE POLICE OFFICERS protecting the scene at the air shaft were starting to get a bit edgy. The place was difficult to find, and it had taken a couple of attempts by the fire service to guide them up the track. Another patrol car had been positioned at the gateway off the A628, but there was no sign yet of the rest of the team – the forensic medical examiner, the CID, the Scientific Support van, or the senior officer who would take charge.

The gradual arrival of daylight made the scene look even worse than it had in the light of their torches. PC Greg Knott was the more experienced officer. He had attended sudden deaths before, and he knew from the smell, and the condition of the area surrounding the body, that this death had occurred some time ago. The gases building up in the body as decomposition set in had begun to expel the contents of the stomach and intestines, and blood from the victim's nose and ears caused a confusing picture of the injuries he had sustained.

Worst were the eyes, though. In the place where they should have been there were black, clotted pools that almost seemed to match the unnatural colour of the victim's face.

With every moment that passed, PC Knott was getting more and more worried that there were things he ought to be doing. It had been a long, tedious night shift. And now, right at the end of it, Knott and his partner actually had an interesting call to attend. They were FOA at a suspicious death – the first officers to arrive. And that brought sudden responsibilities, the knowledge that the actions they took, or didn't take, right now could affect the whole investigation, if it turned out to be a case of murder.

Their first priorities had been to assess and protect the scene. And he knew the first rule was not to interfere with anything at the scene, once they were sure that the victim was actually dead. But he hated standing around doing nothing. It went against his instincts. Knott wanted to poke around, to identify the victim, to try to figure out what had happened.

As more time passed, the urge to do something was becoming stronger. Knott told himself it would impress the senior officers when they arrived. But he looked at his partner, who was trying to find something secure to fasten the end of the blue-and-white tape to, and he was glad he wasn't on his own. A bad mistake would be too easy to make. Above all things, any evidence at the scene had to be preserved from contamination. Knott looked at the sky, praying that the rain would hold off, because they had no means of protecting the body if the weather broke.

There was the noise of a car engine, whining as it approached.

'Who's that coming?' said Knott.

'Let's hope it's the medical examiner.'

They both looked down the hill, watching the spot where the track crested the rise and emerged from the banks of heather. Nothing appeared. Yet the sound of the engine became louder and louder, until it almost seemed to be on top of them.

'Bloody hell!' said Knott, spinning round. A black Mitsubishi pick-up was only a few yards away from them. But it was travelling down the hill, not up.

'Where did that come from?'

'I don't know, but he's going to drive right through the tape, if we don't stop him,' said Knott.

'He'd better not, or we're dead meat.'

'Stop him, then.'

They both began waving and running towards the vehicle. The driver had already slowed to a crawl as he bumped over the stony track, and he finally came to a halt a few feet from the air shaft. He lowered the driver's window.

'What's the problem?' he said.

'I'm afraid you can't come through here, sir. This is a crime scene.'

'A what?'

'A crime scene, sir. There's been a fatality.'

'Oh.'

'So if you don't mind, sir –'

'Has somebody been hurt, then?'

'Yes, sir.'

'Who is it?'

'We don't know. But I'm afraid I'll have to ask you to reverse back up the track. You need to turn round and go back the way you came.'

The driver leaned out of his window to look down the track. 'I could just about squeeze past. The ground's quite dry here, so I think the four-wheel drive could cope.'

'No, sir. Go back, please.'

'It's a damned nuisance.'

'Could I ask your name, sir?'

'It's Dearden.'

'And whereabouts do you live?'

'Over the other side of the hill. Shepley Head Lodge.'

Knott looked at his partner, who shrugged. 'Surely you could take the road through Withens, Mr Dearden?' he said.

'Maybe.'

'It would be much easier than negotiating this track, I would have thought. You'll get a lot less damage to your suspension and your tyres, anyway.'

'I suppose so.'

'Where are you heading for, sir?'

'Glossop.'

'Glossop? Well, this isn't even a shortcut. You'd have to go back up the A628 to where the Withens road comes out anyway.'

'All right, all right. I'm going.'

He revved the Mitsubishi, looked over his shoulder and began reversing up the hill towards where the track widened out at the old quarry.

Knott looked at the body of the young man. 'If Mr Dearden lives nearby, maybe we should have asked him if he recognized the body,' he said. 'He might have been able to give us a quick ID.'

'This lad won't be from round here,' said the other officer confidently.

'You sure?'

'They never are. Besides …'

'What?'

'I didn't like the look of Mr Dearden too much. What was he doing driving over this way, when he could have gone up the Withens road? It would have been a lot easier and quicker for him. It doesn't make sense.'

Knott shrugged. 'Beats me. But take a note of his registration number before we lose sight of him anyway,' he said, as he watched the Mitsubishi do a three-point turn. 'We'll pass his name on to CID. When they arrive.'

'Who do you suppose we'll get?'

'Some bugger who'll tell us we've done everything wrong,' said PC Knott.

DETECTIVE CHIEF INSPECTOR Oliver Kessen was a recent arrival in E Division. Some of the CID officers in the sections didn't know him very well yet, but they were allowing him time to settle into the job.

His predecessor, DCI Stewart Tailby, had moved to his new job in the Corporate Development department at county headquarters in Ripley. Yet it was surprising how often he was to be seen hanging around West Street like a ghost, trying to engage his old colleagues in conversation. It was as if he was reluctant to let go of his old job, to leave his old patch behind. Maybe he was frightened that everyone would forget him, once he had truly gone. But gradually he was losing touch with what was going on in E Division. More and more new officers were arriving at the station who had no idea who he was.

By the time Kessen arrived at the scene by the air shaft, the forensic medical examiner had already attended, and the machinery for an enquiry into a suspicious death was starting to get into action. PC Knott was being kept occupied controlling access and recording the names of everyone who arrived in the scene log.

'The victim is male, appears to be in his early twenties, and has suffered serious head injuries,' said DI Paul Hitchens, as DCI Kessen struggled up the last few yards of the slope.

The track below was already filling up with police vehicles. Their white and orange looked ludicrously out of place in the dark, bare expanses of peat moor.

Kessen simply nodded, and took up a position from where he could see the body without entering the taped-off area. He was wearing a heavy overcoat that made him look twice his normal size and hid his real shape. He had a habit of keeping his lips pushed together, and he rarely smiled. When he did, he revealed crooked teeth that would have benefited from an orthodontist.

'The doctor thinks that death occurred over twenty-four hours ago, from the condition of the body. The attendance of the pathologist has been requested, I understand?'

Kessen nodded again. He found a packet of mints in the pocket of his coat and put one in his mouth. He didn't offer Hitchens one.

'The SOCOs are here. At least they can start getting their photographs and videos before the pathologist arrives. If we get Mrs Van Doon, things should move quickly. The body was discovered by a couple of firefighters from Glossop. Luckily, they had the sense not to mess around too much with the scene.'

The DCI didn't reply. His mouth moved as he sucked his mint. His eyes were fixed on the area marked off by tape, where the scenes of crime officers were clustering.

'The Crime Scene Manager has established an approach path, and the major incident vehicle is on the way,' said Hitchens. 'And the really good news is that we've found an unattended car, parked in a lay-by just below here on the A628. It's an old Volkswagen Beetle. If it turns out to belong to the victim, we could be in luck. This could be a forty-eight-hour job.'

Kessen coughed. Hitchens looked at him as if he thought he might actually be going to say something. But he wiped his mouth with a handkerchief from his pocket, and began to chew his mint again.

'I assume you want to assess the body with the pathologist?' said Hitchens. 'Or would you rather I briefed you later? Perhaps you have other things to do?'

'I want full forensic exploitation of the scene,' said Kessen, without looking at him. 'Tell them to extend the tape three yards up the hill, and two yards beyond the scene on the other side. There's a disturbed area of bracken to the east of here that must be preserved. I want soil samples taken from three sites I'll mark on the map. And get all these vehicles moved back down the track fifty yards. Nobody comes beyond that point, except the pathologist and the SOCOs. And for God's sake, keep that person with the video camera away from whatever this stone structure is. He's leaving his traces all over the bloody thing.'

'It's a ventilation shaft,' said Hitchens.

'I'll be in my car. Let me know when the pathologist is ready for me.'

'Yes, sir.'

'Would you like a mint, Inspector?'

Hitchens took a mint from the packet he was offered, and stood with it in his fingers as he watched DCI Kessen walk back down the track to his car. Then he turned to look for the Crime Scene Manager.

THE SMELL OF a dead body was unmistakable. Ripe, sweet and intimate. Ben Cooper could detect it hanging around in the vicinity of the air shaft as soon as he arrived. It was as if an obscene tropical plant had suddenly flowered in the middle of the peat moor, spreading its noxious scent for hundreds of yards downwind.

By the time Cooper had made his way past the cluster of police vehicles, a small group of white-suited and masked figures was already moving forward beyond the tape to approach the body. Though they were difficult to identify, one would be the pathologist, Juliana Van Doon, and the others the Crime Scene Manager and the Senior Investigating Officer. He thought the stiff, stocky figure whose suit didn't fit properly was probably DCI Oliver Kessen, who was therefore presumably SIO. Their approach was being recorded on video by a scenes of crime officer.

Cooper joined the officers he could see standing back from the scene. DI Hitchens was talking on his mobile phone, maybe trying to round up more specialized help for a search, or the attendance of a forensic scientist. There was also a detective sergeant he knew, but no sign of Diane Fry.

Though the day was mild and a breeze blew across the moor, a trickle of steam was drifting from the mouth of the air shaft, as if it were a kettle that had recently finished boiling.

A hundred yards into the heather, a pair of lapwing lifted and began to circle at a distance. A curlew was calling, but it was impossible to locate it against the landscape. Its bubbling song rolled around the slopes of the surrounding hills like running water.

The air shaft itself was at least twelve feet high, and about eighteen feet across, much too high to get a look inside without a ladder. It had been rebuilt at some time – and the builders had used any piece of stone that came to hand. Some were the original dressed chunks of sandstone, blackened by soot from the steam trains that had passed below ground. But in between there were smaller pieces of clean stone, their golds and reds mortared together with the black in a rough patchwork. From a distance, the result gave the air shaft a look of being in camouflage. It blended in well against the hillside behind it. It looked solid enough, but on the windward side the mortar was already beginning to crumble. No trained waller had rebuilt this.

It was one of those spells when there was nothing to do but wait. Cooper walked a little way across the peat from the air shaft. A snipe took off from almost under his feet, where it had been nesting invisibly in a boggy patch, hoping no one would notice it.

All around him, he could see the wet, black mounds of the moors, broken by small valleys. In some of these places, the peat had been eroded right to the bedrock, worn down to the bone.

Cooper tried to orientate himself to figure out which valley had Withens somewhere at the bottom. He located it by the trees and a glimpse of a road disappearing over a rise. He thought this air shaft was the one he had been able to see from the roadside above Withens.

He could see patterns burned into the heather moors below the road. They were so precise that they looked almost like giant letters, with exact verticals and horizontals linked neatly together. In fact, the series of shapes could have been a message designed to be read only by aliens in outer space. Cooper hoped the aliens had good dictionaries – the message seemed to consist entirely of 'H's.

In the midst of the high, empty spaces, the skyline was broken by a line of lorries heading towards Manchester on the A628. Somewhere up there were the remains of one of the ancient guide marks for the old packhorse roads. They were the only remaining signs of the trade that had once passed across these moors before the turnpike roads and railways had arrived. Medieval salters and badgers had relied on those stone markers to guide them across featureless terrain in all kinds of weather. The Dark Peak moors had created an almost impassable barrier. Even now, there was only the one road through Longdendale.

Activity behind him made him turn and join the group of officers. A quick search of the area around the body and the victim's clothing had produced a wallet, with identification. The information was passed back from the area cordoned off at the air shaft.

'Name of Neil Granger, with an address in Tintwistle,' said DI Hitchens.

'That's only a few miles down Longdendale from here, sir.'

'Good. Let's hope we can keep it local.'

After a few minutes, DCI Kessen made his way carefully away from the body via the approach path that had been marked out. The protective suit did him no favours – his paunch protruded like a round cushion. Kessen stood a few feet away and waited patiently until he had everyone's attention.

'We have an ID, as you know,' he said. 'There are cash and credit cards in the victim's wallet, so it seems we're looking for a motive other than robbery. And down in a lay-by on the main road, we have a vehicle whose registered owner matches the ID from the victim.'

The DCI spoke in a flat, matter-of-fact tone that made him sound almost as if he were bored. But Cooper decided he quite liked it. It had an air of calmness and confidence that was sometimes lacking at the start of a major enquiry.

'It's an open scene, of course, but the perpetrator must have left some traces on his approach or departure, so I intend to fully exploit all forensic opportunities. And if the victim came up here voluntarily, then he came for a reason – and possibly in the company of his attacker. A check on the victim's associates and his recent movements will produce some early lines of enquiry, I'm sure. Where's the nearest civilization – anyone know?'

'A village called Withens, sir,' said Cooper. 'Down in the valley to the east.'

'Know it, do you?'

Kessen's gaze was steady, almost impersonal. Cooper wondered whether the DCI had forgotten his name.

'Yes, sir. I'm seconded to the Rural Crime Team for some enquiries down there, and I'm in the middle of conducting interviews. In fact, if this is the same Neil

Granger, he's related to several of the residents of With-ens, and the vicar was expecting to see him yesterday.'

'Ah. Keep on it, then. There's a local connection here, I'm sure of it. And while you're in Withens, you can have a word with this Michael Dearden, who the FOAs had to turn back from the scene in his car. In fact, perhaps you can do that first, in case there's anything of interest. Find out what he was doing up that track in his four-wheel drive when there's a perfectly good road. We looked at the maps, and he must have driven up past a disused quarry called Far Clough.'

'I'll find it.'

DI Hitchens rubbed his hands. 'Yes, it could be fairly straightforward, sir,' he said. 'That was my own feeling from the start.'

Kessen looked at him, and said nothing. Behind the DCI, Neil Granger's body was being turned over for the video cameras. And everyone could see that the victim's face was covered in black make-up, streaked by the blood from his wounds.

Chapter Eleven

_____

IN WITHENS, A few elderly people were arriving at the church as Ben Cooper drove past. Perhaps the vicar held an afternoon service for them. Cooper looked for the Reverend Alton in the churchyard, but couldn't see him.

At Waterloo Terrace, some children watched him pass. Their bikes lay on the ground in a tangle, the spokes of their wheels lying on top of each other in complex patterns. There were two boys around the age of fifteen, one with short-cropped hair and the other with gelled spikes. There was a girl of about the same age, and a smaller boy who couldn't be more than ten, who leered aggressively at the car. Behind them, Cooper glimpsed a taller figure, a well-built young man in his twenties. Could that be Scott Oxley, the eldest son?

Cooper barely had time to think about it before he found himself driving out of the village to the east, where he passed an old man standing in the road. In fact, he had to slow right down to avoid running him over. The man was wearing a tight tweed jacket and a pair of baggy trousers that had been made for a younger, bulkier man – a man who had worn them until the seat shone and the edges of the pockets were frayed like lace.

Cooper wound down the window of the Toyota.

'I'm looking for Shepley Head Lodge,' he said. 'Am I on the right road?'

'There isn't any other road.'

'That's what I thought.'

'It's just over the next hill. But I wouldn't go up there, if I were you.'

Cooper laughed at his ominous tone. It sounded like a line from an old black-and-white horror film, but it ought to have been delivered by a Transylvanian coach driver, or some other superstitious yokel.

'Especially not at this time of night?' said Cooper.

'Eh?' The old man looked at him as if he were stupid.

'No, I meant – the name of the people is Dearden, not Dracula. It isn't even an anagram.'

'You can laugh, if you want.'

'Sorry. And have you heard of a place called Far Clough?'

'Over there.' The old man pointed across the road to the south. 'Do you see a series of little valleys in the hillside? We call 'em cloughs in these parts. There are three of them over there, and they're called Near Clough, Middle Clough and Far Clough.'

'OK.'

'Near Clough is the closest to the village, you see – that's why it's called Near Clough. It's a shorter walk from here. The other two are further away.'

'Yes, I see.'

'Unless you drive there. In that case, Near Clough is the furthest, and Far Clough is the nearest.'

'How do I get there by car?' said Cooper, squinting up at the moor.

'You can't, there's no road.'

'But you just said –'

'If you had a good tractor,' he said, with a pitying look, 'or maybe one of those ATV things, you could drive there. But not in that car you've got.'

'It has four-wheel drive,' said Cooper, feeling defensive about his Toyota.

'Ah, well. Try it if you want to. You don't have to listen to me. I'm only a daft old bugger who doesn't know any better. But think on – there won't be anybody around to rescue you, when you get stuck. Nobody goes up to the cloughs from one month to the next.'

'OK,' said Cooper. 'I think I'll walk.'

'Do you good, I reckon, instead of sitting in a car all day.'

'Do you live in Withens, sir?' said Cooper.

'Aye. What about it?'

'It's a bit out of the way, isn't it?'

'That has its advantages, I reckon.'

'What advantages?' said Cooper as he studied the view over Withens. 'I mean, where's the nearest shop, for example?'

'Shop? Shop? Do you think there's a supermarket round the corner here somewhere?'

'Well, I just wondered …'

'Oh, aye. There's probably a whole bloody Meadowhall shopping centre behind the bus shelter. Not to mention the cinema and the drive-in chuffin' McDonald's.'

'I was just wondering where the nearest shop is,' said Cooper.

'Glossop that way. Or Holmfirth that way. And bloody great hills in between, whichever way you go.'

'Thanks.'

The man began to walk off, his shoulders stiff with affront.

'Thanks a lot, anyway!' called Cooper.

He shrugged as he watched the old man leave.

'I'd better go and face the undead on my own, then.'

A hundred yards further up the road, Cooper crested a rise, and a house came into view on his left. It stood on an elbow of land nudging into the valley and had been hacked out of the hillside, with high stone walls behind it and a small copse of trees beyond a range of outbuildings. The copse was unusual in this landscape. It must have been deliberately planted and nurtured many years ago, probably when the lodge was built. The front windows of the house had a terrific view over the valley. And the road stopped at the gateway, where a gravel drive swung up towards the house. Beyond that, there was a field gate leading on to the moor.

Shepley Head Lodge was actually over the border in South Yorkshire. There was no sign at the county boundary, only a stone that someone had erected on the grass verge. On the hill above the house, Cooper could see a line of grouse butts near the western edge of Winscar Reservoir. Streams ran out of the cloughs towards the reservoir. On the steeper slopes, they formed tiny waterfalls, white and glittering, cutting into the rock like diamonds.

Why would anyone build a house way out here? It would have to be someone who loved the view, because it would send most people scurrying back down to the shelter of the valleys or the streets of a town.

The clouds were heavy and grey, and there was more rain on the way. There was no sign of castle battlements or bats circling overhead, and no sound of wolves howling in the trees, but Cooper did feel the first hint of doubt. Once he had turned the corner and come over the hill, he had left traffic noise behind him, even what there was of it in Withens. Shepley Head Lodge was rather a lonely spot.

He shook the feeling off, blaming the old man for his ridiculous warning. And he began to walk the last few yards to Shepley Head Lodge.

MICHAEL DEARDEN TURNED out to be a lean, awkward man with a cold air. When Cooper showed him his ID on the doorstep, Dearden put on a poor pretence of incredulity and amazement.

'So somebody has actually come to see us?' he said. 'Gail! Somebody from the police has come to see us!'

'Were you expecting someone to call?' said Cooper.

'Expecting, no. Hoping, yes. But hoping doesn't get us anywhere. We've phoned the police station so often that it's on our "Friends and Family" list for discount calls.'

'Actually,' said Cooper, 'I think you've probably been contacting South Yorkshire Police, haven't you?'

'Yes?' said Dearden.

'Well, I'm Derbyshire CID. You're a bit out of my patch here, Mr Dearden. You're over the county boundary. If you've been having problems of some kind, South Yorkshire will deal with them for you.'

'Oh, will they?'

'Yes, I think so.'

'Well, think again. And think differently this time.'

A pale woman had appeared from upstairs and was staring at Cooper from the bottom step.

'Gail, can you believe this?' said Dearden. 'Someone from the police finally comes to see us, and he turns out to be from the wrong force.'

'I'm Derbyshire, not South Yorkshire,' Cooper explained again. But the woman said nothing.

'Ah, but,' said Dearden, wagging a finger at him, 'Withens is in Derbyshire, isn't it? Withens is on your patch.'

'Yes, sir.'

'So you can talk to us about the Oxleys.'

'If you'd like to, Mr Dearden, I'd be happy to listen.'

'THIS WAS THE old gamekeeper's lodge, which the estate sold off,' explained Dearden as he led Cooper through the house.

'It was certainly built to last.'

'Built to stand the climate, you see.'

There were thick internal stone walls and solid floors that absorbed the sound of their footsteps. There was a stuffed fox's head mounted on an oak shield in the hallway, but it seemed to have been left purely as a reminder of what the house had once been. The rooms had been filled with furniture covered in bright covers and white tablecloths, cabinets of blue-and-white pottery, and stands of smaller items – a collection of snuff boxes here, a display of gleaming brass there.

'Now, the Oxleys are a problem to everyone,' said Dearden. 'What I can't understand is why the authorities don't introduce one of those local child-curfew schemes. The power to do it is there. They can ban children from being in a public place after nine o'clock in the evening, and the police can take them off the streets. But they won't do it. It would be too politically incorrect, I suppose.'

'And perhaps impossible to put into practice.'

'Ah. Because there are no police officers around to enforce it. That's right,' said Dearden with exaggerated glee.

'Besides, those curfew orders only apply to children under ten, sir.'

'The ones beyond the criminal law. Well, there are some of those around here, too, believe me.'

'What sort of problems have you had?'

'Thefts, damage. For about eighteen months that's been going on. Then they set fire to our old garage. Burned it out completely.'

'Can I see?'

Dearden took him through a side door, past some outbuildings and into a yard, where he showed him a garage made of timber and corrugated iron. Though the structure still stood, its interior was blackened and charred, and the door had been destroyed by the fire.

'The trouble is, we can't see from the house when they come into the yard here. They've broken into the garage before, and into the other buildings. Nothing seems to stop them. We've got fed up of phoning the police. We've phoned so often that it's on our "Friends and Family" list –'

'Yes, you said.'

'Then we started using the internet.'

'You did?'

'Online Police.'

Cooper had never before come across anyone who used the Online Police website. It had been set up to allow people to report non-urgent minor crime, with the aim of freeing up telephone systems, particularly the 999 service. The site did make the point that it shouldn't be used for crimes that were happening right then, or where the offender was still nearby, or where there was a witness, or evidence left at the scene.

He wondered if that warning was necessary. Did anybody think people would actually do that? Would a member of the public see a crime being committed, sit down at the computer, log on to www.online.police.uk and spend ten minutes filling in forms with details of their name and address, date, time and place of the crime? Maybe they would, these days.

'They did all these break-ins, and then they burned my garage down.'

'Who did?'

'The bloody Oxleys, of course. You did say you were listening?'

'Yes, sir. But how –'

'The bloody Oxleys from bloody Waterloo Terrace. Those kids burned my garage down. They came from Withens, on your patch, and they crossed into Yorkshire, my patch, and they burned my garage down. It's only a mile from here to Withens, but you'd think we had to call the FBI to do something about it, all because there's a boundary stone in between.'

'When your garage was set on fire, did nobody come from your local police?'

'Some woman came and looked for fingerprints and stuff,' said Dearden grudgingly. 'But she wasn't a proper policewoman. She said she was a civilian.'

'A scenes of crime officer.'

'Yes. Well, she didn't seem to hold out much hope, anyway.'

'You're a bit vulnerable out here, aren't you?' said Cooper.

'Ah. You've noticed. Vulnerable is the word – and there's nobody interested in protecting us.'

Mrs Dearden had brought some tea. She hadn't spoken to Cooper yet. He smiled at her, but she didn't smile back. Her lips were tightly pressed together.

'Do you have any evidence to blame these incidents on the Oxley children?'

'Oh, you think I'm just making it up, don't you? Well, check their records. You'll find that two of them were convicted for a burglary at this property eighteen months ago. It didn't stop them. But that was the only one they were ever caught for. And that's because they tried to sell an electric drill they stole, and it was traced.'

'Which two were they, Mr Dearden?'

'Ryan and Sean. A right couple of teenage tearaways.'

'But since then?'

'We've never managed to catch them.'

'Mmm.'

Dearden started to go red when he detected Cooper's tone of scepticism.

'Have you been into Withens? Have you seen Waterloo Terrace?'

'Yes, sir.'

'Well, you'll have an idea what they're like,' said Dearden. 'I mean, look at the mess they leave. There's mud and rubbish all over the place. They're always dropping bits of broken pallet right the way along the road into Withens. One day I nearly hit a pile of roof tiles that had fallen off their lorry. They've even churned up the edge of the road by their houses, because they had a JCB parked there for a while. I never saw them actually do anything with it, either. It was just in the way for a week or two, then it was gone again. But it left the damage to the road, and all the water collects there now when it rains. You can bet the council won't make the Oxleys pay for the repairs, though. It'll come out of our Council Tax.'

'Is that why you started driving out of Withens via the old quarry track?' said Cooper. 'Because of the state of the road?'

Dearden hesitated. 'It's quicker sometimes.'

'You have a four-wheel-drive Mitsubishi pick-up?'

'That's right.'

'But even so, I would have thought it was pretty tough on your tyres and suspension.'

'Perhaps that's cheaper than ripping up my chassis on a pile of roof slates.'

'Perhaps. But you're taking a big risk of getting stuck.'

Dearden shrugged.

'Do you know Neil Granger, Mr Dearden?' said Cooper.

'Yes, I do. He's one of the Oxleys. Related, anyway. One day, somebody ought to look into just how closely some of those Oxleys are related. They're a bit too reluctant to share their gene pool, if you ask me.'

'Did you ever see Neil Granger on the old quarry track when you drove over that way, Mr Dearden?'

'I don't believe so. Well, no, I'm sure I didn't.'

'Anybody hanging around the air shaft?'

'I saw a couple of the Oxley lads trying to climb it once,' said Dearden.

'Oh? When was this?'

'A few weeks ago. God knows what they were up to. It's not as if they could steal anything. Even if they got down into the tunnel, they wouldn't be able to get out again.'

'No. Did you say anything to them?'

'Not likely. I'd only have got a mouthful of abuse.'

'Which of the Oxleys did you see?'

'That I'm not sure about. They're much of a muchness, unless you actually see them standing next to each other. And every one of them should be in jail, in my opinion. Not that you want my opinion. The police have made that clear enough. The laws of the outside world will never come near the Oxleys.'

IN THE LAY-BY on the A628, Ben Cooper could see that a cordon had been taped off around a light blue Volkswagen Beetle. He recognized Liz Petty pulling on her white suit, getting ready to approach the vehicle.

'They've asked me to do the car, to avoid cross-contamination,' said Petty. 'So let's hope that Locard's Principle is working in our favour today. Every contact leaves a trace. If the perpetrator travelled in this vehicle with the victim, he'll have left traces of himself for us to find, and carried others away with him. It's quite an old vehicle, which is good, because there are more likely to be distinctive traces on the seats and the floor.'

'It's been standing here overnight at least,' said Cooper.

'Yes, I noticed the spider's web. It's been spun from the hawthorn shrub to the wing mirror.'

'The doctor says the body's been lying up there over twenty-four hours.'

'Don't come any closer,' said Petty, reminding Cooper of Lucas Oxley and his dog.

'Why?'

'Be really careful of where you tread. There look to be some interesting traces on the ground here. Anyone getting into or out of this vehicle will most likely have got something on the soles of their shoes. Or anyone using another vehicle, for that matter.'

Cooper studied the surface of the lay-by. 'All I can see are chocolate wrappers, sweet papers and the remains of a burger and fries.'

'Exactly.'

'Why don't people use the litter bins?' said Cooper.

'In this case,' said Petty, 'we might be grateful that they didn't.'

'I see.'

'The interior of the car could be what matters most, though. By the way, there's a box of some kind in the footwell at the back,' she said, peering through the car window.

'You realize the perpetrator probably didn't arrive in this car, Liz?'

'We can hope, can't we, Ben?'

'He might not even have come this way. Apparently, there's a track to the air shaft from the other side of the hill, from a place called Withens.'

'Never heard of it,' said Petty.

'You will.'

'Tourist hot spot, is it?'

'Hardly.'

Cooper couldn't recall seeing anything picturesque about the village where the Oxleys lived. No wonder there were never any tourists passing through, as there were in other Peak District villages.

But at least there was one good thing about Withens. It was a long way from Diane Fry.

WITH A SLAM of the door, DC Gavin Murfin started the car and turned out of the West Street car park towards Edendale.

'So how the hell do we get to this Withens place?' said Fry. 'Have you any idea, Gavin?'

'Why don't you find it on the map?' said DC Murfin. 'I put a couple in the glove compartment.'

Fry found two thick, badly folded Ordnance Survey maps from the Outdoor Leisure series, covering the whole of the Peak District at two and a half inches to the mile.

'We want Dark Peak, right?' she said.

'Hey, you're learning the lingo.'

'I just try to remember that it gets dark if you go north and lighter if you go south. Can't go wrong then.'

'I suppose so.'

Before she had unfolded the map even halfway, Fry realized that it was huge. It was so big that it was almost the size of the Peak District itself. There was no way she could open it fully inside the car, not without covering the windscreen and blocking Murfin's vision. Then she discovered that the map was printed on both sides, too.

'All right – Dark Peak West or Dark Peak East?' she said.

'West, I think,' said Murfin.

'You think?'

'Pretty sure.'

'You don't sound certain enough for me. You *do* know this place we're heading? It *is* in Derbyshire, isn't it?'

'Just about. But it isn't the kind of area you really know unless you live there, like.'

'What do you mean?' asked Fry suspiciously.

'You'll see.'

'Oh, I can hardly wait.'

'Dark Peak West,' said Murfin. 'I'm sure.'

'Stop the car for a minute, then.'

'Why?'

'Because it's on the other side of the map, that's why. I need some space.'

Murfin pulled into a gateway. Fry got out and began to unfold the map on the car roof so that she could turn it over. When it was opened up, the map almost covered the roof of the Peugeot completely. She cursed steadily as the wind blowing down the valley snatched at the corners of the map and pulled sections of it from her hands, slapping them against the roof and tearing the folded edges.

'Right, I've got Dark Peak West,' she called to Murfin. 'I'm looking at the top right-hand corner, and I can see a place called Holmfirth. Anywhere near there?'

'Not far off. Holmfirth is a few miles over the border into West Yorkshire. Come south a bit, and you'll be about right. It's just this side of the national park boundary, in an area called Longdendale.'

'South a bit? But there's nothing there.'

'Well, not quite nothing.'

'Gavin, I can see the national park boundary, and I'm telling you that there's nothing anywhere near it on this side.'

'We'll find it,' said Murfin.

Fry ducked her head and got in the car. She pulled down the visor to look at herself in the little mirror. Her hair had been pushed up on end by the wind in old-fashioned spiky punk style. Murfin was also going to have to apply a bit of Sellotape to his map to hold it together, or buy a new one.

'Drive then,' she said. 'But as far as I can see, we're heading towards – what do they call it around here? – the moon's backside.'

'The Back of the Moon,' said Murfin.

'All right. But I think I prefer my version.'

A FEW MINUTES later, they were out of Edendale and heading north into the Hope Valley, approaching the village of Bamford.

'Are you planning to go over the Snake Pass?' said Fry, trying to follow their route on the map.

'Yes.'

'Is that the best way, Gavin?'

'Definitely.'

Fry looked for the area called Longdendale. This was where a body had been found early that morning, but it was a long valley, which ran right across the map. She studied the adjacent terrain in growing disbelief. Apart from the thin red ribbon of the A628 trunk road snaking its way from east to west through the valley, and the blue of the reservoirs in the valley bottom, the map had no features at all. No, that wasn't quite true. There were masses of thin brown lines that swirled everywhere, clustering tightly together here and there. They were contour lines. The closer together the lines were, the steeper the slope of the land – she knew that from some distant geography lesson. But crossing these brown lines were almost as many pale blue ones – little snaky things that ran down from all the summits, branching and trickling away in every direction. They looked like the worst case of varicose veins she had ever seen.

Many of these pale blue lines were labelled 'cloughs', 'slacks' or 'groughs'. They were streams and rivulets feeding down into the valleys. She could imagine how boggy the ground between them would be, because this was certainly peat moor.

Sure enough, there were lots of little clusters of black dots on the map, too. Fry checked the key for the meaning of the symbol. Rough grassland. In some places, those flecks turned blue. That meant marsh – a polite name for boggy ground that was like wet Christmas pudding to walk through, the sort of ground that the Dark Peak seemed to specialize in. She sighed. If anyone tried to persuade her to walk across one yard of those barren acres of peat moor, she would refuse. There had to be a tarmacked street somewhere in this place.

Fry looked closer, searching the map for features she could recognize. Some of the moors had their own names – she saw Dead Edge Flat, Bleakmires and Withens Moss.

She could make out the line of a disused railway tunnel running under the hills. But the moors themselves were empty.

Then she laughed. Not quite empty. There were actually some features to be found marked among the brown contour lines and the tangled systems of cloughs and slacks. The features were labelled on the map as 'mound' and 'pile of stones.'

'Unbelievable,' she said.

But Murfin just smiled.

Chapter Twelve

THE RENSHAWS' SITTING room was almost colourless. There were no reds or blues in the décor or in the furniture, only shades of brown, cream and off-white, as if the life had been bleached from the house. Diane Fry wondered if it had always been like this, or whether the Renshaws had changed the look of the house since Emma had disappeared, consciously or unconsciously reflecting the draining of the colour from their own lives.

Sarah Renshaw showed Fry and Murfin into the room and made them sit together on the leather settee. Murfin sat down gingerly, trying not to touch the teddy bear that sat at the end of the sofa, against the arm. It was about eighteen inches tall, and it had a red ribbon tied round its throat. Its eyes stared glassily at the Japanese screen in front of the fireplace, and one of its arms was raised as if to take an invisible cup of tea.

Despite the washed-out look of the room, Sarah Renshaw seemed to gain vitality from the moment she was given a chance to talk about Emma. It was the one aspect of her life that seemed to mean anything at all to her now. That, and the endless analysis of her own guilty feelings.

'We can still sense Emma in the house,' said Sarah. 'Can't you?'

'No, I'm sorry. But I never knew her.'

'The house is full of all the things that mean a lot to Emma. Her books, her drawings, and her poems. Her violin and her paints. And, of course, her teddy bears.'

'Teddy bears?'

'Yes. Emma was starting a collection. We gave her a big eighteenth birthday party here, you know. It was a wonderful party, with all her friends, and a disco and everything. Emma said it was the best day of her life.'

Sarah Renshaw's voice died, and her thoughts seemed to drift away for a moment. Fry could almost see the little black fist of reality that was trying to break through her bubble in those few seconds. It hammered, but failed to get in. Fry felt her throat constrict, and experienced a brief pain in the exact spot where the surgeon had left a small, fleshy vestige of her tonsils when he removed them years ago.

But then Sarah recovered herself and was just as composed as before, smiling at Fry as if she had made some small social gaffe.

'Anyway, Emma was starting a collection of teddy bears,' she said, 'and lots of people brought her teddies for her collection on her birthday. Most of them are in her room upstairs, but we keep her favourite ones down here. Edgar there was her very first one, and he's rather special. We gave him to Emma ourselves. He's sitting there waiting for her to come home.'

Murfin looked at the teddy bear on the settee, and tried to edge further away from it. But he found himself nudging up against Fry. She gave him a look, and he edged back again, his trousers squeaking on the soft leather.

'You know,' said Sarah, 'every morning when I wake up, there's a moment when I feel like my old self again. It's a wonderful moment, when Emma is about to arrive home, just as she was that day two years ago. And for a brief time it feels as though nothing was ever wrong at all. I always try to cling on to that moment and bring it into the world with me as I come awake. If only I could manage to hang on to it for long enough, I could make it real. But I've never been able to do it. Every time, the moment slips away from me.'

Sarah sighed, and looked up at something above Fry's head.

'Then I open my eyes, and everything falls back into perspective. And suddenly two years have gone by, and here I am. Here, today. My new self takes over again.'

Howard had pulled up another armchair to be near her. He leaned over and touched her shoulder.

'She'll be back soon,' he said.

But Sarah didn't seem to notice him or feel his touch. 'I always keep Emma's clock going in her bedroom,' she said. 'I make sure I replace the batteries regularly.

It's important that the clock shouldn't stop. As long as it's ticking, it's counting down the minutes until Emma comes home. It mustn't stop, until then.'

'Mrs Renshaw, when Emma went missing –' said Fry.

'When she didn't come home,' Sarah corrected her gently. But she had a resigned note in her voice that suggested she had said it often before, had said it too many times to too many people.

'When she didn't come home,' said Fry, 'you said you spoke to all her friends.'

'Yes, of course we did.'

'By that, do you mean the young people she shared the house with?'

'Yes, and a few others, such as some of the girls she knew on the same course.'

'Was that before or after the local police had spoken to them?'

'Before,' said Howard. 'If they bothered to speak to them at all, that is.'

'The West Midlands officers went through the correct procedures at the time, Mr Renshaw.'

'I suppose you have to say that. You have to stick together.'

'They've sent us copies of all their reports. I read through them yesterday.'

'A journalist on one of the local newspapers told us nine months ago that the police had arrested a man for attacks on two other female students in the area around the same time,' said Howard.

'Yes, I'm aware of that.'

'He told us that the police had tried to make out a case that this man had done something to Emma, too. He said they had no evidence, but they were connecting it. "Tying it in," he said.'

'Yes.'

'I think they've given up. They decided to use that as an excuse.'

The man convicted of attacking the students was in the files, too. One of his victims had died some days later, and it had become a murder charge. Those incidents had been in Birmingham, a few miles from Bearwood, but within easy reach. The defendant had refused to accept responsibility for the disappearance of a third student, and the police had been unable to prove a connection. They said this was probably because the body had never turned up. Fry hoped they hadn't said that to the Renshaws.

'We looked through her diary for clues,' said Howard. 'We'd heard it was the sort of thing the police do. We were looking for indications of her state of mind, mentions of people she might have been meeting up with. The names of any boyfriends.'

'And?'

'She was planning on coming home for Easter. That was all.'

'When was the last entry in the diary?'

'On the Wednesday, the day she rang us.'

'No appointments for the following couple of days?'

'No.'

'Emma wrote in her diary a lot,' said Sarah. 'She is a very thoughtful, sensitive sort of girl. Very artistic, you know. She wrote about her feelings all the time. She wrote poems, too, sometimes.'

'In her diary?'

'Yes.'

'This diary of Emma's – did you find it at Bearwood?'

'That's right.'

'And where is it now?'

'In her room here, with the rest of her things.'

'I wonder if I might see it?'

'You'd be welcome to.'

'She won't need it when she comes back,' said Sarah. 'We've bought her a new one for this year.'

And now Fry thought she could guess the answer to her next question, but she asked it anyway.

'Have you kept Emma's room as it was?'

'Yes,' said Sarah.

'May I see that, too?'

'I'll show you,' said Howard, and jumped up, as if relieved to have an excuse for moving around again. Perhaps the atmosphere had become that little bit too cloying for him. Fry was certainly glad of the cooler air in the hallway and the light from the big picture window at the top of the stairs. In the kitchen, she glimpsed a despondent-looking black Cocker Spaniel – presumably the source of the dog hairs on Sarah Renshaw's skirt.

'How long have you lived here, Mr Renshaw?' asked Fry.

'More than twenty years. Before that we lived in Marple, over in Cheshire.'

'Nice place?'

'It's a very nice place, yes. We had a lovely house, too, and lots of friends there.'

'But Emma always lived here, until she went to the Black Country?'

'Yes.'

'Do you like it here?'

'Certainly. The only problem we've ever had was a burglary a few months ago. But everybody has had them around here. We didn't lose very much. The sad thing is, we wouldn't even have been out of the house at the time, but we'd had some guidance on where we should look for Emma. Sarah was a bit upset about that.'

'Of course.'

As Fry had expected, Emma's bedroom was a shrine, complete in itself. There were pictures on the wall and stacked on a desk, and there were framed photographs of Emma as a girl, from a toddler of about two through to a teenager with long hair. A small dressing table contained bottles of scent and pots of make-up, and a bathrobe hung over the chair, as if it had just been draped there a few minutes ago. No doubt the wardrobe was packed full of Emma's clothes. The bed was neatly made and ready for use, apart from the fact that the duvet and pillows were partly occupied by teddy bears of various colours and sizes.

'By the way, I'm sorry about Edgar,' said Howard.

'Oh, the bear?'

'At first, Sarah used to hide him when people came to the house. She was embarrassed to be asked questions about it. But it was more embarrassing for visitors, when she saw the look on their faces and could see they didn't know the right words to say. After a while, though, we decided to leave the bear where it is. Now, it would seem like an insult to Emma to hide it away. It's just our way of coping. I hope you don't mind.'

'No, of course not.'

'I thought your colleague looked a little uncomfortable.'

Fry was going to explain that Gavin Murfin didn't do sensitive, but she held her tongue and asked instead about the items the Renshaws had brought back from the house in Bearwood.

'These are the pictures on her desk, here.'

'Do you mind if I take a look?'

'Not at all.'

Fry flipped through the pictures. Some were pencil or charcoal drawings; some were done in watercolours or gouache. There were landscapes and abstract designs, and some of them seemed to be sketches of fashion models in bizarre clothes, or simply fancy typefaces with 3D effects. Others were computer graphics in odd colours, like photographic negatives. Fry didn't consider herself any kind of expert, but she saw very little that she would have considered talent.

'Those are the best ones,' said Howard. 'We've been sorting them out ready for bank holiday Monday. We're holding an Emma Day.'

'You're doing what?'

'We're holding an Emma Day. We've found all Emma's drawings and her poems, and we're going to display them for everyone to see, so they'll know what she is like.

We want to share her with people. Share her talent. We've advertised it in the local paper, and in the shops, and we've put posters up in the village hall and at the pub. We've phoned all our friends and sent invitations out. We're going to make all Emma's favourite food, and play her favourite music, so that it will be a complete experience. And then people will be able to know her, almost as we do. It'll be wonderful.'

'Yes, I'm sure,' said Fry, cringing inwardly and trying not to show it. She stared at a drawing of a hillside with a full moon coming up behind it. In the middle foreground was a figure in a floaty dress and with floaty hair, walking up a long, winding path towards the top of the hill. The picture was done in watercolours, with carefully toned blues and greys. But it looked as though it hadn't quite been finished, as if the artist might, perhaps, have lost interest in the idea. The journey towards the rising moon had never quite been completed.

Fry saw that there were poems too, written out carefully on pages taken from an exercise book and mounted on coloured card. She took in a few lines, felt her stomach clench in reaction to their sentimentality, and couldn't bring herself to read any more.

But Mr Renshaw had picked one up and was reading it himself. As he read it, the tears were already starting to form in his eyes.

'It'll be wonderful,' he said.

'Yes.'

He turned to Fry. 'Will you be here on Monday?'

'Er, no, I don't expect to be on duty next Monday,' said Fry.

'If you aren't working, you can come. You will come, won't you? The house will be open all day.'

Howard handed her a hardback diary, of A5 size. Fry glanced inside and saw it was a day to a page, and Emma had found a lot to say.

'Thank you. You'll have it back safely.'

Although the bedroom contained so much of Emma's, it was obvious that there were also things of hers dispersed all around the house. A pair of her shoes stood next to one of the chairs in the sitting room. Another of Emma's teddy bears sat on one of the spare chairs at the kitchen table, where the Renshaws usually ate breakfast. And as they walked from the sitting room to the dining room, they passed a bookcase, full of books in perfectly neat rows.

'These are Emma's books,' said Howard, though it was unnecessary by now.

Fry was starting to see the way the Renshaws' minds were working. They were trying to convince themselves that Emma still lived with them, every moment of the day. For them, each teddy bear contained a lingering fragment of Emma's personality, just like the shoes and the books, and the scent bottles on her bedside table. And perhaps they were right. Perhaps each of their daughter's possessions retained faint strands of her spirit, her essence and her memories, locked inside their plain physical reality. And no doubt the Renshaws prayed that all these small parts of Emma might one day be brought together to re-create her, in the same way that scientists could bring extinct animals to life from the DNA traces in their bones. Fry felt sure that Sarah Renshaw believed it could happen. She believed with all her heart that it could happen.

'Mrs Renshaw, do you really still believe Emma is going to come home one day?'

'Of course.'

'And you, sir?'

Howard laid a hand on his wife's shoulder again. 'No one has shown us any proof otherwise,' he said.

Sarah nodded. 'People seem to think that we should give up hope. But how can we? We'd be letting Emma down, if we did that. We have to do everything we can for her. We have to keep trying all the ways we can think of. Because if we stopped trying, we might miss the one little thing that would lead us to her. I couldn't bear the thought of that.'

Gavin Murfin had been very still for a while. Fry looked at him to make sure he was awake. She was amazed to see that he was surreptitiously trying to wipe moisture from his eyes with his finger. Sarah Renshaw had noticed, too, and passed him a box of tissues from the side table without a word.

'Mr and Mrs Renshaw,' said Fry, 'I know you've gone over all this many times before, but I have to ask what Emma's exact relationship was with Alex Dearden and Neil Granger.'

'The only relationship Emma had with Neil Granger was that he was a fellow sufferer,' said Howard.

'Sufferer?'

'Migraines. Granger has them, too. Apparently, his are so severe that he can black out completely.'

'I see. And Alex Dearden?'

'We had hopes of Alex. But he has another girlfriend now.'

'Oh? Someone he met at university, or since he came back?'

'I wouldn't know.'

But Fry remembered Alex Dearden complaining that Mrs Renshaw rang him every week. What was she really trying to find out from him? Did she really think he might hear from Emma? Wouldn't she ask him about his new girlfriend? Or was that another thing she didn't want to face – another indication that life had moved on and left Emma behind?

'I understand you've had counselling,' said Fry.

Sarah laughed. 'Oh, yes. We learned phrases like "Letting go", "Moving on", and "Closure". But all the time I kept asking myself: "How could I have allowed it to happen?"'

'We've talked about it a lot,' said Howard. 'We thought it was important to talk. We decided it isn't about letting go, but about getting a new perspective on your life. It's more like turning over a piece of earth. Everything on the surface disappears, and new things appear in their place. But it's still the same piece of earth, isn't it? It's still the same life.'

Fry had been told different. She had been advised that sometimes people felt the need to clutch their suffering to them, fearing that if they 'let it go', they would themselves vanish. Their suffering began to define them.

But Sarah Renshaw was right – commemoration was important. A person you had lost could touch you sometimes, in unexpected ways. You might glance into a room and see her sitting on her bed, or catch a fleeting trace of her familiar scent passing along the corridor. You could hear her voice in the silence at night, or her footsteps crossing the floor above your head as you watched television in the evening. Commemoration was an important thing. It was like reaching out to let her know you were there for her. Commemoration was like returning the touch.

ON THEIR WAY back through Withens from the Renshaws' house, Diane Fry and Gavin Murfin noticed the police Vauxhall immediately.

'Anyone we know?' said Murfin.

'I doubt it.'

'I'm not so sure. Who's that coming across the road?'

Fry stared. 'What the hell's Ben Cooper doing here?'

'Not sightseeing, that's for certain,' said Murfin. 'This place looks like something the cat ate and sicked up again.'

'Pull up in front of the pub, Gavin.'

'Ah. Now you're talking.'

Fry wound down the window of the car as Cooper came across.

'Well, well. I thought we'd lost you,' she said.

'It's wonderful how people worry about me.'

'No such luck, though, eh?'

'No such luck. This is Tracy Udall, by the way, from the Rural Crime Team.'

Fry looked her up and down. Confident, capable-looking. Pretty much as she had been herself once, before she joined CID.

'Hello.'

Gavin Murfin gave a cheerful wave from behind the steering wheel.

'Hi,' said Udall. 'Withens hasn't seen so much police activity for years. Folks round here will be getting paranoid.'

'Some already are,' said Fry.

'Where have you been?' asked Cooper.

'To see the Renshaws.'

'Ah,' said Udall. 'I see what you mean. Though paranoid isn't quite the right word.'

'Emma Renshaw's parents,' said Cooper. 'I'd forgotten they lived in Withens. What's happening with that? Have I missed anything?'

'Well, that's what happens when you get promoted to the Rural Crime Team.'

'Has Emma been found? It can't be a murder enquiry, I would have heard. Wouldn't I, Diane?'

'Well, I expect so.' Then Fry took pity on him. 'Of course you would have heard, Ben. I'd have been kicking up all kinds of stink to get you back, no matter what the Rural Crime Team said.'

She didn't look at PC Udall, but Udall seemed to get the message.

'Tell you what, I'll see you back at the car, Ben,' she said. 'I've got some calls to make.'

Fry watched her walk away, giving a hitch to her duty belt. Full of confidence, totally unfazed.

'She's a good officer,' said Cooper.

'I'm sure.'

Fry saw the stubborn set of his face and suppressed an urge to wind him up some more. She had promised herself she was going to be nice to him. Besides, loyalty was one of his strong points, as she well knew.

'So it isn't a murder enquiry?'

'Not until we get the bloodstains analysed,' said Fry. 'And then we'll let you know.'

'Where are you heading now?'

'Tintwistle. To see if we can track down one of Emma Renshaw's housemates. A young man by the name of Neil Granger, who we can't seem to catch at home.'

Cooper put his hand on the car to stop them driving away.

'Don't be in too much of a rush,' he said. 'Somebody's already found him for you.'

DI PAUL HITCHENS was in the incident room at Edendale, where a team was being set up for the enquiry into Neil Granger's death. No decision had yet been taken to activate the HOLMES procedures. If an obvious suspect presented himself during the initial enquiries, there wouldn't be any need for the drain on staff and resources that was involved in a major enquiry. If E Division had too many major enquiries, it would miss its annual targets for house burglary and street crime.

Diane Fry thought Hitchens seemed a bit distracted these days. Maybe the new DCI was giving him a hard time. There were changes in the air around E Division, but then things didn't stay the same in the police service very long. Hitchens might be feeling the draught a bit.

'Well, if there's a link with the Emma Renshaw case, I'm sure we'll find it, Diane,' he said.

'Neil Granger was next on my list for interview,' said Fry.

'I'm aware of that. But who could possibly have known that there was a new line of enquiry in the Renshaw case?'

'Her parents. And I've already spoken to Alex Dearden as well, sir.'

'But Diane, Neil Granger has been dead since Friday night or the early hours of Saturday morning – before you talked to the Renshaws or Dearden.'

'Still …'

'I know it's frustrating that you've lost a witness. But come to the briefing in the morning, and you'll see that there are some important developments in other directions.'

'I see. The link to Emma Renshaw is a low priority in the DCI's thinking?'

'Yes, but you'll see why in the morning, Diane.'

'I'd like to make one request then, sir.'

'What's that?'

'I'd like to attend the Neil Granger postmortem.'

Hitchens paused. 'Well, I don't see why not. Mrs Van Doon never objects to an audience. I'll clear it with Mr Kessen.'

'Thank you, sir.'

'This theory isn't actually set in stone, Diane,' said Hitchens smugly. 'But it involves something equally solid.'

Fry waited for him to explain, but instead he smiled and changed tack.

'You don't remember the original Renshaw case yourself?' he said.

'No, sir. Why should I?'

'West Midlands – that's where you served before you came to Derbyshire, wasn't it?'

Fry watched him carefully, wondering what he was leading up to.

'It's a pretty big area, sir. I mean, we're talking cities here, large populations, high-volume crime. Lots and lots of missing young people. Besides, I worked in Birmingham, not the Black Country, though that's where I lived.'

'Ah, well. It could still be useful.'

'What do you mean?'

'I'm thinking that it might be helpful if someone went over the ground again in Bearwood. You know that ground, Fry. You're from that area.'

'Yes, sir,' said Fry reluctantly.

'You don't have a problem with that, do you? No personal problem, I mean.'

'No.'

'Mr Kessen has read your personnel file, so if you feel …'

'There's no problem, sir.'

'Good, good. Who will you take with you? We have Ben Cooper back with us. That's what you wanted, isn't it, Diane?'

Fry looked at the face of her senior officer, and thought about taking Ben Cooper with her to her old childhood haunts. He was the only one here who had any idea of what had happened to her during her childhood in Warley, or had any inkling of the existence of the sister she was still looking for after all this time. Cooper would be sympathetic. He would allow her time to visit places that had no relevance to the enquiry, without asking difficult questions. He would understand. He would be willing to listen, if she felt she wanted to talk about it. And he wouldn't think any worse of her if she wasn't able to maintain a professional exterior but showed her emotions, even broke down and cried. He would probably think better of her. He might even encourage her. All the things she didn't want.

'I'll take Gavin Murfin,' she said, and sighed when she thought of the newly pristine state of her car.

Chapter Thirteen

NEIL GRANGER'S HOUSE was in the middle of a terraced row on the main road through Tintwistle. At one end was a small Congregational chapel, where some women in hats were just leaving from a side door, perhaps from an evening service or a ladies' group meeting.

The row of houses had been clad with stone and modernized piecemeal. Many of the upper windows had been replaced with modern aluminium-framed versions, yet one house still had a cluster of little mullioned windows. Someone had built a low wall to separate the house from the pavement. It achieved little else, being too narrow for anything but a bit of concrete and a plastic tub containing some dead geraniums. The wall had been constructed from imitation stone, topped by pre-cast concrete blocks that formed diamond shapes, and there was a black wrought-iron gate.

Inside the gate, the flagstones were covered in a layer of dead leaves, which no one had bothered to clear away from the previous autumn. The house to the right had a neat garden and empty milk bottles left on the step for the milkman. To the left, there was a door painted in vibrant green and purple, while the windows had been edged in equally bright red. A small, yellow smiley face had been attached to the fanlight over the door. Ben Cooper wondered what sort of people lived there. Not one of the old ladies from the chapel, surely?

'I don't know what to do. I suppose that I'm Neil's next of kin.'

Philip Granger looked pale and ill. But the impression was perhaps exaggerated by the blackness of his hair and the dark stubble on his cheeks. He gazed around him in a daze, as if he wasn't quite sure where he was, or who these people were that he was with.

'Yes, sir,' said Cooper. 'But there are people who will give you advice and support. There will have to be an inquest first, anyway.'

Police officers had collected Granger from his job at an industrial insulation factory on the outskirts of Glossop, where he had been approaching the end of a long shift. Cooper could see that he was tired, and still in a state of shock from formally identifying his brother's body. They had been lucky to get an ID confirmed so quickly, and to get access to his brother's house. But Philip Granger wasn't going to be much more use to them until the reality of Neil's death had a chance to sink in properly.

Cooper watched him pick up some letters that had been lying in a wire basket behind the letter box. He looked at his brother's name and address typed on them, frowned, and put them down on the window ledge. Then he picked them up again, shuffled through them, and put them back in the wire basket with a guilty look, as if deciding that he shouldn't have touched his brother's mail.

'Do you live nearby, sir?'

'In Old Glossop, not far from the factory where I work.'

'So I take it you'll have visited this house sometimes, sir?'

'Yes, of course.'

'And have you travelled in your brother's car? The VW?'

'Once or twice. Why?'

'We'll need to take your fingerprints, for elimination purposes.'

Granger just stared at him blankly.

'Tomorrow will do, sir. When we get a formal statement.'

'Yes. Whatever.'

The house was sparsely furnished, without much effort to make everything match perfectly – but it was no more than he would have expected from a man living on his own. There was a stereo with sizeable speakers in the sitting room, and a TV in the other corner, with a remote sitting on an arm of the settee.

'Did you help Neil move in?' asked Cooper.

'Yeah. The furniture is a bit of a mixture. Some of it he was given, some he bought second hand. There were some new things. The stereo is new.'

Cooper walked over to the stereo and popped open the caddy of the CD. Nirvana. For some reason, he was surprised. But he didn't really know much about Neil Granger yet. He turned back to Philip, who was standing staring vaguely at the remote control on the settee.

'Are you sure there's no one you'd like to call, who can be with you? We could get a doctor, if you're not feeling well.'

'No, I'm OK.' But Granger sat down suddenly in one of the armchairs, as if his legs had failed him. 'Actually, I could do with a stiff drink.'

'We'll try not to keep you too long.'

'It's all right. You want a statement, you said?'

'Tomorrow. A formal statement tomorrow. But anything you can tell us right now to help us catch your brother's killer quickly would be very helpful.'

'I don't know what to say.'

'Had your brother lived here long?'

'He only moved in last summer. He'd been working away for a while to save up for a deposit.'

'It can be hard getting on the property ladder these days. Did he have a good job?'

'He worked at Lancashire Chemicals after he came back to this area. They thought a lot of him there. He was earning more than me, anyway.'

'Do you know how much he paid for this house?'

'No, I can't remember. Is it important?'

'Don't worry about it.'

It was something they could find out. Also what Neil Granger's mortgage payments had been, in relation to his wages at the chemicals factory. Cooper wasn't sure whether his curiosity on this was personally influenced. He knew all too well how difficult it was to get enough money together for a deposit on a house in Derbyshire and feel able to meet the mortgage commitment. It was taking him a long time on a detective constable's salary, even after ten years in the force. But perhaps house prices in Tintwistle were lower than in desirable Edendale.

Cooper looked into the kitchen. Surprisingly clean and neat. Carpeted stairs started near the back door. He wondered where he should go about finding a diary, letters or an address book.

'How many bedrooms are there?'

'Oh, two,' said Philip. 'Neil has his computer set up in the small one.'

'I see.'

It wasn't a bad little house. It had been kept in good condition inside. It would be ideal for one or two people setting up for the first time.

Cooper went out into the back garden to look at the area where Philip said his brother had kept his car. There were distinct wheel marks in the ground, which the SOCOs could compare to the VW's tyres, if it was thought useful. But there had been showers since Friday and the outline of the car had vanished.

The stone cladding on the front of the terrace had been only a façade. The cladding ended suddenly, presumably because it hadn't been worth the expense of covering the back of the houses. It had been all about outward appearance.

Cooper went back into the house and found Philip Granger sitting on a chair in the kitchen.

'And there's no girlfriend around?' he said.

Philip had already been prompted for the names of anyone in a close relationship who might need to be contacted before news of his brother's death began to leak out. But it was surprising what important details slipped the minds of bereaved relatives, only to be remembered at the second or third time of asking.

'Neil had a lot of girlfriends, on and off,' said Philip. 'I don't think there was anyone particular recently. I suppose I'll have to do some phoning round.'

'Please let us have any names and phone numbers, too. We'll need to speak to them. Also to any other friends or associates.'

'Associates?'

'Work colleagues, perhaps. I don't know. Anyone your brother had connections with. Particularly anyone he might have fallen out with.'

Granger looked up from his feet and tried to focus on Cooper. 'Who do you think did it, then?'

'We don't know at the moment, sir. That's why we need any leads you can give us.'

'You think it was someone Neil knew?'

'Yes, it seems likely in the circumstances.'

'Somehow, that makes it even worse,' said Granger.

'Yes, it always does. Are you older than your brother?'

'Yes, by three years. It isn't much, but it always seemed a lot between us. He was always my little brother. I felt quite responsible for him after our mum died. She had cancer of the stomach, you know.'

'What about your father?'

'He was sent down for burglary when we were teenagers, and we never saw him again. He was let out a few years ago, but he didn't bother coming home. Mum wasn't too upset about that.'

'Did he come to her funeral?'

'No. We've never heard anything from him, and we haven't tried to find him either.'

'So you don't even know whether he's still alive?'

'I suppose not.'

'He ought to be told about Neil, if we can trace him.'

'Well, I'm sorry, but I can't help there.'

Cooper caught sight of himself in a mirror on the wall near the front door. He looked more at home here than Philip Granger did. Briefly, the thought crossed his mind that the house would be coming on the market. He pushed it away guiltily.

'When did you last speak to your brother, Mr Granger?'

'A few days ago. I'm not sure exactly when.'

'During the last week?'

'Yes.'

'The beginning of the week?'

'I'm not sure.'

Granger was starting to flag a bit. He probably wouldn't be able to provide any more useful information at the moment.

'But you said earlier that Neil was in Withens on Friday evening, is that right?'

'Yes,' said Philip. 'He was at a rehearsal.'

'You weren't there yourself?'

'Oh. Yes.'

'And you didn't speak to your brother at the rehearsal?' said Cooper.

'Not really. It was kind of busy. And, you know – noisy.'

'This was a rehearsal for …?'

'The Border Rats.'

Philip looked around the room with a puzzled frown, cocking his head as if listening for a voice that wasn't there.

'They'll have a vacancy now,' he said.

BEN COOPER WAS glad to get back to his flat in Welbeck Street that night. Withens and all the people connected with it had started to depress him, and he wasn't quite sure why. Maybe it was the air of distrust he had met from everyone he had spoken to. They had been suspicious either of the police, or of each other, or even of the world in general. A police officer lived with suspicion, of course. But when it was unjustified, it was peculiarly depressing.

Cooper knew he was due to get a new neighbour in the upstairs flat. The previous tenant had been there for years, but had started to get a bit frail and had taken the chance of sheltered housing when she received an offer. Cooper expected his landlady, Mrs Shelley, to advertise the vacancy, as she had done with the ground-floor flat. 'Reliable and trustworthy professional people only'.

That's what the advert had said in the bookshop that day, when he had seen it by sheer chance.

But Mrs Shelley showed no signs of advertising the flat, or even getting any maintenance work or decorating done when the old tenant's belongings had been moved out. Cooper was curious to know what was going on. He had heard almost no noise from the old lady, but if someone less quiet moved in upstairs, it could have an impact on his life.

Funnily enough, Mrs Shelley had taken to him in a big way. He had thought she might have blamed him for the death of her nephew, who had died during the course of a murder enquiry three months earlier, with Cooper the only person present. But when everything had been explained to her, Mrs Shelley had decided that Cooper was a hero. In a way, he had actually taken the place of her nephew, and now she took a special interest in him. He thought he could probably have asked for anything and she would have said 'yes'. But it was unfair to take advantage of her.

Mostly, he wanted to establish the flat as his own private territory and he was nervous of encouraging her too much, in case she decided to pop in every few minutes to see how he was. The bolts helped there, of course. Though she had keys for the locks, there was no way she could just walk into the flat when he was there. That privacy felt very precious to him at the moment. It was a privacy he had never enjoyed before, since he had lived at Bridge End Farm with his family all his life. Finally, approaching his thirtieth birthday, he felt free for the first time. He could create his own world in this little flat. And he was surprised at how territorial he had immediately become.

He forked some duck-and-turkey Whiskas into a bowl for Randy, who rubbed himself briefly against Cooper's legs. Though they had met each other only a few months before, the cat was very much part of the scenery in Cooper's new life – which went to prove that you didn't need to work at a relationship for years and years, didn't it?

'Where's your friend, Randy?'

He called the other cat Mrs Macavity, because she came and went so mysteriously. In fact, Cooper wasn't sure where she really lived. Apart from the couple of months she had spent in his conservatory, caring for the five rather scruffy black-and-white kittens she'd produced in her basket one morning, her presence was unpredictable. He thought she might have an entire list of homes she called on when she felt like it. A meal here today, next door tomorrow.

Once new homes had been found for all the kittens among his family, Mrs Macavity had returned to her old ways. She was much more of a free spirit than Randy, who didn't wander far from his warm basket next to the boiler in the conservatory. He used the cat flap to do whatever he needed to do in the garden, weighed up the weather, and either lay for a while in the sun or came straight back in to his basket. He was an animal with a fixed routine and firm ideas about what was his territory and what wasn't. Cooper liked that. He thought there was something in that attitude that enabled a person to establish a home.

He'd asked Dorothy Shelley if he could be allowed access to the back garden. There was a door in to it from the conservatory, but the conservatory wasn't part of his flat, according to the tenancy agreement, so he had no rights over it. In fact, it belonged more to the cats than to him.

Of course, the cats didn't seem to belong to anyone, either. But that was perfectly normal. He had cleaned the cat hairs from the floor of the conservatory and washed the black specks of mould off the raffia chair that stood under the side window. He'd have liked to throw the chair out, but it wasn't his property. He'd have liked to have a bonfire in the garden, and put the chair on top of it. But the garden wasn't his.

The few possessions he had brought with him from Bridge End Farm were mostly in the sitting room – a Richard Martin print of Win Hill, a wooden cat on the window ledge. And, of course, the photograph over the fireplace – the one showing rows of solemn-faced police officers lined up in their uniforms, with Sergeant Joe Cooper standing in the second row. That would be his inheritance for ever.

'I'm afraid I've let this garden go a bit since my husband died,' said Mrs Shelley that evening, gazing vaguely through the glass of the conservatory as if she had completely forgotten there was anything out there. 'The one at number six is enough for me to manage on my own, so this has got a bit neglected.'

'I could tidy it up for you,' said Cooper. 'You've got some mature trees out there, but the rest of it is a bit overgrown.'

His landlady didn't seem too sure why she had come next door, though Cooper had been asking her to for weeks, so they could talk about the garden.

'I can't actually see it from my own house,' said Mrs Shelley, 'so it hasn't really bothered me.'

'It's a shame to let it deteriorate any more. Besides, the neighbours might start complaining.'

'I suppose they might.'

'Do you have a key for this door?'

Cooper could have opened the door easily. The wood was rotten around the lock, which was only an old barrel lock anyway. At some time, a small piece of wood had been screwed into the jamb to hold the catch in place where the wood had crumbled completely. A few seconds with a screwdriver, and he could have been out in the garden to take a look round, then put the piece of wood back, and Mrs Shelley would have been none the wiser. But he was on her property, and he had to abide by the rules.

'There's probably a key in a drawer somewhere,' she said.

'In your house? Or in here?'

Mrs Shelley looked around. An old table stood at one end of the conservatory, underneath a shelf of dying geraniums in plastic pots. The paint flaking from the table revealed that it had been several different colours in its lifetime, but most recently daffodil yellow.

'Try the table drawer.'

Cooper had a rummage. 'I think we're in luck,' he said, pulling out an iron key.

With a bang, Randy came through the cat flap. For the past weeks, it had been a source of increasing frustration for Cooper that the two cats had been free to come and go from the outside, while he was kept from it, able only to peer at the scenery sideways through panes of dusty glass. He put the feeling down to the arrival of spring. He could feel it in the air every time he went out of his front door on to the street or opened his kitchen window to let out the smell of his cooking. Even here, in the middle of Edendale, he could catch the scent of the fresh grass growing and the new leaves opening on the trees. He had started to get desperate for contact with nature.

Spring in Welbeck Street wasn't like spring back at Bridge End Farm, where he had grown up and had lived until so recently. But the chance to touch something green and growing would help. Visiting his brother Matt and his family at the farm only made things worse. There were too many memories now.

The cat rubbed its long black fur against his leg. Randy was already starting to change into his summer coat. His winter fur was gradually coarsening and falling out bit by bit each day, so that his outline became sleeker and darker. Since Cooper had taken over his feeding, Randy had become slimmer and much fitter. Occasionally, he returned the favour with a dead vole or shrew he'd brought into the flat from the garden. Often, by the time Cooper got home, they were already smelling and attracting flies. The distinctive smell of death seemed to follow him around these days. It even arrived, as a gift, on his kitchen floor.

Chapter Fourteen

DCI KESSEN TOOK up a position at the front of the room for the morning briefing. In front of him on the table were a series of exhibits relating to the Neil Granger enquiry.

'He looks like a Greek god to me,' said Gavin Murfin, taking a chair next to Ben Cooper.

'Well, I think he's more like Neptune,' said Cooper.

'Why?'

'It's the beard. The way it's sort of ... forked.'

'Yeah. Like the Devil.'

Kessen was waiting impassively for everyone to settle down. Diane Fry came in and sat on the front row, where no one ever wanted to be.

'I bet he's worth a lot, though,' said Murfin. 'Thousands.'

'I've no idea.'

'How old would you say?'

'A century or two, that's all,' said Cooper.

Kessen cleared his throat. The room gradually fell silent.

'I know what you're all wondering,' he said. 'I've decided to call him Fred.'

The DCI smiled without showing his teeth. The expression lacked humour. In fact, it looked more like a challenge to anyone who might dare to laugh.

'Oh, my good Lord,' said Murfin quietly.

Using both hands because of its weight, Kessen held up one of the evidence bags. It was made of clear plastic, and everyone could see what was inside it. There was also a large colour photograph of the item pinned up on one of the notice boards.

'An antique bronze bust,' said the DCI. 'This was found in a vehicle belonging to the victim, Neil Granger. The vehicle in question is a Volkswagen Beetle, which had been left parked in a lay-by on the A628, a few hundred yards down the hill from where Mr Granger's body was found.'

The bust was about nine inches high, with a dull green patina, and stood on a solid base. It represented the head of a man with a Roman nose, curly hair and a rather forked beard. Whoever he was, he gazed with blank eyes into the room. Cooper was reminded of a corpse he had once seen on the dissection table at the mortuary – a homeless Irishman who had been killed in a hit-and-run incident and left in a ditch. The Irishman's hair had been black, but his face had carried a similar green tinge.

'We know that there have been a number of burglaries from homes in the Longdendale area during the last few months,' said Kessen. 'During these burglaries, small antique items have been taken. This is a small antique item.'

The bust was heavy, and it landed with a thump when he rested it back on the table.

'Initial enquiries into Neil Granger's circumstances and his associates suggest that he may not have come into possession of this item in the normal manner.'

Kessen hesitated, and looked at the faces of some of the officers in the back row with an expression of disappointment.

'We think it may have been stolen,' he said.

'Are we going to put photos of the bust in the media, sir?' asked one officer.

'Not just yet.'

'We could get a quick identification that way, if the legitimate owner comes forward. Someone would be sure to recognize it if they saw it on TV or in the papers. It's very distinctive.'

'But we would also tip off the thieves that we have it,' said Kessen. 'I don't want to do that yet. That's a fact we're going to keep to ourselves. Understood, everybody?'

There were nods, and a few shifty looks from officers who might already have mentioned the bronze bust to their wives or husbands.

'We do have a bit of information about this item,' said Kessen. 'DI Hitchens will fill us in.'

'Well, we e-mailed pictures of the bust to a couple of experts yesterday and asked them to give it the once-over,' said Hitchens. 'Apparently, it's a copy of an original in marble that can be found in a museum in Florence. The character with the curly hair and beard is Lucius Verrus, an obscure Roman emperor. Closer to home, though, there's a larger copy of this in Chatsworth House. That's the Duke of Devonshire's stately home, a few miles east of here.'

'I think we know what Chatsworth House is,' said Kessen.

Gavin Murfin put his hand up. 'Have Chatsworth had any antiques lifted recently?' he said. 'I mean, I went in there once with the wife and kids, and the bloody place was stuffed with them. You could hardly move for antiques. God knows what the old Duke's insurance premiums must be like.'

'Thank you, Murfin,' said Hitchens, with an uneasy glance at the DCI.

'In fact, while we were there, I said to the wife that if I ever got kicked off the force I thought I'd go into the antiques trade. I could train the kids to sneak a few bits of china and silver out of Chatsworth now and then, and they'd never be missed. The place is massive. In fact, can you believe there was no one even living in the part of the house that we went in? So how would they know what they've got, and what they haven't? Someone could make a mint that way, I reckon.'

'Gavin ...'

'Yes, sir?'

'We're investigating a suspicious death,' said Hitchens. 'Not planning *The Italian Job*.'

'Sorry.'

'Are there prints on the bust, sir?' asked Cooper.

'Yes, the victim's. Neil Granger's.'

'He left his fingerprints on it? That's a bit amateurish, if he's involved in an organized gang.'

'Well, they always make a mistake.'

'Everybody knows not to leave fingerprints these days. It doesn't feel right.'

'It's evidence,' said Kessen. 'Let's see how it all adds up.'

Murfin leaned towards Cooper. ''Course it's evidence,' he said. 'Why does he have to state the bleedin' obvious all the time?'

'What were the victim's movements after he left the church at Withens?' asked Cooper, trying to pretend he hadn't heard Murfin.

The DCI looked at Hitchens, as if to suggest it was time he did something to earn his pay.

'It seems he drove straight home,' said Hitchens. 'His next-door neighbours noticed Granger's Volkswagen arrive. That was about twenty minutes after the Reverend Alton says he left the church.'

'The neighbours saw him?' said Cooper, who would like to have been able to speak to the neighbours himself, but hadn't been given the task.

'No, but the VW has a distinctive engine noise, they say. They also heard Granger's front door close, and then some music later on, for about three-quarters of an hour.'

'What music?'

'Does it matter, Ben?'

'I'm just wondering how thick the walls are. If the neighbours could tell what the music was, it might mean the walls are thin, and they would hear more of what went on next door.'

'His neighbours are a different generation to Neil Granger,' said Hitchens. 'I don't suppose they would have recognized the music if they'd been sitting with it blasting down their own headphones.'

'Anyway, I think it was Nirvana,' said Cooper.

'How do you know that?'

'The CD was still in the player when we visited the house with Granger's brother. I checked. And it lasts about three-quarters of an hour.'

'Brilliant.'

Cooper was conscious of a few heads turning towards him around the room.

'But the thing is, the neighbours never heard Granger go out again,' said Hitchens. 'They seemed confident of it, too. They say they usually recognize the sound of his door closing and his car engine. I think they're right – they would have noticed the same noises later at night, when it was quieter. But they sleep in a bedroom at the front of the house, and Granger keeps his car on some spare ground at the back.'

'So Granger went out again after the neighbours had gone to bed.'

'And now you're going to ask what time that was,' said Hitchens. 'You might think they were early to bed, because they're middle-aged. But in fact, the neighbours stayed up watching a late-night film on ITV.'

'*Schindler's List*,' said Cooper.

'Now, how the hell did you know that, Ben?'

'I watched it myself. It finished at 1.30 a.m.'

There was a strange silence from the officers immediately around him. Even Gavin Murfin seemed to be trying to use his body language to pretend that he was sitting next to someone else entirely. Cooper realized he would probably get ribbed mercilessly in the CID room afterwards. His fellow DCs would be calling him Sherlock for weeks. But he never had quite learned when to keep his mouth shut.

DI Hitchens was staring at him with something like pity. Mr Kessen had gone all glassy-eyed, not unlike poor old Lucius Verrus on the table in front of him.

'Damn right, Cooper,' said Hitchens. 'So the chances are that Neil Granger went out of the house some time between 1.30 a.m. and the time he was killed on Withens Moor later that morning. Unfortunately, we can't be exact about the time he was killed. Or Mrs Van Doon can't.'

Another officer across the room took up the challenge. 'Granger's VW was parked in a lay-by on the A628, so somebody might have noticed it.'

'We've got teams tracking down lorry drivers who were on that route in the early hours,' said Hitchens. 'There's an all-night roadside café a couple of miles down the road, and we're hoping the owner might be able to put us on to some of his regulars who were on the road at that time. That might narrow the time down for us. If we're really lucky, they might have seen another car in the same lay-by. Or even a car and occupants.'

'Why did Granger park on the road when he could have driven up the track right to the air shaft? Wasn't there a car that came down the track over the hill? It was seen by the first officers at the scene.'

'Ah, yes,' said Hitchens. 'DC Cooper?'

'The driver's name is Michael Dearden,' said Cooper. 'I went to see him yesterday. He lives just outside Withens at a house called Shepley Head Lodge, and he says he uses the track for a short cut. It's an old quarry road, but it isn't suitable for anything apart from a four wheel drive. Granger's old Volkswagen wouldn't have made it up the hill.'

'Whoever met him might have had a four-wheel drive,' said Hitchens. 'So we have to bear in mind that they might not even have approached the scene from the A628. If this Dearden came over from the Withens direction, someone else could, too. There's no restriction on the access at Dearden's end, Cooper?'

'No, sir. There's an open gateway. Withens Moor is access land.'

'We mustn't neglect the possibilities. We'll get someone to check out the lie of the land there.'

'We're going to take our time at the scene, too,' said DCI Kessen. 'We need to exploit every forensic opportunity.'

'Unfortunately, sir, the SOCOs say the ground had been trampled thoroughly before the scene was secured.'

'How did that happen?'

'Well, the firefighters do tend to have rather large boots. On the other hand, we've had more luck from the lay-by where Granger's car was parked. One of the SOCOs scraped up quite a wide range of samples from the ground there. If we can match the right combination to a suspect's footwear, it would help us enormously.'

'Thank you,' said Kessen. 'I want to make it clear that we're going to limit the amount of information we release – particularly what we allow Neil Granger's associates access to. So we should be circumspect.'

'Yes, sir.'

DC Murfin leaned towards Cooper again. 'What does that mean?' he said. 'I thought it was when you were Jewish, like.'

'He means watch what you say.'

'Ah. As if I'd do anything else.'

Cooper saw Diane Fry turn slightly to look at them over her shoulder, frowning as if she had caught a couple of pupils misbehaving in class.

'Miss isn't pleased,' said Murfin.

'Shhh.'

'I can't emphasize enough that we must be meticulous in preserving evidence,' said Kessen. 'This is going to be a real team effort, so we must work together and communicate fully. And remember, everybody – there's no "i" in "team".'

Cooper heard Gavin Murfin muttering under his breath.

'There's a "u" in bullshit, though,' he said.

Before the briefing broke up, everyone seemed to need to take another look at the photographs of the victim from the scene. The colours looked so unreal, as if something had gone wrong with the film in the photographer's camera. Granger's face was streaked with blood from his head wounds, but it had dried blacker than normal where it lay against his skin. That was because it had streaked and mingled with the black make-up he wore everywhere but around his eyes.

'If we can find out why and when Neil Granger had blackened his face with theatrical make-up, that might give us the lead we need,' said DCI Kessen. 'But at the moment, we keep this fact to ourselves, too.'

GAVIN MURFIN HAD arrived at the office armed with an enormous Peak pasty and a slab of dark, moist parkin. He'd left the parkin in its cellophane wrapper, but the gingery smell drifting across the office made Ben Cooper's mouth water as soon as he walked in.

DI Hitchens approached them with Diane Fry. Hitchens sniffed at Murfin's pasty with interest, while Fry tried not to look at it.

'Cooper, what are you currently working on?' said Hitchens. 'The Oxley family, isn't it? Excellent. We need to pin down Neil Granger's closest associates, who he spent his time with. Maybe he was close to some of his cousins among the Oxleys.'

'He moved out of Withens some time ago, sir, but we know he's been back there. One of the residents saw him on Friday night, and he helped the vicar to clear up after his church was broken into and vandalized.'

'Exactly. Keep on it.'

DI Hitchens drifted off to speak to Kessen. Cooper waited until he'd gone, and then he looked at Fry curiously.

'You never mentioned the possibility of a connection with Emma Renshaw, Diane,' he said. 'I thought you would do.'

'I've already talked to Mr Hitchens about it. It isn't the main line of enquiry at the moment.'

'It can't be overlooked.'

'No, it won't be overlooked, Ben.'

'I do remember the case. Granger was one of her housemates, too, and he'd known Emma all his life.'

'He was also one of the last people to see her alive, as far as we know. But most of the activity was in the Black Country, where she was last seen. The mobile phone is the first indication we've had that she made it anywhere near home. Of course, there was no direct evidence at the time that any crime had been committed. Emma Renshaw simply disappeared. No body, no witnesses, no apparent motive. And no evidence.'

'Until now. Now we have her phone.'

'I suppose it's still possible that she might have wanted to disappear. That was the conclusion at the time. But who knows what might have happened to her since then.'

Cooper hesitated. 'There's another reason I remember the Emma Renshaw case.'

'Oh, yes?'

'We've been reminded of it fairly regularly during the last two years. There have been several minor incidents that officers have had to deal with. Advice has been given. An informal warning once, I think.'

Fry looked up from the file. 'You mean the parents? Yes, I know about that. But thanks for telling me.'

'And Neil Granger lived in Withens. So he was a near neighbour of the Renshaws, too.'

'Like you say, he and Emma were old schoolfriends.'

'Childhood sweethearts maybe?'

'If they were, it sounds as though they'd cooled off. By all appearances, they were no more than acquaintances in Bearwood.'

'But sharing a house.'

'The general agreement is that it was a matter of convenience, splitting the cost.'

'Childhood relationships never survive adolescence anyway,' said Cooper. 'Girls mature earlier, so boys of the same age suddenly look like children. And the girls develop an interest in the bigger boys.'

'Possibly. We weren't able to prove that they were more than just friends, anyway. But they'd known each other for a long time, so it was quite natural they should share a house.'

'What sort of state are the Renshaws in these days?'

'The state of Cloud Cuckoo Land,' said Fry.

'Right.'

'Don't forget our meeting, Ben.'

'What?'

'We're supposed to be arranging a meeting. I take it you've forgotten?'

'Well, in the circumstances …'

Fry nodded. 'OK. But let's not forget about it altogether, eh? I think we have some talking to do.'

A COUPLE OF hours later, Ben Cooper was watching PC Tracy Udall check her duty belt. She was painstaking in her routine, even as she continued talking to him. But a patrol officer's safety could depend on carrying out this routine properly at the start of every shift. Udall shook her head and tutted when Cooper told her about Lucas Oxley and his dog.

'It was my own fault,' he said. 'I don't think I identified myself clearly enough. He seemed to be a bit deaf or something. A uniform will make a difference, I'm sure.'

'Perhaps it was rather rash, going on your own,' said Udall. 'But you hadn't got the full picture about Waterloo Terrace.'

'Exactly.'

'But you'll be all right with me. I can subdue any savage dog with a single glance. My kids take no notice of me, but other than that, I'm mustard.'

Udall unfastened the four keepers on her uniform belt and clipped her duty belt over it. Cooper could see that she was right-handed – she positioned her rigid handcuffs on her right hip and her baton on the left, her weak side. She drew the handcuffs out of their holster, pushing the single bar through the double bar and pulling it back to the pre-load position before re-holstering them carefully.

'Is your son behaving no better?' said Cooper.

'He had another tantrum this morning about me going to work.' Udall sighed. 'These duty rosters don't help. He doesn't understand the shift system.'

'Does anybody?'

Udall laughed. 'He needs a routine at that age. He needs to know exactly when his mum is going to be at home and when she isn't. A regular routine provides a bit of security in itself. But that's what I can't give him at the moment. Quite honestly, I could do without going through a major guilt trip every time I set off for work.'

'You're not thinking of leaving the force, Tracy?'

'Nah,' she said. 'But it's difficult sometimes.'

After a hastily called briefing at Glossop section station to gather resources, Cooper was about to find himself on his way back to Withens. It was almost as if the body of Neil Granger hadn't been found at the air shaft in the interval since his last visit. Or that he had been in the right place yesterday, but not asking the right questions. Granger was related to the Oxleys, and the Reverend Derek Alton had been expecting to see him the day he died. Cooper had cornered his own line of enquiry, and it centred on Waterloo Terrace.

'By the way, I asked the community constable about the Oxley kids,' said Udall. 'He's only been on the patch about eighteen months, but he's had a few dealings with them already.'

'Any of them in particular?'

'There have been several complaints about the younger ones. The usual sort of stuff – hanging around outside people's houses, making a lot of noise, swearing, running across gardens. You get the picture.'

'Nothing out of the ordinary there.'

'No. Nothing out of the ordinary. Not where there's a group of youngsters gathering together. And of course that means they get blamed for anything that goes off in the village – minor thefts and damage to property. Also any vandalism, graffiti, litter – you name it.'

'Did the community bobby ever get any proof the Oxley kids were involved?'

'Proof's a different matter. But he's spoken to them many a time. Also to their parents. Or he's tried to.'

'I know what he means,' said Cooper, with a sigh.

Udall laughed at him as she tested the security of her baton in its ring on her left hip and switched her torch on and off. She flipped open her medical protection pouch, which contained a face mask, latex gloves, antiseptic wipes and a contaminated-waste bag. The most immediate threat to a police officer often came from an encounter with body fluids rather than with a lethal weapon. Hepatitis B and HIV were on the streets, even in Edendale. But just in case she did need to subdue a violent suspect, Udall had also been issued with a CS spray.

'He says the Oxley adults co-operated to the minimum amount they could get away with. They never became aggressive or argued with him. They always promised to talk to their kids and keep a closer eye on them. They never gave him justification for taking further action.'

'But have the complaints stopped?' said Cooper.

'No. And the Oxleys had quite colourful careers, by all accounts. All the boys have court records. There were even some arson charges at one time. Ryan and Jake are the ones giving most cause for most concern at the moment. Actually, the Social Services case officer is quite optimistic about Ryan – she says he's a sensible lad at heart and will probably settle down.'

'Really?'

'There's no need to sound quite so cynical, Ben. Many of our young offenders settle down and become perfectly respectable citizens.'

'OK,' said Cooper. 'And Jake?'

'He's causing some problems at the moment.'

'Is there nothing that can be done with him?'

'Basically, there are two options. Either we take him away from his parents and put him into local authority care. Or we leave him where he is, until he's old enough to earn himself a spell in a detention centre.'

'And that would be the start of a long cycle of court appearances, and eventually prison.'

'Exactly. But we operate on the principle that the best place for a child is at home, with his family. So, with this kind of case, we're in a cleft stick.'

'What about the older ones?'

Udall hesitated. 'Scott and his cousins, you mean? They're not the concern of Social Services any more, and I only asked about the children. But there'll be court records we can look up.'

'And the girls aren't a problem? Lorraine and Stacey?'

'Not that I know of.'

'Well, if they're clean, let's hope they stay that way.'

'Amen.'

Finally, Udall checked her personal radio and chose a battery. Cooper waited patiently while she made sure the radio was on the right channel and placed it in its holster.

She adjusted the lead to the handset, so that it wouldn't be in the way if she had to draw her baton. Then she gave her duty belt a final tug, and was ready. She lifted an eyebrow at the way Cooper was watching her.

'How do I look?' she said.

'Terrifying.'

'Thanks a lot.'

'But only if I were a criminal,' said Cooper. 'Or an Alsatian dog.'

PC UDALL'S LIVERIED Vauxhall Astra was white, with an orange flash and black-and-white checkerboard patterns down each side, and a blue beacon on the roof. It had those yellow and red diagonal stripes on the tailgate which had been dubbed a 'baboon's bum', after something very similar had been spotted on a BBC wildlife programme. The code number of the vehicle was painted on the roof in large black letters for identification by the air support unit. A bottle of mineral water had been thrown on the back seat.

Ben Cooper had never felt entirely comfortable being driven by someone else. He much preferred being at the wheel than being a passenger. He had always supposed it was something to do with a need to be in control. But maybe today it was also the result of Tracy Udall's tendency to wave her hands breezily as she talked. The B6105 Woodhead Road out of Glossop was narrow and winding, and at one point, as it descended into Longdendale, there was a sharp kink in the road called The Devil's Elbow, which had been a notorious accident black spot for years.

There was a long string of five reservoirs filling the valley bottom. One of them, Valehouse, came into sight as they approached the Devil's Elbow, then they descended the hill towards its neighbour, Rhodeswood. They drove alongside Torside Reservoir for a while, past the national park information point. Although it was Monday, there were small sailing boats on Torside Reservoir. The track of the former railway line ran right by the road here, converted into the Longdendale Trail.

Finally, they crossed the dam between Torside and Woodhead and eased cautiously out into the traffic on the A628.

'This end of the valley has always had a few problem areas for us,' said Udall. 'Hadfield and Hollingworth, particularly. The closer you get to the outskirts of Manchester, the bigger the problems. The motorway makes it so much easier for people to get to Longdendale now.'

'What about the upper end of the valley?'

'Well, not so much. The crime rate tends to decline when the population disappears.'

'What do you mean?'

'Look at your map. See those names along the road? Then look around you here. Where's the village of Crowden? Where's Woodhead? Where's Saltersbrook?'

Cooper looked. 'Judging from this map, we must have driven through all of them in the last half-hour, but I missed them. Did I fall asleep, or what?'

'No. It's because they're not there any more.'

'They just died?'

'They were removed,' said Udall. 'Flattened, cleared, eliminated. Apart from their names, they were wiped off the map.'

'You're kidding.'

'Nope. I'm told there used to be at least five inns along this stretch of road, between Crowden and Saltersbrook. Crowden alone had a school with forty pupils in it. And there was a seventeenth-century Stuart mansion called Crowden Hall. They've all gone.'

'We're not talking about villages that disappeared under the water when the reservoirs were built, Tracy?'

'No, these villages were well above the water line. They were right here, on the road. You can still see where the houses were, in some cases. But a few foundations are all that's left. In fact, take a look at Saltersbrook, and you'll find the ruins of the village inn on the old packhorse road. At Woodhead, there was one house that stood right over the entrances to the railway tunnels. It's just a few square yards of concrete now.'

'But why?'

'Well, this is a water catchment area, Ben – the hill-sides gather the water that feeds the reservoirs down in the valley.'

'Of course.'

'The water companies decided that the presence of people in Longdendale might pollute the water supply for the customers in Manchester and the Lancashire cotton towns. So they moved them all out and demolished their villages.'

'Including a Stuart mansion,' said Cooper. 'But I suppose they didn't care quite so much about those things in the nineteenth century.'

Udall laughed. 'Nineteenth century, nothing. My dad remembers Crowden Hall. In fact, he has a photograph of it in a drawer somewhere. The hall was demolished in 1937 by Manchester Corporation.'

'Damn.'

'One of the pubs survived right into the 1960s. But that went, too. And only a couple of years ago, the water company spent £300,000 moving an entire farming operation a mile further up the hill at Crowden, to get it away from the road. They said it was to safeguard water quality from grazing sheep. They had to build a new house for the farmer in that case. But he was one of the lucky ones, I think. Entire communities have just disappeared from this area.'

Cooper looked back at the boats on Torside Reservoir. Presumably, sailing was an activity that could be trusted not to pollute the water.

'And what about Withens?' he said.

Udall shrugged. 'I don't know. But it doesn't look like a place that will last, does it?'

Chapter Fifteen

AT 7 WATERLOO Terrace, Ruby Wallwin had cooked lunch for herself – stewed beef with new potatoes and baby carrots. But she made no attempt to eat what she'd cooked. She put the food on a plate and sat at the table, but didn't touch a thing. Instead, she stared at the wall and listened to the clock, until her meal time was over. Then she disposed of the uneaten food, poured a half-drunk cup of tea down the sink and washed the pots, taking comfort from the feel of the hot water on her hands and the lemony smell of the washing-up liquid.

Afterwards, Mrs Wallwin turned on both her radios and the television. She had a radio in the kitchen, and another upstairs in her bedroom, while the TV was in the sitting room. It meant there was something she could hear in every room. She didn't know what the programmes were that they were broadcasting – she needed them only for the sound of the voices. Some of those voices had become familiar, and were like friends chatting in the next room, waiting for her to join them. There were other times when she found the voices inside her house only made things worse. Then she would turn them all off, until she could no longer stand the silence again.

When she went out of the house, Ruby Wallwin always left a few lights on and a radio playing quietly. She didn't do it to deter burglars – she had nothing worth stealing, after all. She did it so that the house wouldn't be quite so dark and silent when she came back to it.

Yesterday, she'd been to the morning service at St Asaph's. She had sat on her own, surrounded by empty pews. There were a few people of her own age in church, but Mrs Wallwin hadn't lived in the village very long, so she didn't feel able to sit with them, though they said 'hello' when they saw her.

Ruby Wallwin had particularly wanted to speak to the vicar, the Reverend Alton. She didn't know him all that well, but he seemed like a decent man. She had taken her time leaving the church after the service, hoping that he would notice her. But Mr Alton had seemed very distracted, and he had disappeared into the vestry before she could get his attention.

Mrs Wallwin would have spoken to the vicar. She didn't want to speak to the police.

BEN COOPER STOOD in front of the black brick terrace, watching the grey shapes of the wood pigeons that were flying in a small flock now, out over the fields and back again. The sound of the chainsaw that was still operating somewhere behind the houses only seemed to accentuate the eerie silence. Waterloo Terrace stood below the road, sheltered by its screen of trees as if it lay in a cocoon, separate from the rest of the village.

'Do the Oxleys own these houses?' he asked.

'No, they're rented,' said Tracy Udall.

'Council property?'

'A private landlord.'

'They're a bit run-down, aren't they?'

'I don't suppose the Oxleys are ideal tenants.'

'No.'

'Where would you like to start, Ben?'

'My choice, eh? Let's see the list again.'

Udall's list was very organized. Number 1 Waterloo Terrace was recorded as being occupied by Mr Lucas Oxley. Strangely, numbers 2 and 3 were listed the same way. Why would Lucas Oxley need three houses? But then his family was rather large, according to Derek Alton.

There were certainly more Oxleys nearby. The fourth house in the terrace was occupied by Mr Scott Oxley, and number 5 was Ms Frances Oxley. But 6 and 7 provided a bit of variety – their occupiers were Mr and Mrs Melvyn Tagg, and Mrs Ruby Wallwin respectively. The eighth house was said to be unoccupied.

'Who should we tackle first?' said Cooper to himself. 'Eeny, meeny or mo? Oxley, Oxley or Oxley? I wonder if they've ever thought of starting a firm of solicitors?'

He looked at the terrace of houses again. Logic dictated that he should start at number 1 and see if

Mr Lucas Oxley was home again. But he wasn't feeling logical today, and something told him it might be helpful to approach the Oxleys at a tangent. Besides, he could still remember the dog.

'Number 7 it is, then. Mrs Wallwin.'

Closer to, the bricks weren't really black at all. They had an almost purplish tinge, as if they had been steeped in blackberry juice. Number 7 showed few signs of decoration. Its paintwork was a sort of chestnut brown, or had been at one time. The combination with the black bricks was somehow depressing. There were lace curtains in the windows, which gave it an old-fashioned air. It might have been part of a setting for one of those urban townscapes painted by L. S. Lowry. After all, the painter had lived for a number of years at Mottram, down the valley, so it was possible he had seen Waterloo Terrace.

To reach number 7, Cooper and Udall had to pass a fenced-off area where six green wheelie bins were stored. They reached the front walls of the row of gardens. All the gardens were long and narrow, and all were overgrown, despite the past efforts at growing vegetables. They walked up the path, avoiding the nettles that were spreading from the soil on to the stone flags. Cooper took a quick glance at number 8, which was on the other side of one of the dark brick passageways. Its windows were dirty and curtainless, and it had an air of neglect. There was nothing more depressing than a house that had been left empty for a long time, and in Waterloo Terrace it was more depressing than ever.

'I HAVEN'T COMPLAINED to the police about anything,' said Mrs Wallwin, when she found Ben Cooper and Tracy Udall on her doorstep.

Cooper was surprised at the defensive note in her voice. Though she was slight and rather frail looking, she stood right on the step, as if she hoped to block the doorway. Many old people were far too trusting about who they opened their doors to. But not in Withens, it seemed.

'Mrs Wallwin? Good afternoon. We just want to ask you a few questions,' said Udall in her pleasant est manner. With most elderly people, her charm would have worked perfectly.

'What about?' said Mrs Wallwin.

'May we come in?'

'What for?'

'It doesn't matter,' said Cooper. 'Do you know a young man called Neil Granger?'

And Mrs Wallwin's face softened a bit then.

'Yes, of course I do. I know him and his brother. They used to live here.'

'Here?' said Cooper. 'You mean here, in Waterloo Terrace?'

'Next door. They were looked after by their uncle and aunt when they were teenagers. Their dad was sent to prison, and they never saw him again after he came out. Then their poor mother fell ill with cancer and couldn't look after them herself.'

'Their uncle and aunt would be Mr and Mrs Oxley?'

'That's right.'

'They have quite a few children of their own, don't they?'

'Yes.'

'Do they cause you any trouble, Mrs Wallwin?'

'Not to speak of. They can be a bit noisy, but all kids are like that.'

Mrs Wallwin was wearing rather worn pink slippers, and her legs were painfully thin. Cooper could detect a musty smell, like old newspapers or clothes that hadn't been aired properly.

'When did you last see Neil Granger?' he asked.

'He was by here the other night.'

'Which night?'

'It would be Friday.'

'Do you know what time?'

She shook her head. 'He went off with the others. His uncle and his cousins. They went off up to the pub, I should think.'

'Thank you.'

Beyond Mrs Wallwin, Cooper could see a small table in the hallway. There were a couple of familiar-looking envelopes on it, with red slogans on the outside. 'You're a winner!' 'Open now for some wonderful news!' The usual junk mail, not yet thrown away.

'Neil and Philip don't live here any more,' said Mrs Wallwin. 'The house is empty now. I only got this one because my son works for the company.'

'The company?'

'The water company.'

'Do you live alone, Mrs Wallwin?' said Udall. She sounded genuinely concerned, but it didn't wash.

'Why do you ask?'

'There have been a few problems in this area. A lot of houses have been broken into. We just want to be sure that you're safe and secure.'

'I'm safe, all right. Nobody comes here.'

'Nobody?'

The old lady looked suddenly worried, as if she had given the wrong answer.

'My son comes to see me,' she said. 'Of course he does. Why shouldn't he?'

'As long as you're all right, love,' said Udall.

And this time the sincerity of her concern seemed to get through.

'I wouldn't want to die here alone,' said the old lady suddenly. 'It might be days and days before anyone found me.'

'I'm sure that wouldn't happen, Mrs Wallwin. You've got neighbours here.'

'Yes, I have,' she said. 'I'll say goodbye now.'

And suddenly she began to close the door. But Cooper noticed that she left it on the chain and watched them through the narrow gap as they walked down the path.

'Are you sure about that, Ben?' said Udall as they reached the gate.

'What?'

'I attended an incident once when I was stationed in Chesterfield. Someone living in a block of flats reported to the housing office that she hadn't seen an elderly neighbour in a while. I knew the man was dead before we even got the door open. The smell was on the landing – that smell you know is going to cling to your uniform for ages, until you wash it.'

'I know the smell,' said Cooper.

'But, of course, I had to call for the doctor to certify death. The old man was lying on his bed. There was fungus growing around his eyes and dead maggots lying on the floor all around the bed. The doctor said he'd been dead for quite a long time. Not days, or weeks – months.'

'And you're saying it took that long for the neighbours to notice?'

'It wasn't really their fault. The old man made it clear he didn't want any contact. He always refused to answer the door, even though they knew he was in, because they could hear him through the walls, moving about the flat. Now and then, they'd catch a glimpse of him scuttling towards the stairs like a sneak thief, but that was all.'

Cooper nodded. He knew there were some people like that. People who lived in fear of a human touch. People who were terrified of making contact with another person, perhaps because they were afraid of their own lives being exposed for what they were. They heard a voice outside their door and prayed that whoever it belonged to would walk on past.

'Let's see what the Taggs are like at number 6,' he said.

MR AND MRS Melvyn Tagg turned out to be a young couple, in their twenties, with a harassed air.

Melvyn answered the door with an open bottle of Jeyes Fluid in his hand. When Cooper took a breath to speak, the odour of the disinfectant made his eyes water.

'You'll have to talk while we get on,' said Melvyn. He ran his free hand through a fringe of long, dark hair, leaving it glistening with Jeyes Fluid.

'That's fine,' said Cooper. 'We won't keep you long.'

In the front room, the Taggs had a small baby lying on a towel spread on the table. It was naked, and its legs and arms were wriggling with irritation. Melvyn introduced the blonde woman holding the nappy as his wife Wendy. She looked at their visitors with suspicion, and a hint of panic.

'Mel,' she said, 'what are they doing here? Why did you let them in?'

'I couldn't just stand on the doorstep, could I?'

A slightly older child was sitting on the floor in the corner, surrounded by toys. There were building bricks, wooden blocks, small furry animals and drawing books scattered in a random pattern around. Cooper smiled at the child, and she stared back with her mother's expression. This was a house where he would have to be careful where he put his feet, in case he crushed some treasured plaything and set off a crisis.

'Sorry to bother you,' said Cooper. 'But I'm glad we've been lucky enough to find you both at home.'

'There's nothing lucky about it,' said Wendy. 'We're both stuck here all week. Mel was laid off at the refractory, and now he can't get a job. And as you can see, I've got these two to look after.'

'We're making enquiries about a young man called Neil Granger,' said Cooper.

'Oh, yes. We've heard,' said Melvyn.

'You have?'

'His brother Philip rang Lucas after some of your lot had been to see him. Lucas is their uncle.'

'And he's your neighbour, too. I take it you mean Lucas Oxley?'

'Of course.'

'Word gets around fast then.'

'It does around here.'

'Neil was all right,' said Wendy. 'It's a shame. Do you know what happened?'

'Not at the moment.'

'Philip said it wasn't an accident. Neil had been in a fight.'

'Well, something like that.'

'There was a bit of a rough lot he mixed with in Tintwistle. Bikers, some of them.'

'Do you know any names?'

'No,' said Wendy. 'We hadn't seen much of Neil lately. We don't get involved like we used to – we have our hands full.'

Cooper turned to Melvyn Tagg. 'How long have you been unemployed, sir?'

'About a month. There's no call for unskilled blokes these days,' said Melvyn apologetically. 'I never had much education. Wendy's got GCSEs, though. She ought to go to college and learn to be a secretary or something.'

'How can I work or do college, when there are these two round my neck?' said Wendy.

'Perhaps when they're a bit older ...' said Cooper.

'We'd never be able to afford a nursery. They charge more than I could earn at any job that I could get. Besides, the nearest nursery is in Glossop. Not much use to us, is it?'

'What about family? Or your neighbours?'

'They're never in.'

Cooper noticed there was no suggestion of Melvyn Tagg looking after the children. He quite liked children himself, and hoped he might adjust to being a house husband in the same circumstances. He looked at the nappy and baby powder and the other paraphernalia. Of course, the circumstances might never arise.

'There's your next-door neighbour, Mrs Wallwin. She's at home all the time, she says.'

'Her? We couldn't ask her to look after our kids.'

'Why not?' said Cooper. 'What's wrong with her?'

'She's shifty, for a start.'

Melvyn was still hanging on to his sterilizing fluid, as if he needed it for a reassurance. 'She seems decent enough to me,' he said. 'She's just quiet, that's all.'

'Melvyn, people are quiet because they've got something to hide.'

'Like what?'

'Well, I don't know. Have you looked at her hands?'

'What about her hands? Are they covered in blood, or what?'

'They shake when she's talking to you.'

Cooper felt he was losing control of the conversation. He looked around for Tracy Udall, and discovered she was squatting in the corner, talking to the older child and admiring a picture book.

'That means nothing,' said Melvyn. 'She probably has that nervous condition – Parkinson's Disease, is it? Or she might just be scared of you. I wouldn't blame her for that.'

Wendy tossed her head. 'Oh, ha ha.'

'Er, sorry to interrupt,' said Cooper.

'No, really,' said Melvyn. 'She's probably just very shy and nervous of meeting new people. Some folk are that way.'

'Don't talk daft. She's shifty.'

'But, Wendy, you know nothing about her at all.'

'I know enough. I've got a feeling about her.'

'Oh, right.'

'Don't put on that tone. You know my feelings are usually right.'

There was a brief pause. Cooper saw that the baby's face had started to become screwed up in an expression of serious annoyance. In a moment, there was going to be an ear-splitting noise.

'Have you actually seen Mrs Wallwin recently?' he asked.

Wendy looked at him as if she'd just noticed him come in. 'She keeps herself to herself,' she said.

'So you haven't seen her?'

'No, but she's OK. She's not dead or anything.'

'How do you know?'

'She bangs on the wall sometimes, when we have the telly turned up loud.'

'Do the kids ever bother her?'

'What, these two? They cry a bit sometimes, but not that bad.'

'No, I was thinking of the older kids in the terrace – the Oxleys.'

'I'm not sure what you mean.'

'Well, sometimes, they can be a bit mischievous. Someone living on their own can become a target. Knocking on the door and running away. Shouting abuse through the letter box. Stealing bottles of milk. Writing rude words on the windows.'

Wendy was staring at him. 'You got into bad company when you were a kid, did you?' she said.

'That's just me, is it, then?'

'I don't think the kids here do any of those things.'

'OK.'

'I mean, they've been in trouble now and then. You probably know that.'

'Yes.'

'But they don't do stuff to the neighbours.'

'Are you sure?' said Cooper.

'I'm quite sure. Their dad makes a rule about it. He'd kill them if they did anything to the neighbours.'

'There have been some break-ins in this area recently. There was one at the church on Friday night.'

'Oh, we don't go to church,' said Melvyn.

'No, but –'

'Besides, isn't it antiques and stuff that's being taken? The Renshaws have been done, and the Deardens down the road there.'

'Yes.'

'You want to be looking for some gang from outside, then.'

'We were actually wondering if you had seen or heard anything suspicious.'

'We're stuck in the house,' said Melvyn. 'And you don't see much from down here, you know.'

'Let us know if you think of anything.'

The baby began to cry. It started quietly, but threatened to build up quickly. While Wendy swore over the nappy, Melvyn began to show Cooper and Udall to the door.

'So what do you think about living next to so many members of the Oxley family?' said Cooper cheerfully, as he paused on the Taggs' doorstep. A tense silence fell. Melvyn stopped smiling. Wendy flushed and walked towards the kitchen without another word.

'Wendy was an Oxley, before we got married,' said Melvyn.

'Ah.'

'She still is, really, if the truth be known,' he added.

'Still is? Do you mean …?'

'Oh, we got married properly, unlike some that I could name. We did it right, in the church with the vicar and everything. We had a reception at the Quiet Shepherd, sausage rolls and cheese on sticks. We even had a photographer, and a honeymoon. In the Algarve.'

'Right.'

'We're still paying for that, though.'

'So ...?'

'So Wendy's a Tagg according to the law, but still an Oxley under the skin. Heart and soul, if you ask me. Nobody ever leaves that family. Not until they die.'

'They must be very close, I suppose. Not many families would choose to live so near together.'

'You can say that again. Personally, I couldn't wait to get away from my lot. My family only came to the wedding because they wanted to see if it was true what everybody kept telling them about the Oxleys.'

'But you fit in all right here, do you, sir?'

'Yes, I do,' said Melvyn. 'When I married Wendy, I became an Oxley as far as they're concerned. One of the family, I am. Don't make any mistake about that.'

'Thank you very much,' said Cooper. 'I wouldn't want to make two mistakes in the same afternoon.'

STANDING IN FRONT of Waterloo Terrace, Ben Cooper looked up towards the road. Melvyn Tagg was right – you couldn't see much from here. Waterloo Terrace was almost completely cut off from view by the thick covering of sycamores and chestnut trees on three sides. Even in the entrance, the track took a forty-five degree turn to reach the road, so that nothing passing could be seen from the houses. Not from ground level, anyway. And probably not even from the upper floor.

He turned back to the houses. Number 5 was next. Its brick façade was indistinguishable from the others in the row, except that the door and window frames had been painted blue, and a plastic water butt stood under the end of the downspout to collect the rainwater. Nettles were growing against the wall, and their tops had already reached the window ledge.

But at 5 Waterloo Terrace, Frances Oxley wasn't at home. Or she didn't answer the door, which wasn't quite the same thing.

'I think Mr Alton mentioned her,' said Ben Cooper. 'This must be Fran, Lucas Oxley's daughter.'

'That's the one,' said PC Udall.

They stood on the step and waited for a moment or two. Cooper rang the bell again. There was something about the house that made it feel as though there was someone at home, but lurking behind the curtains or in the shadows of the hallway. He stood a bit closer to the front door, listening for footsteps in the hall. Udall followed his lead, taking a couple of steps to the side, and casually glancing through the curtains of the front window. She shook her head.

'No sign of anyone.'

'Mr Alton suggested there was a man in Fran Oxley's life, but he seemed a bit vague about his status.'

'Maybe he spends a lot of time away,' said Udall.

Cooper walked backwards to the gate and looked up at the house. The curtains were drawn upstairs, and there was no smoke coming from the chimney, as there was from numbers six and seven. Fran Oxley's house might be heated by gas or electricity, rather than the smokeless solid fuel Mrs Wallwin favoured.

'By "away", do you mean working away, or away at Her Majesty's pleasure?' said Cooper.

'Working, I was thinking. But who knows?'

'Is there mains gas in Withens?'

'I doubt it. The bigger houses have propane gas cylinders.'

'Of course – I've seen them. I suppose it's a bit too remote here. It's easier for the coal man to get here than the gas company.'

Cooper tried the door again, but there was still no response. And it still didn't feel right. People who didn't answer their door to the police were a challenge. They made him want to know more about them.

'Number 4, then,' he said. 'Mr Scott Oxley.'

Cooper knocked on the next door. They were all looking the same already. And at number 4, Scott wasn't in, either.

He shrugged at Udall.

'There are three more houses yet,' she said.

They didn't need to go out of the gate and down the path to the next house, because there was no wall or fence separating numbers 3 and 4. There was nothing to prevent them just walking a few feet along the flags. But they did have to cross the entrance to one of the dark passages that Cooper thought of as a ginnel – though they weren't anything like the usual narrow alleyways that he was familiar with in White Peak villages. Ginnels could be pleasant little thoroughfares, bordered by hedges and trees, and offering glimpses of other people's back gardens or flower-covered walls. They usually led somewhere that you wanted to go, too. But the dark, brick passages of Waterloo Terrace held no temptation at all.

'I suppose these passages lead into a kind of communal yard at the back,' said Udall. 'I don't know what they keep back there.'

'Perhaps Mr Lucas Oxley will tell us.'

But there wasn't much chance of that. Again, there was no response to his knocking.

'It's starting to feel as though we're not wanted,' said Cooper.

And then he heard a very low growl, which stopped almost immediately. It died simultaneously with the sound of his own voice, so that he wasn't entirely sure he'd heard it at first. Logically, he wasn't sure. But emotionally, he had no doubts.

'Well, you got that about right.'

Lucas Oxley was standing just within the arch of the passage that ran between numbers 1 and 2. He was wearing the same suit that he'd had on the day before yesterday, and the same hat. The long snout of the shaggy-haired Alsatian protruded from the corner of the brick wall, close to its owner's leg. Its eyes were fixed on Cooper, and a small string of saliva dripped from the side of its mouth on to the path.

Oxley had been standing so still that again Cooper wouldn't have been aware of him, but for the dog. A man who could keep still, and a dog that could keep silent. They made a formidable combination.

Lucas Oxley looked annoyed. Briefly, Cooper wondered whether he was more irritated by the fact that his dog had let him down and broken its silence, or by his unwelcome visitors. Tracy Udall took a couple of steps to the side to separate herself from Cooper and create two targets instead of one. There was a low brick wall between them and Oxley, but it was no barrier to the dog. Cooper couldn't see the body of the Alsatian, but he was hoping that Oxley had it on a strong leash, for now. He had to be polite, anyway, until other measures were called for. It was procedure.

'Police, Mr Oxley. Detective Constable Cooper and Police Constable Udall.'

'You were here before,' said Oxley suspiciously.

He looked at Udall. Cooper could tell from the corner of his eye that Udall had adopted a non-threatening stance known as the 'Father Murphy', with her palms open and facing upwards, her left foot slightly forward and her body half-turned. Her forearms would be in contact with her baton and handcuffs, and her cuffs could be drawn unobtrusively, if necessary. It had been automatic for her, something deeply ingrained from her training. And it was a sensible precaution.

But Cooper felt a bit more relaxed. He had met this dog before, and he knew it would have attacked by now, if Lucas Oxley intended it to. But this time he couldn't mistake Udall's uniform.

'I was here on Saturday,' said Cooper. 'What's the dog called?'

Oxley shifted his feet a bit. He was a man of so little movement that this was almost a burst of activity.

Watching him carefully, Cooper decided to read it as a form of apology. Oxley gazed down at the dog.

'Nelson,' he said.

'Nelson? That's a grand name.' Cooper could see that the dog had two eyes, so maybe the name had some other significance than a reference to Admiral Horatio Nelson. The row of houses was called Waterloo Terrace. But surely the Battle of Waterloo was on land, won by the Duke of Wellington?

The Alsatian looked pleased to hear its name and get a bit of attention from its owner. Cooper still couldn't see its body for the brickwork, but the angle of its head changed, and he knew it had sat down. He let out a breath he didn't know he had been holding.

'We'd just like a few words, if you don't mind.'

'Well, I mind.'

Cooper took a breath, but pretended he hadn't heard properly. 'We're asking a few routine questions. You know about the death of your nephew, Neil Granger?'

'I heard.'

'It's a quiet village, isn't it? We're hoping that residents like yourself might have seen something. A strange vehicle, or anyone acting suspiciously around the area some time on Friday night or Saturday morning.'

'I saw nothing,' said Oxley. 'Are you finished?'

'Well, we'd like to have a word with any members of your family –'

'They're not at home. You know the way out.'

The Alsatian's ears went up as it heard the change of tone in Lucas Oxley's voice, and it let out another rumbling growl. At this point, the procedure was to retreat.

'Don't you want to *help*?' said Cooper in frustration.

Oxley looked unimpressed. 'We help ourselves,' he said.

Chapter Sixteen

IN THE NEXT lay-by down the valley from where Neil Granger had left his Volkswagen, there was a roadside café in a portakabin, for lorry drivers who wanted to stop on their trans-Pennine runs over the A628. Across the road, black-and-white crash barriers had a strip of red reflectors set into them, warning of the bend as well as the drop.

The lay-by itself contained the usual debris from passing vehicles – fragments of windscreen glass, cigarette packets, aluminium drinks cans, bits of broken pallet, an entire lorry wheel. And, inexplicably, a pair of green serge trousers lay on the grass, with their legs intertwined. The wall was topped by barbed wire strung between rusted iron posts, intended to discourage people from falling over into the stream below. Further up the hill, water ran down a series of natural steps formed from dark, smooth stones.

PC Udall pulled up as close as she could to the café. A huge twelve-wheeler Mercedes articulated lorry rumbled into the lay-by behind them. If it had been a small lay-by, like the one where the VW was parked, the truck would almost have filled it on its own. The grill, with its three-pointed star, was right behind their rear bumper, while the driver's cab was somewhere above them, out of sight. The driver could see down into the car, without being seen himself – until Cooper got out.

There were two women serving inside the café, surrounded by smells of frying bacon and clouds of steam that the ventilator could hardly cope with. They were busy, and they shook their heads briskly when Cooper and Udall began asking questions. They didn't remember any customers, except a few of their regular truckers. They didn't see anything in the lay-by, unless it parked right up by their door.

Even after a few minutes, Cooper was glad to get out of the stuffy atmosphere. He found he was sweating, and took his jacket off. Then he looked at the sky and saw the clouds dragging more showers towards his end of the valley. Above Torside Reservoir, the rain and sunlight were chasing each other across the face of the hillside so fast that it was as if somebody had just turned up the speed on a film.

He sighed, and put his jacket back on before leaving Udall in the lay-by and cautiously dodging the traffic to cross the road. He had noticed a rip in the steel crash barriers where a vehicle had gone through and over the edge towards the River Etherow.

The five Longdendale reservoirs were surrounded by a whole system of channels, weirs and culverts built from square sandstone blocks. They controlled the flow of water to and from the reservoirs, some of them coming into use only for overspill, when the water levels were too high.

Cooper descended a couple of flights of steps from the side of the A628. He could see that very few people walked here now. The steps were almost overgrown with brambles and ferns in places, and the stone was slippery with moss. Dampness hung in the air, and he had to cling on to the iron railings to keep his footing as he turned a corner halfway down the slope.

He found he was looking down into a smaller reservoir or holding basin, with water cascading over a weir right beneath his feet. The water ran into a channel and away through a culvert under massive stone buttresses towards the main reservoir. There was a straight drop of about twenty feet into the channel from the steps where he was standing, and the slopes on either side of him were covered in wire mesh to prevent the loose stone from slipping down and blocking the channel. The mesh didn't hinder the vegetation, which was flourishing in the damp air and the sun on the south-facing slope.

The mesh had held back the stones, but something else was blocking the channel. The carcass of a dead sheep lay in the water, with white foam bubbling through its ragged fleece, and one of its black ears waving slowly backwards and forwards in the current. The animal had obviously been there for some time. Its body was swollen with gas, and the wool had gradually loosened from its head and shoulders, so that patches of mottled skin were visible through the water.

Cooper went back to the car and Udall drove round the bend, where they saw Michael Dearden in the next lay-by, arguing with a uniformed officer guarding the tape around Neil Granger's Volkswagen. They stopped to see what the trouble was.

'Ah, there you are – what's your name,' said Dearden when he saw Cooper. 'How long are you going to keep the track blocked?'

'As long as necessary, sir. We need to preserve any forensic evidence. It can be a long process, I'm afraid.'

'Surely you can leave the track open?'

'No, sir. And I don't understand what the problem is in using the road through Withens.'

'Oh, forget it.'

Cooper exchanged looks with the uniformed officer and got back in the car.

'Can we get a look at the old railway tunnel entrances, Tracy?' he said.

'Of course. At this end, they're right by where the Woodhead station used to be.'

She drove a few yards and turned sharply into a narrow roadway that had no signs indicating where it went. At the bottom, some of the station's platforms were still visible, but the track, sleepers and ballast had all long since been removed.

It was the tunnels that caught the eye, of course. There were three of them, their entrances driven into a rock face that still bore the marks of the navvies' pickaxes. The 1950s tunnel was much larger than the other two. It had been made wide enough to take two lines, and it was a lot higher, too. The two smaller tunnels huddled close together, and the three of them made Cooper think of the ewe and its twin lambs, attached to the same hill in their own way.

To his surprise, he found Gavin Murfin in front of the tunnels talking to one of the maintenance men, who he introduced as Sandy Norton.

'Hey, Ben,' said Murfin, 'did you know you can still travel between Woodhead and Dunford Bridge by rail through one of these tunnels?'

'Really?'

'There's a little railway line in this tunnel for maintenance work.'

'It's just a two-foot gauge,' said Norton. 'It's the quickest way for the engineers to get access to the middle of the tunnel. They have a battery electric locomotive shedded here.'

'My brother-in-law would be down here like a shot, if he knew,' said Murfin. 'He's a big railway nut.'

'Don't tell me that,' said Norton. 'They're always coming here, trying to find some way of getting in.'

Cooper drew Murfin aside. 'What are you doing here, Gavin?'

'I've been given an hour off jankers.'

'How come?'

'For some reason, Miss has gone to the PM.'

'The Neil Granger postmortem?'

'That's right.'

'But I didn't think she was working on that enquiry. I mean – you *are* talking about Diane Fry, Gavin?'

''Course I am. Who else? We're working on the Emma Renshaw case, but Diane is proper put out that she lost a witness before she could get to him. There's no way she's going to accept anybody else's opinion about whether there's a connection or not.'

'She wants to prove it one way or the other for herself.'

'Exactly.'

'Well, I can understand that.'

'So I've been catching up on some other enquiries at the office, and now I'm supposed to meet her at the Renshaws. I noticed the guys working down here and thought I'd take a look at the tunnels.'

'The air shaft where Neil Granger was killed must lead down into here somewhere.'

'I suppose so.'

Cooper turned back to the maintenance man.

'I've just come down from Withens,' he said. 'Do you know it?'

'Oh, yeah.'

'Do you ever get the kids from the village hanging around down here?'

'I know the ones you mean. They ride around here on their bikes sometimes. They're a bit cheeky, but I've not had any real bother with them personally.'

'What are the chances of anyone getting into the tunnels?' said Cooper.

'We never let anyone in,' said Norton. 'Safety reasons.'

Cooper could see the National Grid had been careful with their security. He stood in front of the 1950s tunnel and looked up at the top of the steel-mesh fencing. There wasn't even enough of a gap for a small child to get through.

The reason for the security was obvious. The Longdendale Trail was right behind him. It ended at the old station platforms, and would be thronged with walkers and cyclists at the weekends, and in the summer. All kinds of people would get into the tunnels, if they could.

The surface of the trail had been created by pouring smooth sand over the line of the railway tracks. The sand probably made the going quite difficult when it was wet – in fact, Cooper thought it would be a trail to avoid in bad weather, because it was so open to the elements. A few yards away, in the middle of the trail, lay a dead hare. The skin of its head had been eaten down to the skull, and long, black insects were swarming around its throat, where a wound had been inflicted by a larger animal.

Norton followed his gaze. 'Rats are getting a big problem,' he said. 'Especially in this middle tunnel.'

'But it isn't used for anything now, is it?'

'Not at all. Not for a long time.'

'I can see that rats must have thrived in the tunnels when they were being built. With a lot of workmen around, there must have been a plentiful food supply.'

'I should say. They say there were nearly fifteen hundred men working here at the height of the tunnel project. They would have taken food in with them to where they were working. I expect there would have been plenty left on the floor for the rats.'

'It reminds me of a story that a coal miner told me after the strike back in '84–85,' said Cooper. 'He said there had always been lots of mice underground in the mines. He saw them all the time, hundreds of them, right down at the coalface. But the men were on strike for a year. And when they went back to work, there were no mice at all. They had all died. That was because they had relied on the presence of the miners for their food supply – without the crumbs of bread and pastry, and bits of fruit and chocolate that had dropped from the miners' snap boxes, the mice starved.'

'Arthur Scargill killed our mice,' said Murfin. 'Bastard.'

Cooper remembered Scargill, too. He had been the miners' leader during their turbulent strike in the 1980s. The strike had resulted in many bloody pitched battles between police and pickets, and it wouldn't be easily forgotten in Derbyshire.

'I think he's retired now.'

'Damn, I forgot to send him a card,' said Murfin.

'But the thing is,' said Cooper, 'I would have thought all the rats would die out when the tunnels were finished and the trains began running. Surely the navvies would move on to another job somewhere, and their shanty towns would be demolished? The rats' food source would have dried up.'

'Maybe they did die out,' said Norton. 'But they're back again now. They seem to eat as much poison as I can put down, and thrive on it.'

'Super rats?'

'If you want to call them that.'

Thanks to mild winters, the rat population had been rising fast, and they were getting bigger year by year. They could grow to the size of a small dog where they fed on the leftovers from fast-food outlets. In the country, rats normally ate crops out of the fields and were supposed to be smaller, and easier for a terrier or a cat to deal with. But an increasing volume of human visitors had made a big difference to country rats.

'How often are the tunnels checked?' said Cooper.

'The cableway is inspected regularly. The others not so often. Why?'

'If feasible, it might be an idea for someone to check inside the old tunnels. At least as far as the first air shaft.'

Norton looked at him, but for some reason he didn't ask the obvious question. Perhaps it was the expression on Cooper's face that told him the answer would be something he didn't want to know.

'How long have the high-voltage cables run through the other tunnel?'

'A long time. Since 1969, well before the line was closed in the new tunnel.'

So four hundred thousand volts had been buzzing below the hill for the last thirty-four years. Maybe that was what had re-energized the rat population.

'Of course, it'll be different if they re-open the railway line,' said Norton.

'Do what?'

'Through the newer tunnel, of course, not these old ones. They'll have to re-electrify it. Twenty-five thousand volts, they say. Because the Channel Tunnel won't take diesels.'

'Channel Tunnel? What on earth are you talking about?'

'I suppose it might not come off,' said Norton. 'But that's the plan. A rail link all the way from Liverpool to Lille in France, through one of these tunnels here. Nine trains an hour in each direction. They reckon it could take two million lorries a year off the motorways. Imagine driving your lorry on to a train in Liverpool and driving off in France. And all thanks to these tunnels. Just think about the men who blasted their way with gunpowder through these hills for three miles to make them.'

'They were navvies, like the men who built the canals?'

'That's right. Not Irish, though. For some reason, almost all of the navvies on the Woodhead tunnels were English. The conditions must have been pretty awful for them up here.'

'You're not kidding,' said Murfin. 'It isn't exactly the Riviera now, is it?'

'No. Actually, a lot of the men died, in one way or another. Accidents of various kinds, and illness. The first tunnel killed thirty or forty men, and injured over six hundred. They built the second tunnel from arches in first bore, and that killed dozens more. Woodhead was known for death and disease in those days. They called it the Railwaymen's Graveyard.'

'Bloody hell,' said Murfin. 'You're starting to scare me. I think I prefer Diane Fry.'

Norton looked at him, puzzled. 'Well, they were short of food, and had no clean water,' he said. 'They worked seven days a week in appalling conditions, constantly soaking wet and freezing cold in the winter. It's not surprising so many of them died. Someone worked out that the death rate among the Woodhead navvies was higher than among British soldiers who fought in the Battle of Waterloo.'

'Hold on,' said Cooper. 'Waterloo?'

'It was about twenty years before the first tunnel was started.'

'Right.'

'The navvies were very superstitious, you know. They had so many disasters that they thought their digging and blasting had disturbed some evil spirit that had been sleeping deep under the hill. According to the stories, they carved symbolic faces over these portals to control the evil.'

Cooper followed his gaze. 'I can't see anything.'

'No.' Norton sighed. 'No one cared about those navvies at all, you know. It was only afterwards that the conditions they worked in came to light. There were springs that caused flooding, and the men were always soaking wet. They had fumes and gas to deal with, and there was twenty-four-hour shift work, with no time off. Those first tunnel builders just had a shanty town, with mud huts shared by fifteen men at a time, and all their supplies brought over the moors. They paid into a club for a doctor for themselves – the company gave no help. The only thing that was cheap was beer, so a lot of them would have been alcoholics by the time they finished the tunnels. There were no old navvies, anyway. They were lucky if they lived to forty.'

'Do they send you down here to entertain the tourists?' said Murfin. 'Or are you practising for a job at the Count Dracula Experience?'

But Norton ignored him. 'And you know what?' he said. 'There were steam shovels available for tunnelling by 1843, but they didn't use them here. Men's lives were cheaper.'

'Where was this shanty town?' said Cooper.

'Where was it? What are you asking me that for? You said you've just come from there.'

Cooper stared at Norton. 'From where?'

'Withens, of course.'

'Withens started as the navvies' shanty town?'

'Fifteen hundred men used to live up there when they were working on the tunnels. All they had were huts made out of mud and piles of stones, with heather chucked on top for a roof. It doesn't bear thinking about, does it? Not in the winters they get up here.'

Cooper looked at the dark mouths of the old railway tunnels again, expecting to see rats scuttling across the dirt floor. Apart from steel fences and gates, the newer tunnel had been left unobstructed. With a new track-bed, it was almost ready for those Euro expresses to go through.

Somewhere along the three-mile length must be the lower opening of the air shaft that emerged on Withens Moor, two hundred feet above. He wondered if the rats could run up the inside of the air shaft, too. He could picture them spiralling their way upwards between the courses of stone, jerking and stopping, sniffing the air, then running ahead again. He imagined they would climb almost in silence, dragging their tails on the stone as their pale feet and long claws found a purchase in the crumbling mortar and they gradually emerged from the darkness on to the moor. On to the moor where Neil Granger had lain dying.

Chapter Seventeen

'SMASHED LIKE A clay flower pot,' said Juliana Van Doon, running water on to her dissection table to rinse away the blood and body fluids.

'Forgive me,' said Diane Fry. 'But that doesn't sound very scientific.'

She looked at the pathologist curiously. There weren't many cases that moved Mrs Van Doon to metaphor. The killing of children, yes, or something else particularly tragic. But a young man who had met a violent death? She must see plenty of those.

'The skull,' said the pathologist. 'It's a wonderful thing, the skull, and it does a terrific job of protecting our brain. But hit it hard enough, and you soon find out how brittle it is. The seat of our intelligence becomes no more than a few dying roots, and dirt trickling from a smashed flower pot.'

Fry shivered at the tone of the other woman's voice. Her own fragility was something she didn't care to think about just now. She was already seeing the bones. She didn't want to see what else lay beneath.

Mrs Van Doon looked at her, and smiled sadly. 'I'm sorry. Memories, you know. Even pathologists aren't entirely immune from personal feelings. We can't all keep up a constant stream of jokes as we fillet a fresh cadaver.'

'That's OK,' said Fry, though the apology and the reference to memories had made her feel even worse. If Mrs Van Doon was going to burst into tears, Fry would have to leave the room, or she'd be liable to join her.

DCI Kessen was standing with the Scientific Support Manager. He gazed at Fry over his mask, with that air of infinite patience that seemed so unnatural.

'We have an open skull fracture,' said the pathologist, returning to her usual brisk tone. 'The scalp laceration is consistent with an impact on the stones found at the scene, which are rather rough and sharp. I think we'll get an exact match. The *dura mater* membrane is broken, which resulted in considerable leakage of cerebrospinal fluid. And there's a compression of the brain in the area adjacent to the site of the injury.'

'It looks like his head hit the stone when he fell.'

'Yes.'

'The pattern of the blood spatters seems to tell the same story.'

'And that was the injury that killed him,' said the pathologist.

'You're sure? Could he have survived?'

'Without rapid surgical closure of the membranes, infection would have set in very quickly.'

'There was a lot of blood at the scene, too.'

'Scalp injuries bleed a lot,' said Mrs Van Doon, with a shrug.

'What about the other head injury?'

'There's a contusion to the back of the head, caused by a hard, smooth object. This blow caused a diffuse brain injury, probably resulting in concussion from the impact of the brain against the inside of the skull.'

'How serious?'

'A short period of coma. And he would almost certainly have had a bad headache when he woke up, maybe nausea and dizziness.'

'*If* he had woken up.'

'Of course. The blow to the back of the head would probably have rendered him unconscious and caused him to fall. But it wasn't fatal. The impact with the stone was.'

DCI Kessen spoke then, and everyone turned towards him to listen.

'You realize this is crucial? It might be the evidence that makes the difference between a charge of murder and manslaughter. The blow to the back of the head may have been intended only to stun, and the victim's death wasn't intentional.'

'You'll have the full opinion in my report, Chief Inspector,' said Mrs Van Doon.

'Thank you.'

The pathologist looked at him for a moment, expecting another question, which didn't come.

'Then we have the face …' she said.

Cleaned up and with his eyelids closed, Neil Granger's face looked almost normal. But it hadn't been like that when the firefighters had found him.

'The face was painted with some kind of water-based theatrical make-up. Black.' The pathologist looked up at the police officers. 'Do you know of any reason for that?'

'Not yet.'

'Just curious.'

'And the eyes?' said Fry. 'The eyes were full of blood. Were they injured separately?'

'Injured?' said Mrs Van Doon. 'They were removed.'

'You're kidding. Now you *are* cracking jokes.'

'No. But don't worry.'

'Don't worry? You say the victim had his eyes removed, and you're telling us not to worry?'

'It was done postmortem.'

'Great. A killer who steals his victim's eyes.'

'And it wasn't done by the killer, I'd say.' The pathologist indicated a couple of evidence bags being sorted by the scenes of crime officers. They contained Neil Granger's clothes and various traces scraped and swabbed from them. 'You have a feather, black. And some bird droppings, white. The eyes have been torn out roughly, not cut. I'd say one or more members of the crow family did the damage.'

'Well, that's something.'

'Yes. Also, the victim had blood on his hand. And not only blood, but cerebrospinal fluid.'

Fry screwed up her face in distaste. 'From the skull fracture. He touched the injury. But didn't you say …?'

'The victim was already unconscious before his head hit the stones, yes. So it's very unlikely that he touched the head wound himself. Impossible, I'd say.'

'Just spell that out for us again,' said Fry.

'Well, I would suggest the blood and cerebrospinal fluid were transferred to his hand by means of some third party.'

'Someone else. Someone touched his head wound, and then his hand. His killer? Or one of the firefighters who found the body?'

'Possibly.'

'Maybe even a police officer. Some of them can't keep their hands to themselves at a crime scene.'

'But there's one other injury to consider,' said Mrs Van Doon.

'Really?'

Fry looked at the head, but could see only the lurid colour of the bruised and broken skin near Neil Granger's right temple.

'Somewhere else on the body, then?'

'You can't help sounding hopeful,' said Mrs Van Doon, with a small smile. 'You'd like evidence for a murder charge, after all. That's usually what investigators want. A manslaughter conviction just isn't satisfactory, is it?'

'Maybe not,' said Fry impatiently. 'I hadn't really thought about it.'

'There's an ulna fracture.'

'Wait a minute – ulna? In the arm?'

'Correct.'

'He had a broken arm?'

The pathologist lifted a side of the plastic sheet. 'See?' she said.

Neil Granger's left forearm was badly swollen and bruised. But something else looked wrong with it. Fry bent to look more closely, then pulled away suddenly. The skin below the forearm was broken or torn. Burst was the word that came to her mind. Granger's skin hadn't been broken by a blow from the outside, but ripped open from the inside. The end of a bone was poking through the hole, like an obscene creature emerging from its cocoon, a white grub seeking the light.

The idea of things emerging from the body made Fry feel sick and cold. It was the most horrible thing she could imagine. During her teens she had consistently refused to watch a video of the film *Alien* with her schoolmates, because she had heard about the scene in which a creature burst from the body of actor John Hurt, where it had been growing in his chest. She knew she would probably have fainted, and that would have ruined the tough-girl image she was cultivating at the time. Even now, she never wanted to see the film. Nor did she ever want to see internal organs spilling from a belly wound. She never wanted to see the bones under the skin. Neither real, nor imaginary.

Fry swallowed. 'Was his arm broken in the fall?'

'No,' said Mrs Van Doon. 'By another blow. Possibly from the same weapon that caused the head wound. We can make the comparisons for you here.'

'Two blows. I don't suppose there's any way to tell which came first? That would be too much to expect, I'm sure.'

'Actually, it isn't.'

'You can tell?'

'Well, I'll leave the deductions to you, as usual. But what I can say is that the blow to the head was probably struck while the victim was standing. If you find the weapon, we'll have a good chance of establishing that more definitely.'

'But?'

'But the injury to the arm was inflicted when the victim was already lying down. There's bruising on the other side of the arm, where it was impacted on the ground. Again, if we had a weapon, we could do some angle tests. A heavy wooden stick of some kind. That's what you should be looking for. Unfortunately, the weapon doesn't seem to have splintered, as it hasn't left any splinters in the wound that I can see. So unless the lab can find some traces, there's no way of telling what kind of wood.'

'Someone knocked him unconscious, then hit him again, breaking his arm?'

'Perhaps. But remember that he struck his head when he fell.'

Fry looked up, dragging her eyes away from the protruding bone. 'You mean he was already dead when his arm was broken?'

'It wouldn't have happened quite so quickly,' said Mrs Van Doon. 'But he was certainly dying.'

'NEIL HAD LIVED in Tintwistle for about nine months,' said Philip Granger. 'His house is right on the main road.'

'Yes, we know. You went there with DC Cooper and some other officers yesterday,' said DI Paul Hitchens patiently.

Granger nodded, but didn't look at Ben Cooper, who was sitting next to the DI. Cooper gathered the impression that Philip Granger didn't remember him. He'd already made a formal statement this afternoon about his brother, which had been pretty comprehensive. There were details in it that would be gone over again later, but not just now.

In the interview room at West Street, Granger looked as ill as he had the day before. Either he hadn't shaved before he came out, or he had a bad case of five o'clock shadow. Cooper wanted to ask him if he was experiencing the survivor's guilt that members of a victim's family often suffered from – the irrational feeling that the wrong person had died. It should have been me, not him. And all those 'if onlys'. Maybe it was even worse for an older brother.

'Neil was forever complaining about the traffic jams in Tintwistle,' said Granger. 'They've been talking about a Longdendale bypass for years and years. He even went to some of the meetings of the campaign committee, but he didn't like the other folk who were on it. He said they were pretentious gits with too much time on their hands.'

'We're continuing to examine your brother's house, Mr Granger,' said Hitchens. 'As next of kin, you have the right to be present, if you wish.'

'Next of kin,' repeated Granger.

'Do you understand what I'm saying, sir?'

'It doesn't matter. You've got Neil's car, too, haven't you? The Beetle.'

'That's right.'

'Have you found anything yet?'

Hitchens perked up with sudden interest. 'In the car? Why do you ask?'

'I thought there might be some clues in it. I mean, Neil might have given someone a lift that night, mightn't he? He had a habit of doing that. I wouldn't pick anybody up myself, because you never know who they might be these days. But Neil didn't always see sense like that.'

'I understand.'

Granger looked at Cooper for the first time.

'It was the vicar that phoned me, you know,' he said. 'Mr Alton.'

'Yes, you mentioned it in your statement,' said Cooper. 'Mr Alton was expecting Neil to help him in the churchyard on Saturday morning.'

'I went round to Neil's house, but there was no sign of him.'

'Yes, sir.'

'But I didn't really think there was anything wrong. I didn't think ...'

Granger stopped. He seemed to feel the need to go over again some of the things he'd said in his statement. But only some of the things – those that affected himself. Perhaps they were the only facts he was sure of, and the rest of it he couldn't believe.

'The next-door neighbours couldn't give a toss,' he said.

'Did your brother not get on with them?'

'I don't think they liked the look of him any more than me. But they hated me coming to his house on my bike.'

'You don't live too far away yourself, do you?'

'I share a place with some mates in Old Glossop.'

Hitchens glanced at Cooper.

'Five or six miles, something like that? So you're only a few minutes away.'

'It depends on the traffic.'

'It must have been quite different for both of you, when you moved away from Withens,' said Cooper. 'You had plenty of family living nearby when you were there.'

'We lived at Waterloo Terrace, near our uncle and aunt. Number 7.'

'Number 7?' said Cooper, surprised.

'Yeah, why?'

'For some reason, I thought it must have been number 8. It's the empty one.'

'That house has been empty a while,' said Granger. 'But we lived at number 7. My uncle fixed all that up with the landlords.'

'So Mrs Wallwin has only been there a few months.'

Granger looked puzzled. 'Who?'

'The lady who lives in number 7 now.'

'Oh.'

DI Hitchens coughed impatiently.

'I'm sure you have a lot you need to do, Mr Granger. But one more thing I must ask you about before you go is this.'

Hitchens produced the bronze bust in its evidence bag. Granger reached out a hand to straighten the clear plastic, but made no attempt to touch the bust itself.

'Do you recognize it at all, sir?'

'No. I'm sorry,' said Granger.

'Do you recall your brother possessing something like this?'

'Not at all.'

'But you're familiar with the interior of his house? Have you been inside recently? Before his death, I mean.'

'A few days ago, yes.'

'Did you see anything resembling this?'

'No, I'd have noticed it. It would be out of place.'

'Might your brother have bought it as a gift for someone, do you think? A girlfriend? Is there someone in his life who likes antiques?'

'I'm sure there isn't. It certainly doesn't belong to Neil. It isn't the sort of thing he would have in the house. I don't remember seeing it when I was there yesterday –'

'No, sir.' Hitchens put the bag aside with a satisfied air. 'It was in your brother's car.'

Granger shook his head. 'Could Neil have found it? Or I suppose somebody could have given it to him.'

'Unlikely, sir, don't you think? We understand it could be rather valuable.'

'I can't help you, then.'

Hitchens stood up and shook Philip Granger's hand. 'On the contrary, sir,' he said. 'You've been very helpful indeed.'

DIANE FRY LOOKED at the photographs of the crime scene. In particular, she studied the pictures showing the body lying at the base of the air shaft.

Neil Granger's skull had been split open like a clay plant pot, according to Mrs Van Doon. Or maybe like one of those chocolate Easter eggs all the children had been eating a couple of weeks ago. Part of his scalp had peeled away, and the bone underneath had been shattered, ripping the membrane that covered the brain. His cerebrospinal fluid had leaked from the tear on to the stones – stones that were already covered in blood that was spreading from his scalp wound.

In the photos, Fry could see that the blood had matted his hair and trickled in rivulets down his face and neck until it touched the stones and ran into the ground, his life seeping away into the peat.

In a way, Neil had been lucky. He had never recovered consciousness after the first blow to his head. He would not have known what happened later. He would never have seen the crows landing and hopping closer to his face, or felt the stab of their beaks in his eyes. He would not have experienced the slow deterioration of his body as his tissues decomposed and gases forced out the contents of his stomach and bowels on to the peat.

Fry wondered whether he would have been able to see the steam in the dark. The photographs taken at the scene showed the steam clearly. It looked almost as if the old trains were still running in the tunnels two hundred feet below Withens Moor. But the trains hadn't run for more than twenty years.

Chapter Eighteen

CARL WAS IN his twenties. He lived at home with his elderly mother, worked in the family business, and led a prosperous life. One morning he answered a phone call, told his mother he had to go to Newcastle – and failed to return. He took neither his car, money or credit cards. Fifteen months later, when police were notified, he was still missing.

After enquiries drew a blank, the case was referred to the National Missing Persons Helpline, who distributed posters and checked their usual sources, but found no official records of Carl. So they appealed for news of him on their weekly page in the Big Issue *magazine*. Nearly twenty people called after seeing Carl's photo, to say: 'That's the chap I buy the magazine from!'

The NMPH faxed a letter for him to the Big Issue, and Carl called. He knew the photo was of himself, but didn't recognize the name: he had invented one for himself. All

*he could remember, he said, was being chased through the
streets of Newcastle and then getting a lift from a truck
driver. When they stopped for coffee, the driver said: 'You'd
better wash your face.' In the mirror, Carl saw blood from
a head injury he hadn't been aware of.*

*The driver dropped him off in Manchester, where Carl
wandered the streets for three weeks, still not knowing who
he was. His sole possessions were a St Christopher medal
and a keyring holding a snap of himself with a woman.
Eventually he sought help from the Citizens Advice Bureau,
who told him of a hostel in Stockport and gave him the bus
fare. He lived there for a year, started selling the Big Issue
under his alias, found a flat, began to build a life for himself – but was haunted by the fear that something terrible
had happened in Newcastle. What had he done?*

*The NMPH reassured him that he wasn't in trouble
with the police. His brother said it sounded like Carl, and
that he had had an accidental blow to the head three days
before he vanished. The NMPH arranged a meeting. Carl
recognized his brother, and it turned into a happy and
emotional reunion. Finally, Carl went home to see his
mother again.*

'YOU SEE?' SAID Sarah Renshaw. 'That could be Emma.'

Diane Fry handed back the paper. Her eyes had automatically been drawn to the next case study below it, which
was headed 'We find long-lost sister'. She didn't want to
read that one. She suspected how easy it would be for her,
too, to become convinced that her case would be the next
success story for the National Missing Persons Helpline.

'We're in touch with all the agencies,' said Sarah. 'They send us news regularly. We have Child Find and Missing Kids in the USA. The NMPH, of course. UK Missing Persons. People Searchers. We've listed Emma with them all, and we check regularly. If she turns up somewhere, they'll let us know.'

'You shouldn't put too much faith in the system, Mrs Renshaw.'

'Oh, but they get results all the time. I've looked at their websites on the internet. They have wonderful successes every week for somebody. They find missing persons who have been suffering from amnesia and don't know who they are, or people who have gone off for some reason and then haven't been able to get up the courage to contact their families. Every week, they find people like that. One week, it could be Emma that they find.'

'But there's no way you can keep up with every single missing or homeless girl in the world, is there?'

'We have to try.'

Then Fry took out the photograph of Emma taken in Italy.

'Who's the other girl in this photograph?' she asked.

'One of the students on the same course,' said Sarah. 'I forget her name.'

Fry turned the photo over. 'Emma and Khadi, Milan' was scrawled on the back, with the date.

'Her name seems to be Khadi. Do you know anything about her?'

'No. I think she's a local girl – from Birmingham, I mean.'

'Did Emma know her well?'

'I don't think so. She isn't one of the friends she socializes with. I think that's a problem when students are local – they don't live in the halls of residence, or in student accommodation, so they don't mix in as much socially.'

'Also, it probably means they're still living at home with their parents,' said Fry. 'That can hinder their social lives a bit, in some cases.'

'Yes, especially –' Sarah Renshaw stopped.

'Especially what?'

'Well, she's an Asian girl, isn't she? I understand some Asian families don't give their daughters quite as much freedom as we do. It's different for sons, of course.'

'Is that right?'

Fry had dealt with many Asian families during her time in the West Midlands. She had encountered young women with Asian backgrounds who had every bit as much freedom as Emma Renshaw had been given. Probably more, in fact. But it was true that if the girl called Khadi had lived with her parents, that could have been the reason she hadn't socialized with Emma and her friends, whatever her background.

'We never spoke to her, did we?' said Howard. 'I don't think she can be a particular friend of Emma's.'

'I'm sure the local police would have spoken to her anyway, if she was,' said Fry.

'Well, I'm not sure of that at all.'

'Very good, sir.'

Khadi. It sounded like a shortened form of some other name. Fry racked her brain, trying to cast her mind back to Birmingham and the Black Country. She seemed to have lost most of her cultural awareness in just a few months spent in the Peak District. There were a few Asians in Edendale, but most of them were Chinese and ran restaurants and take-aways. Sometimes, there were parties of Japanese tourists. But seeing a person from the Indian subcontinent, or an Afro-Caribbean, was still quite a rarity.

Khadija. Was that it? She made a note to get someone to contact the art school in Birmingham and track down a student with that name. The school would grumble, no doubt, but it was worth following up. It felt like a loose end.

'I take it you've heard about what happened to Neil Granger?' she said.

'Yes, we heard yesterday.'

'Yesterday? The day he was found?'

'Gail Dearden told us. She's a friend of ours.'

'The Deardens live up the road a little way out of Withens,' said Sarah. 'They bought the former game-keeper's lodge.'

'Is that Alex Dearden's mother?'

'That's right. She said her husband Michael saw the body, and he thought he recognized Neil Granger.'

Fry frowned. She remembered that Dearden's car had been intercepted by officers at the scene where Granger was found. She hadn't visited the air shaft herself, but she was surprised that Dearden could have been allowed close enough to identify the body.

'What was Mr Dearden doing there?' she said.

'We've no idea.'

'Alex doesn't live with his parents now, does he? He has a house in Edendale.'

'He never really went back home after he graduated,' said Sarah. 'He got a job with a computer company in Edendale, and he moved to live there. I don't think Michael and Gail see as much of him as they'd like. But he has a girlfriend, and it seems serious, so he has other things to think about than his mum and dad.'

'Unfortunately, I never did get the chance to speak to Neil Granger about Emma.'

'That's a shame. Do you think he might have known where she is? We've never asked him, not since we went down to Bearwood two years ago.'

'You've asked Alex Dearden often, he says.'

'Yes, but that's different. The Granger boys weren't people we talked to very much.'

Fry sighed. It didn't make sense to her. It seemed the fact that Sarah Renshaw had pestered Alex Dearden for news of Emma, but not Neil Granger, didn't actually mean she thought Alex was more likely to know something.

'If you don't mind, I'd like to go over that last day again with you,' she said.

'Last day?'

'The day Emma went missing.'

'Ah.'

'As I understand it, she was planning to get a taxi from the house at 360B Darlaston Road, Bearwood, to New Street railway station in Birmingham.'

'Yes.'

'Are you certain she was getting a taxi? It's only a few miles. Might she have caught a bus, as she did when she went in to college?'

'I don't think so, do you?' said Sarah.

'Well, I don't know, Mrs Renshaw. Emma was a student – she might have decided she couldn't afford a taxi. If she was a fit girl, she might have preferred to walk to the bus stop, even with her bags.'

'But the others said she was getting a taxi.'

'But did Emma tell you that herself?'

Sarah looked at her husband for guidance, but he shook his head. 'Well, I don't think so. Not in so many words.'

'OK, thank you. Now, we believe Emma was due to catch a train from New Street station a few minutes before eleven o'clock that morning, and she would have to change at Manchester Piccadilly to get to Glossop, where you were supposed to collect her at twenty past one.'

'That's right. We tried to call her mobile phone, but we only got the message service.'

'Mrs Renshaw, would you have expected Emma to have phoned you at some stage?'

'Well, if her train was late, or she missed one ...'

'But before that? Wouldn't you have expected her to phone to tell you she was setting off? Or to call you from the train? Or to let you know she'd arrived at Manchester?'

'Well, perhaps. But she might not have been able to reach us,' said Sarah. 'I think I was in and out of the house all morning. I had some shopping to do, because we were having a dinner party to celebrate Emma coming home, and there were a few things I had to get.'

'No messages? You have an answering machine?'

'Call Minder. But there were no messages. Anyway, I think Emma would have been more likely to ring Howard's mobile, since she knew he was driving to collect her at Glossop. But Howard was out on business all morning. You had some meetings, didn't you, dear?'

'Yes. I was trying to pack everything into the morning, so I was very busy.'

'No voice mails?'

Howard shook his head.

'In fact, it was a bit of a rush for Howard to get back here and pick up me up before he drove to Glossop,' said Sarah, with a smile. 'He arrived a bit stressed, poor man, because he'd been battling through the traffic in Sheffield and he thought he was going to be late. He said it would have been easier for him to have gone to Glossop on his own, but I wanted so much to be there to meet Emma.'

Fry wanted to stare at Howard Renshaw to see what she could read in his face, but she resisted the temptation.

'So you both went to Glossop to meet your daughter. You hadn't heard from her, so you assumed she was arriving on the twenty past one train. And when she didn't get off the train, you waited for the next one.'

'Yes.'

Fry had a painful image of Sarah standing on the station platform at Glossop, getting excited as the diesel units pulled in from Manchester, her hand already half-raised, ready to wave the moment she set eyes on her daughter.

And when Emma didn't arrive? Had Howard reassured his wife, checked the time of the next train, and taken her across the road for a coffee while they waited? How had he coped as the hours dragged on, and Emma still hadn't appeared? How had Sarah herself coped?

But Fry didn't need to wonder about that. Sarah had remained hopeful. Her hope had never died – it still shone from her face now, as she was obliged to go over the story for the umpteenth time.

Every time she spoke to the Renshaws, Fry found their air of belief palpable, even contagious. A few minutes later, as she was sitting in their lounge talking about Emma, someone rang the doorbell. Both the Renshaws gave a sharp intake of breath, and Sarah looked immediately at the clock. While Howard jumped up and went to the door, his wife fussed with the cushions and smoothed her dress, as if an important visitor were about to walk in.

The expectation was so strong inside the room that Fry felt obliged to get out of her chair to look out of the window. She half-expected to see Emma herself standing in the drive, two years older than her photos, but restored to living flesh and still wearing the blue jacket and jeans that Fry had so often seen mentioned in interview reports. But it wasn't Emma Renshaw. Instead, it was a pale woman in a green jacket.

'Who was that?' she said, when Howard returned.

'Gail Dearden. She had some news.'

'Oh?'

'Another sighting.'

'Of what?'

'Of who,' Sarah corrected her with a smile. 'Gail helps us to collect cuttings for the album.'

'What album is this?' said Fry, with a sinking feeling.

The album was sitting right there on a bookshelf. It was a thick volume with heavy blue covers that had been well-thumbed. Howard picked it up almost reverentially and passed it to her, with a glance at Sarah for her approval.

Reluctantly, Fry opened the album and glanced at the first few pages. She had been right to be apprehensive. A few minutes ago, she had casually remarked that the Renshaws couldn't keep up with every single missing or homeless girl in the world. Mrs Renshaw had said that they could try. And boy, how they were trying.

'Take it away with you for a while,' said Sarah. 'There are plenty of possibilities for you there, I think.'

BACK AT THE station in West Street, DC Gavin Murfin was watching the TV news with two other detective constables. They were waiting to see an interview with DCI Kessen about the Neil Granger enquiry.

'What's all the interest?' said Ben Cooper, draping his jacket over a chair.

'We've got a bet on about how many times he states the bleedin' obvious,' said Murfin. 'I'm backing him for a full half-dozen.'

'Oh. Well, for goodness' sake, don't let Diane catch you.'

'Nah. She's miles away. She's gone to see the Renshaws again. They'll be skipping happily through Wonderland together for a while yet.'

'Well, be discreet, Gavin.'

'Hey, here he comes,' said Murfin. 'Somebody get a notebook out and write them down.'

'The murder of a young man is totally unacceptable,' said DCI Kessen from the screen.

'There you go!' said Murfin. 'That's a cracking start. In fact, I think it should count as two.'

'No way,' said one of the other DCs.

'Well, no worries. He's got plenty of time, like.'

'The police will be taking measures to identify the person responsible for this crime.'

'Two!'

'And we're hoping to get the full co-operation of the public in this matter.'

'Three!'

'Hold on.'

'That's obvious, isn't it?'

'Not to the public.'

'True, my son. But we're not the public, are we? If I was having a bet with the general public, it'd be different, like.'

'Make it half a point.'

'Give over.'

'Shh!'

'Neil Granger's family and friends are very distressed,' DCI Kessen was saying, 'and everyone who knew him will be saddened by what has happened.'

'Four. And five,' said Murfin. 'That's my boy. Now see him go for the big finish.'

'We're keeping an open mind on the motive for this crime.'

'No,' said the DC. 'Not that one.'

'Mmm.'

'But we'd very much like to hear from anyone who was in the vicinity of Withens Moor on Friday night or early Saturday morning.'

'I hope you're not going to let me down, sir,' said Murfin. 'There's a pint of beer riding on this.'

'He's not going to do it,' said the DC. 'Start getting your money out, Gavin.'

'A young man is dead.'

'Yes! I knew you could do it. You beauty! What a finish! Here's Detective Chief Inspector Oliver Kessen to talk about the progress the police are making in the enquiry into the murder of twenty-two-year-old Neil Granger, "A young man is dead," says Mr Kessen. What a genius!'

'And we believe we are seeking an individual who is prepared to resort to violence.'

'Just a minute, that's seven.'

'Oh, damn. The daft bastard. Why couldn't he have stopped when he was winning?'

'When *you* were winning, you mean.'

'Seven. Who had seven?'

'Nobody.'

'No one had enough confidence in the lad. Who'd have thought he could manage seven statements of the bleedin' obvious in one minute?'

'Has he done much media work before?' asked Cooper.

'I dunno, Ben. But he won't be doing much more, if he performs like that. The one thing HQ like in their senior officers is a good media image.'

'What about the media liaison officer?'

'Dan Simmonds?'

'Oh, yes.'

Murfin sighed. 'Ah, well. Better get back to work on this murder enquiry, I suppose. I believe we're seeking an individual who's prepared to resort to violence, like.'

THE REST OF the CID team were already starting to drift away home for the night by the time Diane Fry got back to her desk. She barely noticed them leaving as she logged on to the website of the National Missing Persons Helpline and looked through the photos of missing people. Ironically, Emma Renshaw was one of the most recent additions. The other cases made Fry very depressed, but there was no denying that they were compulsive reading.

There was Kevin, who had vanished in 1986, aged sixteen. He had left his home to buy some eggs for a cookery exam at school the next day. Before he went out, he'd had a bath and emptied his pockets, so he took only £1 with him to pay for the eggs, and nothing else. Kevin hadn't been seen since.

There was Dan, from a village near Southampton. He was only fourteen, but the eldest of five children. He was last seen in January 2002, after spending an evening fishing with some friends. An adult thought he had seen Dan in the village square later that night, but Dan never returned home.

And then there was Carly, twenty-six, who vanished from Sheffield in November 2001. She had just returned from travelling abroad and was busy sorting out her things. When her mother came home, it looked as though Carly had popped out. She had taken her keys with her, but little else. She never came back.

Fry sat back, staring at the windows of the CID room without seeing them. At one time, that gallery of missing children on the NMPH website would have included Angela Fry, aged sixteen, last seen in Warley, West Midlands.

Diane had been fourteen in 1988, when Angie had left the foster home they were living in. It had been the year of the Lockerbie bomb, the year Salman Rushdie went into hiding and George Bush Senior had become president of the USA. But it had also been the year that Angie had left the foster home where they lived, and she was never seen again. Not by her sister, anyway.

Other kids remembered that year for Mutant Ninja Turtles and *Bill and Ted's Excellent Adventure*, for Cagney and Lacey, and the Goss brothers with their mascara and lip gloss. Some of Diane's friends had been such huge Bros fans that they had worn black puffa jackets and ripped jeans, and Doc Martens with Grolsch bottle tops attached to the laces. But Diane had been fourteen then, and her foster parents hadn't allowed her to wear ripped jeans. She had made do with a Garfield toy with sucker pads on its feet that she had stuck to the window of the car when they had gone anywhere. Garfield had been helping her look for Angie in the Black Country streets they drove through.

But even Garfield had failed her. At nights, she had sat in her room and listened to pop music, wondering where Angie might have gone. Angie had mentioned Acid House raves, taking ecstasy and KLF. But Diane was listening to Belinda Carlisle 'Heaven is a Place on Earth' and Bobby McFerrin – 'Don't Worry, Be Happy'. The world had seemed a grey place. School had lost any interest for a while. West Bromwich Albion had been swilling around in Division Two, changing managers nearly every year. Ron Atkinson was the manager the boys had been talking about.

The small details were impressed on Fry's mind as if they might have been immensely important for capturing the memory. The last memory that she had of her sister, unusually excited as she pulled on her jeans to go out that night. She was going to a rave somewhere. There was a boy who was picking her up. Diane had wanted to know where, but Angie had laughed and said it was a secret. Raves were always held in secret locations, otherwise the police would be there first and stop them. But they were doing no harm, just having fun. And Angie had gone out one night, with their foster parents making only a token attempt to find out where she was going. Angie had already been big trouble for them by then, and was getting out of control.

Looking back, Fry knew she had worshipped her older sister, which was why she had been unable to believe anything bad of her. Every time they had been moved from one foster home to another, it had been their foster parents' fault, not Angie's.

And when Angie had finally disappeared from her life, at the age of sixteen, the young Diane had been left clutching an idealized image of her, like a final, faded photograph.

WHEN HE GOT home to 8 Welbeck Street that evening, Ben Cooper found Mrs Shelley standing in the tiny hallway shared by the two flats. She was clutching something in a paper bag with mauve stripes, and she looked a bit surprised to see him.

'Oh, it's you, Ben.'

'Yes, I still live here, Mrs Shelley. Were you waiting to see me?'

'No. I'm going upstairs.'

'Oh, I see.'

'She's very nice. You'll like her.'

'Will I?'

'Oh, yes.'

'Who will I like?'

'Peggy,' said Mrs Shelley, raising her voice a bit, as if she thought he might have gone deaf.

'I don't know any Peggys. Wait a minute ... is this somebody who's moving into the upstairs flat?'

'Of course. I told you it was all arranged.'

'No, you didn't.'

'Well, it's all arranged anyway.'

'Who is she, Mrs Shelley?'

'Quite by chance, I have a friend who lives in Chicago. She emigrated to the USA with her family nearly thirty years ago.'

'That's nice.'

'We're old schoolfriends. I was very sad when she left. But her husband lost his job here during the seventies when the company he worked for went out of business, and they wanted to make a new life for themselves. I can't blame them really. He's in research.'

'Very interesting.'

Cooper had learned just to make neutral noises while Mrs Shelley was speaking. Eventually, she might get round to telling him what he wanted to know, with a bit of nudging. But it was best to let her talk and get there at her own speed, otherwise she felt harassed and got irritable.

'And this is the lady who's taking the upstairs flat?'

'No, of course not. Peggy is her daughter.'

'I see.'

'Now, Ben, I don't want you to be rude to her.'

Cooper raised his hands. 'Why on earth should I do that?'

'Well, she's American, you know.'

'There's nothing wrong with Americans.'

Mrs Shelley looked doubtful. 'I'm not sure about that. She seems rather, well ... exuberant.'

Cooper smiled. 'I'm sure she'll be fine.'

'She doesn't seem anything like my old friend, considering she's her daughter. I don't know what could have happened to her in Chicago. I suppose she must have got it from her father's side. What do you think of this? I bought it in a craft gallery in Buxton, near the Crescent.'

Mrs Shelley opened the striped bag and showed him the contents.

'What on earth is it?'

It looked like an empty wooden shuttle from a cotton mill, but with dozens of little openings along its length, like tiny mouths with pouting lips. There was something slightly obscene about it. But maybe that was just his own imagination.

'It's an Australian Banksia nut,' said Mrs Shelley.

'A what?'

'Well, that's what the label said. An Australian Banksia nut. It cost me £4.'

'A bargain.'

'Do you think she'll like it?'

Cooper raised her eyebrows. 'Is this for my new neighbour?'

Mrs Shelley hesitated. 'It's a house-warming present. I thought it might make a talking point.'

Cooper looked again at the object. The tiny mouths pouted and smirked, as if they were forming lewd words.

'Well, I suppose that'll work,' he said.

As soon as he had settled in at Welbeck Street, Ben Cooper had asked Mrs Shelley if he could have bolts put on the front and back doors of his flat. The locks were OK, but they didn't give much security on their own. Diane Fry had warned him about living too close to the patch where he was so well known, and had advised him to have a spy-hole fitted on the front door, too, so that he could never be surprised by a caller. But that seemed to be going a bit too far; it was a little too paranoid. This was only Welbeck Street, Edendale, after all.

When the ring came on his bell, Cooper almost jumped with surprise. He had not thought a spy-hole was necessary. Now, though, he experienced a strange reluctance to open the door without being able to see who was on the other side. He couldn't call it foreboding exactly, more a need to be careful, a suspicion that opening the door could change his life.

The woman who stood on the doorstep was a complete stranger. She was in her thirties, thin, with straight fair hair. A battered blue rucksack was slung over the shoulder of her cotton jacket.

'Oh, I think you rang the wrong bell,' said Cooper. 'You'll be for the upstairs flat, won't you?'

She looked confused. 'Are you Ben? Ben Cooper?'

'Yes.'

'Then, it's you I've come to see.'

'Aren't you my new neighbour?'

'I don't think so.'

'Sorry. You're not Peggy, then?'

The woman shook her head. With each moment that she stood on his doorstep, she was starting to look more and more familiar. Each movement rang a bell in the back of Cooper's mind. Yet he was sure he had never met her before.

'No, I'm not Peggy,' she said, 'whoever she is.'

'I don't really know who she is,' said Cooper. 'Just that she's supposed to be moving into the flat upstairs. Are you sure you're nothing to do with her?'

'Sure.'

'So you must be selling something?'

'No, not that either. My name's Angela. They call me Angie.'

'I'm sorry, but I really don't know you.'

She laughed. 'Angie Fry. Does that help?'

Gradually, Cooper began to recognize the resemblance around the eyes, the slim shoulders, and the way she stood, all the things that had rung so many bells. But he was still completely unprepared for the shock when she finally explained.

'I'm Diane's sister,' she said.

Chapter Nineteen

HOWARD RENSHAW TURNED off the TV set when the news had finished. He and Sarah sat in silence for a few moments.

'That chief inspector seemed a very sincere sort of man,' said Sarah. 'He gives you the impression that he'll get things done.'

'Yes,' said Howard.

He played with the remote control for a while, switching the power on and off, so that the red light on the set blinked and the static hissed.

'Perhaps we should have talked to Neil Granger,' he said.

'He's dead. It's too late.'

'He might have mentioned Emma to someone.'

Sarah lifted her head and looked at her husband with interest. 'There's Lucas Oxley. That's his uncle.'

'I was thinking of the brother.'

'Oh. Philip.'

'That's him. I'm not sure where he lives now, but I could find out.'

'Why not?' Sarah hesitated. 'In fact, I'm surprised we haven't thought of it before.'

'It was just this business of him getting killed that put it into my mind.'

Sarah stood up and moved towards the bookshelves, as if drawn by some force to caress the spines of the books, as she had so often.

'I seem to remember you saying that the Grangers and the Oxleys weren't people that Emma would have bothered with. You said she would never have kept in touch with Neil Granger.'

'Did I say that?'

Sarah frowned at one of the books, straightened a bookmark, then picked it up and held it to her face to smell it.

'I'm sure you did.'

'I might speak to this Philip anyway.'

With a sigh, Sarah leaned to rest her forehead against the wood of the bookshelf, closing her eyes as if in meditation or to see an internal vision more clearly.

'I wonder what Emma is doing now,' she said. 'What do you think?'

Howard turned away when she couldn't see him. He switched on the TV again, but turned the volume right down as he saw the adverts were still on.

'I can't picture it,' he said.

'I can. I picture it all the time, trying to see what she's doing at each hour of the day.'

'Sarah,' said Howard, 'have you ever thought it might be better if we knew that Emma wasn't alive any longer?'

His wife froze. Her eyes remained shut, but she was watching her internal vision shatter.

'How can you say that?'

'It was just that, listening to the chief inspector on the news talking about Neil Granger, it occurred to me that at least Granger's family would know what had happened to him and could say, "That was where it ended, this is where we start the rest of our lives."'

'I don't want to hear you talking like that again,' said Sarah, trying to keep her voice steady. 'You know as well as I do that Emma is alive.'

'Of course,' said Howard. 'I'm sorry.'

Sarah turned and looked at him. But she could only see the back of his head, and his growing bald patch. Beyond him, the television screen was flickering into the opening credits of a wildlife programme. In the branches of a tree, a hook-beaked predator swivelled its head and stared with unblinking yellow eyes at the camera, ignoring the struggles of a small lizard that writhed in its talons.

BEN COOPER REMEMBERED the first time Diane Fry had mentioned her sister to him. It had made him feel guilty, as if he had dragged something painful out of her that she would rather have kept to herself. And he knew that Fry had been searching for that missing sister ever since she'd transferred to Derbyshire from the West Midlands. In fact, she had told him herself that it was the only reason she'd come to Edendale, desperately following a rumour that Angie was somewhere in one of the big cities to the north.

Cooper felt sure that it was desperation and hope that had driven Fry this far. Desperation to find the one remaining link to her own past, and therefore perhaps the confirmation she needed of her own identity. And hope that she might find her sister before it was too late.

Now he thought about it, Cooper knew he had never really believed that Diane's hope would ever be justified. Too many possibilities awaited someone who had been a heroin addict by the age of sixteen – as Angie had been, according to her sister. Yet that desperate faith had actually been strong enough to produce Angie herself, right here in the flesh, in the sitting room of his flat at 8 Welbeck Street.

Cooper was so surprised by the fact that for a few minutes he could only stare at his visitor stupidly. He sat down on the arm of the sofa, suddenly feeling so disorientated that he was afraid his knees might otherwise crumple and leave him sprawled on the floor in an undignified heap. Then he stood up again immediately and opened his mouth to speak. But the only questions that came into his mind were 'Why here?' and 'Why me?', which sounded too discourteous to be uttered to a visitor.

'How did you find out where I live?' he said at last.

Angie Fry brushed a strand of hair from her forehead in a familiar gesture that he saw almost every day. 'Oh, they told me at the police station.'

'I see. They gave you my address?'

'Yes. I hope you don't mind. It's important, or I wouldn't have come here bothering you.'

Cooper realized his mouth was hanging open. He could neither believe what he was seeing, nor what he was being told. But the person standing in the middle of his rug was too like Diane Fry to be anybody except who she said she was. And his upbringing prevented him from blurting out what was in his mind.

Angie looked at him and smiled briefly. Cooper thought for a moment that it was a mocking smile, but it disappeared from her face too quickly for him to be sure.

'Well, aren't you going to offer me a coffee or something?' she said. 'You might even ask me to sit down, rather than leaving me standing here.'

'Of course. Would you like coffee? Or would you prefer tea?'

'Coffee would be great,' she said. 'White, no sugar.'

'Just the way Diane has it. No sugar.'

'Like they say, we're both sweet enough already.'

'Maybe.'

The kitchen of the flat was near enough for Cooper to continue holding a conversation with Angie while he made the coffee and lifted down a pair of Simpsons mugs from the dresser.

'Did you call in at the station, or did you phone?' he said.

'Oh, I phoned.'

'Who did you speak to?'

'Does it matter?'

'Just wondering. Did you get put through to CID, or did you talk to someone on the enquiries desk? Male or female?'

He got no answer. Eventually, he went back into the room with two mugs of coffee and found Angie Fry sitting on the floor with her back against his sofa, staring at the ceiling. She'd taken off her rucksack and jacket, and he could see she was wearing an old sweatshirt with lettering that might have been the name of a university or a rock band, but was too worn to read.

'Are you all right?'

'Questions and more questions,' she said. 'I knew you'd treat me like this. You *are* a copper, after all. Suspicious lot, aren't you?'

'We're trained to be. But, whether as a copper or just as another human being, I prefer to be told the truth.'

'I *am* telling you the truth,' she said.

'I don't think so.'

She said nothing, but sat and looked at him for a moment. He was relieved that she didn't try to bluff it out, to bluster and lie barefaced, as he had heard so many people do in the interview rooms at West Street. So he didn't hesitate in explaining what he meant.

'They would never give out a police officer's home address at the station,' he said. 'It's the number one rule. You really ought to have known that.'

For a second, he thought she might laugh. But that mocking half-smile flitted across her lips again, then vanished. She nodded, lowering her eyes. Her shoulders slumped a little inside the sweatshirt.

'I'm not a very good liar,' she said. 'I should have known not to try to lie.'

'We get plenty of experience of hearing good liars,' said Cooper.

'Yes, I expect you do.'

'So?'

'So what?'

'Are you going to tell me the truth?'

'Perhaps I'd better,' she said. But Cooper, listening carefully to the intonation of her voice, thought she might as well have shaken her head and said 'no'. Unlike some of the regular customers they had to interview at West Street, Angie Fry had learned to lie only through her words. She hadn't mastered the techniques of controlling her voice and the expression on her face, of disguising the tension in her body and the look in her eyes. He had listened to scores of much better liars than Angie Fry. Much better.

'I heard you were a farm boy, Ben. So I looked in the local Yellow Pages for farmers called Cooper. Though I can't imagine Di ever having any interest in farming.'

'Di?'

The mocking smile was there this time, definitely. Cooper felt himself go a little pink in the neck. 'Of course. Diane.'

'We were always Di and Angie to each other, when we were little.'

Cooper nodded. 'Go on.'

'Well, I was lucky for once. The first number I tried was the wrong Cooper, but the second was right. Bridge End Farm, was it?'

'Yes.'

'And was that your dad I spoke to?'

Taken by surprise, Cooper tensed painfully, his fingernails stabbing into his palms as his hands clenched. The physical reaction to any unexpected mention of his father never failed to embarrass him.

'I think it would have been my brother,' he said.

'Oh, right.' She raised an eyebrow slightly. 'An older brother, is he? Interesting.'

That smile was starting to become annoying. Each time it appeared, it seemed to linger a bit longer, and looked a little more openly mocking.

'Yes, an older brother. What's interesting about that?'

'I don't know really. Just the older brother/older sister thing. It can be complicated, can't it?'

'I wouldn't know,' said Cooper, who had decided he wasn't going to give away even the slightest detail of his private life that she didn't know already.

'Anyway, I made out I was an old college friend of yours who'd lost touch with you. I asked if you still lived there, at the farm. And your brother told me you'd moved out, and he gave me your new address. He's not like you, is he? He wasn't suspicious of me at all. I take it *he's* not a copper.'

'Of course not. He's a farmer.'

That part of the story, at least, would be easy enough to check out with Matt. Bridge End Farm was certainly in the Yellow Pages, but Angie could have thought that through. As for where she had heard that he was a farm boy in the first place, it seemed to Cooper that there was only one person who might have told Angie Fry that. And it made no sense at all.

'What else did you hear about me?' he said.

'Not very much.'

'Are you sure?'

'Yes. What else is there to know about you?'

'Not very much. But I'm curious where you heard anything about me at all.'

She hid her face in her coffee mug, lowering her eyes. 'I asked around. Everyone knows you.'

That last bit was true, at least – Cooper could hardly deny that. There were far too many people in Edendale who knew all about him. Diane had told him he was mad to move into this flat in the centre of town, where he would be so close to so many people who knew exactly who he was and might have reason to bear a grudge. But it had caused no problems for him. Not until tonight, anyway.

'You're looking happier,' said Cooper.

'What?'

'You're smiling a lot. You weren't smiling like that when you arrived.'

'It must be because I feel at ease with you.'

'Really?'

'Well, you're a good listener. But then, I suppose you'd say you're trained to be.'

Cooper put down his mug. 'You'd better get to the point and tell me what it is you want from me.'

'Oh …'

He could feel himself starting to lose patience then. Angie was intruding into his private life uninvited and without a proper explanation, and he really didn't have to be polite to her all evening, if he didn't feel like it.

'There's no point in pretending you don't want something,' he said. 'I'm sure you wouldn't have gone through all that business with the Yellow Pages and phoning up farmers called Cooper if you didn't want something from me, Angie. So I don't want to hear any more of this rubbish. Just cut to the chase, and tell me what you want. Then I can say "no" and go back to my own life.'

Angie looked down at her coffee mug. She was still clutching it, though he had watched her tip back the last drops of coffee several minutes ago. Her fingers were tight and white at the joints. They moved restlessly against the smooth porcelain, tracing the slightly raised shapes of Homer and Marge. Backwards and forwards her fingers went, following the shapes, keeping themselves moving. Reluctantly, Cooper found he couldn't hold on to his burst of irritation.

'Have you spoken to Diane recently?' he said.

Angie shook her head.

'When? Not since you left Warley?'

'No.'

'But that was years and years ago.'

'It's fifteen years.'

Cooper restrained an exclamation. It was beyond his comprehension how sisters could be apart for fifteen years without getting in touch with each other. But stranger things happened in families.

'I know Diane has been looking for you,' he said. 'In fact, she's been looking for you very hard recently.

She once told me it was the reason she'd come to Derbyshire, because she'd managed to track you down as far as Sheffield and this was as near as she could get.'

'Yes, I know she's been looking for me.'

Cooper began to get impatient again. 'Well, if you know *that*, what's the problem? You've found me, so I'm sure you could have found Diane a whole lot easier. What do you want me to do? Do you want me to talk to Diane for you? Maybe arrange a meeting? You want to do it gradually, is that what you're worried about? I know it's going to be a shock for both of you, after so long.'

Angie listened him out with a defiant stare. 'No, you've got it all wrong,' she said. 'Completely wrong.'

'What then?'

She leaned forward suddenly, thrusting her narrow face towards him, so that he couldn't avoid the stare of her pale eyes or miss the tiny lines clustered around her temples, lines etched by years of pain.

'I want you to explain to her that I never want to see her again,' she said. 'I want you to tell her to leave me alone.'

Cooper sat back, shocked by the vehemence that was suddenly in her voice. 'You don't mean that.'

'Mean it?' Now she put the mug down on the table, with a crack like the noise of an air rifle. 'Believe me, I don't want my little sister back in my life. And I'm damn sure she doesn't really need me back in hers. But there's no way I can try to tell her that myself. She's so damn stupid and pig-headed that she wouldn't believe me. I know from past experience that she only believes what she wants to hear, and I could never do any wrong as far as she was concerned. She never saw the real me, no matter how much I shoved it in her face.'

'People change a lot in fifteen years,' said Cooper quietly.

'Do you think she's changed? Or would you say she was still like that?'

He sat back. 'Go on.'

'But *you* could convince her, couldn't you? Diane would believe you. They say you're the man who believes in things like telling the truth. Is that right? Or are you going to be another one who just pisses me about?'

'If Diane wants to make contact with you again, who am I to make a different decision for her?'

'It's not your decision, it's mine. And I'm her big sister, so I know best.' Angie sighed. 'OK, what can I do? Will you listen if I tell you the whole story?'

Cooper hesitated. From the little Diane had said, he wasn't sure it was anything he really wanted to hear. But what else was he going to be doing this evening?

'Like you said, I'm a good listener.'

So Angie told him. It took fifteen to twenty minutes, with frequent pauses. But Cooper got the sense of the girl who had rebelled against her family situation, who had been desperate to escape from the nightmare she had got herself trapped in. Any escape route must have looked attractive to her then. But she had only been leaving one trap to enter another.

'We were both taken into care by Social Services. I was eleven, and Diane was nine. They said my parents had been abusing me. Well, of course they had. My dad anyway, and my mum knew. No point trying to pretend it didn't happen.'

'And Diane, too?' said Cooper.

Angie hesitated. 'Has she said so?'

'She says she can't remember.'

'Yeah, right.' But then her tone changed. 'Well, she was only a kid. Maybe she can't. But you see why I know she won't have changed now. The fear goes way back when.'

'You were fostered together, weren't you?'

'Yeah. They kept moving us on to different places, though. So many different places that I can't remember them. It was because of me that we didn't stay anywhere long. I was big trouble wherever we went. But Di thought the sun shone, and she screamed the roof down at the idea of being split up from me. In the end, I couldn't stick it any longer. I left our last foster home when I was sixteen, and never went back. I haven't seen Diane since. And it's much better that way, believe me.'

'I know you were already using heroin,' said Cooper.

'So she told you all about that, too? She must really think a lot of you, Ben.'

'I think it just slipped out.'

Angie raised her eyebrows. 'Oh, yeah? My little sister doesn't let things slip out, unless it's for a reason.'

'I wouldn't know.'

'Well, you're right. The thing is, I was stealing stuff from the house to pay for it. Stealing from our foster parents. That's why there was so much trouble. They just couldn't deal with it, with the idea that this was the way I showed my gratitude. So I had all this shit flying around my head all the time until I thought I was going to be sick on their Axminster carpet, and all I could think about was the next hit. You know, as long as you get your daily fix, you don't care about anyone. You'll use anybody, steal or rob, just for a hit. They always say it's the needle that some people get addicted to, not the drug. They call it needle fever. So it was better for me to leave – better for Di, too. I couldn't stand the thought that she would follow the same route.'

Angie was staring at the ceiling again, rather than look at Cooper. As he had expected, tears began to form in the corners of her eyes as she spoke. She made no attempt to wipe them away, and they streaked her face as they trickled across her cheekbones.

'So it's not quite true that you didn't care about anyone,' said Cooper.

Angie flushed. 'Don't try to trap me. I'm telling it like it was. You need to know that, no matter how strong you are, heroin is stronger. I've done cold turkey many times, and they've had me on a detox programme. Do you know how long you have to wait for help from the Drugs Service? Up to twenty-eight weeks for an appointment. Six months. Do you know what can happen to you in that time? Do you know how easy it is to die? It doesn't take six months. I went through hell doing all that, but I always went back to the drugs. No matter how strong you are, heroin is stronger in the end. It's always there in your brain, and it just calls you and calls you. I know Diane would try to make me stop, but I couldn't deal with that. Neither of us could deal with that.'

Cooper was silent. Despite the deception and the performance he was watching now, the feeling was creeping over him that Angie Fry was essentially telling him the truth. He wasn't entirely convinced, but there was sufficient doubt in his mind.

'I'm still not sure that I shouldn't phone Diane right now and tell her you're here,' he said.

'They told me you were Di's friend. If you care anything about her, you won't let this happen to her. You won't let *me* happen to her.'

Cooper shook his head. 'The trouble is, I really don't think there's anything I can do.'

'She has false hopes, don't you realize that?' said Angie, with a brief flash of anger that Cooper found familiar. 'Diane has expectations that I can never live up to. Quite the opposite. When she found out the truth about my life, she would be so ashamed of her sis that it would knock the bottom out of her world. She always had a kind of fragile sense of security. She always needed something to hang onto to make her feel safe in the world.' She paused, and gave him that challenging smile, even through the tears. 'Aren't you going to tell me that people change in fifteen years?'

Cooper wanted to tell her exactly that, but sensed that Angie was right. It fitted in with his own impressions of Diane. He had always thought there was an underlying fear that she barely kept suppressed by hanging on to the stable things in her life – her job, and her promotion ambitions. And her memories of her sister.

'Are you on or off it right now?' said Cooper.

Angie Fry smiled that slow, sad smile, but with the instant deviousness in her eyes, the expression that told him she was wondering what lie to use.

'Maybe I'd better not tell you that,' she said. 'You being a policeman, and all. I wouldn't want to compromise your principles.'

And Cooper knew she was right. If Angie was using heroin now, he would be in difficulties. If she had to get her fix while she was here, he didn't want to know. He didn't want to be forced into that position.

But he couldn't help studying her eyes, an automatic reflex from his training. Of course, Angie saw him doing it, and met his stare with undisguised challenge.

'Red eyes, it's dope,' she said. 'Dilated means amphetamines. But "pinny" eyes – then, it's heroin.'

Cooper kept on looking. But something must be wrong with his powers of observation. When he looked into Angie's eyes, he couldn't see any of the symptoms of drug abuse. All he could see were the pain and the loneliness. And beyond them, that brief flicker that turned his heart for a moment as he looked deep into the eyes of Angie's younger sister.

He watched her pick up her rucksack from the floor. 'Where are you staying tonight?'

She straightened up, pushed the hair from her forehead, gave him that smile. 'I don't know. Can you recommend a good shop doorway somewhere? I've got the sleeping bag.'

'You're living rough?'

'I'm on the streets. What did you think? That I was staying in some smart little hotel with room service and an en-suite bathroom?'

'Haven't you got any money?'

'I haven't had a chance to get any today.'

'How do you usually get money?'

'How do you think?'

He hoped she meant by begging, but he decided not to press it. 'You shouldn't be sleeping on the streets, Angie.'

'Tell me about it.'

'It isn't safe.'

'So? If you're so concerned about it, what are you going to do? Are you going to ask me to stay the night here?'

'No.'

'No, I thought not. It wouldn't do, would it? What would people say? What would our Di say?'

She went out into the hallway and opened the front door. Cooper held it for her while she pulled her rucksack over her thin shoulders, and watched her step out on to the pavement. She looked around, weighing up which way to go, trying to remember where the shops were, or whether there was a park she might find, and a shelter with a vacant bench.

'There are plenty of benches by the river walk, but it'll be colder down there,' said Cooper. 'Water loses heat faster at night.'

'Thanks for the tip,' she said.

'The market square is quiet, but only after about three o'clock in the morning, when the night-club crowds have gone home. And it's market day tomorrow, so the market staff will arrive at 5 a.m. to start setting up the stalls. That can be a bit noisy.'

'Thanks a lot.'

'And if you slept on my sofa, you'd have to put up with the cats. They're a complete pain. Diane hates cats, so I expect you do, too.'

She looked down the street again. Cooper could hear the sound of the cars on Meadow Road. There was a car stereo playing rap music far too loud, and somebody burning rubber off their tyres as they accelerated from the lights. A traffic patrol would be hanging around later to discourage the boy racers. There was a burst of raucous laughter and the rattle of a can on the pavement.

'I'm not like Diane at all,' said Angie. 'I'm quite the opposite, in fact. I thought you would have realized that by now.'

Cooper looked at her slim hand brushing away the hair, the narrow shoulders, the wiry body, the challenging look in her eyes as she turned towards him. 'You're not *entirely* the opposite,' he said.

'Maybe not. But I'll tell you something – I don't mind cats. I quite like them, within reason.'

'Reason has nothing to do with it.'

'I know.'

'And you'll have to be out of here by 8 a.m.'

'Do you have to be at work?'

'Out by 8 a.m.,' said Cooper.

'OK, it's a deal, then. Cats and all.'

He took her rucksack off her as she walked past him back into the house.

'Thanks, by the way,' she said.

'Right.'

'It's OK, there's no need to say "you're welcome". Because I know I'm not. You just had a sudden vision of me being attacked by some pervert on a bench by the river during the night. And then it might have come out that the friendly local bobby, Constable Cooper, had told me that was the best place to sleep. Not good for your reputation, eh?'

'I'll get you some blankets,' said Cooper.

'Yeah. Thanks.'

For a moment, Cooper remembered the feeling he'd experienced just before he answered the door to Angie. That premonition of disaster.

But he pushed the feeling aside. She'd be out of his flat by 8 a.m. tomorrow – he'd make sure of it. And that would be the last he would ever see of Angie Fry. He'd make certain of that, too.

Chapter Twenty

TUESDAY

FOR THE PAST three nights, Diane Fry had dreamed that she found Emma Renshaw's body. Emma had been dead for two years, and the skin had shrunk to pale tatters on her skull, so that it had become a rubber mask that could be twisted and rearranged into any shape you wanted. For Fry, it transformed into the face of a sixteen-year-old girl – a face as familiar to her as her own, and yet alien. A face that left her sweating, and thrashing her limbs in tangled bedclothes.

Fry knew this fear. This kind of fear was insidious. You could go to bed at night feeling free of it. Yet when you woke in the morning, you found it had descended from the darkest corners of your room and clung to you like cobwebs.

So the smell, the sound or the movement that she knew ought to be innocent, suggesting safety, now brought with it not a specific fear, nor a memory of the event that had scarred her in the first place. Instead, it created a sort of general dread, a vague, shapeless terror of something she couldn't picture or name. In everything now she saw something to fear. The blood in the poppies, the mould in the grass. The bones under the skin of the girl.

That morning, something finally occurred to Fry that she should have known for a long time. She might well be living in a fantasy world of her own making, just as much as the Renshaws were. Angie Fry was no more likely to come home now than Emma Renshaw was. After all, Angie had been gone for fifteen years. A decade and a half. Fry had to repeat it to herself, but it still didn't mean what it should. Hardly any time at all had passed in her own mind – not in that corner where Angie was still a teenager full of life, setting off for a rave somewhere, leaving the house with a laugh and a brief kiss for her younger sister, vanishing into the night in a whiff of scent and the smell of dope.

Fry knew she wasn't immune to the tricks that the mind played. Why should she be free of the need to cling to a desperate, mistaken belief in the face of reality? Was she, too, blind to the bones?

Angie had already been using heroin by the time she disappeared, and the life of an addict was brutish and short. Fry had seen enough of other people's brothers and sisters to know what happened to them. Fifteen years was a long time in an addict's life. And if Angie had still been alive, she would have found her by now.

Fry found herself facing a decision that had slipped through the gap in her curtains like the dawn replacing the yellow glare of the streetlights outside her window. She had to accept that Angie was dead. Otherwise there was nowhere for her to go, except into the dark alleyways of obsession.

For the first time in months, Fry spent some time doing her exercises, emptying her mind, searching for the energy that she needed to get her through. She positioned herself on the rug in her bedroom and went through the movements, gradually losing sight of the faded wallpaper and the floor as her eyes looked beyond them and into herself. Finally, she began to feel the first whispers of the physical intensity that would provide her with the strength that she had lost.

It was a start, but not enough. She needed to put all thoughts of Angie out of her mind, and let the knowledge of her sister's death steal up on her quietly without her noticing. And, perhaps most of all, she needed support in dealing with the Renshaws – the kind of support the presence of Gavin Murfin couldn't give her.

THE CATS HAD been hunting during the night. One of them had been eating its catch in the back garden of 8 Welbeck Street. There wasn't much left of the victim now – only the stomach and intestines, and some other internal organs. They lay on the stone flags, still glistening, dark green and red. And there was something else left, as well – two tiny feet, long and pale, and tipped by white claws. One of the feet was curled into a sort of fist, but the other was stretched out on the ground as it would have been in life. They were the remains of a rat.

Ben Cooper looked around the area for signs of a scaly tail, to get an idea of the size of the dead rodent. Cats didn't normally eat the tail either. They would consume the head and the front feet, but not the back feet, or the stomach, or the tail. If he could find it, the size and thickness of it would give him an indication of whether Randy or Mrs Macavity had caught an adult rat, or a young one freshly out of its nest. Were rats breeding nearby? If so, there would be more remains to come, now that the cats had located their nest.

But there was no sign of a tail on the flags. Cooper shrugged. It was possible some bird had flown away with it, thinking it was a worm. There were magpies in this area – they were frequently mobbed by the smaller birds when they landed in the trees. Magpies were carrion eaters. They also took young songbirds, and even the eggs from other birds' nests. They were ideal for clearing up the leftovers from other predators.

'One of you isn't going to want any breakfast this morning, then?' he said, as the cats came fussing around his legs.

But he put their bowls down anyway, and they ate as eagerly as always.

COOPER STRAIGHTENED UP, and found Angie Fry watching him from the door of the conservatory, with that smile on her face. He felt a surge of unreasonable anger that a private moment was being observed by this unwelcome stranger. Somehow, it seemed to make it worse that this was the first morning he had been able to establish the back yard as his territory. He hadn't even had time to explore the overgrown garden.

'You have to leave now,' he said.

'OK, OK. You said by eight o'clock, and I'm on my way. I just wanted to say thanks before I went.'

Cooper felt himself begin to flush. It was amazing that Angie Fry should have the same casual ability to sway his emotions that her sister did. His annoyance had turned immediately to remorse for being rude.

'That's all right.'

'I hope you'll remember, though, what I said last night.'

'I'll remember.'

'That's good, Ben.'

He accompanied her to the door of the flat, but she paused on the doorstep.

'I may see you again,' she said.

'I don't think so.'

Then the door of the other flat opened, and suddenly a dark-haired woman stood in the hallway, swaying forward slightly as if she'd been forced to stop suddenly, to avoid bumping into him. Another complete stranger to Cooper, she looked to be in her late thirties, and was wearing a black jacket and blue jeans.

'Oh,' she said.

Cooper could see an expression of alarm cross her face. He could forgive her if she took him to be a mugger.

'Hi, I'm your neighbour,' he said. 'Ben Cooper.'

'Oh, right.'

She visibly relaxed, and held out a hand. 'Peggy Check. So you're the young man downstairs. That's what Dorothy Shelley calls you.'

Cooper shook her hand. He looked around for Angie, but she'd vanished into the street without a word. He found Peggy smiling broadly at him, as if at some huge joke. She had a smile that transformed her face and brought out a depth of humour in her eyes, and Cooper suddenly felt at ease with her. It made him realize how on edge he'd been for the last few hours, ever since Angie Fry had arrived on his doorstep.

'Yes, that's me,' he said. 'The young man downstairs.'

'You're a policeman, right?'

'Yes.'

'Dorothy says I'll be perfectly safe with you around. But it isn't too dangerous around Edendale, is it?'

Cooper could feel himself relaxing more and more by the second. All the instincts he'd been repressing while talking to Angie were coming to the fore again. He detected a natural warmth that had been uncomfortably missing from his earlier visitor.

'No, you'll be fine,' he said. 'Watch out for the cats, though. They're killers.'

Peggy looked as though she wanted to close her door and leave, but she couldn't do it with Cooper blocking the way in the little porch. He stepped back over the threshold into his own flat.

She smiled again. 'See you around, I guess, Ben.'

'You must come in and have a coffee some time.'

'Love to. Just let me know. Catch you later.'

Cooper watched her head off down the street towards the market square, walking with a brisk confidence. She might be a stranger here, but she would be all right in Edendale. There was no doubt about that.

And he felt sure of one other thing. If she did take up his invitation to come in for a coffee one day, Peggy Check wouldn't sit in his flat and tell him lies all evening.

BEN COOPER FOUND Diane Fry standing in front of his desk when he arrived at West Street. She had an armful of files and something that looked like a photo album. She seemed a bit subdued, but that wasn't what Cooper noticed most when he looked up at her. He found himself automatically looking for the similarities to her sister. The slim shoulders and straight fair hair were recognizable. But there was something else, too – something about the look in the eyes that he couldn't quite put his finger on.

Fry brushed a strand of hair from her forehead. Another familiar gesture.

'Is there something wrong?' she said. 'What are you staring at me for?'

'Oh … nothing.'

'If you say so. Ben, I want you to take a look at this. Tell me what you think.'

'What is it?'

'It's Sarah Renshaw's cuttings album. She let me borrow it because she's just started a new one.'

Mrs Renshaw had collected a thick album of cuttings from newspapers. They were mostly reports of missing children who had been reunited with their families, some of them after several years. There were also stories about young people living rough on the streets of various cities, or in squats, or even in the temporary camps of New Age travellers and environmental protesters.

There were scores of them, and Cooper was astonished at the range of newspapers represented. All of the nationals were there, both tabloid and broadsheet. There were Scottish papers, and local weeklies from Yorkshire and the Midlands, in fact from all over Britain. Some of the stories, he realized, were printouts of pages from the websites of foreign newspapers, mostly American. Cooper turned to one from the *Milwaukee Journal Sentinel*, featuring a girl injured in a car accident on Highway 54 and left unconscious in hospital. The police in a place called Oneida were trying to identify the victim, and were appealing for help from the public. The phone number had been circled in blue ink. He guessed the Oneida cops would have had a call from Sarah Renshaw. He hoped they had dealt with her sympathetically.

Cooper checked the dates of the cuttings. The earlier ones began almost immediately after Emma's disappearance, but were mainly local stories, and they were weeks apart. But as the album filled up, the dates got closer together, their sources more far-flung and international, until the most recent pages were packed with stories culled from the internet day after day.

It gave Cooper a dizzying glimpse of the world as seen by Sarah Renshaw. In this world, it was as if Emma had started off as just a single missing person in North

Derbyshire two years ago, but had steadily multiplied herself over the months. In her various incarnations, she had spread out and scattered all over the globe, invading the world like an army of clones, or a virus proliferating at an unmanageable rate.

These multiple Emmas had ended up in all kinds of places, some of them lost and anonymous, some hungry or injured, alone or finally reunited. And Sarah Renshaw had spent hours at the computer tracking them down. Perhaps she had become increasingly desperate in her efforts as she realized the numbers involved, and discovered the speed of the virus that she was trying to keep up with. There were more young people going missing every day than anyone could imagine.

Cooper closed the album with a sigh. They were far from being clones, but the young women featured in these cuttings did have a few things in common, and one big difference from Emma Renshaw. Each of them was someone's daughter, of course. Many of them would have parents worrying about them at home.

But most of all, every one of them was still alive.

'It's sad,' said Cooper.

Fry nodded. 'The most worrying thing is the guilt factor.'

'What do you mean?'

'Sarah Renshaw keeps talking about this "belief" business. I think if Emma turns up dead, she's going to interpret that to mean she didn't believe hard enough. She'll think Emma is dead because *she* failed her.'

'That isn't rational at all.'

'There's nothing rational about guilt. There's nothing rational about the Renshaws at the moment.'

'That bad, eh? I've heard a lot about them, but never actually met them.'

'It would be interesting to see what you think of them, Ben.'

'Yes.'

Cooper wondered if Fry had actually told the Renshaws that anyone who had been missing for years was unlikely to turn up again some day. He didn't feel like supporting her in that opinion just now. He knew only too well that it could really happen.

Fry straightened her shoulders and her manner changed.

'And how are you getting on with the Oxleys, Ben?' she said. 'Are you one of the family yet?'

'Oh, yeah. An in-law that nobody speaks to.'

'Well, you'll have to keep trying,' said Fry. 'Use a different approach or something.'

'A different approach. Right.'

DCI KESSEN DIDN'T have to wait as long for the room to settle down this morning. His silent, patient style was unsettling some of the officers. They didn't quite know what to make of him. What was he thinking behind that thin smile? Even DI Hitchens seemed unsure of how to behave.

Ben Cooper saw that Tracy Udall was here this morning with some of the Rural Crime Team, including Sergeant Jimmy Boyce. He waved to Udall, then hesitated, realizing he should be careful who he sat with, in case it was taken as signifying something. Then he sat on a chair at the back of the room, perching on it as if suggesting that he had to make a quick getaway on urgent business.

'All right, thank you,' said Hitchens as he opened the briefing. 'Those of you who've been working on leads connected to the bronze bust we found in Neil Granger's car will know that we've had some results. The bust turns out to have been stolen right here in Edendale, from a house called Southwoods Grange, which was burgled two weeks ago. The property is owned by the National Trust, so all the items were recorded and photographed for security. There's no doubt it's the same one.'

'How much is it worth?' asked someone.

'Difficult to say, but I'm told it's insured for five thousand pounds.'

'Nice. And have we detected this theft, sir?'

'Er, no. But the bust was part of a haul of small items worth considerably more, I'm told. By the time a unit responded to an alarm at Southwoods Grange, the perpetrators had got well clear. There were no solid lines of enquiry to follow, and no sign of any of the stolen property turning up anywhere. Until now.'

'Sir, do you think it might have been the Gavin Murfin Gang practising for the Chatsworth House job?'

From his seat at the front of the room, Kessen turned his head slowly to look at the DC who had spoken. Very few people laughed, except Murfin, who chortled loudly and winked at his colleague. DI Hitchens smiled, but managed to keep his face turned away from his boss and his voice steady.

'Well, facetiousness aside, we do have some similar MOs on a series of other incidents in the past few months, including some in Longdendale, near where Neil Granger lived.'

Hitchens looked around the room and found Ben Cooper. 'As some of you know, the Rural Crime Team have been working on these burglaries in Longdendale for a while. Their intelligence has proved very useful. Also, we have some ongoing checks on a number of Granger's associates, which will take some time. But a few of them are already looking very promising. Very promising indeed. There are a couple of Neil Granger's friends who have a string of theft convictions between them.'

'Where are these associates, sir?' said Cooper. 'In Tintwistle? Or back in Withens?'

'No, not in Withens. I'm thinking particularly of two former colleagues of Granger's at Lancashire Chemicals in Glossop, who were recently sacked because they were suspected of pilfering. They've both spent time inside on unrelated matters, and Granger has been associating with them. They drink together occasionally at a pub in Mottram. There was some good work done there, establishing that fact so quickly.'

Hitchens turned to look at Kessen, who nodded and gave everyone his smile. It actually felt as though he had offered effusive congratulations.

'That's not to say there isn't a lot more work to be done on Granger's associates,' said the DI. 'Including those in

Withens, Cooper. Granger has some relatives there who might be a bit dubious, I gather.'

'They're mostly kids,' said Cooper. 'Nuisance and vandalism, yes; maybe nicking from cars. But I don't think there's any suggestion they're into antiques.'

'Well, we'll see. We need more information yet before we close down that possibility, so keep on it. The RCT are going to help with that aspect of the enquiry, so we're lucky to have some help. Neil Granger seems to have known quite a lot of people.'

'The family in Withens, the Oxleys, aren't terribly co-operative,' said Cooper.

'Well, stick at it. Try a different approach.'

'Yes, sir.'

Cooper could feel DCI Kessen's eyes on him, and decided to keep quiet. A transfer to the Rural Crime Team might come quicker than he expected, if he wasn't careful.

'Unfortunately, we're still waiting for any useful forensic results from the scene. The lab has promised us something shortly.'

There were a few muffled groans. That probably meant that evidence taken from the crime scene had gone to the Forensic Science Service at the cheap rate, so it would take longer to be worked on by the lab. The police had to pay for the services of the FSS per item, so there were budget considerations to take into account. Promises, on the other hand, didn't cost anything.

'However, if we can line up a few prime suspects, we're hopeful there will be some contact traces we can use to tie them in to the scene, both the air shaft and the lay-by where Granger's car was parked. The enquiry team tracing lorry drivers who used the A628 that night is having some success.'

'So what's the theory?' said Cooper, forgetting that he had decided to keep quiet. 'That Neil Granger was a member of a gang of antiques thieves operating in the area?'

'It seems the likeliest explanation for the presence of the bronze bust in his car. It was part of the haul from Southwoods Grange. It's possible the members of the gang fell out over the proceeds. It happens all the time. Maybe Granger had been trying to keep some items for himself, and the others found out.'

'Why do you think they would meet at that particular spot?'

'It's quiet enough. And the access is reasonably easy, especially if the rest of the team had a four-wheel-drive vehicle and drove up to the air shaft.'

'It wasn't particularly convenient for Neil Granger. He left his car in the lay-by, and walked up.'

'We don't know that he walked up. He may have been in someone else's vehicle.'

'True.'

'At the scene, we're intending to do a search of the surrounding area, but it's mostly heather and bare peat – not much scope for hiding anything.'

'And what about the air shaft?' said Cooper.

'What about it?'

'There may be no scope for hiding anything in the heather, but what about inside the shaft?'

'It's too high to reach,' said Hitchens doubtfully.

'If there was a vehicle here, they might have had a ladder. An aluminium stepladder in the back of an estate car or something. You could do it easily. In fact, if you piled some of these loose stones on top of each other, I reckon one person could give another a leg up, and they could get over the edge.'

'I'll make a note,' said Hitchens. 'And we'll let the task force do it. They have ladders.'

'Was there anything in Neil Granger's house?'

'Nothing that has been recognized as an antique, anyway. Not unless you count a set of plaster ducks on the wall in the spare bedroom.'

'Hey, those fetch quite a bit now,' said Murfin. 'I saw some at an antiques fair the other day. I couldn't believe the price. But the guy on the stall said they were kitsch, and most people had chucked them away when they went out of fashion. So they have a rarity value, if they're genuine.'

'But would you think of nicking them if you broke into somewhere full of proper antiques, Murfin?'

'Probably not.'

'And would you then hang them on the wall in your spare bedroom, with the grottiest wallpaper you could find?'

'No.'

'All right. So there were no other items that looked like stolen antiques. A team is going through all the addresses and phone numbers they could find in the property, but Granger wasn't very organized, I'm afraid. And none of the names match any of the suspects on the Rural Crime Team's list of possibles.'

'He'd have to be more than disorganized to leave a list of his criminal associates lying around for us to find,' said Cooper.

'Stranger things happen. Stupider criminals have been known.'

'This one wasn't stupid, sir. He hasn't been making many mistakes.'

'Apart from the one that got him killed.'

'What about this black make-up business?' said Murfin.

'OK, it's an unusual form of disguise, but the make-up seems to have been conveniently at hand because of some theatrical group he was involved in rehearsals for.' Hitchens looked around the room. 'Anything else we haven't covered?'

Diane Fry began to stir slightly on her chair near the front.

'Oh, yes, we haven't forgotten the possibility of a link to the disappearance of Emma Renshaw, who still hasn't been found,' said Hitchens.

It didn't sound convincing to Cooper, and Fry didn't look happy about it. There was a definite air of afterthought. But to his surprise, DCI Kessen seemed to latch on to the subject.

'DS Fry, did you want to explore that a bit?'

'Thank you, sir.' Fry took a moment to gather her thoughts. Maybe she was equally surprised at being asked for her opinion. 'I do think we should bear in mind that Neil Granger was supposed to have been the last person to see Emma Renshaw before she disappeared. But we only ever had his word for that.'

Hitchens slipped naturally into the role of devil's advocate.

'Yes. But bear in mind that he didn't have time between leaving the house and arriving at work to do anything much more than drop Emma off somewhere,' he said. 'If he didn't drop her at the railway station, where did he take her? And why should he lie about it?'

'It's also true that we only have Neil Granger's word for the time he left the house.'

'But again, there was only a few minutes' margin there. Alex Dearden left no more than ten minutes before Granger says he did. So the most we could allow him would be, say, twenty minutes.'

'That's time to do quite a lot,' said Fry stubbornly.

'To kill Emma and dispose of her body? I don't think so.'

'If he killed her in the house, her body could have been in the boot of his car while he was at work.'

'Was his car forensically examined at the time?' asked Kessen.

'No, sir.'

'That's a pity. A wasted opportunity. It would at least have eliminated that possibility. Did he have the same car as the one we have in our possession now?'

'I'm not sure, sir. I think so.'

'If Emma Renshaw's body was ever in the boot of his car, Forensics may still be able to get some traces.

Bloodstains perhaps, or fibres. You could get that checked out at least, Fry.'

'What about Alex Dearden?' said Hitchens.

Fry shook her head. 'I don't see how he had time to do anything. Neil Granger saw him leave. And Granger admitted to being the last to see Emma.'

'There's always the possibility that they were in this together.'

Kessen looked at Fry apologetically. 'I'd be more open to that kind of suggestion if you could offer me a motive. One of the boys, yes – an attempted rape, a rejected sexual advance, or something of the kind. We've seen it often enough. But two of them conspiring together? Were they particularly friendly?'

'No, sir.'

'So why should Dearden help out Granger, or vice versa?'

Even Diane Fry was silent at that.

'Of course, Emma Renshaw might have decided she couldn't afford a taxi,' said Hitchens. 'She might have set off to walk to the station, or to catch a bus, or hitch a lift.'

'No one along the route to the station reported seeing her,' said Fry. 'In any case, it's over four miles and she was carrying a bag. Bus drivers didn't remember her, and no motorist ever came forward to report giving her a lift, or seeing her hitching.'

'That's not to say it didn't happen, of course. It's still open as an option.'

WHEN THE MEETING broke up, Cooper watched Diane Fry walk over to speak to DI Hitchens. Perhaps she was pressing her case for Emma Renshaw not to be forgotten. Or maybe she just wanted to be seen to be with the senior officers, and not part of the crowd now squeezing their way towards the door. He waited, and after a few minutes, Fry came towards him.

'OK, I've fixed it, Ben,' said Fry.

'Fixed what?'

'I've fixed it for you to come to see the Renshaws with me. I want to get your view on them. Then you can go on to the Oxleys later.'

'Oh, great.'

'Have you thought of a new approach?'

'Yes, I'd thought I'd just take a pile of interview forms and fill in the answers myself right now.'

Chapter Twenty-One

ON THE WAY into Withens, Ben Cooper and Diane Fry saw a youth walking along the side of the road. He was wearing cargo pants, a parka jacket and a black woollen hat pulled down over his ears.

'Would that be one of the Oxley boys?' said Fry.

'Where?'

'Walking along the road up ahead.'

'It could be. Sean? Ryan? One of the two.'

'And they're what age?'

'Fourteen, fifteen.'

Fry looked at her watch. 'Why don't we ask him why he isn't at school? If he doesn't actually have a note from his teacher on him, we could insist on giving him a lift home, then talking to his parents.'

'It's worth a try, I suppose.'

The youth glanced over his shoulder when he heard the car approaching. Maybe he had been intending to thumb a lift, but he didn't bother when he saw them. He just carried on walking at the same pace, plodding along the narrow grass verge with his shoulders hunched inside his parka.

Fry slowed, indicated and pulled into the side of the road in front of him. The boy didn't look up, but waited until the car had stopped, then suddenly turned and raced off across the heather away from the road.

'Watch out, he's legging it!' said Fry.

'Damn.'

By the time Cooper had released his seat belt and got out of the car, the youth was a couple of hundred yards away, his arms and legs flailing as he weaved and splashed across the boggy ground towards the nearest clough, where he would soon be out of sight.

Cooper sighed, recognizing the futility of a chase on foot.

'Was it Ryan or Sean?' said Fry.

'I don't know.'

'Well, great.'

'It was a good idea,' said Cooper. 'Just not good enough.'

'Ben, what do you think of this antiques angle?' said Fry as they got under way again.

'It's not for me to say, really.'

'That's cautious.'

'But if there are some potential suspects …'

'You're thinking you might be wasting your time with the Oxleys?'

'I *know* I'm wasting my time with the Oxleys, Diane. They're never going to talk to me. It's starting to make me feel like a leper.'

'Don't worry,' said Fry. 'The Renshaws will be happy to talk to you. But only about one subject.'

FRY INTRODUCED COOPER to Howard and Sarah Renshaw, and he was allowed to sit on the settee next to Edgar the teddy.

'Can I ask you something that may not appear very relevant?' said Fry.

Howard Renshaw smiled faintly. 'We've been asked so many questions that we're hardly in a position to know what's relevant and what isn't any more. So go ahead.'

'You've told me about your house in Marple, and how much you liked living there …'

'Yes.'

'From what I've heard, it sounds a very pleasant area. Nice neighbours, good schools, close to the countryside but near enough to get into Manchester or Sheffield easily. And you said you made lots of friends in the neighbourhood.'

'That's right. So what did you want to ask?'

'What on earth,' said Fry, 'made you move to Withens?'

Sarah laughed. 'Well, first of all, you have to realize that it was over twenty years ago, when Emma was very small. We were different people then.'

'We were twenty years younger ourselves,' said Howard. 'I think that had a lot to do with it.'

'Yes, you're right.'

Howard perched on the arm of Sarah's chair. Fry expected her to touch his arm or even hold his hand. Previously, it would have been the sort of gesture she would have noticed between them. But Sarah didn't do that. Instead, she rearranged her skirt and held her hands in her lap.

'The thing about Withens,' she said, 'is that it's a kind of separate world on its own. When we saw it, we realized it was nothing like all those nice commuter villages we'd known before. It was much more *real*. Do you know what I mean?'

'Not exactly.'

'There was something rather spiritual about it. To us, then, it seemed like the sort of place we wanted to bring up a child.'

Fry sneaked a glance at Cooper. His expression told her what she wanted to know. Maybe he was thinking of the Oxleys and having difficulty locating the spirituality.

'We fell in love with Withens almost as soon as we saw it,' said Howard.

'Did you?'

'It was summer when we first came,' said Sarah.

'Yes?'

'It *can* be a little difficult in the winter.'

Sarah laughed at her husband. 'We were so innocent, weren't we? One of the first things we did was take down a big stone wall at the back of the house. It must have been ten feet high, and we couldn't understand why anybody had built it there. It didn't seem to have any purpose at all – not something of that height.'

'We made jokes about how high those nineteenth-century sheep must have been able to jump.'

'Well, *you* made jokes,' said Sarah.

'As far as we were concerned, a wall that height was just blocking the view up the valley from the house. So we took it down.'

'We had a much better view,' said Sarah. 'For a while.'

'What happened?'

'Winter came. And it snowed.'

'We realized why they had built a wall ten feet high,' said Howard. 'It was because that was the height of the snow drifts. The snow came down the valley on the north winds, and we were the first place to get snowed in that winter. And since we'd taken the wall down, it drifted against the side of the house instead of being stopped by the wall.'

'The first morning, we had to dig our way out of the door.'

'That *was* a particularly bad winter,' said Howard. 'But that's one of the things about Withens – you get the feeling that something like that could happen at any time. It's as if nature is waiting to give you a sharp little nudge whenever you seem likely to forget about her.'

'And that's what makes Withens seem real?' asked Fry.

'It's *one* of the things,' said Howard. 'It seemed to us that a child should grow up knowing about nature and the seasons. And I think we were right. Emma is the sort of girl who belongs in the countryside. She has a special relationship with nature.'

'You said one of the things. What else?'

'There are the people, of course. They're wonderful.'

Fry stared at him. 'Sorry. Are we still talking about Withens?'

'Don't you think they're wonderful?'

'Detective Constable Cooper knows the people here better than I do.'

'They're interesting,' said Cooper. 'No doubt about it. And some of them I can't imagine living anywhere else.'

Both the Renshaws looked at him as if he had said something very profound.

'I've been trying to persuade Sergeant Fry to come to our Emma Day,' Howard told him. 'You're going to come, aren't you, Sergeant?'

Fry wanted to bolt for it, but she couldn't. Sarah seized on her hesitation eagerly.

'Yes, you must both come. We need all the support you can give us, so we know you'll come.'

'That would be wonderful,' said her husband. 'We're so grateful. So grateful for everything you're doing for us.'

Fry began to shake her head, but Sarah Renshaw had fastened her intense gaze on her.

'Bring Constable Cooper with you,' she said. 'He'll appreciate Emma's work.'

'There'll be a little display in the garden, if the weather's fine,' said Howard. 'Down in Emma's Corner.'

'What's that?'

'Well, we decided to plant a tree on Emma's eighteenth birthday, and we wanted something significant. She always loved the buddleia, because of its scent and the way its flowers attract the butterflies in summer. They call it the Butterfly Bush, don't they?'

'I wouldn't know,' said Fry, her gardening experience having been limited to dandelions growing in a window box.

'We planted another one on the anniversary of the day she disappeared, as well as on her birthday. And the same again the following year. Now there's a little grove of bushes at the bottom of the garden that holds another bit of Emma.'

'Marking the days is important. The day she was due felt a bit like Easter.'

'Easter? Not – resurrection?'

'In a way. If we think about Emma hard enough on that day, it seems as though she will actually walk in through the door and say she's sorry for taking so long to come home. It hasn't happened yet, of course. But perhaps that's because we haven't wished hard enough. What do you think?'

'I really don't know.'

Then the Renshaws looked at each other, and flushed a bit pink. Both of them now had the beginnings of tears in their eyes.

'Are you thinking what I'm thinking?' said Sarah to her husband.

'It would be the ideal time to make contact,' he said.

Fry thought they were still talking about support. It was a strange way of putting it, but lots of things were strange about the Renshaws.

'Yes, that would help you a lot, wouldn't it?' said Sarah.

'Sorry, what would?'

'Making contact.'

'I don't really follow you. Contact with who?'

'With the Other Side, of course.'

'We thought that while you're here,' said Howard, 'it would be the ideal opportunity to have a séance.'

'We've been consulting a psychic, and using a pendulum to try to locate Emma,' said Sarah. 'It seemed very appropriate, because they're things that Emma is interested in herself, anything mystical or supernatural. If we held a séance, you could ask all the things you want to.'

An uncomfortable silence followed. Fry wished that Cooper would say something. Why had she bothered going to the trouble of arranging for him to come with her, if he was just going to sit there and take it all in, saying nothing?

But then he did decide to speak. And Fry blessed him for changing the subject.

'Mr and Mrs Renshaw, I wonder if you have any more photos of Emma? From around the time she went to university, I mean.'

'Once she'd gone to university, we didn't manage to take as many,' said Sarah. 'But there are a few.'

Howard fetched an album. 'If we let you have this,' he said, 'we need it back for Monday.'

'That's all right.'

Cooper opened the album and turned over the pages rapidly. Towards the back, he seemed to find something that interested him. Fry leaned over his shoulder.

'What on earth is that?' she said. 'Was your daughter going to a fancy-dress party or something?'

Fry began to laugh, but she met Cooper's eye, and the laughter died in her throat.

'Oh, that,' said Sarah. 'It was something Neil Granger got Emma into. I really don't know what she saw in it.'

'In what?'

'It's a group they have here in Withens. I don't really understand it, but it seems to be a local tradition.'

Emma was dressed all in black, which wasn't unusual for a girl of her age. In fact, Fry had a fondness for black, too. But the outfit Emma was wearing consisted of a black tail coat, black leggings, a black top hat, and Doc Martens boots. She looked tall and very slim – just not the right shape for the outfit. She was also wearing reflective sunglasses, and carrying a recorder.

'This was something to do with Neil Granger?'

'He's one of the group. Or he was,' said Sarah. 'As you can see, Emma's a musician. She's a very talented girl in a lot of ways.'

'I'm sure.' Cooper held the page open, and Fry turned it slightly towards herself, trying to puzzle out the meaning of the photo.

'But what I'm wondering, Mrs Renshaw,' she said, 'is why Emma has her face blacked up.'

DEREK ALTON LAUGHED to himself, and sat down in one of the front pews of his church. There was a strange smell in the aisle this morning. It was a musty odour, as if the windows and doors hadn't been opened for months. He wondered if there was damp rising through the stone flags and rotting the oak of the pews, or soaking into the fabric of the kneelers.

Perhaps he would come back into the church tomorrow and find green shoots bursting through the floor, as they had broken through the paths in the churchyard. He knew he would be powerless to fight back the invasion, and would have to watch helplessly as nature pulled apart his aisle, ripped up the pews, clambered into the pulpit and clawed at the altar rail.

Three of the Oxleys had come to see Derek Alton at his bungalow the previous evening. There had been Lucas, smiling and in his suit. There had been the old man, Eric, nodding and winking knowingly. And young Scott, too. Scott Oxley had sat behind the two older men. Yet his stare was the one that Derek Alton had felt the most.

'Vicar, you know that we lost Neil ...'

'Yes, I'm so sorry.'

'We wanted to ask you a bit of a favour.'

'Oh, of course. You want me to conduct the funeral? That's no problem.'

The two older men looked at each other, but said nothing.

'When do you want to have it? Do you have a date in mind?'

'No, no,' said Lucas. 'Neil's going to be cremated. The service will be at the crematorium in Edendale.'

'I see. But you'll need someone to lead the service.'

To his surprise, the three men began to shift uneasily in their chairs.

'We've got someone from the Humanist Society,' said Eric. 'We reckon it's what he would have wanted.'

'Oh.'

'You're welcome to come along, of course.'

'Thank you.'

'It was something different we wanted to ask you.'

'What then?'

'Vicar, we want you to take his place.'

'What?'

'We want you to join the Rats for May Day. Well, you know all the stuff we do. There's no time for anyone else to learn it in time, you see.'

'Well, I don't know what to say.'

'You'll do it, though, won't you?'

'Well, I'm not sure it would be appropriate, Eric.'

Despite his words, Alton found a surge of excitement building up inside him. It was a warm churning, which started in his abdomen, almost like a sexual excitement. He tried to be calm, and hoped the Oxleys wouldn't see his reaction. But then he glanced at Scott, and saw the smirk on the young man's face.

'I'm a Church of England clergyman,' said Alton.

'And we're your parishioners,' said Eric. 'You're not going to reject us, are you? This is important to the community. You're always talking about the importance of community.'

'Yes.'

With a smile, Lucas produced a thick blackthorn stick that he had been holding inside his coat, and held it out towards the vicar.

The old man had spoken then. 'The darkness and the light,' he said. 'Will you be the darkness or the light?'

'YOU'RE NOT GOING to do it, are you?' said Ben Cooper. 'I mean, you won't go with them to see a psychic, Diane?'

'You're kidding. I'd rather read all Emma Renshaw's sickly poems ten times over. Besides, I don't think it was me the Renshaws really wanted. They think you're the sensitive one.'

'Oh.'

'What do you think, Ben? Fancy playing the part of Gypsy Rose? Knock once for yes and twice for no? I can just picture it. You'd have the Renshaws in the palm of your hand. They'll believe anything, those two.'

'Like the psychic.'

'Yes, like the bloody psychic. You know, I think they've finally gone completely nuts.'

'Completely?'

'Well, they're still functioning on some basic level. But they've lost touch with reality. They're delusional. They could end up being a danger to themselves.'

'According to the Traffic crew who picked them up, that's exactly what they were doing at the underpass. Being a danger to themselves.'

'Well, yeah. And all these little rituals they go through – it seems to me that they're all designed to bolster the Renshaws' conviction that their daughter will come home some day. Mrs Renshaw said it herself – "you have to believe", she said. I think they're terrified that they'll start having doubts. And once they start to have doubts, that's when they'll fall apart. The Renshaws will just crumble if their delusions are ever shattered.'

'How fragile are those delusions?'

'At the moment, they seem to be feeding off each others' belief. But, of course, if Emma Renshaw's body is ever found ...'

'It would bring them back to reality, surely?'

'But it would also take away their last hope. The only thing that's keeping them going.'

'I'm sure they've been offered counselling.'

'Several times. They went through some sessions, but there was always a problem. The counsellor would talk to them about closure, about letting go. And the Renshaws can't understand that. How can they let go, they say, when Emma will be coming home soon?'

'I think Emma's body will be found one day, don't you? The circumstances don't look like a voluntary disappearance.'

'Maybe. But some victims are never found.'

Cooper shuddered. 'How long can the Renshaws keep it up?'

'I don't know,' said Fry. 'And I don't want to be around to find out.'

'No.'

'What about the Oxleys? More down to earth, I hope?'

'I sort of meant what I said at the Renshaws. My impression is that the Oxleys are synonymous with Withens. They could never live anywhere else. I mean, I can't imagine the Oxleys doing the opposite of what the Renshaws did, and moving from Withens to Marple.'

Fry thought about it. 'I'm still not clear on the reasons the Renshaws had for moving.'

'Because it was more *real*, man.'

'That's just it – it sounds too, sort of, New Age for them. Too dreadlocks and dope, if you know what I mean. The Renshaws aren't old hippies, are they?'

'I don't think so. But it's kind of difficult to tell with most of them, after all this time. Unless they've got pony-tails and kaftans and they're running shops selling crys-tals and runes, they look pretty much like anyone else in their fifties. They grow out of it – outwardly anyway.'

'Yeah. Outwardly.'

Cooper looked at her. 'I know the Renshaws have turned a bit wacky with all this stuff about Emma, but I don't think they're actually sharing a spliff every time we're not looking.'

'No.'

'What are you thinking, Diane?'

'I'm thinking it can be very dangerous when people believe every word that you tell them. Dangerous – or very convenient.'

THEY DROVE INTO the car park in Withens. Fry switched off the engine, and they sat for a few minutes looking at the square stone houses, the tower of the church beyond the yew trees, and the background of black hills.

To Cooper, the hills seemed to have moved in a lit-tle closer every time he came here, making Withens a bit more claustrophobic, a bit more impermanent. What had Tracy Udall said? It didn't look like a place that would last. But surely it *had* lasted. The railway navvies' shanty town had been here in the middle of the nineteenth century, and the farms must already have existed long before that. So why did it feel so temporary?

Cooper wondered where exactly the shanty town had been. Where had fifteen hundred navvies lived in such appalling conditions? Was it here, where the village now stood? Or further down the road, past the church, among the banks of bracken and peat bogs?

'You're meeting PC Udall here?' said Fry.

'At the church.'

'What's she like?'

'She's very sound. Dedicated. Good at her job.'

'Great. I think you ought to try harder on the Oxleys. I don't think you're wasting your time.'

'You think if we dig hard enough, we'll find some connection with Emma Renshaw?'

'Ben, if you can find what this blacked-up faces thing is all about, it would help.'

'Neil Granger might just have been using it as a form of disguise, or camouflage at night. It's only theatrical make-up. Anyone could get hold of it, but if he had it lying around anyway for rehearsals for this dance group –'

'Yeah, a dance group. What did the Renshaws say it was called?'

'The Border Rats.'

'Peculiar sort of a name.'

'Granger was at a rehearsal the night before he was killed,' said Cooper. 'Down at the village pub there – the Quiet Shepherd.'

'Have you been there yet?'

'No.'

The Yorkshire Traction bus came into the car park again and did its circuit. Today, there were three old ladies sitting on the bus. They gazed down at Cooper and Fry without curiosity. None of them made any move to get off, and the driver accelerated away again.

'So,' said Fry. 'What was your impression of the Renshaws?'

Cooper hesitated. 'Howard,' he said. 'What does he do? For a living, I mean?'

'He's retired now. But he was Sales Director for a steel refractory in Sheffield. A very successful one, by all accounts.'

'Yes, I can imagine.'

'What do you mean, Ben?'

'It just seemed to me,' said Cooper, 'that Howard Renshaw was trying to sell us something. And doing it very well.'

Fry sighed, but with a sense of relief. 'That's what I think, too,' she said. 'I was worried that I was being paranoid.'

BEN COOPER FELT pleased that Diane Fry had valued his opinion enough to go to the trouble of getting him along to the Renshaws. As they sat in the car in Withens waiting for a shower to stop, he felt as though he had temporarily come closer to Fry than he had managed to be for a long time. It was a chance, perhaps, to talk to her properly – if the right moment came.

'By the way, I have to go on a trip tomorrow,' said Fry.

'Yes? Anywhere nice?'

'The West Midlands. We have to interview Emma Renshaw's other housemate, Debbie Stark. And a girl called Khadi who she went to Italy with. No one seems to have bothered with her before. Then we have to call at Smethwick OCU to see the officer who dealt with the case two years ago. We might take a look at the house in Bearwood, too.'

'Yeah,' said Cooper.

'You don't sound too impressed. They're sound leads that need following up.'

'I was just wondering – will you be all right?'

'All right? I'll have Gavin Murfin with me, if that's what you're worried about. The only danger I'll be in will be from coming home smelling of curry.'

'The Black Country, though,' said Cooper. 'That's where you're from, isn't it?'

'Of course it is. You know that.'

'It's where you were living when you were stationed … When you decided you had to leave.'

'Yes. This has nothing to do with you, Ben.'

'Is Bearwood near where you lived as a child?'

'Ben –'

'You were living with foster parents there when your sister Angie left home.'

'I could really regret ever having told you any of this. It isn't some kind of soap opera that I expect you to keep track of. It's just my life, that's all. And it's in the past now.'

'Not entirely,' said Cooper.

'What do you mean? I've barely even seen my foster parents since I moved from the West Midlands. I had a Christmas card from them last year, and they write occasionally. Apart from that, the rest of it is history. It's over. I've forgotten all about it.'

Cooper shook his head. 'You haven't forgotten Angie.'

The windows of the car were starting to steam up. Maybe it had turned a bit colder outside since the shower started. Or maybe it was the fact that Cooper was starting to sweat. He felt like Daniel entering the lion's den.

'You know, I definitely think I could regret ever telling you anything about my life.'

'But you wouldn't give up on trying to find Angie, would you?'

'Have you never noticed,' said Fry, 'that the world is full of people who've given up trying, in one way or another?'

'No, I hadn't noticed that.'

'Well, take a look around. You can't miss them.'

'It's only because I'm concerned about you, Diane.'

'I don't need anybody to be concerned about me.'

'I just –'

'Ben, drop it.'

'But –'

'I don't ever want to hear you mention my sister again. Got it?'

Cooper stared out of the windscreen. He couldn't see much outside because of the condensation. But he knew that Withens was out there, waiting for him to have another go at getting into Waterloo Terrace.

'Got it,' he said.

'Now go and try the Oxleys again.'

'Diane, you don't know what they're like.'

'I'm sure you can get something out of them. Use your charm, Ben. Talk their language.'

'For heaven's sake, Diane, *you* try – see how you get on!'

Fry leaned a little closer to him.

'I don't have the charm,' she said. 'Or so they tell me. And I certainly don't have the language. Not like you do, Ben.'

'It doesn't work in this case,' said Cooper. 'I don't get near enough to use the charm. They don't listen to me long enough for me to start speaking their language. So maybe I should start doing it *your* way.'

'That *would* be a first.'

'So what do you suggest?'

'Well, I suppose we might need to try someone else with the Oxleys. Amazing as the idea seems, it's possible they just don't like you, Ben.'

'Really? I thought you were in a minority of one there.'

Fry looked at him coldly, but didn't reply. Cooper could see the tired edges of her eyes and the tense lines around her mouth. He sighed.

'I mean it, Diane. Trying to talk to the Oxleys is like drawing teeth. And I never had any ambitions to be a dentist.'

'I know what you mean,' said Fry. 'I couldn't imagine that job. All those people with decaying teeth. Some people should just keep their mouths firmly shut.'

Fry gathered the files together as Cooper got out of the car and walked across the road. He was glad of the cool air, and let out a deep breath that he had been holding.

Something odd and surprising had struck Cooper while Fry had been tearing him off a strip. While the Renshaws were convinced that their missing daughter was alive and well, and would be found very soon, Diane Fry might be living in the opposite fantasy. Despite the effort she was putting in to track down her sister, Cooper was beginning to get the feeling that deep down she actually believed that Angie was dead.

Chapter Twenty-Two

BEN COOPER MET PC Tracy Udall outside St Asaph's church. Withens was starting to get him down, but he wasn't in a position to complain. Diane Fry had to enter the fantasy world of the Renshaws, and he didn't envy her. Yet his own role wasn't going to be simple, either. To pull apart the Oxley family, he had to get a chance of speaking to each member of the family separately. And that was easier said than done. The Oxleys seemed to cling together, and hardly wanted to let each other out of sight. It was an admirable closeness in a family. Or was it something else?

Perhaps it was time for a change of strategy. He'd tried to be friendly and polite, and it hadn't worked. It had been too much to hope that it would, with the Oxleys. A bit of subtlety was called for. An oblique approach, so that they didn't see him coming quite so easily.

Udall looked a bit tired today, too. Cooper wondered if her son had been causing her problems. For a moment, he was on the point of asking her, but it occurred to him that he didn't know whether Udall welcomed his interest in her private life any more than Diane Fry did.

A group of boys were hanging around near the bus stop again. Two of the lads were the fourteen- or fifteen-year-olds he had seen before, but now with Sheffield Wednesday football shorts over their jeans. The third was the smaller boy with close-cropped hair, but a distinct family resemblance.

Cooper thought he was at least starting to get an angle on the names now – the two teenagers he reckoned were Ryan and Sean, of which at least one was Lucas Oxley's son. The smaller one was undoubtedly Jake, the Tiny Terror.

Each of them seemed to be wearing a personal stereo, with the wires of their earpieces trailing into the pockets of their jackets. No doubt they were enjoying their personal choice of pop, which seemed to dominate everyone's life as a teenager. Ben Cooper's father had called it 'puberty set to music'.

But there was something a little strange about the Oxley boys. They were each plugged in to their own world of sound, yet they seemed to be able to communicate with each other by using their eyes and their body language. They turned to watch Cooper drive down the road. The Oxleys seemed the sort of family who were close enough to be able to send their thoughts to each other in some mysterious fashion. Perhaps Lucas Oxley had already been alerted by some psychic means to his approach. Cooper wondered if a telepathic communication from the Oxley boys would be accompanied by a hip-hop backing track.

At Waterloo Terrace itself, the children had been building a sort of fort on the waste ground in front of the gardens. They had dragged lumps of wood from the yard behind the terrace to make the walls, with sections of drainage pipe standing on end at each corner like little towers. The wood had been stacked only three feet high or so, but it looked pretty unstable. It certainly wouldn't meet with the approval of the council if it had been an official play area.

'I understand the landlords sent some of their workmen to dismantle this once,' said Udall. 'But the kids just built another one.'

'It looks almost as though they're expecting a siege,' said Cooper.

The sound of chainsaws seemed to provide a constant background accompaniment whenever he visited Waterloo Terrace. He pictured the muscular Scott and his cousin, Glen, cutting up the heavy railway sleepers he'd glimpsed in the yard. But what would they use them for? Building an even bigger fort?

'You know, it reminds me a bit of the place up at Townhead,' said Udall. 'I don't suppose you know it? It's a kind of commune, I think. They converted a couple of terraces of railwaymen's houses.'

'A commune? But this is different. These are all members of the same family.'

'I know. You wouldn't think they'd all want to live together, given the choice. I know I wouldn't want to live with my family. We usually try to keep as far away from each other as we possibly can.'

Cooper knocked at number 5, Fran Oxley's house, but got no reply. He listened at the door, thinking he heard voices. But he wasn't quite sure where the sound was coming from. He tried a bit harder, in case the knocker wasn't loud enough, or the occupier was at the back of the house. But there was no response. It felt almost as if the house itself were ignoring him.

'I wonder why no one has ever fitted door bells,' he said.

'Probably not worth their while.'

'I'm going to put my card through the letter box,' said Cooper. 'Then at least we'll have made contact, of a kind.'

He scribbled a note on the back of the card and pushed it through the door. At number 3 he did the same thing, after he got no reply to his knock. But then he looked at Tracy Udall.

'Can you hear it?' he said. 'There's definitely someone at home somewhere. It sounds like children.'

'I think you're right. It's coming from that direction.'

Cooper walked along the row of houses towards the sound of laughter. He followed the muddy track past the front gates to the end of the terrace. Here, the track made a sharp turn at the last house and vanished behind it. He kept walking, skirting the deep puddles that had gathered in ruts underneath the shadow of the blank gable end. A skim of oil had formed on the surface of the water in the puddles.

Ahead of him, the track continued for another fifty yards, towards more trees. But on his right must be the yard that the brick passages ran into.

Then Cooper stopped. He was amazed to find that there was another row of houses facing the back of Waterloo Terrace. There were eight of them again, all of the same construction – black brick, with an arched passageway between each pair. But all of these homes were unoccupied, and had long since been abandoned. Their windows were broken and their doors stood open, or had been removed altogether. Some of the slates were missing from the roofs, and grass was growing in the guttering. One of the downspouts had collapsed, and water was dripping from the end of the amputated section of pipe. The wall of the house clearly showed the path of the water, where it had discoloured the brick as it trickled towards the ground. In the middle of the row was its name, marked out in a decorative brick panel a couple of feet below the roof. Trafalgar Terrace.

Cooper looked at the yard. On this side, it was protected by a six-foot wire-mesh fence. Inside, he glimpsed stacks of railway sleepers, roof tiles and old tyres. Just on the other side of the fence, two girls were standing barefoot in an old tin bath of the kind that miners once used to wash themselves in front of the fire. The girls were each holding the hand of a woman who stood outside the bath, and they were paddling excitedly in a thick, viscous substance like heavy brown mud. It had splashed up their legs and on to their clothes, but they didn't seem to care. They were having a wonderful time.

It was the first time Cooper had seen anybody in or near Waterloo Terrace enjoying themselves, and it was like a breath of fresh air. He laughed.

'That looks fun!' he called.

But their laughter stopped immediately, and their smiles faded when they saw him.

'I hope your mum doesn't mind you getting mud on your clothes. My mother always did when I played in the mud.'

All three of them stared at him silently. Cooper felt irrationally disappointed and hurt. He recognized a tinge of guilt, too – guilt that he had been responsible for destroying that moment of innocent enjoyment.

The mud they were trampling was almost red, and he could smell the earthy aroma from here. But there was no clay soil in this area. The Dark Peak was on acid, peaty soil that formed a different kind of mud altogether – the black, slimy stuff that hikers sank up to their knees in on the summit of Black Hill and Bleaklow. The clay must have been brought in specially. But for what purpose? Was it just for the girls to play in? Or had they borrowed it from some other job their parents were using it for?

'I don't want to stop you,' he said. 'Don't mind me.'

But the girls continued to stare at him until he walked past them and on to the back lane. Cooper thought of his nieces, who weren't far from the ages of the two Oxley girls. He thought about how devastated he would be if Amy and Josie began to regard him with the same fear and suspicion that he had seen on the faces of the Oxley girls, the same dislike and refusal to communicate.

But Amy and Josie weren't Oxleys, they were his nieces. He was their uncle Ben, and they had known him all their lives. They were family to each other, and it made a difference.

At least, it made a difference in the Cooper family.

He looked again at the ruins of Trafalgar Terrace. This was obviously where most of the pigeons lived. They sat in fidgeting rows along the roof ridge, and they were nesting on the window ledges on the upper floors, where a few bits of straw lay among shreds of rotten wood and broken glass from the windows.

'You've no right to be down here.'

Lucas Oxley was standing in front of a gate in the wire fence of his yard. He had a hammer in one hand, and a dozen rusty nails clutched in his other fist. Cooper looked around for something that Lucas might have been nailing, but could see nothing new among the debris on the grass.

Cooper could hear a sort of scurrying and rustling sound behind Oxley. It was coming from among the railway sleepers and tyres stacked in the yard, or perhaps from one of the passages that ran between the houses. Somebody was busy back there. Cooper pictured some of the other Oxleys going about their business, whispering to each other cautiously – knowing, without being told, that there was a stranger nearby. He was becoming convinced that the Oxleys could smell him coming. Maybe if he chose a different aftershave and deodorant next time he made his Sunday-morning trip to Somerfield's, it would confuse the scent, let him get closer to the nest before they recognized him.

'Good afternoon, Mr Oxley,' he said.

Oxley put the handful of nails into a pocket of his jacket, leaving one hand free. He shifted his grip on the shaft of the hammer. Then he looked at Cooper for a while.

There was a smothered laugh from the yard. It was a male laugh – one of the older Oxley sons. Whoever was back there, they sounded to be dragging something heavy across the ground, something that scraped on the concrete and landed with a thud when it was dropped.

Tracy Udall came to stand at Cooper's side, but sensibly said nothing. Lucas Oxley ignored her.

'Weather's not too good this morning,' said Cooper. 'A bit wetter than it has been lately.'

Oxley nodded cautiously.

'But you're still managing to get a few jobs done outdoors, I see.'

'What?'

'You're getting a few jobs done. Mending a fence, are you?'

'What's that supposed to mean?'

'Nothing. And you're keeping your lads busy round the back there, by the sound of it?'

'They're good lads.'

'I'm sure they are.'

'Lads always get into a bit of bother now and then. It means nothing.'

'No.'

'They're good lads.'

'We only wanted a few words, sir.'

'About anything particular? Or were you just wanting to pass the time of day? Because if you have, you've come to the wrong place.'

'It's about Neil Granger, sir.'

'Aye?'

'We're trying to find out how he died.'

'We have to bury him. It's your job to find out how he died. If you've a mind to.'

'Of course we've a mind to. But we need help.'

'Aye. You come asking for help now, but you're never around when other folks need help.'

'Do you remember Emma Renshaw, Mr Oxley?' said Cooper desperately.

'Of course I do.'

'Neil knew her very well, didn't he?'

'Everybody knew her. Now, if I ask you to leave my property, you have to – I know that. Unless you're here to arrest somebody. Are you going to do that?'

'Not today, Mr Oxley.'

Cooper turned away, and looked up towards where the road should be. He couldn't make it out because of the thick screen of trees in the way. Out of the corner of his eye, he saw Udall raise her shoulders, as if adjusting her belt. It was a discreet shrug, and a question: *Are we wasting our time here?*

'You really can't see much from down here, can you?' said Cooper.

'They built the houses like this so nobody had to look at them,' said Oxley sourly.

Was that almost a bit of conversation?

'So what were they originally?'

'Railwaymen's cottages. You'd think they'd have built them in stone, wouldn't you?'

'Yes.'

'But the railway company said they had a policy to build their workers' houses all the same. Well, if you ask me, they had a big contract with a brick company, and got their bricks dirt cheap, like everything else.'

Cooper felt they were making contact, even striking up a conversation. He took a step forward towards the fence, so that he didn't have to raise his voice quite so much. The Alsatian stood up. Cooper stopped.

'What about members of your family, Mr Oxley?' said Udall, recognizing the moment to divide attention. 'Might some of them have been around at that time and seen something?'

'Scott was probably at the pub Friday night. You could ask him. But he isn't home.'

'No, we've tried.'

'The young ones would be home at that time,' said Oxley.

'Are you sure?'

'Sure. They're good lads.'

'What about Frances?' said Cooper. 'Or is it Fran? At number 5 – she doesn't seem to be home either.'

'Fran has a job.'

Oxley said it as if he expected them to be surprised. Cooper found that he actually was, and mentally chided himself for forming pre-conceptions. Lucas might have a job as well, for all he knew. And Scott, too.

'Is Fran working today, Mr Oxley?'

'She works in a café, over in Holmfirth. She won't be back until later. She has to use the bus.'

'Right.'

'Did you see some kids up on the road?' said Oxley.

Cooper nodded. 'There were a bunch near the bus stop.'

'Was Jake among them? Little lad, younger than the others. He has a bad leg.'

'I didn't notice.'

'There's nothing wrong with any of them,' said Oxley. 'They're all good lads.'

'I'm sure they are, sir.'

'And I'll tan the hides off them, if they're not. Now, you've been asked to leave, and you're trespassing.'

COOPER TOOK A last look at the yard as he turned to leave. He took particular note of the vehicles he could see parked in among the pallets and old tyres. There was a light blue Transit van and a small flat-bed lorry, but they were at the wrong angle for him to make out the registration numbers.

Tracy Udall made a helpless gesture at him as they walked back up the track past Waterloo Terrace.

'Where does Lucas Oxley work, Tracy?' said Cooper. 'What's his job?'

'I think you're asking the question wrong,' said Udall. 'I don't think he has a job exactly.'

'He isn't registered for unemployment benefit. I checked.'

'No. I suppose you might say he's self-employed. And he works wherever work is to be had.'

'Mmm. That sounds like a definition of "criminal" to me.'

'Did you notice all the stuff round the back of the houses in Waterloo Terrace? Stacks of pallets? Roof tiles? Tyres? Fence posts? He's trading, that's what he's doing. I imagine he'll pick up anything that he can get cheap – maybe just for the cost of a bit of effort by his lads to collect the stuff and bring it back to Withens. Then, if anyone around here wants some fence posts or roof tiles, they know where to come. I'm betting he sells some of the stuff out of the back of a van at car boot sales and cattle markets, too.'

'Legally?'

'It's mostly legal, I should think.'

'Tell me about the bit that isn't.'

'Well, let me put it this way – I wouldn't take the tiles off my roof and leave them by the roadside overnight. And I wouldn't park a lorry with empty pallets on it anywhere accessible.'

'But who's going to know one pallet from another?'

'Exactly.'

'Some of the sons work, though, don't they?'

'You mean, do they have jobs?'

'Yes. Jobs where they go off to work and earn an honest living, like you and me.'

'They do bits of casual labouring, I think. There's still some farm work to be had at certain times of the year, and beating for the shoots. But, mostly, they'll be hiring themselves out as labour with the van or the flat-bed lorry.'

'They don't sound like they're your antique thieves, anyway.'

'No, I never really thought they were.'

'Are we no nearer getting a lead on the thefts?'

'The people we've interviewed so far are small-scale. We don't think they're responsible for the majority of thefts. It's going to take a lot more work.'

AS THEY HEADED back towards Udall's car, Cooper saw the bus coming down the hill. A woman got off at the stop in the car park and began to walk across the road towards Waterloo Terrace.

'I'll catch you up, Tracy,' said Cooper. 'I won't be a minute.'

The woman was wearing jeans and a dark coat and carrying a shoulder bag. Cooper watched her approach the terrace. She went straight up the path of number 5 and used a key to enter the house.

'Fran Oxley,' Cooper said to himself. 'So you're home, then. And you can't pretend that you're not.'

BY THE TIME he got to the house, Fran Oxley had already gone inside and shut the door. Cooper waited a couple of minutes to let her see his card and read it, then he walked up the path and knocked.

She must have been standing right behind the door, because she opened it with his card still in her hand. She looked at him blankly, then at the card, and he could see her putting two and two together without any trouble. The Oxleys had no trouble recognizing a police officer when they saw one. He might as well be carrying a neon sign around on his head.

'Is this you?' she said, tapping the card.

'Yes. Are you Frances Oxley?'

'I don't have anything to say.'

'If I could just ask you a few questions.'

'I don't have to answer any questions.'

'I was talking to your father earlier on –'

'You've been talking to Dad?' she said incredulously.

'Yes, Mr Lucas Oxley.'

'Then you'll have found out everything you're going to hear from this family.'

Cooper tried to look past her into the house. He had been concentrating on his body language as much as his words. He was hoping Fran would be the one member of the Oxley family to recognize that he wasn't a threat. He was hoping that she might even invite him into the house. But she hadn't quite gone for it yet.

'It's about Neil Granger,' said Cooper. 'Your cousin Neil.'

Fran Oxley hesitated, looked at his card as if to give it back to him, but hung on to it instead. She looked up the terrace along the row of doors.

'I'd like you to leave now,' she said.

BEN COOPER HAD rarely felt so impotent as he stood in the track watching the houses. He could hear children running up the passage behind the terrace, whispering to each other and brushing against the fencing. Smoke began to rise from one of the chimneys, and the smell of cooking was coming from somewhere, maybe from the open window at number 1. If he wasn't mistaken, the children were going to be served microwaved pizza for tea. He couldn't quite name the flavour, but it was something with onions, and the smell was making him salivate. Even worse was the feeling of isolation when Cooper heard a back door slam and the voices of the children were cut off as they entered one of the houses. That eerie Withens silence fell again, broken only by a clap of wings from pigeons taking off from the roof.

He began to feel foolish and lonely standing there trying to picture the scene indoors. He was frustrated not to know for sure which of the houses the children had gone into, or which adult was in charge of the microwave. Or was it an adult? Any one of the older Oxley children would be perfectly capable of taking a couple of pizzas out of the freezer and opening a family-sized tin of baked beans. Or maybe even one of the younger kids. Some children learned to look after themselves from a very early age, out of sheer necessity. And the Oxleys were nothing if not independent.

'Damn and blast.'

Cooper began to walk back to the car, feeling like the single person at Christmas, shut out of all the family fun just when everybody was supposed to be enjoying themselves most. He felt exposed, too, as if the whole population of Withens was watching him from behind its curtains, laughing at his powerlessness.

'Diane, you don't understand,' he said. 'It's time you came down here and saw for yourself.'

But not all the Oxley children were home for their tea. There were three boys standing in the road in front of the bus shelter. They had been playing with a football, but now one of them was holding it under his arm. As Cooper watched, the youngest one, Jake, began to make his way across the road towards the other two boys. He walked with a noticeable limp, as if one leg were shorter than the other. But it didn't seem to hinder him too much. When one of the others threw the ball down again, he ran for it nimbly enough, and kicked it with his good leg towards the car park.

It was the stationary car standing in the middle of the road that drew Cooper's attention from the boys. The vehicle was a Mitsubishi pick-up, with its engine still running as if it had come to a sudden halt. But it stood in the centre of the carriageway, where it would cause an obstruction if anyone wanted to get past.

Then Cooper recognized the driver. It was Michael Dearden, frozen behind his steering wheel, staring at the Oxley boys like a rabbit caught in headlights. Cooper had rarely seen a grown man look so frightened.

Chapter Twenty-Three

WEDNESDAY

RANDY HAD SPILLED soil out of a plant pot in the conservatory. Ben Cooper brushed it up, rearranged the pots more neatly on their shelves, pushed the cat's basket back into its corner and straightened the plaid blanket it was using as a bed.

He looked for other things to tidy, decided that the back door needed painting some time soon, brushed some cobwebs off a pane of glass. He stared through the glass, where he could make out the shapes of the trees against the lights of the houses in Meadow Road. The branches were just starting to come into leaf, and their outlines against the light were fuzzier and less stark than they had been all winter. Growth was progressing here, too.

He went back into the kitchen and shut out the sight of the garden. In the porch, there were some letters behind the front door. One advantage of living in town was that his mail came early in the morning, before he left for work if he was on a day shift. At Bridge End Farm, out there beyond even the smell of the town, the mail was delivered about lunchtime.

'What have we got today then, Randy? Would you like a new credit card? A loan to help you pay for a foreign holiday, perhaps? Want to join a book club?'

Randy looked at him contemptuously and licked his lips.

'Yes, I know what you want. I was only kidding. Hello, what's this? A postcard.'

The postcard had a picture of Chatsworth House on it. He always liked to try to figure out who a postcard was from before he turned it over to look at the message, but he couldn't think who would bother to send him a card from Chatsworth, when it was only a few miles away.

When he finally looked and saw who the card was from, his first uncharitable thought was that she must have stolen it from the souvenir shop. But that didn't make sense, really. She would have had to pay to get into Chatsworth House in the first place.

The message said: 'Sorry about the other day. You were great, so thanks. I know you'll make the right decision.' It was signed: 'Love, A'.

'It's from Angie,' said Cooper.

Randy made a noise like a bird chirruping, then began to cough, as though trying to clear a hair ball from his throat.

'Give over,' said Cooper. 'You're not dying of starvation just yet.'

The cat got up and stalked off towards the kitchen with its tail twitching.

'Angie,' said Cooper, reading the postcard again. 'What does she mean by "I know you'll make the right decision?" What right decision?'

This time, the cat didn't answer. It was in the kitchen and pretending it couldn't hear him. Cooper turned the postcard back over and frowned at the picture of Chatsworth House, as if it could have some hidden significance he was supposed to figure out. Chatsworth? Was there a connection? Was she trying to tell him something?

'It's too subtle for me,' he said.

He dropped the mail on the table and headed towards the kitchen. 'Randy,' he said, 'why the hell have I started talking to myself?'

COPIES OF THE Social Services report on the Oxleys had arrived on Cooper's desk at West Street. The visits to Waterloo Terrace were summarized, along with meetings at the Social Services offices. It took several sheets. Cooper knew he was unlikely to have time to read the older stuff. The visits had started in 1986, and the most recent was four weeks ago, at the beginning of April.

Taken together with visits by their landlords, Peak Water, by officials from other council departments such as environmental health and education, and from the police, it would make a pretty intimidating list. No wonder his own appearances day after day had failed to impress the Oxleys. He must have seemed the latest of a long line of official busybodies, anxious to interfere in their lives, poking their noses in, demanding information about their private affairs. And all, obviously, with the purpose of finding an excuse to get them out of their homes. The fact that any of the Oxleys had spoken to him at all ought to be taken as a compliment. Even 'bugger off' was more than some of the council representatives had achieved.

Cooper took a call while he was reading the reports on the Oxleys boys again. It was Fran Oxley.

'Do you still want to talk?' she said.

'Of course.'

'I thought you might have given up by now.'

'I won't be giving up.'

'Can you come to see me tonight? It'll have to be latish, about nine? I'll be home from work then.'

'Yes, I'll be there. What do you want to talk about?'

Fran hesitated a moment, but seemed to make up her mind. 'If you come tonight,' she said, 'I'll tell you about Neil.'

Cooper was smiling when he put the phone down. The fact of somebody actually speaking to him gave him a surge of satisfaction. For a moment, it crossed his mind that it might be a con, a practical joke by the Oxleys. But Fran had sounded sincere, if a little hesitant.

Humming quietly to himself, he went back to the reports. It was then that he noticed the Oxleys had an Anti-Social Behaviour Order in force against them.

'For goodness' sake. No wonder Lucas Oxley made such a point of saying he wouldn't tolerate his lads getting in trouble.'

Cooper looked up guiltily, hoping no one in the office had heard him. He didn't even have the cat for an excuse.

An ASBO made a difference. Persistent juvenile offenders were a thorny problem for the police. Experienced defendants knew to plead 'not guilty' to charges every single time. They had learned that it meant their case would have to go to a crown court trial and a jury verdict. Well, you have to try your luck, they would say. Then they would make up a story to explain their actions – any story at all, it didn't really matter. Often, they put up no defence at all, but left it to their defence lawyer to pick holes in the prosecution case and expose any procedural flaws that could be found.

Some defenders had become expert at getting an acquittal on a technicality, picking at the threads of the procedural detail, so that even the most damning evidence of guilt might never be considered by the court. Police officers had learned that the most important thing in their lives was to follow correct procedure, if they were ever going to get a conviction. The fully documented chain of evidence, the properly executed search warrant, the interview conducted to the letter of the rule book – those were the only real strengths they could call on, under the scrutiny of a court. Justice, truth, and the suffering of victims were insignificant side issues.

And even time could be against them. The defence might find ways of delaying a case so long that witnesses forgot what they had seen, or changed their minds, or decided it might be more sensible, after all, not to appear in court.

But an Anti-Social Behaviour Order could be taken out in civil proceedings, which meant the same burden of proof wasn't needed. Just the number of complaints from neighbours could be enough for the council to obtain an ASBO, which obliged the family involved to refrain from anti-social behaviour for a specific period – in this case, five years. But the sting in the tail was that, although an ASBO was a civil action, breaking one was a criminal offence and could mean a jail sentence.

Of course, the threat posed by an ASBO might also mean that people would go to greater lengths to conceal offences.

Cooper thought about Lucas Oxley. He seemed like a man genuinely passionate about keeping his family in line, but also obsessive about preserving their privacy. What lengths would Lucas go to if he thought one of his family had stepped over that line?

Also in the heap of paper on his desk, Cooper found copies of the conviction records for the Oxleys and began to thumb through them. He saw that three years previously, Scott Oxley had been convicted of criminal damage, and given probation. No surprise there. But he had been charged jointly with Craig Alan Oxley, aged sixteen.

'Who's Craig?' said Cooper.

Then there was another conviction. Two years ago, for taking a vehicle without the owner's consent, Scott had been sentenced to fifty hours community service. He was charged jointly with Craig Alan Oxley, aged seventeen.

'Craig? There isn't a Craig.'

Cooper scanned the rest of the records. He wondered if that was how most of the Oxleys spent their time – doing community service instead of working for a living.

'But the point is, who's Craig?'

Was he a middle brother? A cousin? Cooper searched for a separate record for Craig Alan Oxley. His address was given as 5 Waterloo Terrace, Withens. That was Fran Oxley's house.

If only the Oxleys were on the electoral roll, it would help a lot. But the Oxleys probably believed that if they were on the electoral roll, all sorts of people would come looking for them, to make them pay Council Tax and income tax.

And Fran's husband – what was his name? Barry Cully, that was it. But he wasn't her husband. Fran had told him that Barry was an electrician and was away working in Saudi Arabia at the moment. So Craig could be living at Fran's house.

But then Cooper turned to the last page of Craig Oxley's court records. No, he wasn't living in Fran's house. He was in Lancashire. For his last offence he had been sent to the Young Offenders' Institution at Hindley.

Cooper thought about trying to obtain school records for the Oxleys. Of course, he wasn't even certain that they were all Lucas's children. But one thing he felt sure of – for the Oxley boys, school would mean social isolation. Only at home in Withens were they among their own kind.

DI HITCHENS PUT his head round the door of the CID room and called Cooper away from his reports.

Cooper had already stopped humming after reading about the ASBO and Craig Oxley. But this wasn't a good sign, either.

'We've pulled in one of Neil Granger's associates, by the name of David Senior,' said Hitchens. 'He seems to have the closest links to Granger, and he was actually seen near his house on Friday night, a few hours before Granger was killed.'

'Are we interviewing him, sir?'

'No, he's stewing in his own juices at the moment, waiting for the duty solicitor. But interestingly, we had a call from Granger's brother, who wants to talk to us.'

'You think he has some information on this Senior?'

'It seems likely. I'm scenting a breakthrough. You met Philip Granger, didn't you, Ben?'

'Yes, sir.'

'Let's go and see what he has to say, then.'

PHILIP GRANGER was looking a bit better than last time Cooper saw him. The initial shock had perhaps worn off now, and some more useful information might well be coming back to him. This was a strange time for relatives, following a suspicious death. Until someone was charged with murder, or twenty-eight days had passed, Neil Granger's body wouldn't be released for a funeral, so his brother might have to wait a month or so yet before he could start to put the whole business behind him.

'I heard that you've arrested David Senior,' he said.

'No. At the moment, he's helping us voluntarily,' said Hitchens.

Granger nodded. 'Right. But I think there might be something you haven't realized.'

'What's that, sir?'

'Neil was gay.'

Hitchens shrugged. 'So?'

Granger looked surprised at the DI's reaction and didn't seem to know what else to say for a moment. Cooper felt surprised, too, but concentrated on not giving it away in his expression.

'Neil didn't make any big deal of it,' said Granger. 'But he did get the piss taken out of him by some of our cousins. That's one reason he was keen to move out of Withens, you see. I thought it might make a difference – Neil being gay, I mean.'

'It doesn't make any difference to us, sir,' said Hitchens. 'These days we aim to treat everyone fairly, regardless of ethnic origin, religious belief, gender or sexual orientation.'

'Oh.'

It might have been the first time that Philip Granger had heard the words, but they were familiar to Cooper. In fact, he was fairly sure they were on a noticeboard somewhere in the station under the heading 'Statement of Purpose'.

'I mean, the time has long since passed when the fact that your brother was gay would lead to us making any assumptions about his lifestyle or his associates,' said Hitchens.

'I see.' Granger looked almost disappointed. 'I thought I was helping.'

'Unless you're suggesting this has some direct relevance to the enquiry into your brother's death?'

'Well, I'm not sure,' said Granger. 'It's just that David Senior ... well, I don't know what connection you think he has to Neil. But they were ... they had a relationship.'

'Do you know anything else about David Senior?'

'He used to work at the chemicals factory with Neil. That's where they met, but that's all I know about him.'

'Does he ride a motorbike?'

Granger frowned. 'Not as far as I know. Why?'

'We were told that some of your brother's friends were bikers.'

'If it was Neil's neighbours who told you that, they probably meant me. I ride a motorbike.'

'Probably,' said Hitchens, as if that had confirmed what he suspected.

Now Granger looked a bit uncomfortable, perhaps feeling that he hadn't helped as much as he hoped he would.

'There *was* something else.'

'Yes, sir?'

'You were asking me about antiques and things ...'

'Have you remembered something?'

'I'm not sure. But there was a small box on the mantelpiece in Neil's house when I went there on Saturday. I didn't think much of it at the time, but I don't remember ever seeing it there before.'

Cooper searched his memory. He thought he had done pretty well checking the CD player, but he had never noticed the box.

'What was it made of?' he said.

'It was metal. Bronze or brass, I couldn't tell. About this big –' Granger held his hands a few inches apart.

Hitchens looked at Cooper, who shook his head. 'Well, well,' said Hitchens. 'Let's see if anyone else has noticed it.'

As soon as Philip Granger had left, DI Hitchens' manner changed. Cooper had to lengthen his stride to follow the DI back to his office.

'Is there a rush, sir?' he said.

'We have to get on to it straight away,' said Hitchens.

'This bronze or brass box, you mean?'

'Well, there's that as well.'

'And …?'

'I need to get somebody to work turning over the local arse bandits. They'll be shitting themselves knowing one of their bum chums has got himself done in.'

'But, sir, didn't you just say …?'

'Of course I did.' Hitchens stopped suddenly. 'You've got to be sensitive with bereaved relatives, you know, Cooper. Didn't they tell you that in training?'

'Yes, sir.'

'Well, then. Do you want to do bandits or box?'

'Box,' said Cooper.

Diane Fry and Gavin Murfin were on the M6 motorway, approaching the junction with the M5 north of Birmingham. They were already well inside the vast urban sprawl at the heart of the Black Country. It couldn't have looked more different from the empty wastes of peat moor around Withens.

'Is the Black Country the place where black pudding comes from?' said Murfin.

'Of course it isn't.'

'Well, I just wondered, like. I know Bakewell pudding comes from Bakewell, so I thought –'

'No, Gavin, it doesn't.'

'OK.'

They were passing through the western edge of Smethwick, having taken the wrong exit from the M5 when Murfin got excited about seeing the West Bromwich Albion football ground. Fry was starting to feel edgy as they came closer to her old stamping grounds. The feeling of tension was like steel springs trying to pull her into the air, so that she hardly seemed to be touching her car seat. But she knew she mustn't take out her own edginess on Gavin Murfin.

'What about blackberry crumble, then?' said Murfin.

'No, Gavin! Now, will you shut up about it?'

'All right.'

Fry remembered all too clearly shopping with her friends in Birmingham or at the Merry Hill shopping centre, touring the Birmingham clubs, drinking lager while she listened to the boys talking about West Brom.

They drove through Langley and hit traffic at the junction with the A4123 Wolverhampton Road, where the signs all seemed to point to the Merry Hill shopping centre. It had been Fry's shopping mecca as a teenager, the place where all her friends had gone to meet on a

Saturday – not to spend money, because they didn't have any. Well, not unless somebody had nicked a few quid from their mum. They went just to walk around, to be there and be seen there. It made you part of the crowd, part of the Merry Hill lot.

With her friends, she had come to know the place so well that it was like a second home. They had learned all the ways of avoiding the security guards and the CCTV cameras. But there had been others attracted to Merry Hill shopping centre, too – men who had money, and had seemed attractive. And perhaps a little dangerous, too.

'Black Forest gateau?' said Murfin.

THEY TURNED SOUTH on Wolverhampton Road and headed towards Warley and Bearwood. And as soon as she saw the big white cross picked out in brickwork on the tower of Warley Baptist Church, she knew she was back home.

There were starlings roosting on the high ledges, their white droppings streaking brickwork that had always seemed a little ornate for a Baptist church. They stopped to fill up with petrol. On the forecourt of the petrol station, Fry saw the familiar blue-and-cream buses passing, and heard the sound of a genuine West Indian accent.

Murfin was intrigued by the Caribbean restaurants and Punjabi food stores they passed along the road.

'A Somali takeaway!' he said. 'We don't get those in Edendale.'

'You're not getting one here, either,' said Fry. 'Turn left up ahead.'

They turned into a housing estate and drove through the streets to Hilltop. Murfin didn't question her directions, knowing that she was familiar with the area. They passed Warley High School on Pound Road. It was the middle of the morning, lesson time, so there were no kids hanging around outside. Fry heard a bell ring somewhere and was glad they were already past. She didn't want to be in sight of the school when the kids appeared.

Warley Baths were now called a swimming centre. Further up Thimblemill Road was the library, where Fry had spent even more time, sitting among the books, looking for something she could relate to, something that told a story similar to her own. She had never found anything.

At the infant school someone had planted a yucca in a concrete flower bed, and there were security shutters over some of the windows. But it still looked much the same. Next door was the King's Community Church. Had it been called that back in the 1980s? She had a feeling that 'community' had been an invention of the eighties. Before that, people hadn't felt the need to use the name. A community was something you just *were*.

They negotiated their way through a series of little roundabouts, each with its cluster of shops and a pub. And on George Road she found the Plough still there at one end of the road, with the George Hotel at the other, near the infant school. Familiar places, all of them. Yet alien now, too, like backdrops for a recurrent bad dream.

From the roundabout near the Hilltop shops, she could see the view across the valley to more houses.

There were some masts on the horizon, but she couldn't remember what they were for.

'Do you want to stop, Gavin?' she said. 'You can get a pie in the shop over there.'

'Why, sure,' said Murfin, surprised.

While he went into the shop, she walked a few yards back to the roundabout. Yes, the little brick semi was still there, too. It wasn't a council house any more, by the look of it, but had probably been bought from the council by its occupants. The new owners had put in a Georgian-style front door and leaded windows, removed the crumbling rendering from the walls and covered them with artificial stone. They had painted all the woodwork white, and they had even erected a little wooden fence, which symbolically separated the house from the pavement.

For many years, Fry hadn't been able to hear certain songs cropping up on the radio without being transported back to Warley. Anything by Right Said Fred or Salt 'n' Pepa turned some kind of switch in her mind, and she instantly found herself again in that crumbling council house on the Hilltop estate. She would be lying on her bed in her own room, listening to a cheap stereo and holding the diary she had hidden under her spare sweaters in a bottom drawer, just as Emma Renshaw had done.

In those days, there had been particular pieces of music that she had used to try to lift her mood, and others she had chosen because they matched her depression, or because their words allowed her to wallow in tearful self-pity. Now, they all meant the same thing. They all

recalled the bedroom and the diary, the painful recording of the details of her life, the failure of a miracle to
happen.

Fry stood for few moments longer, looking at the window of the front bedroom. Then, beginning to get embarrassed, she turned away.

Murfin was waiting for her by the car, smiling content-
edly. Food always made him happy. Fry could get envious
of him, if she spent too much time in his company.

'We can cut through this next street, Gavin,' she said.

'OK.'

They passed Warley Water Tower, so like a medieval
fortress from a distance that it had fuelled her fantasies
as a child. And beyond the golf club were Warley Woods.
The woods seemed to mark the southern boundary of her
territory, with Wolverhampton Road at the western edge,
providing the escape route into town. The woods looked
neater and more well trained now, less threatening in
their orderliness, but also less like a place that might offer
a refuge when you needed one.

In a short time, the place had changed a lot. Yet Fry
knew she would have difficulty putting her finger on what
exactly it was that had changed, what the subtle differences were that made this place so alien from the world
she had known as a teenager.

She was glad she'd come, though. Warley was the
physical link to her past, and seeing it had helped her
to put it into perspective. Finding that the house on the
Hilltop estate was nothing like it had been fifteen years
ago gave her the power to sever the link in her memory.

The bedroom and the diary couldn't exist behind that stone cladding and the leaded windows. The music had faded with the sight of the little white fence.

And now, maybe, she could put the whole of her past to rest.

Murfin had stopped the car at a crossroads, where there were long rows of shops running to right and left.

'This is Bearwood,' said Fry. 'Where Emma Renshaw went missing, too.'

Chapter Twenty-Four

IT TURNED OUT that the search of Neil Granger's house had recovered the box. It had been logged by the exhibits officer, but its existence was buried in a mass of paperwork. It was even smaller than Neil's brother had recollected – about four inches long and three inches wide, and it was made of brass, not bronze.

'It looks Indian,' said Ben Cooper.

'Expert, are you?'

'No, sir.'

'You won't mind if we get a second opinion then?'

Cooper could see that the DI was irritated to have had to wait for a member of the public to point out the box. It was the only item that resembled an antique in Neil Granger's house, and now he would have to explain to Mr Kessen why it had only just turned up.

'Fingerprints?' said Cooper.

Hitchens sighed. 'Two recent sets. Neil Granger's and his brother's. We took the brother's prints for elimination when we knew he'd been in the house.'

'He must have touched it when he noticed it on Saturday.'

'Check with him anyway.'

'I don't suppose there's anything in it, sir?'

'Not a thing,' said Hitchens. 'It would have been nice, wouldn't it?'

He passed the bag containing the box to Cooper. 'See what you can do with it, then. Origin, value – ownership, if you can.'

'OK.'

'That'll take you a while, I expect. What else were you supposed to be working on?'

'Withens,' said Cooper. 'The Oxleys.'

'Ah well, you'll probably get round to them later this afternoon. I don't suppose they'll miss you.'

'I think I'm the highlight of their day, sir,' said Cooper.

AFTER SEVERAL FRUITLESS phone calls trying to establish the ownership of a brass box that everyone agreed might or might not be Indian, Ben Cooper finally tracked down a dealer in Crookes who offered to take a closer look at the box. Crookes was on the western outskirts of Sheffield, and could be reached via the A628. It was too tempting to resist. He made an appointment that allowed him plenty of time to take another quick look at Withens on the way.

It was nearly four o'clock by the time Cooper reached the village. He saw straight away that the postman came late in Withens. It was probably the last place he reached on his delivery round from Sheffield, or wherever the nearest sorting office was. A distinctive red van was parked outside the Quiet Shepherd, and Cooper walked over to wait for the postman to come out. The postie was in his thirties, fair-haired and blue-eyed, and wearing a navy blue Royal Mail body-warmer. He agreed he was nearing the end of his round, and seemed quite happy to spend a couple of minutes talking about his customers in Withens.

'They're a mixed bunch here,' he said. 'Take the folk at Waterloo Terrace, the Oxleys. They don't seem to want their letters at all. At number 1, they nailed the letter box up once. I had to report it, back at the office, and the manager spoke to them. But you'd be surprised at the attitude some people have. I mean, it's not my fault if they don't like the mail they get, is it?'

'No.'

'But there's the lady at the opposite end. Mrs Wallwin, number 7. She hardly gets anything. Sometimes, I collect together a few bits of junk mail and stuff that's been sent to other people, and I put it through her door, just so that she's got something to open now and then.'

'You do?'

Cooper remembered the envelopes he had seen on Mrs Wallwin's table. 'You're a winner!' 'Open now for some wonderful news!' He had assumed Mrs Wallwin used them for lighting her fire, like everybody else. But perhaps she kept them as a sign that somebody out there was thinking about her. Did she realize it was only the postman?

The postman seemed to misread Cooper's expression as disapproval. 'Of course, I know I shouldn't do that, really. I'd probably get the sack if some busybody shopped me for it. But it's doing no harm. It's only stuff nobody else wants, isn't it?'

'You're not kidding. I'd *pay* you not to deliver my junk mail,' said Cooper.

Since he'd moved into his flat three months before, he'd been gathering mail addressed to every previous tenant. Some of them had been dead for years, according to Mrs Shelley. And some of them had strange tastes in mail-order items, too.

The postman was reassured. 'The other lot who can be a bit of a nuisance are the Old Rectory folk. Name of Renshaw.'

'Oh?'

'They hang around at the gate waiting for me to get there. I think they must be at the upstairs window watching for me coming down the hill, because by the time I get to them they're jumping up and down with impatience and snapping at me for being late. Which I never am, I might say. I get up here pretty much on time, no matter what the weather's like in the winter. They don't seem to appreciate that.'

'So the Renshaws are eager for their mail?'

'Aye.' The postman sniffed. 'Trouble is, by the way they react, I don't think I've ever brought them what they're hoping for. I suppose *that's* my fault, too.'

'The Oxleys,' said Cooper, 'do you ever have any problems with a dog there? A long-haired Alsatian?'

'No, I never have a problem,' said the postman. 'I know it's there, all right, but they keep it shut up in the yard. They never let the dog out at the front of the house. Well, not unless they *really* don't like the look of you.'

COOPER WAS SURPRISED to find a Peak Park Ranger in the car park. Of course, the village was within the national park, though it was difficult to remember sometimes. He supposed the area was valued more for its surrounding habitat of peat bogs than for the village itself.

Cooper introduced himself and asked about the moorland fire that had been burning since Friday night.

'There are still a few patches smouldering under the surface,' said the Ranger. 'They might persist for another week or so. Some fires last for months in the peat, you know. We're lucky it wasn't a summer one. But that's another few acres we've lost up there. With fires and erosion, we'll lose the whole bloody landscape in a few years.'

'Is it that bad?'

'Have you seen the erosion recently? The moor is eroding, the sphagnum moss is dying, the peat is disappearing down to the bedrock.'

'Yes, I know.'

Many thousands of pairs of feet were wearing tracks across the plateaux of the Dark Peak every year, and water running through hundreds of groughs and channels was washing away yet more peat. In places it had been scoured away down to depths of twenty feet, creating deep valleys in the black crust and washing the peat away year by year. It ran down into the water catchment area and into the reservoirs, where the water was brown and tasted peaty.

'Acid rain is the real problem though,' said the ranger. 'Long term.'

'Really?'

'It's been falling on us for decades – for centuries. It's been falling on us ever since the factories in Manchester began to belch out their pollution over there. The prevailing wind blows all the pollution in this direction, and it falls in the rain when it reaches high ground. It's the acid rain that's killed the moss. And it was the moss that bound the surface. Now the moss is gone and the peat is exposed, so it gets washed away year by year, inch by inch. Eventually, the hills will be nothing but bare rock. No more banks of purple heather in the summer, no sheep, no grouse, no songbirds. No wildlife of any kind. That's what acid rain means to us.'

'The moors are a sitting target, I suppose?'

'Absolutely. It's only a matter of time before they're gone. And fires like this one don't help. Some fourteen-year-old kid on a school outing from Manchester started it. We don't know whether he was smoking a fag and dropped it, or whether he lit a fire deliberately, which is just as likely, in my view. But a fire takes days to put out and longer to damp down, and this one has already destroyed thirty acres of moor. Another thirty acres gone. Maybe the acid rain isn't quick enough. Now Manchester is sending its kids out here to destroy the moors faster.'

'Long-term damage, I suppose?'

'I said "destroyed", didn't I? How long do you think it takes peat to form?'

Cooper shook his head.

'Two hundred thousand years. Even presuming we're still around after all that time, would we see new peat? Well, the fact is that peat forms from the undecomposed remains of – guess what? – sphagnum moss. No, when this peat is gone, there won't be any more.'

'Do you know Withens? There's a family down there at Waterloo Terrace I'm interested in – the Oxleys.'

'Don't tell me about the Oxleys. Their kids like to set fires, just so they can hear the sirens and see the flashing lights as the fire appliances arrive. It breaks the boredom a bit. When we turn up, there's always a little crowd of excited youngsters. The ones that started the fire are probably among the spectators. But we're never going to be able to prove it.'

'There's a burnt-out house at the top of the road,' said Cooper.

'I remember that. It was empty for years and getting derelict. It had got so bad that nobody wanted to spend money on repairing it, I suppose. The local kids broke in and were using it. Then it started getting fires. We were called out there several times. Each time, there was a bit less of the building left. The roof fell in quite early on, and it wasn't really considered dangerous any more after that. But it still got set on fire regularly. I reckon the kids were dragging bits of wood up there to burn, once all the beams and doors and window frames had gone up in smoke.'

'Whatever happened to saving up the wood for bonfire night?' said Cooper.

'You're joking. What century are you living in?'

'It's what we did when I was kid. And that's only –'

'Last century, I expect.'

'Kids never did that where I lived,' said Cooper. 'They used to let other folk collect wood and pile up their bonfires, then they'd sneak in and set fire to them a few days before the fifth. They thought that was much more fun than collecting their own.'

The Ranger looked at him. 'Do you have any children of your own?'

'No.'

'Let me know in a few years' time, when you've managed it, and I'll come and give them a talk about fire safety.'

'Thanks a lot.'

The Ranger looked over Cooper's shoulder and gestured at something behind him. 'Well, look at him.'

Cooper turned and looked. It took him a moment to register what he was seeing. A small boy was walking past him, leaning forward to pull on a rope that was attached to a makeshift trolley. Its wheels rattled on the pavement as he passed. The trolley was full of sticks, perhaps a dozen of them, all a yard long and solid-looking.

'Hold on, son,' said Cooper.

But the boy was already a few yards past him and heading down the hill towards the Quiet Shepherd. He showed no intention of stopping.

Cooper began to walk behind him in the same direction. He noticed the limp in his left leg, and felt sure this was Jake Oxley.

'Where are you going with those sticks?'

'To the pub,' said the boy.

'What for?'

'You're a copper, aren't you?'

'Yes. What are you doing with those sticks?'

'That's my business. It's not copper's business.'

'It might be. Tell me, and we'll see. Where did you get the sticks from?'

The boy began to speed up as he approached the pub car park. The sticks bumped together and clattered as the trolley went over a kerb. Cooper lengthened his pace, aware of the ranger watching him.

'Stop a minute, son. I want to ask you something else.'

'You can't talk to me,' said the boy. 'I'm only nine.'

'So?'

'It means you have to talk to my dad.'

'And who's your dad?'

'I don't have to tell you that. I don't have to tell you anything. I'm only nine.'

Cooper noticed that the boy's limp didn't seem to hinder him.

'Is your name Oxley, by any chance?' he said.

'I'll report you to the Social Services. Then you'll get in trouble. You're not allowed to talk to me, because I'm vulnerable.'

'And you're only nine,' said Cooper.

'Yeah.'

The boy broke into a run across the car park and vanished into a side door of the pub. Cooper wasn't going to run. He didn't want to appear to be pursuing a nine-year-old child. It never looked good.

'With any luck, you won't make it to ten,' he said to the closed door.

Then he looked at the hill he would have to walk back up. With a sigh, Cooper sat down on the low wall around the pub car park. The parking area consisted of a wide patch of crushed stone, and large boulders had been left in position near the entrance and exit. There was even an outcrop of rock right in the middle. He couldn't figure out whether the rocks had been too big to bother moving when the car park had been created, or had been left there for picturesque effect.

Cooper noticed a building at the back of the pub. It was some kind of storage shed or garage, with wide doors that stood open at the moment. The interior looked intriguing.

He got up and strolled over towards the door, hoping no one was watching him from the windows of the pub. Inside the doors, trestles had been set up. At the moment, they supported wooden boards, much like the ones he had seen being fished out of the river a few days ago. If these were the same ones, they had been washed clean of slime and duckweed. They'd also had hundreds of nails hammered through them, so that the points protruded above the surface of the wood by a centimetre or so. Each board might have been a bed of nails for an Indian fakir, except that a layer of clay had been spread over the nails and smoothed out. A skin was starting to form on the clay.

Cooper shrugged, imagining some garden feature. Perhaps the landlord of the pub had been watching one of those gardening makeover programmes on TV.

He looked at the pub again. There was no sign of the boy with the sticks. But Cooper was sure he had been speaking to the Tiny Terror.

'WELL, WE ALL need a moment's rest from our labours.'

Cooper turned to find the Reverend Derek Alton watching him. Either he had moved very quietly, or Cooper hadn't been paying attention.

'I wasn't actually thinking of going into the pub. Not when I'm on duty.'

'Well, I'm off duty. Besides, I have a special dispensation.'

'Mr Alton, there was a young boy here a minute ago. Nine years old, with a slight limp.'

Alton nodded. 'That would be little Jake Oxley. Lucas's youngest boy.'

'I thought so. What happened to him? Did he have an accident?'

'You mean his leg? Yes, he was knocked down in the road, right in front of Waterloo Terrace there.'

'He was? By somebody passing through? No. I don't suppose so …'

'It would perhaps have been better that way,' said Alton. 'But not many people pass through here. Only those going to Shepley Head Lodge.'

'Did one of the Deardens knock him down?'

'Yes, it was Michael, in his four-wheel drive. It wasn't his fault, by all accounts. Jake seems to have run out of the entrance to Waterloo Terrace, right in front of him. Michael wasn't even speeding, but he couldn't stop in time. In fact, Jake was lucky – the car only caught him a glancing blow, but his leg was shattered. Because his bones are growing, they haven't healed properly, I think.'

'The Oxleys must have been very upset.'

'Oh, yes. But so was Michael. He was never charged with any offence, but guilt can be a terrible thing, all the same.'

Cooper looked up the road towards Shepley Head Lodge. 'Is that why Mr Dearden tries to avoid driving through Withens?'

'Well, wouldn't you? He has to drive past the same spot every time. And the Oxley children are always out playing by the side of the road, including Jake. Michael would rather go out of his way to avoid seeing Jake every day.'

'Thank you, Mr Alton.'

'Have I been of some help?'

'Yes, I think so.'

'I'll leave you to your work, then.'

Alton walked across the car park and went into the pub through the same side door that Jake Oxley had used. He was carrying a long bag over his shoulder, like a cricket bag or a soft case for a musical instrument of some kind.

Cooper watched him go. Maybe it was time to pay a visit to the pub. If he was lucky, he might be able fit it in after his drive into Sheffield.

'Well? Did you find out anything from the boy?' asked the Ranger, as Cooper struggled back to the car.

'Oh yes,' said Cooper. 'I found out he's only nine.'

THE HOUSE IN Darlaston Road was occupied by another group of students now, of course. As far as they were concerned, Neil Granger, Alex Dearden and Debbie Stark might as well never have existed, let alone Emma Renshaw.

But Diane Fry found it helped her just to stand outside the house and look up the road towards Birmingham, to note that the nearest bus stop was only about fifty yards away and to imagine Emma walking along the pavement towards the stop.

Emma could easily have walked that distance with her luggage. But did she? Or had Neil Granger or some-one else given her a lift? How could she ever know? No witnesses to Emma's last journey had been found at the time, let alone more than two years later.

Nevertheless, Fry had to make the attempt. She and Gavin Murfin took a side of the road each and tried des-perately to jog people's memories, with the help of the photographs of Emma.

'Most of them weren't even living around here then,' said Murfin, crossing the street to speak to Fry in between houses. 'Even those who were in the area two years ago look at me as though I'm round the twist.'

'I know.'

Fry looked at the fifty yards of pavement between 360B Darlaston Road and the bus stop, as if it might tell her something. She found it as difficult picturing Emma here as she had in the area where the mobile phone was discovered.

'I think Emma was picked up by someone,' she said. 'But it had to be someone she knew. So why didn't she tell any of the others that's what she was doing, Gavin?'

Murfin shrugged. 'Maybe the person picking her up was somebody she didn't want them to know about.'

As Fry watched, a cream-and-blue double-decker bus slowed down and stopped, blocking her view of the house completely.

'But who?' she said.

Chapter Twenty-Five

BEN COOPER HAD to steer the car carefully to avoid scraping his paintwork on the boulders as he drove into the entrance of the Quiet Shepherd's car park. He was already in a bad mood.

For a start, he was convinced the antiques dealer in Crookes had simply wanted a bit of attention, and that the leads he'd offered would turn out to be useless when they were checked out. After he had finally escaped from the dealer, Cooper had realized how hungry he was. He had no idea whether the pub in Withens served food, so he had grabbed a cheese sandwich from a corner shop on his way out of Sheffield. The cheese had been greasy and unidentifiable, and it lay uncomfortably on his stomach by the time he arrived at the Quiet Shepherd.

Inside, the pub was gloomy. The lower parts of the walls were dark wood panelling, with even darker wallpaper above it in a deep, sombre blue. Black-and-white photographs hung in frames on the walls, some of them showing views of an old railway station with steam trains standing at the platforms and dark tunnel mouths visible behind them. Either Woodhead or Dunford Bridge, he supposed.

But the first thing Cooper noticed was that a lot of noise was coming from the room above the bar. An awful lot of noise. In fact, it sounded as though several people were kicking their way through the floorboards, screaming at each other while they did it. There were other noises, too, like someone smashing up wooden furniture. The lights in the middle of the bar were swinging under the vibration.

Cooper looked at the landlord behind the counter. He was polishing glasses, apparently unconcerned that his pub was being demolished over his head. Cooper thought he could detect some kind of music behind the noise, too, so perhaps he had just happened to walk in while the local thrash metal band was practising. It might explain why there was no one else in the bar.

'We don't get much custom on a Wednesday night,' said the landlord, as if reading his mind. He put his towel down and smiled at Cooper. He had a couple of amalgam fillings on either side of his lower jaw that had gone black with age.

'So what's going on upstairs?' said Cooper.

'Old folk's bingo evening. They can get a bit rowdy. Some of them are terrors on those zimmer frames, you know.'

'Right.'

'They don't usually injure each other too much. But I'll give you a shout if I need any help chucking them out.'

The landlord began to edge away, snuffling a bit, as if to suggest that he really needed to find a man-sized tissue or he was going to do something disagreeable. Cooper listened to the noise for a while as he sipped his drink. There wasn't a great deal else to do, expect to study his own distorted reflection in the bottles hanging upside down in the optics behind the bar. There wasn't even a jukebox in here. He could see one through the other side, in the public bar. But judging by the colour of the walls in there, he knew the room would stink like a smoker's armpit.

'Did you know a young man called Neil Granger?' said Cooper.

'Yes, I heard about him. He used to come in here with the others.'

'The others?'

'His family. Friends. You know.'

'You heard he was killed?'

'Yes, very sad.'

'He was in here on the Friday evening, a few hours before he died,' said Cooper.

'Yes, that would be right.'

'Did he seem any different from usual?'

'Not at all. Though he left a bit earlier than the others.'

'There was a rehearsal that night.'

'Yes,' said the landlord cautiously.

'Just a minute – is that what's going on up there tonight?'

'Happen.'

'What do they call it?'

'The Border Rats.'

'What sort of thing is that? It sounds very noisy.'

'They're a bit secretive about it. Nobody's supposed to know until they do the performance.'

'Oh? And when is that?'

'Next weekend. May Day bank holiday.'

'I saw the Reverend Alton come in.'

'Did he?' said the landlord, surprised. 'Well, now.'

'And little Jake Oxley.'

'Yes, he'll be with his dad and his brothers.'

'Can I go up and see what they're doing?'

'No, I'm sorry. Like I say, it's all confidential. They've booked a private room, and that's that. I can't let anyone in.'

'You know I'm a police officer?'

'Yes, I know that,' said the landlord, and began to polish some more glasses. 'Did you want another drink?'

In one of the bottles lined up on the optics, Cooper glimpsed a twisted shape that appeared over the shoulder of his own reflection. It looked like a head and face, but the strange thing was that it seemed to be black and shiny, and the only features he could make out clearly were the eyes. He waited, hoping the person would move into his field of vision. But instead it vanished into the distortion caused by the curve of the bottle, and then it was gone. Cooper turned, but was too late to see anyone. From the direction of the reflection and the background he had been able to see in the bottle, he guessed the person must have been standing right over by the door that said 'Toilets'.

He walked over and looked at the door that led upstairs. There was a sign on the handle, and the door didn't move when he turned the handle carefully.

Cooper looked at his watch. He was due at Fran Oxley's in five minutes, and he daren't be late. He couldn't risk losing the first chance he'd had to talk to one of the Oxleys. Pity. He would have liked to hang around a bit longer.

He was halfway across the road to Waterloo Terrace when the noise hit him. Cooper stopped in amazement and turned to look at the pub. It was the first time he had heard the screaming.

NEIL GRANGER HAD been rehearsing for something the night before he'd been killed. And Emma Renshaw had been a member of the same group two years ago, according to her parents. But what was it all about?

Cooper hesitated, remembering that Diane Fry was in the Black Country with Gavin Murfin. Then he rang her mobile number anyway.

'Diane, what was the play that Neil Granger was supposed to be rehearsing for?'

'Something called *The Border Rats*,' she said.

'What's that?'

'I've no idea. Why?'

'I'm outside the pub in Withens now. The landlord's a bit coy, but it sounds like they're rehearsing again. And I've never heard anything so noisy in my life.'

'What do you mean? Is it a musical?'

'There seems to be music, but no singing. Just stamping and banging.'

'Something modern and avant-garde, then.'

'In Withens? Are you kidding?'

'Call in and see what they're doing.'

'I've tried, but the door's locked, and there's a sign that says "private function".'

'Oh, well. I don't see that it really matters.'

'I'd like to hang on until they come out, and find out what it is. But I'm supposed to be at Fran Oxley's in a few minutes. It could be my only chance ever to speak to an Oxley and get a reply.'

'You can ask somebody another time.'

'I suppose so. But won't we be interviewing the other members of the cast and the stage crew? Maybe someone noticed something wrong, or Granger said something to them.'

'We'll get round to that, if necessary. But his brother was there, too, and he says Neil was fine when he left. I really don't see that it matters.'

'Maybe not. I'm just curious.'

'Anyway, it isn't a priority at the moment, if at all,' said Fry. 'We're concentrating on the weapon, the forensic evidence at the scene, and the contents of the car. We're working on a theory that Granger had an argument with one or more of his associates in the antiques gang. We think they had either had just done a job, or were making some arrangements for disposal of the stolen items.'

'We?' said Cooper. 'This is DCI Kessen's theory?'

'He's SIO. In Mr Kessen's assessment, that's likely to be the most fruitful line of enquiry and therefore the best uses of resources – which, as usual, are insufficient.'

'Well, if he thinks he can justify his decision in the Murder Book,' said Cooper, thinking of the log that the Senior Investigating Officer had to complete meticulously, in case he was ever challenged on a decision in court.

'Well, your friends in the Rural Crime Team are sharing their leads on the antiques thefts, so no doubt we'll be picking a few people up for questioning. With a bit of luck, they won't have thought to dispose of the clothes they were wearing, and we'll get a DNA match from Neil Granger's blood. They're bound to have got blood on them somewhere, if only their shoes. Those head wounds of his bled profusely.'

'And there's the bronze bust, of course.'

'Absolutely. That has to have been their big mistake. Maybe they didn't know Granger had it in his car. There are no fingerprints on it, but it's distinctive, so we'll almost certainly be able to trace it to an owner. If we locate other items from the same property in somebody's possession, we're laughing. Yes, this one could be over bar the shouting within forty-eight hours, just the way we like them. Then you can go back to rural crime, Ben.'

'And you can go back to the Renshaws.'

'Yeah, thanks.'

'I suppose the possibility of a link to Emma Renshaw isn't a high priority either?' said Cooper.

'Lowest of the low, I'd say. We don't even want to think about going down that route. Apart from the fact that they knew each other, where's the link anyway?'

'Apart from her mobile phone having turned up just now?'

'Coincidence. The best bet there is that somebody found the bag and grabbed it, thinking it might be something worth nicking. When they realized it wasn't, they dumped it again. Originally, it could have been anywhere. The laboratory might be able to give us something more specific, but we'll be lucky. If some thieving little sod with a record has left his prints on the phone, he's in for a rough time, sure enough. But the most we're going to get is the original dump site for the phone.'

'Emma's body could be in the same area,' said Cooper.

Fry was silent for a moment. He knew she hadn't overlooked that fact, but was choosing not to consider it for now. 'We'll cross that bridge when we come to it,' she said. 'Was there anything else, Ben? Only Gavin wants to get on with some interviews. You know what he's like for dedication to the job.'

'Diane, I have one more chance with the Oxleys tonight, when I'm seeing Fran. But if I'm still having difficulties tomorrow, would you help me?'

'Yes.'

'I mean, if I go up there much more often, they're going to start complaining about harassment. My options are getting increasingly limited. We have no grounds for bringing any of them in for questioning.'

'Yes, I'll help.'

'You will?'

'I said yes, didn't I? Talk to me tomorrow. I'll look forward to visiting the Oxleys.'

BEN COOPER STOOD outside Waterloo Terrace and studied the black brick houses. So what was going on behind the doors of numbers 1 to 5? How many of the Oxleys were here, rather than in the upstairs room at the pub? Did they know he was out here, or were they oblivious, locked up in their own isolated little lives? It wasn't only Mrs Wallwin who was isolated here in Waterloo Terrace. But what was the difference between the Oxleys standing against a world that wanted rid of them, and Mrs Wallwin, alone in a world that just didn't care? The difference was that the Oxleys had each other.

Cooper paused at the thought. He had taken the Oxleys' closeness for granted. For years, he had been taught not to assume anything, but the Oxleys had pushed him into the wrong response. Did they really have each other? Or was that only a front they presented to the outside world? Who could know what was going on within the walls of Waterloo Terrace, except the family themselves?

He didn't think Mrs Wallwin was suspicious at all. She wasn't creepy. And she wasn't unfriendly. But also, she wasn't an Oxley.

Could the Oxley family really be afraid of her, feeling they had to keep her at bay and defend their territory from her? Mrs Wallwin was an unlikely invader. But, to the Oxleys, she was an alien, a stranger in their midst – and therefore as threatening as a full-scale siege might have been. Mrs Wallwin, the Trojan horse.

Then Cooper remembered Mrs Wallwin mentioning her son, who worked for the water company. Was it possible that the company had put her into the house at Waterloo Terrace as a spy? Could the Oxleys be right to be suspicious of her?

REMEMBERING THE SILENT Alsatian, Cooper hesitated before he went through the gate. Some body armour would have been nice, and gloves and a riot helmet. Maybe an entire set of flame-proof overalls, boots and shin protectors, like the public-order teams wore. But he had nothing at all to protect him. Finally, he shrugged and walked up the path to ring the bell at number 5 Waterloo Terrace. There was no barking or growling, no scratching of claws on the tiles in the hallway behind the door. There was just the sound of the bell itself, which in fact was more like a buzzer. He pressed it again, and waited. Nothing.

Wearily, Cooper rang the bell again. Was it for the fifth time, or the sixth time in just a couple of days? He listened to the buzzing in the house, noting a slightly different tone to the noise. It was somehow clearer today. Maybe Fran Oxley had cleaned the cobwebs away from the box. Inevitably, he got no reply, so he knocked on the door, giving it a good double rap that anyone in the house ought to hear. He found the door moved under his fist, swinging inward slightly. It hadn't even been on the latch, let alone locked.

He pushed the door a bit more, until he had a view into the hallway, but without moving from the outside step.

'Hello!' he called. 'Anybody home?'

There was silence from the house. He could see right down the hallway to a set of stairs leading to the first floor, and at the end of the passage a door was open into a small kitchen. The silence here wasn't threatening, but worrying in a different way.

'Anybody home?'

There was no answer.

'It's the police. Detective Constable Cooper, from Edendale.'

Still no answer.

'I called the other day. I was with PC Udall, from the Rural Crime Team. You asked me to come and see you. Hello?'

Now he was in a quandary. He had to make a judgement on whether he was justified in entering the house. He had no grounds for suspicion that a crime was taking place. He had been invited to the house by the occupier, but not actually invited in. Indeed, all along this terrace it had been made clear to him that he wasn't welcome in their houses by the Oxleys. If he entered, he would have to be able to justify it later. Worse, he might be giving the Oxleys an excuse to treat him as an intruder.

But somewhere in Fran Oxley's house he could hear a rustling. It was a surreptitious movement, perhaps the sole of a shoe moving cautiously across a bare floorboard, or a sleeve brushing against the wall. It seemed to be coming from the hallway, or from the bottom of the stairs. Cooper felt his way across the kitchen, conscious of his feet sticking to the vinyl flooring as he passed the cooker. Before he could reach the door, he trod in something particularly sticky, and his shoe left the floor with a tearing noise. He froze, with his foot in mid air. There was a moment of silence. Then he heard somebody scuttling back down the hallway and out of the side door of the house into the passage.

'Damn.'

Cooper tripped over a loose flap of vinyl as he ran through into the hallway. Despite the lack of light, he could see that the side door was open, but just beginning to swing shut. He reached it and paused, putting out his hand to stop the door closing fully. Slowly, he pushed the door open again, careful to make sure that no one was standing on the other side of it in the dark passage. The door met no resistance, but went back against the wall of the house with a small thump. He wished he'd brought a torch with him from the car – but who would have expected to need a torch inside a house?

He had no need to let his eyes get accustomed to the darkness, as it was actually less dark out in the passageway than it had been indoors. He checked the passage was clear to the left, then walked carefully towards the back garden. He could no longer hear anyone running, which meant either that they had been too quick for him and had got well away from the scene already, or that they were hiding nearby in the darkness.

In the Oxleys' yard, the fusty smell of old timber was overpowering. There were a couple of old outhouses built of the same black brick as the terrace itself. They must have been outside toilets once. Privies. These things were tourist attractions in some places. There was even a book about them. But Cooper was sure that the Oxleys' outhouses wouldn't feature in any book. If a writer had ever dared to venture into the yard behind Waterloo Terrace to get a glimpse of them, he was probably even now lying dead and mouldering behind the sagging wooden door with a broken hinge on the end privy.

A ragged black-and-white cat was patrolling the stacks of pallets. As Cooper watched, it slithered slowly into the darkness in the middle of one of the stacks, vanishing bit by bit until only the white tip of its tail could be seen, twitching slowly. Then even the tail disappeared. There must be at least mice living under there, maybe rats. But if there were rats, what the Oxleys needed was a good terrier.

The thought made Cooper remember the dog. The one he had encountered four days previously had been a long-haired Alsatian, and it had been as silent a killer as the cat.

He stopped at the corner of the pallets and listened, trying to orientate himself. He wasn't sure how big the yard was, or even whether it ran parallel to the terrace, or at an angle. The dog had come down the passage between numbers 1 and 2, which must be towards the far end. But if he walked along the back wall of the yard, would he be getting further away from the houses, or nearer?

At the moment, there was no sound that would suggest the presence of the dog – no click of claws on concrete or of a chain rattling. The fusty smell of wood and rusted iron was too strong for him to pick up a canine scent. But he would have to watch out for a kennel or a pen of some kind when he got closer to number 2. The dog had been taught not to bark or growl before it attacked, and that had two results. It would give him no warning of an attack, but it also meant the dog could listen more acutely without the noise of its own barking to hinder it. Cooper knew that it would hear him much sooner than he heard it. There would be no contest. If the dog came for him, his only hope might be to climb the pallets and hope the stacks were more stable than they looked.

His foot nudged something heavy that made a metallic scraping sound as it moved. Cooper leaned down and felt what was on the ground. Something round and heavy, and made of steel. He moved his hand along, but had the sense of something that stretched several yards ahead of him. There were more lying next to it, too. Scaffolding pipes.

It was becoming more difficult to move around here. The ground was littered with unidentifiable objects, and the path between them wasn't clear. But up ahead, Cooper could see the outline of the flat-bed lorry the Oxleys used.

He looked towards the houses. Apart from number 7, where Mrs Wallwin lived, none of them had their curtains drawn closed on their downstairs windows. Numbers 2 and 4 had lights showing, and Cooper could see into their kitchens. Presumably, the Oxleys weren't concerned about people peering into their windows from the back. Who would be in the yard behind Waterloo Terrace at night, anyway? Nobody with any sense, thought Cooper.

Mrs Wallwin, though, had different habits. Either she had good reason to expect someone to be peering in, or she had something to hide. Wendy Tagg would say the latter. But Cooper thought he'd be surprised if Mrs Wallwin didn't get some level of harassment from the Oxley children, even if it was only banging on her windows and shouting insults. Even the youngest children would soon have picked up on the atmosphere of hostility towards her, and weren't so restrained in expressing it.

Cooper made the decision not to venture any further, but to go back down the passage or through the house to his car, where he could call in and fetch a torch. But before he could turn round, he became aware that he was seeing a movement just beyond the garden – the movement of a dark shape against the stacks of pallets in the yard and the slightly lighter tree cover on the hillside behind Withens. He watched the shape move along the fence, then stop and turn towards him.

Cautiously, Cooper felt his way towards the fence and found he could see a gap where a gate must be open. He edged sideways, manoeuvring for a better angle from where he could see the figure against the sky.

It was a person, certainly, but it seemed unnaturally tall. Scott Oxley was tall – but not that tall. There were other things wrong, too – the silhouette didn't quite gel with what a human outline should look like. Cooper was squinting to try to make out details of the odd shape, when he realized there was another standing within a couple of feet of it. Then a third and a fourth became visible. There was a line of them along the inside of the fence, standing among the pallets and scaffolding pipes and piles of old tyres.

There was a scratching sound and a spark of flame from a match as one of the figures lit a cigarette. Cooper saw the heads and shoulders of four people. He saw four black faces, but no eyes. Where their eyes should have been, there were only a series of metallic flashes reflecting the flame of the match before it died.

But it wasn't the sight of the reflected flames that stirred the hairs on the back of Cooper's neck. It wasn't the whiff of sulphur from the match, or the acrid taste of the cigarette smoke on the air. His overwhelming memory of the moment would be the bittersweet mingling of sweat, leather and beer. And the faint jingling of tiny bells.

Chapter Twenty-Six

As SOON AS they turned off the motorway and headed back into Derbyshire, Diane Fry and Gavin Murfin began passing through fields of oilseed rape that Fry had noticed on their way to the West Midlands. She had the window open, and the ammonia reek of the crop filled the car. She had surprised herself earlier by knowing that the yellow flowers were oilseed rape. Ben Cooper's world must be rubbing off on her.

'Well, that was a bit of a waste of time,' said Murfin.

'Not entirely.'

'Eh? That Stark girl was a dead loss. She has a short-term memory problem, if you ask me.'

'She certainly couldn't remember anything that wasn't in the West Midlands reports at the time.'

'She remembered the Renshaws.'

'Yes. In fact, you'd almost think she wanted to forget all about it.'

'But Emma Renshaw was supposed to be her friend,' protested Murfin.

'Mmm. But people deal with these things in different ways, Gavin. Maybe Debbie Stark had it right. She said she was upset for a while, but then she managed to put it behind her. Like she said, she had to move on, and get on with her life.'

'I wouldn't forget my friends so quickly.'

'I don't know. Old schoolfriends, old college friends – we soon lose touch with them, because it doesn't take long before we have nothing in common any more.'

'I didn't go to college,' said Murfin.

'You know what I mean.'

'Yeah, I suppose so. But I've missed my tea because of her, that's all.'

Fry knew that, whatever Gavin Murfin's drawbacks, he had served in CID for years and had a lot of experience of interviews and had come across all kinds of suspects.

'Gavin, what do *you* make of Howard Renshaw?' she said.

'Our Howard? He's one of those people whose brain is way ahead of his mouth.'

'What do you mean?'

'He never uses a single word that he hasn't thought about before he says it,' said Murfin. 'I hate that kind. Give me somebody whose mouth keeps working when their brain's stopped completely. That's the kind of person I like to interview. It gives me a chance for a kip between questions. It can be a bit wasteful of tape though, like.'

'Ben Cooper said that he got the impression Howard was trying to sell us something all the time.'

'You took Ben to see the Renshaws?'

'Yes. Is that a problem, Gavin?'

'Nope. I just thought he would have had his hands full with the Oxleys and rats, and stuff.'

'Rats?'

'It was nothing important. We had a look at the old railway tunnels the other day when we were down that way.'

'Oh.'

'Ben asked the bloke there to check out the tunnel under the air shaft where Granger's body was found.'

'Why would he do that?'

'He seems to have a thing about air shafts. Maybe they're phallic symbols. I reckon I'd see phallic symbols everywhere if my sex life was as bad as Ben's.'

Fry looked at Murfin. It had been a good idea to make him drive. The trip to the Black Country had been the longest uninterrupted period she had ever seen him go without eating. What's more, the withdrawal symptoms were making him unusually talkative.

'Does Ben Cooper talk to you about his sex life?' she said.

'Nah. But I can tell. Trouble is, he always picks the wrong ones, and then he gets let down. I mean, there was that Canadian bird –'

'Yes, I remember that, Gavin.'

Murfin glanced at her. ''Course you do, that's right. But I don't think he blamed you for that, Diane. Not entirely.'

'Thanks.'

'You see, when something like that happens, it takes him time to get over it. He goes all funny and starts talking to himself.'

'You're kidding.'

'Haven't you noticed?'

'I can't say I have.'

'Ben's a mite over-sensitive, if you ask me. But I suppose it takes all sorts.'

'You're getting to be a proper little psychologist, Gavin.'

'That's me. Clement Freud.'

Fry looked at Murfin again to correct him, and noticed that he was chewing something.

'What are you eating?'

'Just some chocolate I had stashed away for emergencies, Diane. Do you want some?'

'How long has it been in your pocket?'

'A day or two.'

'No, thanks.'

'I need the energy for all this brain work.'

'Particularly your psychological insights.'

'I know about phallic symbols, anyway. The more sexually frustrated you are, the bigger the symbols you see everywhere.'

'I'll take your word for it.'

They drove on for a while, heading towards the A6, which ran right through the heart of Derbyshire and the Peak District.

'Those air shafts,' said Murfin. 'How deep do they go?'

'Two hundred feet,' said Fry.

'Right.'

DIANE FRY HAD brought Emma Renshaw's diary with her, and found she couldn't leave it alone.

'What do you think these initials mean, Gavin?' she said. 'LDBAT.'

'I've no idea. The Renshaws said they didn't know. Debbie Stark didn't know. And Khadi Whatsit didn't know.'

'So they said.'

'You don't believe anything that anybody says, do you?' said Murfin.

Fry turned over a page, then turned over some more. 'She's repeated the same initials day after day.'

'Perhaps they were something to do with the lectures she had to go to. Like a reminder.'

'But why the same every day?'

'*I* don't know.'

'And another thing,' said Fry. 'Emma wrote in her diary all the time. So how come her parents found it in her room at Bearwood? Why didn't Emma take it with her when she went home for the Easter holiday? Surely she didn't just forget it?'

'Well, from what I've seen of Withens,' said Murfin, 'it was probably because she knew nothing could happen there that would be worth writing down.'

'Maybe.'

Fry stopped turning pages. A memory was coming back to her of another diary, one not unlike this. It had been a teenage girl's diary, though the girl had been a few years younger than Emma Renshaw. That girl had been living with foster parents in a semi-detached house in Warley. She had been an unhappy girl.

Suddenly, the letters made sense. It was almost as if Emma had spoken the words to her. There was no room for doubt in Fry's mind.

'Life Didn't Begin Again Today,' she said.

Murfin stared at her. 'What did you say?'

'LDBAT. It means Life Didn't Begin Again Today.'

'How do you know that?'

'I just do, OK?'

'But –'

'Gavin, trust me for once, will you? She's written it in her diary day after day. She didn't need to spell it out, because she knew exactly what the letters stood for. It's on page after page. It becomes a kind of mantra. Life Didn't Begin Again Today. Life Didn't Begin Again Today.'

'OK, OK. I hear what you're saying. I suppose it's as likely as anything.'

'Yes, it is. A bit immature, perhaps. But that's the impression I have of Emma – too immature to be safe when she was away from home for the first time. She was brought up in Withens. Living in the Black Country must have come as a shock.'

'OK, so what did she mean by it?'

'Something didn't happen that she wanted to. A man, I'd guess.'

'It usually is,' said Murfin. 'One of the boys? Neil Granger? Not Alex Dearden?'

'Somebody she got a bit obsessed with, but who wasn't interested in her. It could have been one of her lecturers at the art school.'

'You could be on to something there, Diane. They're a funny lot, artists.'

'Emma might have found one of them rather more interesting than the people she knew back in Withens anyway.'

'I'll grant you that.'

'Job for you tomorrow morning then, Gavin. Phone the art school again and get a list of all the staff who would have had contact with Emma. Some of them were spoken to at the time, but we'll need a complete list. Their ages would be useful, too. Then you can contact Debbie Stark again and go through the list with her. She was on the same course.'

'Waste of time, she is,' said Murfin.

'See if you can't jog her memory a bit.'

'I just hope there aren't too many. It could take weeks.'

'That's the way it goes, Gavin. But a couple of weeks won't make any difference now.'

'It will to my ulcers.'

'I didn't know you had ulcers, Gavin.'

'I haven't. But I'm expecting them any day, like.'

They were on the A6, and only a few minutes from Edendale now. Fry gazed at the White Peak scenery going past the windows with mixed feelings. She didn't know where home was any more. But maybe she never had.

She turned the pages of Emma's diary again.

'She ought to have used his initials,' she said. 'If she liked initials, she should have referred to him that way. Or at least the initial of his first name. That's what I would have done.'

'I never kept a diary,' said Murfin. 'It seems a bit sad to me.'

'It would have helped a lot,' said Fry. 'But I can't see anywhere she's done that.'

'Maybe she didn't feel she had to. She knew who she was talking about, so why should she bother with initials?'

'But when she first met him –'

Murfin made the final turn into the Eden Valley and began the long descent towards Edendale.

'That diary,' he said. 'When does it start?'

'January, of course.'

'I just wondered. My lad has a diary for school, but it starts in September. They call it an academic year diary.'

Fry stared at him. 'Gavin – you're a genius.'

'Yeah, I know.'

'If this is a member of staff we're looking for, Emma would have met him in her first term at the art school – the previous October. Even if it was a student, the same applies.' She slapped the diary. 'We've only got the last four months here. We need the diary before this one.'

'If she had one.'

'Oh, she'll have had one all right.'

LDBAT. Life Didn't Begin Again Today. The more she looked at it, the more Fry was sure. Emma Renshaw had written it day after day, a sure sign of an obsession.

But on a Thursday two years ago, Emma's diary entries had stopped completely. Life didn't begin again that day, either. But had life ended, instead?

'That's another thing you can do, Gavin. Get on to the Renshaws and ask for a previous diary.'

'Great. The rewards of genius, eh?'

Fry opened her file and looked at the photographs of Emma Renshaw for a long time. In particular, she studied the ones in which Emma was wearing a sleeveless T-shirt or shorts, displaying bare limbs and healthy skin. In one picture, she was posing in a bikini top against a background of sand and sunlit water, with her arms and shoulders an uncomfortable shade of pink. In every photograph, Emma was smiling and happy, a healthy teenager with the rest of her life before her.

Fry found a sentence running through her head. It was something really stupid that she'd heard on a BBC Radio 4 programme a few months ago. It might even have been *You and Yours*. The discussion had been about direct marketing, the posh expression for junk mail, and how it could be stopped – or 'suppressed', as one of the studio guests had insisted on putting it. The presenter had expressed astonishment that every year hundreds of thousands of people who'd died were still being targeted by firms sending them junk mail. The guest had made a statement that had given Fry a little shudder of apprehension. She had said ominously: 'There are ways of suppressing people who've died.'

Fry wondered whether there was a direct-marketing technique she could use in the case of the Renshaws.

Was there really a way of suppressing someone who'd died? Was there a way of putting away the ghost of Emma Renshaw?

Now, when she looked at the photographs, Fry began to see something different. Something that the photographer hadn't captured on film. She had seen the blood in the poppies and the mould in the grass. Now she saw the bones under the skin of the girl.

THE FIGURES WERE moving. They swayed a little, and nodded their dark heads. They did it in unison and in unnatural silence. Ben Cooper wasn't sure whether they had seen him. If he stood quite still, they might not notice him.

He tried to remember what was behind him, whether his outline would be visible. Of course, he was standing against the black bricks of Waterloo Terrace. But then he remembered the uncurtained windows and the light spilling out of two of the kitchens. And he knew that he might as well have advertised his presence.

The four figures suddenly jerked and leaped into the air. When they landed, they hit the ground with a thud of boots and clash of bells. Then they disappeared from Cooper's view below the level of the pallets, and there was a tremendous clattering noise, wood pounding on wood, rhythmic blows coming steadily closer towards him.

Cooper began to back away, trying to make out what was in front of him while feeling for the opening in the fence behind him. The noise was deafening, surely enough to disturb the residents of Waterloo Terrace.

The pounding came slowly nearer, mingled with bells and heavy breathing. But the figures were squatting now, and were no longer recognizable as human. They might just as easily be some kind of shaggy apes, all legs and arms, scuttling towards his feet. Cooper could smell the sweet scent of fresh wood as the edges of the pallets were splintered and bruised by whatever was hitting them.

Suddenly, Cooper came up hard against something metal. Had he misjudged the gap in the fence? Was it a foot or two to the left? But with his hand behind him, he could feel the hard, unforgiving edges of steel scaffolding pipes. A solid barrier, and the pipes were far too big for him to use to defend himself.

The noise changed and the earth vibrated as the weapons began to strike the ground near to his feet. Cooper caught the occasional glimpse of a reflection from a pair of mirrored sunglasses, or a dark, ragged silhouette as the figures came closer, still moving in rhythm, as if to some music only they could hear.

Then the screaming began. It was one voice, but unnaturally high-pitched for a human voice, more like the sound of a pig being slaughtered. Cooper froze at the noise, feeling for the first time that he was seriously in danger. He felt something heavy whistle past his left leg and hit the ground, then the same on the right. A double thud like a jackhammer sent a quiver through his legs. Two more blows followed quickly, an inch or two nearer to his boots.

Cooper moved his feet, realizing he was going to have to fight back. This was the moment when he regretted not attending training sessions at his martial arts dojo, even though it was so conveniently close to his flat. The sessions had started to seem like a meaningless ritual. But now he felt clumsy and unfit, and wished he could summon some of the energy and suppleness that might get him out of trouble.

Because of the screaming, he felt, rather than heard, the next blow land almost on his toes. Desperately, knowing he was close to getting hurt, he kicked out at where he thought an arm might be and was rewarded with an impact and a startled grunt. Feeling the rhythm and knowing that two more blows would quickly follow, he swivelled sideways, waited for the thud on the ground and kicked out again. This time, his boot landed on something hard that jarred the sole of his foot.

There was a brief pause, and the screaming stopped abruptly. Cooper decided to take the chance to dodge to the side, but was too slow. A blow swished past his face and landed with a terrific clang on the scaffolding pipes.

Then, all at once, there was light. Two arc lights popped and burst into life, illuminating the yard as if it were daylight. Lucas Oxley stood in the gateway, frowning angrily at the four figures that crouching sweating and gasping around Cooper.

'That's enough,' said Lucas. 'If anybody takes one more step, I'll break his stick over his stupid head.'

'WELL, I'M SORRY I wasn't here when you arrived,' said Fran Oxley. 'But we were a bit busy at the café tonight, and I missed the bloody bus.'

'That's OK.'

'But I see you met some of the lads. They've been having a practice tonight.'

With the lights on in Fran Oxley's house, Ben Cooper found the four young men looked no less bizarre, and only slightly less threatening. They were all dressed entirely in black, with heavy work boots and coats that seemed to be made out of rags dyed jet black. One of them had a thick cartridge belt around his waist, and another wore black leather wristlets covered in iron studs. They had taken off their black top hats and rested their sticks against the wall. When they removed their mirrored sunglasses, their eyes stared out at him from white patches of skin. The rest of their faces were covered in some kind of black paint that had streaked with their sweat.

'Does the paint come off?' said Cooper, knowing he sounded stupid.

'It's a water-based theatrical make-up,' said Scott Oxley. 'It washes off easy.'

'It doesn't half give you blackheads, though,' said Ryan.

Ryan Oxley was the only one that Cooper recognized. He was one of the teenagers he had seen on the road near the bus shelter, but it was only his hair really that made him recognizable. His older brother, Scott, was a tall young man in his twenties with broad shoulders and fair hair cut very short. Nobody introduced the other two, but Cooper heard one of them addressed as Glen.

Somehow, all the young men looked bigger and bulkier in their strange outfits than they would have been if he had found them dressed in T-shirts and jeans.

'They used burnt cork, traditionally,' said Fran. 'But apparently it causes cancer. This stuff you just put on with a brush or a sponge. It's a bit like wearing a face mask. It feels sort of dry and powdery, not greasy at all, like you might imagine.'

'You do this, too?' said Cooper.

'I play the concertina.'

'Right. And this is the Border Rats?'

'These *are* the Border Rats. It's a group, not a thing.'

'We're only some of them,' said Scott. 'Everybody's in the side. There are a few blokes come over from Hey Bridge, too.'

Cooper noticed that their sweat had brought out their individual smells – leather and rags, feathers and flowers, beer and cigarettes.

'Can I have a look at the sticks?' he said.

'These are blackthorn,' said Ryan. 'That or hazel is best, because it doesn't split as much, you know.'

'I think I saw your little brother Jake with some sticks earlier on.'

'He's the Stick Rat. It's his job.'

'What does your father do?'

'Dad is the Squire – that's the leader. But he's the Beast as well. Granddad used to be the Beast, until he got too old. You have to be a bit nimble on your feet.'

'Beast?'

'Some sides have a hobbyhorse, or something like that. We have a rat. Obvious, really.'

'What we're doing is re-enacting the killing of the rats that lived in the tunnels when they were being built. It's symbolic.'

'But if you want to know any more, maybe you'd better talk to the vicar,' said Scott.

'Mr Alton? What has he got to do with it?'

'He's the bloke who knows about the history – the symbolism and stuff.'

'He knows about the history of the dance? Does he approve of it?'

'Approve? You're kidding. He's been dying to join the Border Rats ever since he came to Withens. He used to be one of those hanky-waving types – Cotswold morris dancers. This is the proper thing.'

'More *real*?' said Cooper, thinking of the Renshaws.

'Well, yeah.'

Cooper knew the four young men couldn't wait to get out of his presence, but they looked a bit abashed – not by him, but by the tongue-lashing Lucas had given them. For a few minutes, at least, they were trying to make polite conversation, as if that might make up for trying to scare him to death in their yard. And almost succeeding.

'Wasn't Neil Granger in the group, too?' he said.

'Oh yes,' said Scott. 'He was the Bagman – the secretary, sort of thing. But he had new ideas.'

'What sort of ideas?'

'Well, this year, he wanted everyone to go and dance up the sun on May Day.'

'Dance up the sun? You mean a ceremony at dawn?'

'That's it. Neil said it was a tradition in other places. If you ask me, he'd got that from the vicar. But Dad told him it's never been a tradition here, so we weren't doing it. And that was that, really.'

'So there was a disagreement? Was that why Neil left the rehearsal before anyone else on Friday night?'

'Could have been,' said Scott. 'But he was stubborn, was Neil. He didn't give up on the idea, did he?'

'How do you mean?'

'Well, I reckon that's why he was up there by the air shaft next morning. He said that was the best place to see the dawn come up. I think he went to prove a point and show it was possible. But none of us would have gone up there with him.'

'Are you sure?' said Cooper.

'Sure. Dad would have killed us.'

The others nodded and laughed. They began to wipe their faces, smearing their black make-up into grotesque patterns as they waited for Cooper to leave.

FRAN OXLEY TOOK Cooper through into the next room to get away from the young men, who had raided her fridge for cold drinks.

'It was just something I wanted to tell you about Neil,' she said. 'I don't suppose you'll believe me, but I had to say it.'

'Yes?'

'I know your lot will be assuming he was up to no good and got himself killed through his own fault.'

'Well, not necessarily …' began Cooper, wondering how she had seen that so clearly. Was the thinking of the police really so predictable?

'You don't need to deny it. I know how it works. I've seen it often enough round here. For what it's worth,

I wanted to tell you that Neil was all right. One of the best. He was a hard worker, and he was honest, too. He wouldn't have got involved in anything he shouldn't. Well, not unless ...'

'What?'

'Well, he had his views on what's right and what's wrong, that's all.'

Cooper wondered how far he could push his luck with Fran Oxley. But he was here now, so he might as well try.

'You know the young woman who went missing – Emma Renshaw? What do you think Neil's relationship with her was?'

Fran laughed. 'Oh, that theory again. You're totally blinkered when you get an idea into your heads, aren't you? Neil must have attacked Emma Renshaw, mustn't he? He must have done her in somewhere. He was just the type, after all. That would be very convenient.'

Cooper began to shake his head. 'That's not quite the way it works.'

'No? Well, you can forget it. Because Neil wasn't in the least bit interested in Emma Renshaw. For a very good reason.'

'You mean because he was gay?'

'You know? Who told you?'

'Neil's brother.'

Fran frowned. 'Philip told you? But why?'

'I'm sure he thought he was helping. He wants us to find the person who killed Neil and not waste our time looking at things that aren't relevant.'

But Fran continued to look baffled.

'Oh, I'm sorry,' said Cooper. 'Have I spoiled your revelation?'

He regretted his tone as soon as her mouth screwed up into an expression of contempt. He might have ruined his one chance of getting some information voluntarily from one of the Oxleys.

'I suppose you'd better go, then,' she said. 'I can't tell you anything you don't already know.'

'There's one other thing,' said Cooper, as she stood to see him out.

'Yeah?'

'What about Craig?'

Fran stopped quite still. 'Craig?'

'Your brother, is he? Or another cousin?'

She stared at him speechlessly. Cooper knew he was close to something. But would she tell him? He was pushing his luck.

'Come on, Fran. Talk to me about Craig.'

She walked towards the door, and Cooper thought he had lost the chance. But then Fran turned, and her eyes glittered when she spoke. Her voice had risen, too. It was as if she had put distance between herself and Cooper to give space for her anger.

'You want to know about Craig, do you?' she said. 'Well, I'll tell you about Craig. He got himself into trouble and ended up in court. That had happened before, but the last time it was serious. When they sentenced him, he should have gone to a local authority secure unit, but there were no places available. They said it was because they'd been having a crackdown on persistent young offenders, and the secure units were all full.'

'So he was sent to the young offenders' institution at Hindley,' said Cooper.

'Yes. But he's not there any more.'

'He's out? Where did he go?'

Fran turned her face away, and didn't answer straight away.

'He's back here in Withens,' she said.

Cooper frowned. Had the Oxleys been hiding Craig after all?

'In that case, I need to speak to him,' he said.

'Oh, yes? If you've got psychic talents, go ahead. But other than that, you're wasting your time.'

Cooper's heart sank. 'What do you mean, Fran?'

'It's as near as you'll get, without going to the graveyard.'

Fran's attempt to seem unconcerned wasn't working. Cooper could see her face starting to redden and become strained with the effort of holding back tears.

'Craig couldn't stand it in Hindley,' she said. 'He didn't see any way that he was ever going to get out of places like that, because he thought the system had him marked down for a life in prison. Worse, he couldn't cope with being away from the family for so long among all those strangers. There was no one he could talk to, to tell them what he was feeling. He was on hourly checks, but it wasn't enough. In the end, he hanged himself in his cell. He wasn't the first, so we're told. And I don't suppose he'll be the last.'

DIANE FRY AND Gavin Murfin were almost home when Fry took a call on her mobile from Sarah Renshaw. It was almost as if they had known she was thinking about them. It was getting very late, but she'd given the Renshaws her number in case they thought of anything useful. And when Sarah rang, she sounded almost panicky.

'There's a teddy bear missing,' she said.

'What?'

'One of Emma's teddy bears is missing.'

Fry stared at Murfin in astonishment. This was a bizarre turn, even for Sarah Renshaw. Murfin leaned over to try to listen to the call, and the car veered towards the centre of the road. But it was quiet at this time of night, and there was hardly any traffic.

'I don't think that concerns me, Mrs Renshaw,' said Fry.

'But where has it gone?'

'Does it matter? It's only a teddy bear. There are plenty more.'

'No, this was a special one,' said Sarah. 'We were looking for it to put on display for our Emma Day, but it isn't there.'

Fry sighed. Another special one. The first that her parents had given her, which now sat on the leather settee. The last one they'd given her, which sat at the breakfast table. So what was special about this one?

'This is a Chiltern golden plush teddy from 1930,' said Sarah. 'It's worth at least five hundred pounds.'

'Really?'

'They're rather rare.'

'An *antique* teddy bear?'

'Yes.'

Fry sat bolt upright with interest. 'When did you last see this bear?'

OUTSIDE THE DEARDENS' house, Shepley Head Lodge, the night was far from quiet for anyone who knew how to listen. Rats began to scurry along the outer walls of the house, stopping suddenly to sniff at small objects and roll them in their claws as they scavenged for food. Tiny pipistrelle bats spilled out of a gap in the roof tiles of the outbuildings and flitted backwards and forwards across the yard, darting at moths and night-flying insects.

Later, a pair of foxes heaved over the dustbin, scattering rubbish on the path and snarling at each other as they argued over the dried carcass of a roast chicken. There was a sudden swish through the air, and a barn owl's talons thudded into the breast of a pigeon that had chosen its roost carelessly. The victim's wings flapped a few times as the owl shifted its grip, then launched itself back into the night. Three grey feathers spiralled to the ground, where they settled and began to soak up the dew. A hedgehog poked its head out of a hole in a pile of dead branches and checked the scents in the air to make sure that the foxes had gone. Its spines scraped against the bark as it came out on to the wet grass and began to hunt for slugs and beetles. As innocent as it looked, it was the most successful predator of them all.

Chapter Twenty-Seven

THURSDAY

IN THE MIST that followed a grey dawn, the Reverend
Derek Alton unlocked the door of St Asaph's church
and let it swing slowly open in front of him. As usual,
he looked for signs of intruders or vandalism, but could
see none. The church had been given a wide berth ever
since the news of Neil Granger's death had spread. But
perhaps it was just the frequent police presence in the
village that was making the difference, rather than any
sense of respect.

It was right here in the porch that Alton had last
seen Neil on Friday night. He wasn't sure whether he
had really experienced a premonition as they had stood
close together in the darkness and listened to the noises
from the village. It felt that way now, but hindsight was
deceptive. And, of course, feelings could be even more
deceptive.

Alton heard a distinctive engine noise that grumbled to a halt beyond the churchyard wall. It was muffled by the trees and the dampness that hung in the air, but it was enough to make the vicar turn away from the door and steady himself with one hand against the oak frame of the porch entrance. The smooth wood was cold to the touch and running with moisture. Alton shivered as he caught the click of the latch on the gate hidden behind the yews.

It seemed to Alton that the figure approaching him through the mist in the churchyard was one that should not have been there at all. It appeared at first to be a shape returned from the grave. Or, if not actually yet in a grave, then escaped from its drawer in a mortuary freezer to haunt the church porch. And to haunt Derek Alton's conscience.

He recognized the creak of a leather motorcycle jacket and saw something familiar about the darkness of his visitor's eyes. Neil Granger had never owned a motorbike, of course. But his brother did.

'Morning, Vicar.'

'Philip?' Alton stared at the young man. 'This is a bit early in the morning for a call. You've only just caught me.'

'Sorry. But I have to be at work in Glossop in an hour.'

'Come into the church,' said Alton. 'It isn't much warmer inside than out, I'm afraid. But at least it's dry.'

'No, it's OK. This won't take long.'

Alton frowned at the young man's tone. Philip wouldn't meet his eye, but fiddled with the strap of his motorcycle helmet and stroked the smooth surface.

The movement of Philip's hands drew Alton's eyes to the helmet. It was bright red, and looked glaringly out of place in the church porch against the dark stone. There were several scratches on it, as if the helmet had already saved its owner from serious injury in an accident. Alton wanted to suggest to Philip that he should replace it with a new helmet, in case it had been damaged and weakened. It might not protect him next time.

But the vicar recognized that his mind was merely reacting to an impulse to change the subject whenever he sensed a difficult conversation approaching. It was one of his weaknesses. He had to learn to face the fire, and hope that he would be made stronger by the flames.

'Well, out with it, then,' said Alton. 'Is it about Neil?'

'Yes.'

'It's such a difficult time for you, Philip. Especially without any immediate family around you to offer support. But I spoke to your uncle a couple of days ago. He explained that it would be a question of cremation, when the time comes. I mean, when the coroner releases ... when the final arrangements can be made. And a humanist service, I gather. That's perfectly understandable – though I did think your brother was becoming a little more interested in the church in recent months. I was quite hopeful, you know ...'

Alton realized he was babbling, and ground to a halt. Philip appeared to be paying no attention to his words at all, but kept his eyes turned down, thinking about something else entirely. The vicar felt himself beginning to grow warm under his coat.

'I went to see the police yesterday,' said Philip.

'Yes, of course. Are they any nearer …? Did they give you an idea …? It's been nearly six days now. Surely –'

Philip shook his head in a gesture of impatience 'Please, Vicar.'

'Sorry.'

A little bit of sun appeared through a break in the mist that hung between the yew trees. It looked as if someone had switched a light on. For now, it was pale and yellow, and ringed with a faint halo. But soon, it would dissipate the mist and the day would be fine.

'It was more a question of me giving them information,' said Philip. 'That's what I wanted to tell you.'

'Information?' said Alton.

'Well, among other things, I thought I ought to tell them that Neil was gay.'

For some reason, Alton found himself latching on to the wrong phrase. 'What other things?'

Philip looked at him then, with an enigmatic smile. 'Nothing else that concerns you, Vicar.'

'I see.'

'But obviously, the police will be wanting to talk to people again now. People who were involved with Neil in some way.'

'Yes, I suppose so.'

'I thought you ought to know.'

Alton had promised himself that he'd make a determined attack on the overgrown churchyard today, provided the weather was fine. That was why he was early this morning, so that he could be outside and ready for action as soon as the mist had gone. He had neglected the job too long already, and no one was going to help him now. He was on his own.

Philip Granger was watching him, waiting for a reaction. 'You get what I'm saying, Vicar? It's something you ought to know.'

'Yes, Philip. Thank you. Thank you very much.'

'It's a good thing to tell what you know, isn't it?' said Philip. 'That is, unless there's a very, *very* good reason not to.'

Derek Alton nodded. But all he could think of were the dock plants growing in his churchyard. He couldn't quite explain why the leaves of the docks disturbed him so much more than the other plants. When he pulled at them, they stretched and wrinkled in his hands, like aged skin. They might be warm on the surface, where they had been touched by the sun. But underneath, they were always cold and damp, like the grave.

PHILIP GRANGER MOUNTED his motorbike and put on his helmet. He looked across the bridge at Withens. He had one more job he wanted to do, one more person to see. Then, perhaps, he could get on with his life and pretend that everything was OK. Then he could leave it to others to sort out the mess.

As he rode north through the village, he looked for his uncle and cousins near Waterloo Terrace, but could see no signs of them. Philip smiled. He knew that the Reverend Alton would be able to tell where he was heading by the sound of his bike engine, but he didn't care.

There was, after all, only one place he could be going once he had passed through Withens in this direction.

WHEN MICHAEL DEARDEN had finishing inspecting the locks and bolts on the doors of the house, he went around all the windows. There were a lot of windows in Shepley Head Lodge, some of them in out of the way corners that could be reached unobserved from outside. He might have to block a few of them up some time.

Gail said it wasn't logical to check the security of the house in the morning when he got up, as well as at night before he went to bed. She said it was obsessive. But Gail knew nothing. If their security had been breached during the night, it was vital to be aware of it straight away. There would be evidence to be gathered, a crime scene to be preserved intact for the arrival of the police. Not that the police would come, of course. But at least they wouldn't be able to blame *him* for not having followed the proper procedures.

So Dearden made it a regular routine to carry out his inspection first thing every morning before he did anything else, particularly before Gail started drifting around the house, disturbing evidence without even noticing anything was wrong.

When he was finally satisfied that the lodge hadn't been ransacked during the night, Dearden looked outside. Because of the elevated position of the house, he had a good view of the frontal approach, where the drive swung up off the road. There was no sign of anyone out there this morning. The postman might be along later on, if he came at all. Dearden had once investigated the possibility of buying the last hundred yards of the road from Withens and closing it off. The road wasn't adopted by the highways authority beyond the village, so it wasn't an official highway. But it had turned out that this section belonged to the farmer who owned the land on either side, and the farmer wouldn't listen to reason when Dearden raised the idea.

The back of the house was the big problem. The yard and the huddle of outbuildings backed into the hillside. He was sure this was the way they had come in when they raided his property before. There were walls built against the hill, but they were bulging and slipping under the pressure and were no barrier to anyone determined enough.

Dearden walked out into the yard and knew immediately that something was wrong. He saw that somebody had knocked over the dustbin. They had strewn rubbish all across his yard.

'Mr Dearden?'

Dearden jumped in alarm. How could he not have noticed the person standing near his side gate?

'How did you get here?'

'On my motorbike.'

'What motorbike?'

'It's here, behind the wall.'

The motorbike was invisible on the other side of the stone wall. Dearden realized he might be making a mistake by only keeping an eye out for cars on the road.

'What are you doing here?' said Dearden.

'Do you know who I am? I'm Philip Granger.'

'Yes. It was your brother who was killed. Alex knew him.'

'That's right.'

Dearden struggled for a moment over what to say. Then he looked at the young man's motorcycle leathers and black hair.

'You're related to the Oxleys, aren't you?'

'Lucas is my uncle,' said Philip.

'I'll give you two minutes to get off my property.'

'Sorry?'

Dearden gestured at the tipped-over dustbin. 'Do you know anything about this? Were you here last night with some of your cousins?'

'No. I –'

'I don't want you here. Your family is nothing but trouble.'

'All I wanted to say was –'

'Now you've got one minute.'

'OK, OK, I'm going.'

With narrowed eyes, Dearden watched Philip Granger start up his bike and leave. Those people from Withens were getting even more brazen if they were wandering on to his property in broad daylight. Serious action would have to be taken.

DEREK ALTON PICKED up the stick that Lucas Oxley had given him. He bounced it in his palm a few times, enjoying the feel of the wood. He liked its solidity, and the smoothness of its grain. It had a satisfying weight and balance, as if it were a natural extension of his arm.

When he held the stick up to the light, he could see the bruises and scarring along the length of the wood. But it was good, thick blackthorn. Blackthorn was best. He was lucky to get it, because there wasn't much of it growing around Withens.

Then Alton frowned at the sight of a stain on the stick. It looked like a splash of red wine. Like communion wine, perhaps? But surely not at the altar of St Asaph's.

With a sudden burst of energy, he swung the stick through the air, as if striking at something around head height. He had to imagine the noise and the impact. But the physical action, the rush of air, and the movement of the muscles in his shoulders all made him feel good, even exhilarated. He wanted to do a little jig on the stone flags, to open his lungs and let out a shout of joy. But this wasn't the place or the time.

'Death and renewal. Winter and spring. The darkness and the light.'

Though his voice was still quiet, it carried the entire length of the church. The sound bounced off the dusty stone lintels and the dark oak roof timbers. The word 'light' seemed to return to him in the cool air with a different note, sharper and more peremptory, as if it had been spoken by someone else. Alton swung the stick again, listening to the swish of its movement through the air. The sound was almost like music, a distant whisper of otherworldly voices, sighing for the coming moment, for the time to be right.

'The beauty and the sorrow, death and renewal. The powers of light and new life.'

Alton wasn't even sure that the Church of England fitted naturally into the landscape in this part of the country. Perhaps Withens needed something more muscular and rugged, more in tune with the cycle of the seasons and the implacability of nature. Perhaps it ought to be able to call on something more in keeping with the preoccupations of those wretched men who had been the first to live and die in Withens – the men killed and maimed in their hundreds building the tunnels. The men no one had cared about.

He had wondered about that when he first came to the place and had learned about its history. It had been the prosperous traders and landowners who had subscribed to build St Asaph's, as an act of charity. But it was the blood of the ordinary working men that had consecrated the landscape.

Now he was getting too absorbed in the past again. It always made him feel depressed. He swung his arm once more, trying to work out what it was about the acoustics that made his voice sound so unfamiliar.

'The darkness and the light. The *light*.'

Sometimes, it seemed to Alton that the entire area might be on the verge of reverting to paganism. Only the previous year, the May Day bank holiday festivities in the town of Glossop had culminated in the burning of a wicker man. Alton had thought this was the sort of thing that only happened in films, and when he had first read about it, he had an uneasy frisson. But he reassured himself that these things were most likely done for the benefit of the tourists these days. There couldn't be any real belief involved in the rituals, could there? Yet local residents in Glossop had written their bad memories in envelopes and attached them to the wicker man, so they would be carried away by the flames. Superstition, that's all.

His feelings were even more confused by the fact that the ritual had taken place at the Glossop Labour Club. Not only that, but events leading up to the burning of the wicker man had included an opening ceremony conducted by the local member of parliament, along with a pie and pea supper, a coffee morning and craft fair. For the children, there had been a short-story competition, a summer pageant, and a bouncy castle. All these were things that in other areas were associated with church fêtes.

There were times when he felt as though he was trying to fight back more than the encroaching nettles and bracken in his churchyard. Now and then, a dark shadow seemed to fall across his day-to-day reality, and he had a vision of himself battling against something just as insidious and persistent, and just as impossible to defeat.

Alton held the stick up to his face and squinted towards the tip. The stain on the wood was dark and had soaked deep into the grain of the blackthorn. Its shape was rather like a map of Derbyshire – a long trickle running away to the north, where it pooled into a smear at the Yorkshire border. He nodded with satisfaction at the image. The village of Withens was somewhere in that smear that was border country, a lost and forgotten speck in miles of empty peat moor. And St Asaph's sat on the edge of the village, gradually disappearing in a mass of encroaching undergrowth, like the burnt-out Ford Fiesta on the grass verge at the top of the road. In most Peak District villages, there would be a committee whose aim was to win the Best-Kept Village competition, and they wouldn't have rested until they had got the abandoned car removed or the churchyard cleared. Not in Withens, though.

All the members of his congregation were either old, or strange. Often both. Services were held at St Asaph's only every alternate Sunday. Most of the elderly residents of the bungalows came, and a few people made the journey from Hey Bridge. But not many others. For the modern generation, attending church was a cause for suspicion. To admit to being a Christian was like confessing to a social problem.

But then again, attending church didn't make you a Christian, any more than standing in a garage made you a car.

Sometimes Alton felt sorry for St Asaph. The saint had carried hot coals in his cloak to warm his master, without burning himself or his garments, which had proved his holiness, or so it was said. But carrying hot coals wasn't much to be remembered for, was it? Some people would suggest it was a foolhardy thing to do.

But if anyone who wasn't holy enough tried to carry those hot coals, they would certainly be burned.

BEN COOPER LOOKED up the road past Waterloo Terrace. He had been planning to call at the church in Withens to see if the Reverend Alton was around. He wanted to ask him about the Border Rats, and maybe to get a look at Craig Oxley's grave, if he really was buried at St Asaph's. Cooper had started to feel that everything he was told by someone in Withens had to be double-checked.

But he had noticed there were cars outside the Quiet Shepherd, and people around the doors of the stone garage where he had seen the clay-covered wooden boards. What was going on at the pub now? Well, the only way to find out was to go and see.

It was only when he saw the baskets of flowers being brought from the cars and the petals being pressed into place in the clay that it dawned on Cooper what he had been looking at on his previous visit. Like many local people, it was something he had taken for granted for years, and had never bothered to wonder about the details of how they came about.

He recognized Marion Oxley, who glowered at him, but carried on with her work filling in blocks of colour with blue hydrangea petals in outlines that seemed to have been created with rows of black coffee beans.

'You're making a well dressing,' said Cooper.

'That's right.'

An outline drawing had been made in the surface of the clay with a sharp instrument – probably one of the knitting needles lying around on a side table. The pattern had been emphasized by pressing in holly, rowan berries and alder cones, with mosses, bark, and lichens. The flower petals were going on last, the picture being created from the bottom upwards so that the petals overlapped and the rainwater would drain off.

If Diane Fry had been here, she would have said it was just another quaint rural custom. But this one was unique to Derbyshire, and attracted many thousands of visitors to the Peak District every year to see the displays. The pictures in the well dressings always told a story, too – often a religious theme, but sometimes subjects with more local significance.

'What's that background made of?' asked Cooper, pointing at the pale grey material backing the picture.

'It's fluorspar. We just call it spar.'

'Of course.' Fluorspar was local, too – the product of a number of quarries in the mineral-rich White Peak.

The women were fussing around him, and Cooper started to feel that he was in the way. He couldn't see yet what the picture was going to be. Only the background had been filled in. But soon a picture would appear in living colour for the display. And it *would* be living too – or almost, since all the materials were natural. Some of the hundreds of well dressings that appeared through the county from April through to September were astonishingly detailed and inventive, and it was no wonder they were such an attraction for visitors. Withens just seemed such an unlikely place to find one.

'This is quite an early well dressing, isn't it?' he said.

'We're the earliest at this end of the county. It means we have to rely on what's in flower.'

'Is the display this weekend?'

'Of course. There wouldn't be much point petalling now, otherwise. It'll only last a few days.'

And the well dressings had started as a way of thanking the water goddess who provided a village's clean water supply. Some villagers had believed that it had been their pure water that had protected them from the Black Death that had ravaged the rest of England in the fourteenth century.

DEREK ALTON'S HANDS were stained green and smelt of leaking sap from the dock plants. Their leaves were large and healthy-looking. But when he grasped them in his bare hands, he could feel both sides at once, the cold and the warmth. Another eternal duality lurking in the undergrowth to surprise him. The cold of death and the warmth of life. The darkness and the light.

Alton pulled his hand away, thinking of the slugs and snails that might be clinging to the undersides of the leaves. He wiped his palms on his trousers, and decided he should have worn his gloves. He hardly dared to pull at the leaves too hard, because they were surprisingly fragile and ripped easily in his fingers. Yet their stems were as tough as any weed he had come across, and their roots were firmly fixed, so that they clung tenaciously to the ground even when he threw all his weight into heaving on them. He ended up with pieces of shredded leaf and tiny bits of their flesh pressed into the creases of his hands, his fingers slippery and stained green by their juice. Their broken stems smelled faintly acid.

It must have presented a major engineering exercise to get the massive flat gritstone slabs into place over the graves. It was almost as if the families who had paid for them had been making absolutely sure that their dead relatives were never going to push their way up out of their graves and come back again. No person could lift one of those slabs on his own. But nature could do it. Nature was pushing them up, sliding them aside, pulling them down into the ground and tilting them at jaunty angles, making a joke of the whole thing.

Saddest of all were the stones at the western end of the graveyard. They were tiny by comparison to the gritstone slabs. In fact, they reminded Alton of the little milestones that could still occasionally be seen on the roadside in the Peak District, relics of a forgotten period when travel was slow enough to see them.

At this time of the year, the tiny stones were just managing to peep above the bracken litter, but they were destined to disappear again within a week or two. Alton had no idea why the people who were remembered by the stones had not even earned their full names on their memorials. They bore only initials and a year. Here were G.S. and M.W., and over there C.S. All of them seemed to have died in 1849.

Was it just lack of money that had restricted the poorer families to a tiny stone with no space on it for a proper inscription in tribute to the dead? Or had it been yet another peculiar local custom?

But when he looked at the huge gritstone slabs nearer the church, with their ornately carved lettering, their biblical texts and complete family histories, Alton knew the answer. The people in Withens had not been divided by belief and tradition, but by wealth and position. So many churchyards in so many thousands of towns and villages were testament to that fact. The rich had been able to buy their way closer to Heaven.

But Christian burial was based on the belief that the dead would rise again one day. Like a seed, the body was planted in the earth to await rebirth.

The worst pest of all in the churchyard was the bracken that had spread down the hillside. Grazing sheep normally kept it down, but in the churchyard it was out of reach of the sheep because of the stone walls. Each year, the bracken grew from the debris of its own dead growth of the previous autumn. Recently, a frost had caught some of the new bracken fronds as they unfurled. They were already brown and dead and brittle, crumbling under his fingers. Even as the rest of the plant grew green and vibrant around it.

In one corner of the churchyard, a sycamore and some young hollies had claimed several graves as their own. Elsewhere, rosebay willowherb was beginning its spring offensive and the rhododendrons were threatening, the chestnuts were unfurling their leaves, the brambles, docks and thistles were spreading unhindered, and underfoot were the small, black, bullet-like heads of the plantains.

Alton knew there were a couple of dozen graves that hadn't seen the light of day for years, and probably never would now. Their inscriptions took on an air of ironic neglect: 'Sacred to the memory ... here lieth the body ... departed this life ... Blessed are the dead which die in the Lord.'

The sycamores had spread through the churchyard like a plague, their whirling seed pods uncontrollable in the wind. When he had first arrived, Alton had persuaded the diocese to pay for the rampant sycamores to be cut back down to their roots, on the grounds that they were damaging the graves, pushing up the horizontal memorial stones. But already the remaining bases of the trees were shooting again – their amputated boles protruded from the edges of the gravestones like fingers trying to lift the stone slabs. Their fingernails were green – the new shoots of spring emerging from the grave.

There was something that no one ever mentioned, but which Alton couldn't help thinking about whenever he saw the virulent green of the plant life burgeoning in his churchyard. Part of the problem was that in the older areas of the churchyard, the vegetation had too many nutrients to feed on. The sides of the ancient burial caskets would have been breached many years ago, allowing the peaty soil to trickle through the cracks in the wood and mingle with the bones and the mouldering clothes of the dead. And with the soil would go the insects and all the things that lived underground in the dark. And behind them, the roots of the plants colonizing the surface – pale, thin tendrils twining into the crevices and attaching themselves to wood and bones and desiccated flesh. Earth to earth, indeed. And then from earth back into the light, in an unstoppable burst of energy as nutrients surged up the stems of the plants into a green eruption every spring. It was almost as if the dead were always able to come back and overwhelm the living.

Because energy never died – it simply dispersed into the rest of the world and re-formed itself. In the churchyard of St Asaph's, it seemed to re-form itself into brambles and thistles, docks and dandelions, everything that was green and damp and grew faster than he was able to control.

The vicar sighed at such thoughts. They had never entered his head until he had arrived in Withens and Hey Bridge. But he couldn't be blamed. Even the bishop didn't blame him. People still died in Withens. But there had not been a single wedding in his time in the village, nor a christening. It was as if the people had no objection to wearing funereal black to enter the church, but they drew the line at the frivolity of a white wedding gown or a christening robe, at bridesmaids in satiny pastels and bright buttonholes.

Alton heaved on the mat of vegetation. It began to come away in a large lump, a long, tangled blanket of it. It had shallow roots that came away in thin, white tendrils ending in clumps of peaty soil that crumbled and trickled back on to the ground. Alton found he had exposed a wide area of ground that hadn't seen the light for many months. There were lots of insects wriggling and scurrying to get out of the way, and small snails dropping from the brambles on to the ground.

He hadn't realized quite how shallow the peat was in the churchyard, but there seemed to be part of the bedrock showing below the surface. It was a wonder that anyone had ever found enough depth for burials. Maybe that was why the huge slabs had been laid horizontally, to conceal the fact that the graves themselves were shallow instead of the traditional six feet deep.

But then Alton frowned. He knew perfectly well that the bedrock here was millstone grit, not limestone – that was further south in the White Peak. The rock beneath the peat should be dark, not light grey, as this lump was that protruded through the surface among the insects and snails.

Finally, his eyes seemed to focus properly, and he saw the other grey shapes exposed on the surface. There was a series of curved strips like the bars of a cage. There was a flattened edge like a spatula. And there were dark holes in the object he had originally taken for a stone – holes full of shadows that seemed to stare back at him accusingly.

'No!'

Without thinking, he threw the mat of vegetation back, covering the bones he had exposed, as if putting them out of sight would make them cease to exist. Alton screwed up his face, wishing that he could reduce the bones to dust by the power of his thoughts.

'Oh, God,' he said. 'Oh, God, why have you done this to me?'

Chapter Twenty-Eight

'FOR HEAVEN'S SAKE, get these people moved away,' said DI Hitchens.

A couple of uniformed officers moved into action. Ben Cooper hadn't noticed the small crowd that had been gathering on the other side of the churchyard wall. He saw some of the Oxley boys among them, and their neighbour, Mrs Wallwin. And there was Fran Oxley, too, at the back of the crowd. Unlike the others, she wasn't staring at the bones on the ground, but at Cooper himself. He met her eyes, wondering what it was she was trying to tell him. Of all the Oxleys, she was the one he felt he had come closest to communicating with. Yet even Fran wasn't able to speak to him directly, to tell him anything of what she knew. Cooper was an outsider. And that was too much of a boundary for her to cross.

'Where's the vicar now?' said Hitchens. 'Mr Alton, is it?'

'He's inside, sir.'

'See if he's ready to make a statement yet.'

Cooper noticed that the ivy covering the wall of the church had been cut back at some time. It had clambered over the guttering and spread right across the roof towards the ridge before a line had been drawn. If it had been left to itself, no doubt it would have crossed the ridge, too, and spread down the other side, until the entire church was covered. But the ivy stems had been brutally hacked off about three feet below the gutter and the suckers had been peeled from the stonework. You could still see the little white marks where the ivy had taken a grip.

But whoever had cut back the ivy here hadn't bothered to remove the tendrils that had been growing through the gaps between the roof tiles. Cut off from their parent stem, they had turned black and dry, some of them still sticking vertically into the air. Cooper supposed that trying to get them out would have pulled the tiles loose. But now there was a little petrified forest on the roof.

Down on the wall, the ivy was re-growing, of course. Bright green shoots were creeping up the brickwork, inching their way back towards the gutter. He could see from the marks on the bricks that the plants had already grown about twelve inches since they were cut back. Well, that was the way of nature. It never stopped. It would always win in the end, if only out of sheer persistence.

DEREK ALTON WAS sitting in one of the front pews of the church. As Cooper walked up the aisle, he could see only the back of the vicar's bowed head, and he thought he must be praying. Alton looked up when he heard Cooper's footsteps.

'Has it gone yet?' he said.

'You mean the remains? No, sir. There are procedures to go through while they're still in situ.'

'Photographs, I suppose.'

'That kind of thing, yes.'

'I don't want to see it again. I don't want to come out until it's gone.'

'That's not a problem, sir.'

'I'm a Jonah, aren't I?' said Alton.

'Jonah? I'm not as familiar with the Old Testament as you are, but wasn't he the one who got involved with the wrong end of a whale?'

Alton smiled. 'Jonah had bad luck. He became the symbol of somebody who brings disaster down on others. When sailors had bad luck at sea, they believed it was because they had a Jonah on board.'

'That's sounds rather superstitious of you, sir.'

'I'm afraid superstition is difficult to avoid in these parts. It seeps into the bones.'

'And why should you think yourself a Jonah?'

'Why? Neil Granger dies a horrible death shortly after leaving me. And now I find there's some other poor soul lying dead in my churchyard, and has been there for years. I disturbed their bones with my interfering. I must have walked over them many times. Neil must have almost walked over them when he left here that night. He walked over those bones on his way to his death, and he didn't even see them.'

Alton shivered. Cooper wondered whether he should offer some reassuring words about the body being merely the vessel, and the spirit going on to better things. But he decided it wouldn't be appropriate. A doctor to check the vicar over would be more the thing.

'I have to ask you this ... We've found human remains in your churchyard. Do you have any idea whose they might be?'

'None at all,' said Alton, raising shocked eyes to Cooper. 'Surely they must have been in the ground long before I came here?'

'We don't know that yet. A body can be reduced to a skeleton quite quickly, depending on the conditions.'

'Oh, I don't think I want to know that,' said Alton. 'I wish you hadn't told me.'

'I'm sorry to distress you, sir. But, obviously, if there's anything at all you can think of that would help us identify this person, it would be very helpful.'

'Of course. But just at the moment, you know ...'

'I understand. We'll need you to come in and make a statement some time. But in the meanwhile, someone has contacted your wife, and she's on her way over.'

'I'll be all right in a little while. I'm not used to this kind of shock. Even in Withens. You want a statement from me? I don't know what I can tell you, though.'

'Was there anything that made you choose to clear that particular part of the churchyard today?' said Cooper.

'What do you mean?'

'I just wondered ... It's one the oldest parts, isn't it? The gravestones there all date from the nineteenth century.

There are no recent burials, so it's not as if they're graves that living relatives are likely to want to visit. If there were a priority for these things, I'd have guessed you'd go for the most recent graves first. It must be distressing for relatives to find their loved ones' graves overgrown and untidy. But not in that area.'

'Yes, you're right,' said Alton. 'That would make sense. But I wasn't thinking logically. It was those old gravestones that made me curious. The small ones, with only initials and a year. Did you notice those?'

'Yes, though you can hardly see them.'

'Exactly,' said Alton. 'They're already anonymous enough, and so small that I thought it was a shame to see them disappear altogether. I thought they were the ones that needed the light most of all.'

'You wanted to bring light?'

'Yes, that's what I wanted.'

'Whoever buried a body there wouldn't have expected that,' said Cooper. 'I'm sure they thought that corner was the most neglected and forgotten. They gambled on the body not being found for quite a while, maybe never.'

'If I'd managed to get help, though,' said Alton, 'I would have cleared the whole churchyard.'

'But no one would help you.'

'No. Well, no one except Neil.'

'Neil? Neil Granger?'

'He was going to give me a hand. He was a good lad.'

'But he never got the chance.'

'No.'

'Mr Alton, did anybody know that Neil Granger was going to help you clear the churchyard?'

'I have no idea,' said Alton. 'Think about it for a while.'

'Well, my wife, Caroline. I mentioned it to her, because I was rather pleased that someone had volunteered.'

'Neil did volunteer? You didn't persuade him to do it? Or offer to pay him?'

'Oh, no. If I could have afforded to pay someone, I would have done it. But Neil volunteered. He heard me complaining about it one day, and I told him how much I was struggling on my own. I think he took pity on me. But I was very grateful.'

'Did you tell anyone else but your wife?'

'I don't think so.'

'Of course, we don't know who Neil himself might have mentioned it to,' said Cooper.

'I did tell the churchwardens,' said Alton. 'I'd been a bit cross with them for not supporting me more than they did, and I thought it might make them feel guilty. It was wrong of me, I suppose, to feel that way.'

'Your churchwardens are Michael Dearden and Marion Oxley?'

'Yes.'

'So all the Oxleys might have known about Neil?'

'I suppose so,' said Alton. 'Does that help?'

'Perhaps,' said Cooper. 'But, knowing the Oxleys, perhaps not.'

'Who is it out there?' said Alton. 'In the churchyard?'

'We don't know, sir. We might not know for some time.' Cooper stood up. 'Your wife will be here in a moment.'

'Yes.'

'I'm sorry that someone should have chosen the churchyard for this. It's consecrated ground.'

'Consecrated? Yes, but consecrated only means that something has been set apart for a purpose.'

'Well, it's sacred, then.'

'Everywhere is sacred,' said Alton. 'I don't believe that God is in some places and not in others.'

IN THE CHURCHYARD, the scene was chaotic. The crowd of people was getting too big for the uniformed officers to manage, and the perimeter of the churchyard was too large. Some of the children were gradually creeping nearer to see what was going on, dodging behind the graves and hiding in the undergrowth until a PC spotted them and chased them off.

A clergyman had appeared in a black overcoat. He had wispy grey hair, gold-framed glasses and a worried frown.

Diane Fry intercepted him. 'Who are you, sir?'

'I'm the Rural Dean. Derek Alton called me to tell me what had happened.'

'You're Mr Alton's boss?'

'Well, we're all employed by God. But He permits me a supervisory role.'

Fry blinked, as if to clear away an irritating speck that had drifted across her vision.

'Can you tell us when Mr Alton arrived at St Asaph's?' she said.

'About eighteen months ago.'

'And did he take over directly from his predecessor?'

'No, there was an inter-regnum.'

'A what?'

'A period of time between incumbents. It happens all too often these days, due to a shortage of clergy. It can take some time to find the right person for the parish.'

'Particularly in Withens and Hey Bridge, perhaps?'

'There are certain challenging elements to the post.'

'How long was the parish vacant?'

'I believe it was twelve months or so. The previous incumbent fell seriously ill and had to retire, poor man.'

'We're going to have to speak to him.' 'I'm afraid not.'

'It's going to be very important to establish when an opportunity might have occurred for a body to be buried in the churchyard. The previous vicar might be able to cast some light on that for us.'

'Possibly. But I'm afraid poor Reverend Clater retired because he discovered he had advanced prostate cancer. There was nothing they could do for him. He died last year.'

'Hell.'

'Let's hope not,' said the Dean with a sad smile. Fry stared at him, puzzled.

'And no one looked after St Asaph's during this inter-regnum?'

'There were services here, but they were conducted by visiting clergy from other parishes. Sometimes by a retired priest who lives in Glossop. There was no continuity, I'm afraid.'

'And the churchwardens don't seem to have put too much effort into caring for the churchyard.'

'Sadly not. But I'm afraid it's difficult motivating people for that kind of thing.'

'Mr Alton is in the church. I'm sure he'd be pleased to see you.'

'Thank you.'

BEN COOPER FOUND his name called as soon as he got outside the church.

'What's going on?'

'Oh, Mr Dearden – nothing to concern you, sir.'

'It is, if it's something to do with the church. I'm a churchwarden. Is Derek all right?'

'Mr Alton is a bit shaken, but he's all right.'

'What have they done now?'

'Who?'

'The Oxleys. Is it that little beggar, Jake? He's the one who likes setting fires, you know, but nobody has been able touch him because he isn't ten years old yet. So many times I've heard politicians say that no one is beyond the law. It's repeated like a mantra, as if it's supposed to reassure us, just in itself. But it isn't true, is it? A child under ten can't be considered guilty of any criminal offence, no matter what they've done. Children *are* beyond the law.'

Cooper thought about Craig Oxley, who had hanged himself in a cell at Hindley young offenders' institution. Where was the middle ground between those who thought young people should be locked up at whatever age they offended, and others who believed they should never be locked up at all? There were few other options. Youngsters below the age of criminal responsibility could be the subject of care proceedings, which would most likely result in them being taken away from their parents. But once they reached the age of ten, they became criminals. There was no longer even that grey area between ten and fourteen, when it had to be proved beyond reasonable doubt that the child understood what he was doing and knew that it was seriously wrong. The presumption in their favour had been abolished by new legislation nearly five years previously.

Michael Dearden was watching him, and maybe he thought that he read a degree of sympathy in Cooper's expression.

'I read a while ago,' said Dearden, 'that the government was planning to lock up people like paedophiles before they did anything wrong, because they could tell from their profiles that they were likely to commit an offence.'

'Yes, I heard that.'

'And then I read the statistics that nearly 70 per cent of crimes in this country are committed by juveniles. And straight away I thought: "Well, there's your answer to the rising crime rate."'

'What answer is that, Mr Dearden?'

'It's obvious. You lock up all the kids, before they do anything. That way, you'd reduce the crime rate by two thirds at a single stroke. Well, you would, wouldn't you?'

Cooper tried to marshal a logical argument. Then he decided it wasn't worthwhile.

'You can't argue with the facts,' said Dearden.

'Mr Dearden, I don't think it's the Oxleys who have been targeting your property.'

'Rubbish. Two of the Oxleys were caught and prosecuted. They had broken into one of my outbuildings and stolen gardening tools and weedkiller.'

'Yes, I know. Ryan and Sean. But that was over a year ago.'

'I've seen them hanging around here plenty of times.'

'Since the court case?'

'Yes. Well, no. Not to actually see them. But I know it's them, still. They're just a bit more careful not to get caught now. They've learned to be cleverer criminals – that's all the court system has done for them, and me. Since they were taken to court, all they want to do is get revenge on me.'

'We think it's more likely that you've been targeted by a gang of antiques thieves than that you're still being troubled by the Oxleys, Mr Dearden. We think Mr Oxley has stopped all that now.'

'But who else would it be?'

'I don't know. But there's no evidence it's the Oxleys.'

'It wouldn't be hard to find some evidence. I've told your people no end of times, you'd only have to raid those houses in Waterloo Terrace, and you'd come away with a rare stash of stolen goods. And I know you could do it, if you wanted to. You did at Hey Bridge the other morning.'

'That operation was based on extensive intelligence.'

'Intelligence?' Dearden laughed. 'Well, that counts me out, then. Obviously, I don't have the intelligence to see what's in front of my face. It's no wonder you lot take no notice of me. I'm just a silly old bugger who's imagining things, as far as you're concerned.'

'I'm sure that's not the case, sir.'

'But I'm sure you'd soon sit up and take notice of me if I decided to do something about these break-ins myself, wouldn't you?'

Cooper looked at him more closely, and noticed the challenging stare and the slightly wobbly smile.

'Do what, exactly?' he said.

'Oh, that would be telling. But I've got something in mind that would put the wind up the Oxleys once and for all.'

'That wouldn't be a sensible thing to do, sir,' said Cooper. 'I'd have to advise you against any unilateral action.'

'Exactly,' said Dearden triumphantly. 'I knew whose side you'd be on.'

'Mr Dearden –'

But Michael Dearden was no longer listening. He got back into his pick-up, revved the engine and spun his wheels as he headed out of Withens. Cooper watched him as he climbed up Dead Edge and crashed his gears as he drove back over the border.

Cooper frowned. Derek Alton had said that Dearden avoided driving through Withens because he dreaded seeing the Oxleys in the road in front of Waterloo Terrace, as he had the day he'd knocked down and injured Jake. That might be so. But Cooper could detect no guilt in Michael Dearden. At least, not about what had happened to Jake Oxley.

FURTHER UP THE village, over the bridge, Cooper could see the supports being set up for the well-dressing boards opposite Waterloo Terrace. The well consisted of a stone trough full of clear water that Cooper knew would be ice cold, though there was no obvious source for it.

But he noticed there was another well near the church. It had water bubbling into it from the wall behind, but it looked abandoned, and it wasn't being prepared for dressing like the one further up the village.

There was a familiar face among the little crowd. Eric Oxley. He was the only adult member of the Oxley family here, though Cooper thought he had seen some of the children darting around, excited by what they had found waiting for them when they got home from school. Soon, the Yorkshire Traction bus driver would be doing extra business running tours to the scene. There were screens around the grave now, but a tent hadn't been erected yet to protect the scene from the weather.

As Cooper approached, Eric Oxley seemed suddenly to remember their first meeting, when Cooper had been trying to find Shepley Head Lodge.

'Shop!' snorted Eric. 'We're bloody lucky we've got a pub.'

'You've got a church too,' pointed out Cooper.

'Aye, there's a church.'

'The Reverend Alton says the congregations at St Asaph's are very small, even when there are services here. I'd have thought the church would have been closed by now, to be honest.'

Oxley looked down the village at the church. 'Everybody here thought they would have closed it, too,' he said. 'But that chap arrived, when we didn't expect it.'

'Mr Alton?'

'Aye, Alton. Have you seen him, messing about in the graveyard?'

'He's trying to tidy it up, to improve the look of the place. He says nobody else will do it.'

'Maybe not.'

'He's fighting a losing battle, Mr Oxley. He could do with some help.'

But Oxley just looked at him as if he were speaking a foreign language.

'Have you done?'

'I see your daughter-in-law has been working on the well dressing,' said Cooper.

'Aye. She does it every year. The younger ones help, too.'

'Right.' Cooper remembered the girls in the bath full of clay. 'Puddling', they called it – making the clay ready for spreading on the boards.

'It'll be up at the weekend,' said Oxley.

'But what about the other well? The one below the church. Why isn't that one dressed as well?'

'That well isn't used. It hasn't been used for a long time.'

'But there's water in it.'

'I know that.'

'So why isn't it used?'

'It's on the wrong side of the church,' said Oxley.

'What do you mean, the wrong side?'

Eric Oxley shrugged. 'People won't use the water down that end. They say it's polluted.'

'But there are no farming activities at the end of the village. The farms are at the other end. Down there, there's just the church and the graveyard, and the village hall.'

'Like I said – people reckon it's polluted.'

'But what by?'

But Oxley either didn't know the answer, or couldn't be bothered to explain it. With a twitch of his shoulder, he began to walk off.

'Mr Oxley,' called Cooper.

'Aye?' said the old man, without looking round.

'Those graves at the back of the church. Were those men some of the navvies working on the railway tunnels?'

'Yes.'

'I noticed that they all seem to have died around the same time. What did they die of?'

Oxley had stopped, but he still didn't answer.

'Was it an accident in the tunnels?' said Cooper. 'I thought perhaps it was a roof collapse, or an explosion, or something like that. But they died over a period of about a week. Was it an accident, Mr Oxley?'

'Not really.'

Oxley turned back towards him at last. Cooper couldn't see any expression in his eyes but for the usual suspicion. Oxley's gaze slid past Cooper towards the graveyard itself, and to the neglected well, full of water that the villagers ignored. When he spoke, his voice was tinged not with suspicion, but with anger.

'No, it wasn't an accident that killed them.'

'Not an accident? What, then?'

Oxley took a deep breath and met Cooper's eyes at last when he spoke.

'It was cholera.'

SUDDENLY, THERE WAS a scuffling and a shout from the churchyard gate, and two people burst through before anyone could stop them. They ran towards the tape, the man in the lead not bothering to stop as he charged into it and dragged it with him towards the makeshift grave. The Renshaws.

'Stop them!'

The nearest scenes of crime officer was taken completely by surprise. He tried to turn, tripped on a clump of weeds and dropped his video camera. He began to swear as Howard Renshaw shouldered him aside and trampled into the middle of the sacrosanct crime scene, destroying evidence with every step.

Before anyone could get near him, Howard had dropped to his knees, plunged his hands into the tangled roots and peaty soil, and picked up the skull.

'He had her here all the time,' he said.

'Mr Renshaw, please!'

Sarah was hanging back behind the cordon, not looking at the remains in the shallow grave, but staring at her husband as he ran his hands over the plates of the skull like a man caressing the head of a lover.

'Emma,' he said. 'She liked me to dry her hair when she'd washed it. I can remember being able to feel her scalp move over her skull when I ran the towel through her hair. I know the feel of her skull.'

As a SOCO took hold of the skull and tried to gently prise it from his grip, Howard looked up and caught Fry's eye. 'And this is her skull. It's my daughter.'

He resisted only a moment more, before allowing two police officers to pull him away.

Chapter Twenty-Nine

DEREK ALTON SAT awkwardly on his chair in the interview room at West Street. He was sweating, but then the room was always stuffy, and few interviewees found it comfortable. The interviewing officers tended to sweat, too. It didn't make them guilty.

Alton was a fidgeter. Some people went very still, as if in shock; others insisted on getting up and pacing the room. There were some who appeared quite relaxed – but they were usually the regulars, who had been here and done it all before.

But Alton was a fidgeter. He sat, but not comfortably, shifting from one buttock to the other, edging his chair a little nearer to the table, then away again. His hands were constantly moving. He squeezed one with the fingers of the other, then turned both hands upside down and looked at his palms, as if surprised to see them. Or perhaps just surprised to see something that he could read there. Then Alton put his hands back flat on the table, hiding the palms. But his fingers were still moving. When he lifted his hands again, his fingertips left faint perspiration stains on the polished surface of the table.

Cooper watched him with fascination. These moments before the interview started were often the most important. The interviewee didn't know what questions were going to be asked, and that allowed him to imagine the worst. If he had enough imagination, Alton might already have mentally painted himself into a corner, in a way that his interviewers were forbidden from doing. Just as they were obliged under the PACE rules to explain to him what his rights were, they also couldn't tell him any untruths about what evidence they might have, or what other witnesses had said, or mislead him about what could happen to him. But Derek Alton could do all of that for himself, given time.

'There's nothing to worry about, Mr Alton,' said Fry. 'You're here by your own free will to make a statement. You're free to leave at any time. Do you understand?'

Alton nodded, but stared at her as if she had threatened him with impending doom and destruction.

'Yes, I understand.'

Fry seemed to hear the same shake in his voice that Cooper did. 'Are you quite comfortable, sir?' she said. 'Would you like a drink of water before we start? A cup of tea perhaps? Coffee?'

'No, I'm fine. Thank you.'

'If you feel the need for a break at any time, just say so, and we'll stop the interview.'

'You're very considerate.'

Fry looked a bit surprised to be regarded as considerate. She was only doing what the PACE rules told her to. She was doing it by the book.

'You've kindly given us a statement about the circumstances surrounding your discovery of human remains in the churchyard of St Asaph's, Withens,' she said. 'This is the church where you are the incumbent.'

She had to read the word 'incumbent' from Derek Alton's statement. It wasn't a job title that she was familiar with.

'I'm priest in charge of Hey Bridge and Withens,' said Alton.

'So you're the incumbent at Withens?' said Fry, unsure whether he was contradicting himself.

'That's right.'

'You've said in your statement that there wasn't anything particular that made you choose that part of the churchyard to clear.'

'Well, only because of the graves there. They're very small memorial stones. They were disappearing completely.'

'When was it last cleared?'

'I really don't know,' said Alton. 'It was already deteriorating when I came to Withens.'

'Have you noticed any disturbance in that particular area?'

'Well, not really.'

'Not really? Was there something?'

'There's litter left. Beer cans, that sort of thing. Sometimes you can tell people have been in that part of the churchyard at night – branches broken off the trees, ground trampled. Once or twice, somebody has tried to start a fire.'

'It's out of sight from the road, isn't it?'

'Yes, indeed. That's the problem.'

'Mr Alton, do you know who comes into the churchyard at night?'

Alton looked a little more nervous.

'Children? Teenagers?' said Fry.

'Yes, I think so. Usually. But I can't imagine they would do anything like this ...'

'Any particular youngsters you might be able to identify?'

Alton grimaced. 'Of course. The Oxleys.'

'Thank you, sir. DC Cooper will make sure you get back home to Withens.'

BEN COOPER HAD noticed Tracy Udall's Astra in the car park at West Street, and guessed she must have been summoned to a divisional meeting that had been taking place upstairs. When he found her, she was in the locker room, cleaning her rigid handcuffs, oiling the boss and ratchet bar with WD40.

'Cholera?' said Cooper.

His dictionary defined cholera as an acute communicable bacterial infection of the small intestine by *vibrio cholerae*, derived from the ingestion of food or water contaminated by human sewage containing the micro-organism. It said the symptoms included the rapid onset of a profuse, white, watery diarrhoea, with muscle cramps, vomiting and progressive fluid loss, resulting in death within a few hours.

Cooper had very soon started feeling unwell.

'I mean, *cholera*?'

'It was a result of the conditions the navvies lived in,' said Udall. 'You know, the shanty town?'

'Yes.'

'They not only had poor food and no health-and-safety regulations, they also weren't provided with any clean water or any toilet facilities. Their food and water got contaminated by human sewage, and men started dying of cholera by the dozen. Some are buried at Wood-head Chapel, above the A628.'

'But others are buried in the churchyard at Withens.'

'That's right. It's ironic, when you think about it. Well dressing is supposed to have started after the Black Death. The villages that escaped being affected by the plague credited the purity of their local water supply for protecting them. So they revived the tradition of blessing the wells as a way of saying thank you. I think Tissington was one of the first.'

'Some of them probably still believed they were pro-pitiating the water goddess in those days,' said Cooper.

But Udall was right. Those Derbyshire villagers did have good reason to be thankful. In the middle of the fourteenth century, Black Death had killed a third of the population of England. Villages like Tissington were very lucky not to have been touched. Five hundred years later, though, it had been cholera that had taken the lives of the navvies building the Woodhead tunnels and living in their pitiful shanty towns.

'So the other well in Withens is avoided because it's on the wrong side of the churchyard – below it, where the cholera from the bodies buried there could get into the water supply?'

'It's nonsense, of course.'

'But you understand how that fear might have arisen. Those men died from drinking contaminated water in the first place.'

Udall dried the handcuff grip and reset the handcuffs to preload.

'You know, a lot of people use the tip of a ballpoint pen to double-lock their cuffs,' she said. 'I always think that looks a bit unprofessional – it gives the impression you've lost the key and you're trying to pick the lock with a pen.'

'Some people *do* lose the key,' said Cooper. 'Or forget to take one with them.'

Udall sniffed. 'Some people seem to want trouble. They go in as if they want a suspect to turn violent. Not me. These handcuffs are the most important bit of equipment I have, and learning touch 'n'cuff has been a godsend. It's saved me a lot of trouble from arrests over the last few years. I'll be happy if I never have to draw a baton. A lot of my arrests don't know what's happening. The first time I touch them, they're under my control. *Then* I tell them they're under arrest. And they come like lambs, by and large.'

She eased the handcuffs back into their pouch and patted it, almost with affection.

'Do you think it helps being female?' said Cooper. He had seen plenty of male officers who had exactly the attitude that Udall had described. When they went in to a situation, it was as if they wanted trouble, either because it made them feel macho, or because they liked the adrenalin rush from the risk of injury, he wasn't sure.

'Oh yes,' said Udall. 'They take one look at me, and they're lulled into a false sense of security. They don't realize how dangerous I am.'

'Want to come and give the Reverend Derek Alton a lift back to Withens?'

'Why not?'

DEREK ALTON DIDN'T seem to want to talk on the way home. He sat in the car staring out of the window at the passing scenery as they descended into Longdendale.

'Will you be blessing the well dressing this weekend?' said Ben Cooper.

'Yes, of course.'

'I always thought well dressings were pagan. Water worship. But the church has taken them over these days, hasn't it?'

'The Church of England is nothing if not pragmatic,' said Alton. 'The early missionaries were told not to destroy the pagan holy places and beliefs but to incorporate them into the new religion. The spring festival of the fertility goddess Oestre became the date of the resurrection. They still name it Easter, which I always think is a bit of a giveaway, myself. And death and resurrection have symbolized the beginning of spring for thousands of years. Winter and spring, death and life, the dark and the light. The natural cycle.'

'Like the mummers' play tradition. The Fool is killed, then brought back to life again.'

'Of course. It's a resurrection play.'

'Except they didn't save a part for Jesus.'

Alton decided not to take the bait. He went back to the scenery as they approached the road over the reservoirs.

'And you're interested in the Border Rats,' said Cooper.

'They're based on Border morris, which was the real workingmen's tradition. It was a way of getting a bit of money during the winter, when their families might have starved otherwise. Since begging was illegal, they blacked their faces up as a disguise. But in Withens, the tradition has developed in its own way. That's the nature of genuine traditions. They're not preserved in aspic, they develop naturally and mean whatever people want them to mean.'

'Some of them told me the dance symbolized killing the rats in the old railway tunnels where the navvies worked.'

'That could be so,' said Alton. 'Nobody can know for sure now. It's passed down from one generation to the next, and it gets changed along the way, because nothing is ever written down. Each year it changes a bit more, depending on the people involved.'

'How is it you know so much about these traditions, sir?'

'I'm a morris man myself, I have to admit,' said Alton. 'I danced Cotswold morris in a previous parish.'

'With the bells and hankies?'

'Yes.'

'Pagan origins again?'

'Pagan or not, every dance has its own meaning. A spiritual dimension. The rituals are important, of course. Dressing up, setting aside a special day, learning the words and the movements. All part of the ritual. There's even a sacred space for the dancers to perform in. In religion, it's called the "temenos". But ritual isn't quite enough. If the moments of spiritual connection are going to happen, you have to commit, you have to invest belief in it.'

Cooper noted that the Border Rats seemed to have sparked a bit more interest than a mention of Jesus.

'But this is very limited. It seems to be entirely members of the Oxley family.'

'Not really,' said Alton. 'These days, some of the Border Rats live in Hey Bridge. The two groups hardly speak to each other outside rehearsals, but when they're performing, they hardly seem to know who's who. There's never any shortage of volunteers to join. Lucas Oxley's rule is to give places to those who live nearest to Withens, but as long as they're willing to give everything when they're Border Rats, Lucas doesn't care. If they treat the Rats as a joke, they're out.'

'Thank you,' said Cooper. 'That was very interesting.'

'And no earthly use to you at all, I'm sure.'

'Well …'

'The thing to remember is that morris isn't really terribly, terribly old. And there's no inherent mystical meaning, only what the individual puts into it.

But it *has* grown out of our own culture and history, and it belonged to generations of our own ancestors. That's why it's important.'

BEN COOPER LOOKED at his watch as he and Tracy Udall turned back on to the A628 towards Longdendale. There were several active lines of enquiry that he could be helping out with now. But as she drove along the reservoirs, Udall was still thinking about cholera.

'Do you know, there was a notorious murder here around the time of that cholera outbreak,' she said. 'It was a case that would have defeated even Derbyshire Constabulary, if it had existed in those days.'

'What was that?'

'The Woodhead Tunnel Murder. Not heard of it?'

'No.'

'It was in 1849.'

'Oh, well. The Constabulary wasn't formed until 1857. Besides, Longdendale was in Cheshire until 1974. There might have been a petty constable or something, but a magistrate would have taken charge in a murder case. Where did it happen?'

'In the shanty town where the navvies lived. The place had already became notorious, but this was just after the cholera outbreak. One of the big problems the navvies faced was the contract system. In fact, it was a complicated process of sub-contracting, called "truck". At every level, there was someone who creamed off some of the money for themselves by reducing supplies, buying the cheapest food, cutting corners. You can imagine.'

'Yes. That hasn't changed much.'

'Well, one of the worst sub-contractors was a man called Nathan Pidcock. He was a local man, who ran a haulier's business from Tintwistle. He jumped at the chance of getting involved in the tunnel project, because there were big profits to be made. By all accounts, he made a lucrative business for himself by supplying rotting food, dirty water, and substandard materials at inflated prices. The navvies hated him, of course, but they were living in their shanty town in the middle of nowhere, and they relied on people like Pidcock for supplies. Anyway, finally he must have gone too far. The outbreak of cholera was blamed on water polluted by human waste. Dozens of men died over a period of days. And one morning, Nathan Pidcock was found dead in a ditch on the edge of the camp. He had been beaten to death.'

'And were there no suspects?'

'Suspects?' Udall laughed. 'That's the question of a twenty-first century policeman. Yes, there were fifteen hundred of them. The theory was that a group of workmen decided to exact their own brand of justice on Pidcock for the deaths of their mates. The rest of the men in the camp must have known what happened, but nobody said a word. So the authorities were helpless.'

'A conspiracy of silence?'

'I expect these days we could have done a mass DNA test or something.'

'Only if there was some blood, or traces of other bodily fluids from the perpetrators at the scene, or Pidcock's blood on their clothing. But basically, you're right – there would certainly have been some forensic evidence to follow up.'

'There was one witness, though,' said Udall. 'Nathan Pidcock had a young assistant, a lad called John Cobb. He helped with deliveries to the camp. But he was only about fourteen, and the attackers left him alone.'

'Wasn't Cobb able to identify anyone?'

'No. He saw the whole thing, but couldn't point out any one of his employer's attackers. His story was that they had disguised themselves. He said they all had their faces blacked up.'

Cooper wasn't surprised. The continuity seemed to be there even now, a tradition passed down through the generations. Maybe the Oxleys were direct descendants of those railway navvies who had died building the tunnels. Maybe their ancestors had lived in the shanty town, which seemed to be treated as the village's dirty little secret.

He recalled the superstition that Sandy Norton had mentioned about the tunnels. Those workmen were right that an evil had been brought down on them by the tunnelling project. But it hadn't been caused by some primeval force that had slept for eons under the hill and had been disturbed by their blasting. It had been a much more human evil. Its cause was greed.

Chapter Thirty

THE SECOND TIME Ben Cooper met his new neighbour, it was on neutral territory again. He had arrived home and was fiddling around in his pockets for his door key. It had been a hard day, and his mind was full of fragments of conversation, and pictures of young Oxleys he couldn't put the right name to.

As he managed to get the key into his hand, the door to the other flat opened. Briefly, he wondered whether Peggy Check had been listening for him coming in. If Dorothy Shelley was the only person she knew in Edendale, she might be getting desperate for a bit of normal human contact. Cooper immediately felt guilty that he hadn't made an effort to be more sociable.

'Hello, how's it going?' he said.

'Great, thanks. And you?'

Cooper knew he was probably a bit dishevelled at the end of his shift, rather unshaven and maybe a bit grubby.

'Fine. I'm sorry, I'm just home from work.'

He opened his door, still feeling a little embarrassed. He thought perhaps he didn't smell too good either.

'You must come in for a coffee some time.'

'Sure. That would be great.'

'Good.'

He nodded and smiled, thinking there was probably a next step, but not quite able to bring it to mind.

'When?' said Check.

'Oh, er … tonight, if you like. Eight? Eight-thirty?'

'Fine. See you later then, Ben.'

COOPER FED THE cats, showered, changed and thought about having something to eat. His stomach told him he was starving. But he couldn't face rummaging through the freezer compartment. Not another frozen Chinese meal for one. But he had time to nip down to the Hanging Gate for a bar meal before Peggy Check called.

During the first week or so after he had moved into his new flat in Welbeck Street he had checked out all the pubs within walking distance. There were several of them, some of which he had visited before, but one or two were new to him. He wasn't a heavy drinker, not like some of his colleagues, who took to it to help them deal with the pressure and some of the depressing realities of the job. A drink or two did help him relax. But most of all, a decent pub provided company.

That was why he needed the right sort of place – not one that attracted only tourists, so that the same faces were never in the bar two nights running.

And definitely not an Irish bar with singing waiters and ceilidh nights.

At night, some town-centre streets became drinking strips. An area around the front door of each pub became a bubble of noise and smells, loud music and scores of young people yelling to make themselves heard above it. Inside, it was like walking into a tropical micro-climate. Hot, sweating faces above yards of bare flesh moved around in the heat and humidity of an Amazon rainforest, exhuding a miasma of antiperspirant and alcohol fumes.

Occasionally there were fights at closing time. And of course, there were the drugs. On Friday and Saturday nights, there was a permanent police presence – a personnel carrier with caged accommodation in the back and a riot visor over its windscreen, multiple foot patrols of officers who had drawn the short straw and been rostered for the late shift.

Tourists learned to avoid those areas at night, when they saw the change that had come over a town that had looked so quaint during the day, with its cobbled alleys and tall stone buildings, its antiques shops and tea rooms. Even the pleasantest of England's market towns could have a Jekyll and Hyde nature.

But to Cooper, Edendale still had character, a proper sense of place. It had its own smells and sounds and sights – that accumulation of sensations that gave it a unique identity, so that you always knew where you were. The same couldn't be said of many towns, whose high streets looked indistinguishable.

On his way to the Hanging Gate, he passed through streets that had rows of terraced houses with names like Riversleigh and Rockside. In the window of a cottage, someone had let a yucca plant flourish, and it had filled the little bay window completely. A small tabby cat had squeezed into the tiny amount of space left on the window ledge, and it peered out at him through the plant's spiky leaves. Antique bottles were lined up in another window next door. They were carefully arranged by size – the largest at either end and the smallest in the middle.

Cooper shook his head. The windows of these houses were so small that they allowed in little enough light already, without being cluttered up with dusty bottles and overgrown yucca plants. Windows like these always made him wonder what the people inside the houses had to hide. Or were they symbolically protecting themselves against the world outside by lining up their peculiar talismans on the edge of their property? Were glass bottles a kind of charm to ward off the evils of the outside world? Maybe there was some psychological reassurance from viewing the world through brown glass or the leaves of a yucca.

He was always curious about people's minds, the bizarre mental processes that made them do the things they did. A part of him would love to be able to knock on a few of these doors to see who was behind them, and then to ask the questions. Why the bottles? What's the yucca all about? Wouldn't you prefer a bit of sunlight in your life?

Like many pubs in the area, the Hanging Gate had scenic Peak District views in framed prints on the walls. The same old CD of 60s and 70s pop classics seemed to be playing, too. But it also had Bank's Bitter and Mansfield Cask Ale and Pedigree, not to mention a choice of lagers like Stella Artois and white wine on draft. On uneven stone flags, the cigarette machine, jukebox and slot machines had been pushed back against the wall, out of the way.

Cooper ordered a steak pie and chips and nodded to a few casual acquaintances as he found a table. He had a paperback novel in his pocket that he'd brought to read if there was no one to talk to.

Stained-glass panels were set into the ceiling and red roses in the pattern of the carpet. None of the colour schemes in the décor seemed to fit together when you took the pub as a whole. One corner might seem to make sense on its own, but when Cooper sat in the middle of the room, as he did now, he got quite a different perspective. Now, there were too many painful clashes, too many choices that made no sense, too many failures of taste and logic. It was chaos – a jumble of pieces that would never fit together as a whole.

A FEW MINUTES later, there was a slight change in the background noise in the bar. Ben Cooper looked up from his pie. He saw the men sitting by the bar turn their heads towards the door. Probably some tourists had wandered into the pub to get out of the rain and were rustling their cagoules in the porch as they shook themselves off like wet dogs. Maybe they had an actual wet dog with them, too.

If they were lucky, someone might make a bit of room for them near the log fire, which the landlord always kept ready and had lit because of the change in the weather. He didn't like anyone being hostile to tourists in his pub, because they tended to buy shorts rather than beer, which made a difference to his profit margin. They might even be tempted to a Hanging Gate All-Day Breakfast.

But no one moved away from the fire. No rustling cagoules passed Cooper on their way to the bar, no flashes of orange and yellow clashed with the purple patterns of the wallpaper as they appeared from behind the glass partition. Instead, Cooper became aware of water dripping on to the end of the polished oak-effect table, and a pair of grubby trainers that stopped on the industrial-thickness carpet just inside his line of sight.

'Hello, Ben.'

'What are you doing in here, Angie?'

'I came in for a drink. You're going to buy me one, aren't you?'

'How did you find me?'

'You're a man of habit. It's not so hard.'

She sat down in an empty chair, smiling as if sure of her welcome. Cooper leaned across the table to speak to her, anxious not to draw the attention of the other customers too much.

'Look, I can't put up with this. I want to know how you got my name and address in the first place.'

'Maybe I hired a detective. There are some good ones around these days.'

'Angie –'

'If you're not going to buy me a drink, I could ask one of those people over there. I don't mind. I'm quite good at asking for money.'

'Sit down,' said Cooper. 'Just try not to drip on my book. What is it you want?'

'For a start, a tonic water would be nice.'

'You drink tonic water?'

'Yes. But I drink it straight from the bottle, to be trendy.'

'OK.'

'Oh, and a packet of cheese-and-onion crisps.'

Cooper went to the bar to get her drink. While he waited, he looked back at Angie Fry. She wasn't paying any attention to him at all, but had picked up his book and was slowly turning the pages. Her pale fingers lying against the cover reminded him of the hands of the skeleton protruding from the shallow grave in St Asaph's churchyard.

He kept his back to the men sitting against the wall. They were silent now, wondering quite what to make of Angie. Normally, they might have ribbed him or given him a friendly wink about having a girlfriend. But even they sensed that there was something not quite right about Angie.

'Do you read books a lot?' she said, when he took her the tonic water and crisps.

'Quite a bit. They're relaxation. Especially since I've lived on my own. I don't want to end up watching telly every night, like a vegetable.'

'It helps to keep the brain active, right? The imagination.'

'Yes, I think so.

She put the book back on the table. Cooper noticed that she had lost his page.

'It seems a funny thing to be doing in a pub, though,' she said. 'Anti-social.'

'I don't do it all the time. Only when I want to be left alone for a while.'

She laughed. 'And now I've come along and interrupted your relaxation. That's not very fair, is it?'

She gazed at him, as if expecting him to take some deeper meaning from her words. Cooper sighed. He was going to have to take a course in communication skills. Everything was going straight over his head these days.

'The world isn't fair,' he said. 'We just have to hope it's unfair in our favour occasionally.'

'Is that the best we can hope for?'

'I'm afraid so.'

'It hardly seems worth bothering.'

'But there are other things in life, apart from fairness. So think about the things that you can get hold of.'

'Like what?'

'Love?'

'You what?' said Angie.

'Well, maybe.'

'You're crazy, do you know that? Love!'

'It was only a suggestion. Think about it.'

'I can't believe you, Ben Cooper. Are you for real? I've never met anybody so naïve.'

'You know, it's funny,' said Cooper. 'But you sound just like somebody else I know.'

Angie laughed again. 'Right. And what have you decided, Ben?'

Cooper thought about Diane Fry. She'd been the bane of his life for months. Yet she'd tried to help him, even when he could see she was having difficulties dealing with the Renshaws. Could he lay the extra stress on her about her sister? In a way, this was keeping her together and focused; while she had hope, she could cope. Angie wanted him to take her hope away.

'I can't do it,' he said.

'You can't? Of course you can.'

'I can't,' he said. 'I can't take Diane's hope away.'

'I heard you were her friend.'

'Yes, you said.'

Angie looked disappointed in him. If that was the way she felt, she should join the queue.

'Well, what sort of friend *are* you? You know it would be the best thing for her, to forget all about me.'

Cooper felt himself weakening. 'Diane wouldn't listen to me, anyway. Not without any proof.'

'Of course,' said Angie. 'I thought you would say that. And that's why I came.'

She reached inside her coat and pulled out an envelope, which she handed to Cooper.

'What's this?'

'Open it and see.'

There was nothing written on the outside of the envelope. Cooper glanced around uncomfortably. A police officer being handed a plain brown envelope in a pub wouldn't look too good. But the customers of the Hanging Gate had lost interest in him and Angie. Some football highlights were being shown on the TV screen.

He opened the flap of the envelope and slid out the contents.

'How did you get these?'

'It doesn't matter.'

'Yes, it does matter,' said Cooper angrily. 'How did you get them?'

'Let's just say I have the right sort of contacts.'

'Criminal contacts, obviously.'

'You stick to your friends, and I'll stick to mine.'

He was holding a death certificate. It recorded the death in Chapeltown, Sheffield, of Angela Jane Fry, aged thirty. It was dated just over a year ago.

'And presumably this isn't your real address,' said Cooper.

Angie laughed. 'That isn't even my name now. I changed it some time ago.'

'Diane would go straight to this address and make enquiries.'

She shrugged. 'Good luck to her. The house was used as a squat, but the owners evicted everyone months ago.'

'I don't understand why you're doing this.'

'From what I hear of Diane, she's persistent. She needs something like this to stop her. She needs convincing.'

'Where have you been hearing things about Diane?'

'She's been pretty active in Sheffield, believe me. She's been making a big nuisance of herself, and there are a lot of people who don't like it.'

Cooper nodded. For once, he did believe her.

'It's making life difficult for me,' said Angie. 'And for some of my friends. I need her to stop.'

'What friends? Anyone I know?'

'Not very likely, is it?'

'Well, *someone* told you about me and how to find me.'

'Like I said, everyone knows you, Ben. You're just going to have to live with it.'

'Do you think I won't be able to find out who it was?'

'Is it that important?' said Angie.

'Well, yes, actually.'

She shrugged, took a drink of her tonic water and pulled a face. Then she pretended to take an interest in the football on TV.

'Who's playing?'

'Just what I was thinking,' said Cooper.

Unfortunately, Angie was right. There were too many possible sources where she could have obtained information about him. On both sides of the law. That didn't stop him itching to find out, though. He would love to give somebody hassle for leaking his address.

Cooper looked at the death certificate. It was a very good forgery, and he would certainly have been convinced by it. Angie must have some interesting contacts. But the odd thing was that, though she said she wanted Diane to stop trying to trace her, she was asking an awful lot of questions about her sister. Cooper was starting to feel that she really wanted to know all about Diane, but at second hand. Despite her façade, she was frightened of having to face her little sister.

'I know I'm taking a big gamble trusting you,' said Angie. 'But I know you're her friend. Do you realize how rare that is? I couldn't find any others. But I do trust you. If you don't do this, you won't just be letting me down. You'll be letting Diane down. She needs to get over all this and put it behind her, for her own sake. I think you know that, Ben.'

Cooper met her eyes. They were disconcertingly familiar – the same eyes that he had to look at when Diane was angry with him. But they were too familiar – they should have looked more different from Diane's. He had seen plenty of smackheads in Edendale, and they were blank-faced and skinny, with discoloured teeth. There was a place on the Cavendish Estate where the kids went to inject themselves every night, and the council came round every morning to pick up the needles. Those smackheads had dead eyes, not like these.

'I'll think about it,' he said. 'That's all I'm going to say.'

'Cool. Thanks for the drink, anyway.'

COOPER WAITED UNTIL Angie had left the Hanging Gate. He watched her walk past the window of the pub, heading towards the Market Square. Then he slipped his book into his pocket, nodded at the landlord and stepped out of the door. He paused on the step with his hand to his head as if to brush his hair into place, and was able to see the figure of Angie Fry as she disappeared into the High Street. He could tell by the way she was walking that she had no idea that she might be followed. She had trusted him too much, in the end.

He found a cap in his pocket and put it on as he crossed the street and walked in the direction Angie was following. He turned the corner of the High Street, and stopped.

A couple of hundred yards further on, there was a line of cars parked on the side of the street, close under the front wall of the old technical institute, which had been converted into offices. The lights came on in one of the cars as Angie reached it, and she opened the passenger door. Cooper stopped behind the last car in the line and bent his head, pretending to be fastening his shoelace on the rear bumper. He had a clear view as the car ahead manoeuvred to leave its parking space. He could see it was a dark blue BMW and, as it pulled out in the traffic, he saw its registration number.

Cooper patted his pockets until he found a notebook and pen, and wrote the number down by the light of a streetlamp before he forgot it. Then he pulled out his mobile phone and called the comms room at West Street to request a PNC check.

'Sorry, DC Cooper,' said the operator. 'I can't give you any information. That's a blocked number.'

'Are you sure?'

'Quite sure.'

A blocked number? Cooper had never come across one before, not in ten years of police service.

'Thanks anyway.'

Well, one thing was for sure. Criminals and drug addicts didn't own dark blue BMWs with blocked numbers. The privilege was only extended to vehicles whose ownership was officially protected. Investigators in vulnerable positions, like the DSS. But mostly police officers involved in sensitive operations. What exactly had Diane Fry been sticking her nose into?

BEN COOPER WALKED back to his flat, but didn't go in. He unlocked his own car and drove out of town on Castleton Road until he found the street where Diane Fry lived. A few minutes later, he was looking up at the window of Fry's flat. This was a student area, and the houses had been converted into as many flats and bedsits as possible, so they would be pretty basic. But Fry was on a sergeant's pay now. Surely she could afford something better than this? There was nothing special about the Peugeot car she ran. She didn't take exotic holidays that he was aware of. But where else would her salary go? Was there something he didn't know about her life?

Well, of course, there were lots of things he didn't know. Would it do Diane any good to find her? Was that where Diane's salary went – on her efforts to find Angie? And then he thought about a heroin addiction. It was an expensive habit to feed.

Cooper had been intending to ring the bell, but for some reason he couldn't quite bring himself to do it. He had been in Fry's flat only once, and that was an occasion he had very vague memories of. All he really knew was that he hadn't been welcome. He had no conviction that he would be any more welcome now.

He thought of Ruby Wallwin. When you live alone for a long time, you become a hermit and the outside world becomes a threat. You hear someone's footsteps in the corridor, and hope that they will pass by. And when they do, you take it as another sign that the world has rejected you, that you're not wanted. In that way, you paint yourself into a corner, building a barrier that the world can never cross. And you hole up for the siege.

Surely this was what she needed? This was the great frustration that caused the chip on her shoulder? But if he got the two of them together, would she move away? She once told him that it was the reason she'd come to Derbyshire.

Besides, why make life any more difficult for himself? Surely he could just go home and forget all about it.

Cooper turned his car, switched on the radio and headed back into Edendale. If the curtains at the window of one of the first-floor flats had twitched as he left, he wouldn't have noticed.

Chapter Thirty-One

FRIDAY

BEN COOPER WASN'T really asleep when his alarm went off next morning. He hadn't slept properly at all, but had spent the night turning restlessly in his bed, worried that he'd miss the alarm. When the high-pitched beeping came, it penetrated a foggy limbo he had been suspended in, a world halfway between waking and sleep. His mind had been groggily circling and circling around the same thoughts, hovering over a deep well of anxiety without being able to see clearly what the cause of his uneasiness was.

Cooper pressed the button to stop the noise, and opened his eyes to stare into the darkness. It was totally black in his room. Black, and silent. There was no traffic on the road outside and no birds singing, no one moving around the house, not even any water hissing through the old plumbing of 8 Welbeck Street. The silence made him feel cold. But perhaps that was only anticipation.

He knew how cold it would be outside, once he had left the house. It was six o'clock in the morning, and it was April.

Cooper swung his feet from under the duvet, sat up and pulled back the curtain. It was also raining.

'Oh, great.'

For a moment, he thought about lying down and pulling the bedclothes back over himself, and staying there until it got light, as normal people did. But then he sighed, switched on the bedside light, and headed for the bathroom. He had no time to waste – he was on an early shift today, and a briefing meeting had been scheduled for 8 a.m.

He skirted the pile of ironing that had been waiting for him to get to it for days, and stumbled in bare feet on the pine floorboards in the passage between his bedroom and the bathroom. It was warmer at this end of the flat, but that only made the thought of going out worse.

He had managed to have a shower and a shave and was trying to drink a coffee when his mobile phone rang on the kitchen table.

'No, I haven't set off yet,' he said to his coffee mug, even before he picked up the phone.

A large black cat walked sleepily into the kitchen and looked at him in a puzzled manner. If Cooper was up and moving around, it must be breakfast time. But it knew something wasn't quite right.

Cooper transferred his coffee to the other hand and picked up the phone.

'Ben Cooper.' He listened for a moment. 'No, I haven't set off yet, Diane. Yes, I know there's work to do before the morning briefing. What makes you think I'll be late? I'll be there on time.'

He pushed the phone into the pocket of his leather jacket, where he had thrown it over a chair the night before. He picked up the shirt, sweater and jeans that he'd put ready. The sitting room was dark, and only a thin sliver of light entered through the curtains from the streetlamp across the road. It glinted off the framed picture over his mantelpiece, as if his father were winking at him from his seat on the second row of the Edendale police line-up. Then Cooper noticed the cat.

'Here, Randy – do you want this coffee? I haven't time to drink it.'

The cat fixed him with its yellow eyes, puzzlement turning to disdain.

'No? Never mind.'

With the cat marching in front of him, its tail in the air, Cooper pulled his clothes on as he headed back to the kitchen. He put two bowls of cat food out and placed them on the floor in the conservatory, near the central-heating boiler. The noise of the rain was loud on the glass roof. Here in the centre of town there was always light, and he could make out the roofs of the houses that backed on to the Welbeck Street gardens from Meadow Road. The rest of the world out there was asleep. He would have to be careful that he was quiet as he left, so as not to disturb his new neighbour.

Cooper looked at his watch. If he didn't hurry, he actually was going to be late.

THE EDEN VALLEY hadn't yet experienced the full impact of its annual influx of tourists, but the May Day bank holiday would make up for that. Everything was geared up for the season – the craft shops were open and full of the aromas of freshly painted and varnished stock produced during the winter, the tourist attractions were spring cleaned and ready, the cafés and pubs were holding their breath, praying for a good summer.

The bank holiday weekend would be particularly busy this year, because Edendale was hosting a day of dance. It was what the morris dancers called an 'ale', though they said the name had nothing to do with the amount of beer that was drunk. Sides from all over the North and Midlands would be converging on the town to perform in the streets and in front of the pubs. With the help of a bit of good weather, the town would be packed.

Recently a television crew had been filming around Edendale, too. Their vehicles and equipment regularly blocked the narrow streets off the market square, irritating the shopkeepers and residents, who had to step over yards of cable snaking across the pavements and cobbles.

TV had a lot to answer for in the Peak District. In Buxton, a new golf driving range had recently opened under the name 'Peak Practice', in reference to a popular medical soap opera.

This morning, the pathologist would have begun to examine the skeletalized remains found in Withens. No doubt officers from other divisions would be phoning the CID room all day with jokes about E Division being so desperate for bodies that they had started to dig up the graveyards.

THE MORNING BRIEFING was a downbeat affair. Many of the officers knew of Emma Renshaw's disappearance two years previously, and they weren't immune from the assumptions being made about the skeleton unearthed in the Withens churchyard. It hardly seemed necessary to wait for the postmortem results. Nobody doubted Howard Renshaw.

For Diane Fry, the fact that the body had turned up in Withens was not what she had expected. But she found it had the result of forcing her to look at the enquiry from a completely different direction. That wasn't a bad thing at all. It was too easy to fall into assumptions.

Now her focus had to be on Withens, and her list of potential suspects had narrowed dramatically, from the entire population of two of the largest cities in Britain to a handful of familiar names, each of whom had a relationship of some kind with Emma. For the Renshaws, the discovery of the skeleton was devastating. But for Fry, it made an impossible task look suddenly like a breeze. Some forensic evidence from the remains and from the scene, a whiff of an opportunity and a motive, and the case could be wrapped up in no time, after all.

Best of all, there were more resources becoming available with the latest development. She wouldn't have to rely on Gavin Murfin alone any more.

As for the Neil Granger enquiry, nearly twenty lorry drivers had been traced who had passed along the A628 in the early hours of the previous Saturday morning, between 4 a.m. and 5 a.m. At that time of the morning, lorry drivers noticed things. Almost all of those spoken to had noticed the VW Beetle left in the lay-by near Withens that morning. Not one of them had seen another vehicle parked near it – not in the same lay-by or in the next one, a few hundred yards up the road.

The associates of Granger's who had been questioned had left the detectives frustrated by the absence of direct evidence, and the convenience of their alibis. The homes of two of them had been searched, without result.

David Senior was one of those who had been questioned most closely. Though a former colleague of Neil's at the chemicals factory in Glossop, he denied that the two of them had been in a relationship recently. 'We were just friends,' he had said, apparently sincerely. No one could demonstrate otherwise, despite what Neil's brother had been anxious to claim.

But when pressed, Senior agreed that Neil Granger was gay. Fry was disappointed when she heard the news. Without even a sniff of a motive for the killing of Emma Renshaw, she was completely in the dark. And surely no one committed murder to conceal the fact that they were gay any more? Neil Granger might have been the person with the best opportunity – in fact, the only opportunity she knew of – but what would his motive have been?

'So, EVEN AFTER the postmortem, we're going to have to wait for a forensic anthropologist to give us an estimate of how long the skeleton had been in the churchyard?' said Ben Cooper.

'Fat chance,' said Diane Fry. 'I bet he won't commit himself to within a year or two.'

'Really?'

'You'll see. We expect too much of these people, and they always disappoint us.'

'But we can't assume the body was buried during the gap between the old vicar leaving and the new one coming.'

'It has to have been since the last time that part of the graveyard was cleared. Otherwise some poor soul would have had the same experience that the Reverend Alton did.'

'I suppose so.'

Cooper was getting ready to go out. He had an appointment in Glossop to see someone at the offices of the Oxleys' landlords, Peak Water.

'What I'd like to know,' said Fry, 'is when exactly the Oxleys lost interest in maintaining the churchyard.'

'Diane, does this mean you want me to have another go at talking to them?'

'Yes, Ben. And try a bit harder this time, could you?'

Cooper sighed. 'You think they're hiding something?'

'Don't you?'

'I'm not sure. But I know they feel threatened in some way.'

'Well, what about this: if the place to hide a body is the graveyard, maybe the best place to hide a murderer is among criminals.'

'You mean one of the Oxleys? You think they're protecting one of their own?'

'Well, the Oxleys may well all be criminals, Ben. But I was thinking of somewhere we put the criminals we've caught. Prison, in fact.'

'But there isn't anyone in prison –' said Cooper, then stopped.

'Not any more.'

Cooper thought of a boy who had hanged himself in his cell because he couldn't stand life in a young offenders' institution.

'Craig Oxley.'

'If what his sister told you is true …'

'But if the Oxleys know who killed Emma Renshaw, would they shop one of their own? I doubt it, don't you?'

'Even in those circumstances?'

'My feeling is that the Oxleys wouldn't even have to think about it,' said Cooper. 'They would know instinctively what was best for the family.'

Fry thought about it. 'Absolute loyalty to family members, no matter what they've done?'

'That's the way it works,' said Cooper. Then he added: 'I'm sorry.'

'Sorry?' Fry stared at him. 'Sorry for what?'

'I don't know why I said that.'

'I do understand family loyalty, Ben.'

'Of course. I didn't mean –'

'I don't want to know what you didn't mean. Even less do I want to know what you *did* mean.'

'Fine.'

'Anyway, there's a line between a family bond and hatred,' said Fry thoughtfully. 'There's no hatred stronger than the one for someone you're supposed to love. So many people cross that line.'

'Yes, you're right.'

'Have you ever felt that line was crossed in *your* family, Ben? What about between you and your brother?'

'I can't imagine it.'

Fry was quiet for a while. He could see she was still thinking about it. She was turning over in her mind all those possible circumstances that might arise between members of a family, between people forced together by the circumstances of being related. She had asked him about his relationship with Matt. But it seemed to Cooper that she had to be thinking about her own relationship with her sister, Angie. It would be unnatural if she weren't.

'It's great to be part of a family,' said Cooper. 'We all feel the need to belong to a family, a tribe, a team or whatever. But the problem with belonging is that, if you get rejected by your family or your team, it really, really hurts. Rejection is the end of the world then, because you're getting rejection from the very people you expected support from. A lot of people can't deal with that.'

'It can be a pretty harsh form of rejection, I suppose.'

'When wild packs of dogs reject one of their own members, they drive it away from food sources and leave it to die.'

'Well, thanks, David Attenborough.'

'A pleasure.'

Fry changed the subject. 'And what do you think the Reverend Alton is keeping to himself?'

'You think he is?'

'Are you losing your instincts, Ben? It's obvious he knows something, or suspects something. But he's the kind who keeps confidences.' She looked hard at Cooper. 'He's the kind who'll keep a secret until it's too late.'

PEAK WATER WAS a small operation, which surely couldn't survive much longer without being swallowed up by one of the larger companies that had come to dominate water supply since privatization. Its offices in Glossop occupied the upper floors of a timber-framed building near the town's market square. There was a building society on the ground floor.

Ben Cooper had made an appointment with someone called J. P. Venables. The medieval appearance of the building's black-and-white timbers must have given him false expectations. To his surprise, Venables turned out to be a man in his thirties, not much older than Cooper himself, but rather overweight, as if he had done a sedentary job all his life. He had shed his suit jacket to reveal a waistcoat with fancy coloured panels, and he wore glasses with tiny rectangular frames.

'Waterloo Terrace,' he said, 'is not the most prestigious property in our portfolio.'

'They were originally railway workers' houses, weren't they?' said Cooper.

'Yes. But of course they weren't required after the stations closed, and they were taken over by Peak Water, which also owns most of the land up there.'

'I'm interested in your tenants at Waterloo Terrace. Particularly members of the Oxley family.'

Venables smiled. 'Now, there's a surprise. I must be psychic.'

'Sir?'

He pointed to a stack of manila files that lay ready on his desk. 'As soon as I heard the words "Waterloo Terrace" and "police", I found my hand moving of its own accord towards the "O" section of my filing cabinet. I wonder how that happened? It's uncanny.'

'You've had a lot of dealings with the Oxleys?'

'Hasn't everybody?'

'Did you know some of their neighbours in Withens have made complaints about them?' said Cooper.

Venables hesitated. 'Yes, we've had a few complaints, which we've spoken to Mr Oxley about.'

'Some of the boys have been in court several times.'

'If there was substantial evidence that they were causing a nuisance to their neighbours, then we might have to take action under their tenancy agreement.'

'You could evict them then?'

'In certain circumstances, yes.'

'I think that's what some of their neighbours would like.'

'We keep the situation under review. We have to, if we keep getting complaints. But it's only the immediate neighbours that are our concern. Other tenants of ours.'

'But all the Oxleys live next door to each other. They only have one immediate neighbour in Waterloo Terrace.'

'Well, of course, that's quite convenient for everyone,' said Venables.

'Convenient?'

'Mmm.'

Venables leaned back in his chair. He looked too relaxed. The water company man had shiny nostrils. When he tilted his head up towards Cooper, he felt as though he was caught in the glare.

'Every time you get a complaint, does someone speak to Lucas Oxley about it?' asked Cooper.

'We try to. There's quite a dossier of reports now. I suppose I could get permission for you to see them if you wanted to. But from what I recall, the interviews with Mr Oxley aren't terribly enlightening.'

'I'll bear that in mind. But I think I can imagine the sort of responses you got.'

'There's Oxley and his wife, and the old man, and all those other members of his family. They seem to form a sort of barrier around themselves, and no amount of argument or appeals to common sense will get through.'

'Has Lucas Oxley ever accused Peak Water of being part of some conspiracy against him and his family?'

'I believe that accusation appears in the reports a few times,' said Venables.

'It's understandable, don't you think?'

'No. What do you mean? There's no conspiracy.'

'I mean, it's understandable that it should seem that way to the Oxleys. To them, it must look as though everyone is against them, and no one is on their side.'

Venables shrugged. 'I can't help that. They've only themselves to blame, after all.'

'Perhaps,' said Cooper. 'Hasn't anyone tried explaining this to the Oxleys?'

'We've written to them several times,' said Venables.

'And?'

'We've never had a reply.'

'But did nobody call on Lucas Oxley to talk to him personally?'

'Well, you've seen yourself what he's like. He sent our man away with a flea in his ear and threatened to set the dog on him.'

'He probably didn't understand what it was you wanted.'

'His behaviour was extremely unreasonable. We would have been within our rights to involve the police at that stage. People can't go around being abusive and threatening to our staff. The company has a responsibility to its employees.'

'And did you involve the police?'

'No. We gave Mr Oxley another chance.'

'Which means?'

'We wrote to him again.'

'Great.'

'We warned him about his behaviour in the clearest terms and told him that he was in breach of his tenancy agreement. We gave him ten days to contact us to arrange a meeting at which the situation could be discussed. We told him we hoped it could be settled amicably on both sides.'

'To which I suppose you got no reply?'

'No. So then we sent him a final warning. Same result. So, regretfully, we began court proceedings.'

'I see.'

'You have to realize that this thing has gone on for months and months. We do try to be patient, but we really haven't the time to be dealing with people like the Oxleys, who refuse to see sense. Whatever the consequences are for the family from here on, they will have brought it on themselves, I'm afraid.'

'So you said.'

Venables shrugged again. 'We've followed the proper procedures, every step of the way. We've bent over backwards to accommodate the Oxleys and come to some mutually acceptable arrangement with them. They can have no grounds for complaint about the way the company has dealt with them. Court proceedings were a last resort.'

'What about the question of the water catchment area? Is Waterloo Terrace a problem? I understand there was a farm that had to be moved recently.'

'Withens is quite different from Crowden,' said Venables. 'The farm had a flock of over a thousand sheep. Besides, it was right by the A628, and there were safety concerns about slow-moving tractors and agricultural machinery having to use a busy road like that, with heavy traffic on it all the time. There's no comparison to the situation at Withens.'

'Has the situation been explained properly to the Oxleys?'

'Mmm. Well, I have to admit that communication might not have been as good as it should be. The fact is, there's been a bit of a problem over jurisdiction.'

'Sorry?'

'We've been experiencing a difference of opinion with South Yorkshire over where responsibilities lie. We don't seem to be able to resolve the situation very easily, I'm afraid. It's causing rather a delay.'

'So the Oxleys slip through the cracks while you argue among yourselves.'

'I wouldn't put it quite like that.'

'I would.'

'As you like. But there are procedures to be followed, and rules to be observed. We can't just go trampling on someone else's territory without being confident of our position. There could be legal repercussions. We have to be very careful, otherwise the company's interests could be compromised.'

'There's another terrace of houses down there, isn't there?'

'Yes, Trafalgar Terrace. They're void properties.'

'Void? That's a good word for it. I'd call them derelict. They look like a health hazard to me.'

'They're earmarked for action in the near future,' said Venables stiffly.

'So neither the Oxleys nor anyone else has tenancy of the empty houses?'

'No. I told you, they're void. Why?'

'We may wish to search Trafalgar Terrace. Do we have your permission for that, sir?'

'Of course. But you'll have to be quick.'

'Why? Is there something you're not telling me, sir?'

'Our contractors will be moving in very soon to start work.'

'You're repairing the houses?'

'Demolishing them,' said Venables.

Cooper stared at him. It was an obvious thing to do, really. In fact, it should have been done a long time ago. But it seemed like another sign of that impermanence that Tracy Udall had put her finger on. It was another bit of Withens about to disappear.

'How did you come to rent all the houses in Waterloo Terrace to members of the Oxley family?' said Cooper.

'I know it looks a little unusual. If the properties were to fall vacant now, I don't think it would happen again. The company would be looking to increase the rents substantially, for a start. But at the time it was thought there was no demand for rented properties in Withens. So the company decided to leave the old policy in place – the policy that tenancies could be passed on to members of the same family. It's a very old principle, designed to ensure a worker's family wasn't turned out on to the street if the man himself was killed during his employment. The early proprietors were concerned about their employees' welfare. They were almost philanthropists.'

'Compared to the present owners, you mean?'

'I couldn't possibly comment.'

'Property values have changed in Withens in recent years, I suppose?'

'There's still a shortage of demand for rental properties. But the company has been approached by a private developer interested in purchasing the entire row of houses.'

'You mean the company is going to sell Waterloo Terrace?'

'It makes sound commercial sense.'

'But new owners would have to take on the sitting tenants, wouldn't they?'

'Of course. The tenants have rights that are protected by law.'

Cooper studied Venables. So often he found himself trying to hear the words that people weren't saying, because that's where the true meaning lay. But there was more than one communication gap involved in the Withens case. In fact, there were as many communication gaps as there were combinations of people trying to communicate with each other. The result was a Babel in his head.

'New landlords would mean big changes for the Oxleys, wouldn't they, Mr Venables?' he said.

'Well, undoubtedly,' said Venables, with a smile. 'Undoubtedly.'

'And do you know what the new owners plan for Waterloo Terrace?'

'Oh yes, I know.'

'Demolition?'

'I imagine that would be the preferred option.'

'But they can't demolish the houses with sitting tenants, can they?'

'Of course not. As I said, they're protected.'

'So the Oxleys would need to be got out of Waterloo Terrace in some way.'

'To make it worthwhile for the developers, yes. But I'm not suggesting there's any kind of conspiracy to intimidate them and get them out. That would be unethical.'

'Not to mention illegal.'

'Quite.'

'It seems to me that no one is making much effort to keep the Oxleys in their homes, either.'

Venables shrugged again. Cooper was starting to get irritated by the shrug. Of all the complacent gestures that people were capable of, the shrug was the second most annoying, after the smirk.

'We believe they've done some unauthorized structural alterations. That will probably be the clincher,' said Venables. 'They're their own worst enemies, I'm afraid.'

'I know. But that doesn't mean they don't deserve to have any friends.'

'Oh? And are you intending to fill that role? A friend of the Oxleys? I know that police work is different these days from what it used to be. But is that really your job?'

Cooper gritted his teeth. Of course it wasn't his job. He didn't need Venables to tell him that. He had Diane Fry to do it for him.

'If I were you, I'd choose my friends more carefully,' said Venables.

And then he smirked.

Chapter Thirty-Two

DC GAVIN MURFIN looked mournfully at the remains of a vanilla slice on his desk. Its enticing yellow smile had disintegrated into a few dusty flakes of pastry before his eyes.

'No signs of a previous diary,' he said. 'No likely looking randy art lecturers. That Stark girl laughed at me when I tried her with some names. She has a colourful turn of phrase, for a lass.'

'It doesn't matter, Gavin,' said Diane Fry.

'Doesn't matter?'

'Not now.'

'I spent hours on that.'

'If Emma Renshaw arrived back in Withens, the person we're looking for is a lot closer to home than Birmingham Art School.'

'Right,' said Murfin. 'You're right.'

He considered it for a moment. 'Tell you what,' he said, 'the day Emma went missing … Do we know Howard Renshaw's *exact* movements that day?'

BEN COOPER WAS remembering the man from the Sunday-morning crowd at Somerfield's supermarket. Last Sunday, he had been trying to tell some story about distraction burglaries in the Southwoods area, and Cooper hadn't been taking much notice. It had sounded pretty small-scale stuff, which someone else would be dealing with, thank goodness. But perhaps he should have listened more carefully. Hadn't the old man mentioned an incident involving genuine antiques? 'They must have driven right past my window to get to Southwoods Grange.'

And what else had he been saying? Cooper thought about Golden Delicious apples and pineapple chunks for a few seconds before he got it. Car registration numbers.

ON FRIDAY AFTERNOON there was a totally different crowd in the supermarket. And many of the staff were different, too. Cooper introduced himself at the duty manager's office and got permission to speak to the checkout assistants and the bag packers, the trolley collectors and the woman at the cigarette counter. One of the older staff on the checkouts thought she remembered the man with the walking stick, but had no idea of his name. She said he was a customer who always paid cash.

'And he always comes in on Sunday, I think,' she said.

'Yes, he does.'

'Like you, in fact.'

'Yes, that's right.'

'You're the frozen meals for one and the Boddington's six-packs, aren't you?'

'Yes.'

'I never knew you were police.'

Cooper moved on. All he had achieved was to let the checkout assistant know more about him than she did about the man with the walking stick.

This afternoon, the supermarket's frozen meat section looked unnervingly like the postmortem room at a giant morgue, with frozen body parts stacked in freezers, neatly packaged and labelled. Fortunately, these weren't human parts, but bits hacked off cows and sheep and pigs. He could understand why people became vegetarians. Perhaps the trick was not to look closely – to see only the price label on the plastic packages and the 'best before' date, not the reality of the meat and bones underneath.

Outside, he tried to remember which way the man went when he left the supermarket. Often, he walked with Cooper to his car and talked to him while he loaded up his shopping. Then Cooper would say goodbye, get in his car and drive towards the exit. Had he ever noticed which way the man with the stick went?

He had a brief recollection of being held up at the lights by traffic one morning and seeing the man waiting at the pedestrian crossing with his shopping bag on wheels to cross to the corner of Eyre Street. From there, he would have only a short walk to the bus stops in front of the town hall, where there were services running to all the areas on the eastern and northern sides of Edendale. It was no help at all.

BACK IN THE office at West Street, Cooper found the rest of the DCs already busy on the phones. He sat down at his desk opposite Gavin Murfin, whose head was bent over some notes in his pocket book that he was trying to transcribe on to a pile of forms. Murfin looked up, shook his head at Cooper in an exaggerated way and sucked his breath through his teeth.

'Late, Mr Cooper? You'll be in trouble. It's a good job Miss is in a meeting.'

'There was just something I had to do.'

'There's plenty to do here,' said Murfin.

Cooper kept quiet. Friday afternoon wasn't a time when he should have been in Somerfield's looking for old men with walking sticks.

But hold on. He shouldn't even be thinking about Friday afternoon. He should be thinking about Sunday morning – that was when the old man did his shopping. In Edendale, the bus companies ran limited services on Sunday. In fact, some routes didn't operate at all. The man with the walking stick left Somerfield's at the same time every Sunday morning, about 10.30 a.m. He walked slowly, too. So, allowing him fifteen minutes to get to the town hall, he couldn't be expecting to get a bus home before 10.45.

Cooper looked around the office. There must be a bus timetable somewhere.

He went to the shelves that contained their reference library. They also contained a lot of other stuff that nobody knew what to do with, including a stack of urgent memos from county headquarters that was about a foot high and threatening to topple over. But Cooper eventually found what he was looking for.

'Route 19. The 10.53 bus to Southwoods,' he said aloud.

Gavin Murfin paused in his transcribing. 'A bus to where?'

'Southwoods.'

'Southwoods? Ah.'

'Do you know it?'

'Of course I know it. There's a decent chippy up there, near the community centre.'

As usual, Cooper found his attention turned off when Murfin got on to the subject of food.

'Would the 10.53 on Sunday morning be a busy route, I wonder?' he said. 'And would it usually be the same driver on duty?'

'Sunday morning? No, that's no good at all,' said Murfin.

'Why not?'

'The chippy isn't open on a Sunday.'

'Gavin, will you get on with your notes and leave me be?'

Cooper got up and crossed the room to get his coat. Murfin watched him until he was nearly out of the door.

'What I can't understand, Ben,' he said, 'is why you're going to Southwoods on the bus, anyway.'

IT TOOK ONLY a couple of phone calls to the bus depot in Baslow to establish that the driver he wanted was currently operating the Route 19 service between Edendale Town Hall and Southwoods Estate. Cooper managed to obtain the times when the bus stopped for a few minutes at the terminus outside the town hall, and he was waiting there when the vehicle pulled in and discharged its passengers.

The bus driver looked at his warrant card. 'You're looking for an old chap with a walking stick and shopping bag? Yes, I know him. I have to help him on board sometimes. He has some days that are better than others, if you know what I mean.'

'That's wonderful. And where does he get off?'

'Corner of Wembley Avenue, near the Unitarian church.'

'Does he live on Wembley Avenue?'

'Well, I couldn't be sure of that. But he heads in that direction. He might be visiting somebody, for all I know.'

'Visiting?'

'Well, a girlfriend or something. Or his mother. I don't know.'

Cooper stared at him. 'His mother. Yes.'

'I didn't mean his mother,' said the driver. 'He's getting on a bit. His mother will most likely have passed on.'

'Have you ever noticed how far up Wembley Avenue he goes?'

'No. He's not too nippy on his pins, so he's hardly got up the street when I pull away. There are two more stops between there and the terminus.'

Passengers were starting to squeeze past Cooper to get on the bus as he stood talking to the driver. He became aware that a couple of old ladies had sat down near the front of the bus and were listening to his conversation, with their hands folded on their laps and their eyes bright with interest.

'Can you drop me off there?' he said.

'Where?'

'Wembley Avenue.'

''Course. But you'll have to wait while I finish getting passengers on.'

Cooper sat down opposite the old ladies, who nudged each other and eyed him eagerly. He looked out of the window at the town hall, desperate not to meet their gaze. He had a horrible premonition of what they were going to say to him, given a minimum of encouragement.

The façade of the town hall boasted four decorative pillars. They stood on ornate bases, which had been partially obscured by the disabled ramps and handrails installed a few years ago to make the place accessible. The building had been edged with decorative stones that had been carved with a wavy pattern. There were so many of them that they were distinctive, and local people had nicknamed their town hall 'The Wavy House'.

He found he was looking at the noticeboard on the wall of the town hall. The building hosted far more than just council meetings. There were notices announcing line-dancing classes, a slimming club, the WI market, Darby and Joan sessions, bridge nights, a book fair, and t'ai chi lessons. He tried to imagine the old ladies doing t'ai chi, just to keep himself amused.

Finally, the bus set off and wound its way through the streets of Edendale town centre before emerging on to Greaves Road and going north. Cooper tried to appear interested in every single thing that they passed. The old ladies gathered their belongings and got off, casting reluctant glances back.

'Next stop Wembley Avenue,' said the driver.

Cooper stood up and waited by the doors. 'Thanks a lot. You've been very helpful.'

'No trouble. Are you sure you don't want his name?'

Cooper paused on the step of the bus as the doors folded open. 'Whose name?'

'The chap with the walking stick, of course. The one you've been asking about.'

'You know his name?'

''Course I do. He's an OAP. He has to show me his bus pass every time he gets on. His name's Jim Revill.'

'I was going to walk up and down Wembley Avenue knocking on people's doors asking for a man with a stick,' said Cooper.

'Well,' said the driver, 'that would have been a bit daft, wouldn't it?'

JIM REVILL WAS totally baffled to find Ben Cooper standing on his doorstep. It was obvious that at first he didn't recognize him at all. Cooper was used to that feeling himself. He had often seen someone walking down the street and felt sure that he knew them, but from an entirely different context. The woman who served him in the petrol station twice a week was very familiar, but she was unrecognizable when she had come out from behind the counter and was dressed up to the nines, having a drink with her boyfriend in Yates's Wine Bar. It was a bit unsettling. People should stay in their contexts, safe and familiar.

'Detective Constable Cooper, Edendale Police,' he said.

'Eh?'

'Sunday mornings at Somerfield's supermarket.'

'Ah! Chinese meals for one.'

'Yes,' said Cooper, with a sigh. 'That's me.'

'But what are you doing here? This is where I live.'

'Yes, I know, Mr Revill.'

'Did you follow me?'

'In a manner of speaking.'

Mr Revill's face took on a stubborn look. 'I don't let people in without seeing their identification and checking up on them.'

'Quite right.'

Cooper showed his warrant card again, and had to wait while Mr Revill phoned the station. But while the old man made the call, he left the front door open, so that Cooper could easily have walked into his house and pulled the phone right out of the wall, if he had wanted to commit a robbery.

But, to be honest, there was very little that looked worth stealing. The shopping bag on wheels stood against the wall near the door. Its handle had worn a bare patch in the wallpaper and its wheels had scuffed the skirting board. There were some cardboard boxes stacked against the wall further along the passage. According to the printing on them, they had once contained tins of cat food and baked beans, though presumably not any more – not unless Mr Revill was stocking up to survive an emergency. If those were the extent of his supplies, Cooper thought the cat would be all right, if it didn't mind a permanent diet of Whiskas beef and lamb. But Mr Revill would be in danger of spontaneous combustion.

'They say you're all right.'

'Thank goodness for that.'

'So is it about the burglaries that you've come?'

'Well, yes.'

'I didn't see anybody. But I've got some registration numbers.'

'You have? Suspicious vehicles? Have you passed them on to the station?'

'They weren't interested,' said Mr Revill. 'Like I told you, nobody bothers coming out for us.'

'Can I have a look?'

'In the front room.'

Cooper followed him through a doorway and into a room full of furniture. A dining table and four chairs dominated the space, and there was hardly enough room to walk around them, because of the sideboard and display cabinets against the walls. And there were more boxes in the far corner. Fairy Liquid and Utterly Butterly.

'Here. I keep a notebook by the window, so that I can write them down straight away. Otherwise, I would forget them, and that would be no use to anybody.'

Cooper looked at the notebook he was offered. He saw a page of car registration numbers, written in large letters in a shaky hand. He turned over a page. There were more numbers. He flicked through the rest of the notebook. Every page was covered in registration numbers. There were hundreds of them.

'These are suspicious vehicles?' he said.

'Yes.'

'What makes them suspicious?'

'They're strangers. I know the cars that come down here regular. There's nothing wrong with my memory. Is it any use to you?'

'Not unless I had a registration number I wanted to compare them to. They aren't even dated. You haven't written down what day you saw them.'

'Well, there's a page for each day.'

'For which days, though?'

'Every day. I start a new page each morning,' said Mr Revill, as if forced to explain it to an idiot. 'Like a diary. You know what a diary is.'

'Right. So I could work my way backwards to say, the sixteenth of last month?'

'Today's the second. So you just turn back sixteen pages, see?'

Cooper flipped back. There were ten numbers on the page he was looking at. 'I don't suppose you can remember what make or model any of these were? Or the colour? Or how many people were in them?'

'No. It never occurred to me to write those things down. I thought the police went off registration numbers. Can't you do a check on the computer, and see if one of them is stolen?'

'Yes, I suppose so.'

'I didn't expect to have to tell you your job, lad. But I suppose you're young yet. Still learning, are you?'

Cooper copied down the numbers. At least there were only ten of them. It would be easier to make a match.

'You've been very helpful, sir,' he said.

'Are we going to catch some burglars? Send a gang of them to prison? Can I tell Mrs Smith at number 16? She says she won't come out again until they've all been locked up.'

'It's a bit early to say that, I'm afraid. But we'll be working on it.'

'Aye. We'll not hold our breath, then.'

BEN COOPER HAD all the registration numbers through the PNC by the communications room. He was aware that he was spending a lot of time on this hunch, especially as he'd had to wait for a bus back into town. He wouldn't have been able to justify it very easily, if he was asked. So the best thing to do was just keep quiet about it, unless it produced results.

As he anticipated, several of the vehicles turned out to belong to local residents, or were registered to companies which might be expected to have a legitimate reason for visiting homes on the Southwoods estate. One was actually in the name of the council housing department. So Mr Revill wasn't too choosy about where his suspicions were directed. Or perhaps he was.

Cooper managed to sift the vehicles down to four that were from out of the area. Two of them were vans, which were of particular interest where burglaries were involved. But he remembered the nature of the items that were being stolen – all small and easily concealed.

Almost the last vehicle he did a PNC check on was an Audi. He was starting to lose interest by now, wondering whether he should leave the rest until later, perhaps tomorrow. There were more productive things to be doing. But then he finally hit a name he recognized.

'No, that isn't possible. Can you check again?'

'That's the name and address of the last registered owner.'

'It just isn't possible,' said Cooper. 'Emma Renshaw has been missing for two years.'

WHEN BEN COOPER got into the CID room he found Diane Fry alone. She had her elbows on her desk, and she was staring out of the window, as if she were wondering where the rest of the world had gone. Cooper was tired, too, but Fry looked exhausted. He glanced at her cautiously as he went through his messages. There was lots of stuff he didn't want to know about. But no invitations from the Oxleys to call for tea. What a surprise.

'Diane, something strange happened this morning. I did a check on some vehicles that were seen at the time of the Southwoods Grange break-in.'

Fry turned her head towards the sound of his voice, but seemed to be looking straight through him.

'One of the cars turned out to be registered to Emma Renshaw. The break-in was two weeks ago. I wondered what happened there.'

'I don't know.'

Cooper watched her for a few minutes. She didn't seem to have been listening to anything he said. Something was definitely wrong.

'Had a bad time with the Renshaws?' he said finally.

'What?'

Fry seemed to wake from her dream and stared at him. He thought she genuinely hadn't even noticed him until then.

'Oh, the Renshaws. Yeah.'

'In a way, you know, it must be a relief to them,' said Cooper. 'After all this time, it ought to help them a bit to know for certain that Emma's dead, instead of wondering about it for ever. At least now they can get on with their lives.'

'Mmm. Yeah.'

Cooper realized that she was avoiding his eye. There was more to her manner than just a harrowing session with bereaved parents.

'What is it, Diane? What's wrong?'

She looked at him properly for the first time since he had come into the room. Her eyes really did look weary.

Weary, and baffled. Like someone who had thought the
end was in sight, but now had to start all over again rolling the boulder back up the hill.

'We got the preliminary report from the pathologist,'
she said. 'On the remains Alton found in the churchyard.'

'It's going to take time to get a definite identification
on the remains, I suppose.'

'Yes, but we have some information.'

'Cause of death?'

'No.'

'No – that was too much to hope for, I suppose. Maybe
later, then. They can probably do some tests –'

Fry pushed the report towards him impatiently. 'You
don't need to read that far. Just take a look at the first
section.'

Cooper started to read. There was some introduc-
tory stuff, then the initial assessment of the state of the
remains – skeletalized, obviously. And a mention of a
missing finger joint on the left hand, which made Cooper frown. Then there was a whole list of measurements
– the cephalic index of the skull, its width and length, the
dimensions of the nasal aperture. From the growing ends
of bones and the gaps between the bones of the cranium,
age had been estimated at twenty-four. Then the report
moved on to a lot of stuff about pelvic width and something called the ischium-pubis index. It said the jawbone
was pointed, the nasal aperture long and narrow, with
rectangular eye orbits and a pronounced brow ridge.

He stopped reading.

'Diane –'

'Yes,' she said. 'It isn't Emma Renshaw. The corpse from the vicar's churchyard is male.'

'But the Renshaws ...'

'I know,' she said. 'The bloody Renshaws. Howard Renshaw held the skull in his own hands. He recognized the shape of it, he said. He knew the skull of his own daughter instantly. Oh yes, and all the stuff about drying her hair. I actually believed him.'

'I'm sure he was sincere, Diane.'

'Sincere? He's certifiable. They both are.'

Cooper looked down at the report again. According to the pathologist, the remains were those of a male aged in his mid twenties, about five feet ten inches tall, give or take half an inch or so. Impossible to establish cause of death. There was minor postmortem damage to the skeleton – caused, no doubt, by the Reverend Derek Alton and Howard Renshaw. Not to mention anyone else who might have taken the chance of poking around in the poor bugger's shallow grave before the first police officers arrived to secure the scene. The entire population of Withens might have been picking over the bones, for all anybody knew. In fact, Cooper could easily picture the Oxleys squatting in a circle around the grave, like a set of cannibals.

'The Renshaws are going to be devastated all over again,' he said.

'Sod the bloody Renshaws,' said Fry.

Cooper looked up then, but she'd already turned away. She got to her feet, with her back turned towards him. She paused only to flick a hand across her face, and strode out of the room.

COOPER HESITATED A moment too long over what he should do. Then he hurried into the corridor after Fry, but was in time only to see the door of the ladies toilet swinging shut.

'Damn.'

'Problem, Ben?'

Liz Petty had been passing along the corridor towards the scenes of crime department. She had stopped, with her camera bag over her shoulder, and was looking at him curiously. No doubt she was wondering why he was staring at the door of the ladies as if he desperately wanted to go in. Petty looked closely at the sign on the door, to be sure.

'No,' said Cooper. 'Everything's fine.'

But it wasn't fine. If he didn't know Diane Fry better, Cooper would have sworn that Howard Renshaw had come closer to reducing her to tears than Fry was ever going to admit.

Chapter Thirty-Three

THE DOOR OF the double garage hummed as it rose and slid into place in the roof. Diane Fry looked at the number plate of the Audi parked next to the Renshaws' Volvo Estate.

'I thought you said this car was two years old, Mrs Renshaw?'

Sarah Renshaw looked confused and shook her head, as if she didn't understand what she was being asked. Fry turned to Howard instead.

'It's a "T" registration,' she said. 'That means it was registered in 1999.'

'Yes.'

'So it isn't two years old.'

'Well, it was …'

'Of course it *was*,' said Fry, irritated to have been given wrong information. 'But it isn't now, is it?'

'No,' said Howard, and began to flush slightly.

Fry stared at him, wondering what was wrong with the man. He wasn't ignorant about cars, and he had bought this one himself. Very few men would have got the age of a vehicle so wrong – especially when the registration system had been changed very recently. Now, the year of a car's registration was identified by numbers on its plate, instead of the old system of letters, which had ended with 'Y'.

'This car is "T" registration,' she repeated. 'It's at least four years old, Mr Renshaw.'

She waited for Renshaw to explain himself, but he didn't seem to want to. He simply looked at the Audi with that pitiful, hangdog expression she had seen before. Then Fry realized the problem. The car had been two years old. It had been two years old when Emma Renshaw disappeared. In the minds of her parents, the car was still the same age, just as Emma was still on her way home from Wolverhampton. Those two years in between might as well not have existed.

'This is ridiculous,' she said.

'I'm sorry,' said Howard.

But Fry couldn't tell whether he was actually apologizing for his behaviour, or simply hadn't understood what she meant. It was her own fault, anyway – she should have checked before now, instead of taking what the Renshaws said as the truth.

'When did Emma last drive this car?' she said.

'She only uses it when she's home from university.'

Fry gritted her teeth, trying to stay calm.

'Mr Renshaw, your daughter hasn't been home from university for over two years. When did she last use this car?'

She saw his adam's apple bob as he swallowed. He was starting to sweat a little. 'It would have been the Christmas holiday,' he said. 'Emma was at home for three weeks, over Christmas and New Year. We had a proper family Christmas together, just the three of us on Christmas Day. But she went out with some friends on Boxing Day and New Year's Eve. She used the car then, I think.'

'I see.'

'I took a lot of trouble over Christmas dinner,' said Sarah. 'We spent weeks doing the tree and the decorations, and months buying the presents. We bought Emma a lot of presents that Christmas. I think it was because she was away from us most of the year, we felt we had to make more effort to show her how much we loved her when she was at home. Perhaps we spoiled Emma a bit, I don't know. But I'm glad we did it. It was the last time. The last Christmas we saw her.'

Listening to Mrs Renshaw's voice growing quieter and quieter in the half-empty garage, Fry began to feel guilty for her impatience and irritation. She felt as though she had trampled on the Renshaws' dreams by pointing out the fact that it was over two years since they had seen their daughter.

'I'm sorry, Mrs Renshaw,' she said. She knew it wasn't enough, not by any means. But she couldn't think of anything else to say to her.

A silence developed between them as Fry examined the car.

'Of course, there'll be even more presents for Emma next Christmas,' said Sarah.

And now her voice had life in it again. There was a rising note of optimism at the end of her sentence that sent a shiver through Fry's spine.

'What?'

'We've saved them all for her, of course,' said Sarah. 'The spare room is full of them. Emma will have such a surprise next Christmas. She won't want to go away again when she sees how much we love her.'

Fry stared at Sarah Renshaw until she couldn't bear to look at her any longer. It was like watching someone trying to get up and walk after their legs had been blown off – and smiling hopefully as they did it. The sight was too painful to prolong, and Fry turned away.

'Mr Renshaw, do you have the keys for this car?' she said.

THEY WERE SQUATTING uncomfortably on seats that had been ripped out of some derelict car. At least, Derek Alton hoped that it had been derelict before the seats were ripped out. The seats were tied to the struts of the van sides with their seat belts, which kept them fairly stable except when the van went round a bend, and then they tended to slide and crash into each other. Alton had been thrown against one of the seat-belt buckles, and now he had a pain in his shoulder, which he knew would be a nasty bruise by tomorrow morning. He bruised very easily. His mother had always told him that when he was a child.

'Where are we going?' said Alton.

'Practice session, Vicar.'

Alton looked round at the rest of the Border Rats. Directly across from him was Scott Oxley, with his brother Ryan. On either side of him were Sean and Glen, and two Hey Bridge men he didn't know were squashed together at the front, just behind the driver's cab, where Eric rode alongside his son. All the team were in full kit, with their top hats and their black make-up and mirrored sunglasses, carrying their sticks and, in some cases, bottles of beer.

'How old are you, Ryan?' said Alton. 'I can't quite remember.'

'Eighteen, Vicar.'

'And how old is young Sean here?'

'Eighteen, Vicar.'

'I see.'

The interior of the van smelled strongly of theatrical paint and sweat, and leather boots, along with the beer that the younger ones occasionally spilled on their trousers or on the floor of the van, which was covered with an old carpet. Alton looked down at the carpet suspiciously. It seemed to be embedded with small pieces of coal and splinters of wood. He wondered what Lucas Oxley normally used the van for when it wasn't serving as the team bus. For a moment, he also wondered whether it was legal – but he put the thought hastily out of his mind as unworthy. It was just that he had never known what Lucas did for a living. Or any of the Oxleys, come to that.

They bumped up a hill and round a few more bends before descending again. There was a steel grille between the body of the van and the driver's cab, and Alton wouldn't have been able to see where they were going, even if he had taken his sunglasses off, which he didn't like to do, because all the others were wearing theirs. He very much wanted to be part of the side, to do whatever they did. Almost whatever. When Scott wiped the neck of his beer bottle and offered it to him, he managed to refuse.

'Yes, it's probably best not to, if you're a bit nervous, Vicar,' said Scott.

'There's nothing to be nervous about really,' said Alton. 'I know the dance perfectly.'

But he could hear the tremble in his own voice, so he didn't expect Scott or any of the others to be in the least convinced. They all looked at him and smiled. He hoped they were sympathetic smiles, but their mirrored sunglasses made it impossible for him to see the look in their eyes, to tell whether they were mocking him.

'Where did you say we're going?' asked Alton again.

'To bring a bit of fertility to our neighbours.'

The others laughed and cheered. Scott Oxley stared steadily at the vicar.

'Do you know,' he said, 'some of them actually believe this fertility stuff. There are women who come to watch us on May Day, then turn up again the following year clutching a baby and telling us we were responsible for her getting pregnant.'

'Aye, but those are all the birds that Scott's shagged,' said Ryan. 'Only they can't tell which of us it was because of the black faces, see.'

Scott continued as if his brother hadn't spoken. 'Fertility ritual! I mean, can you credit some folk? It only ever started off as a joke, to keep people in the crowd amused. You hear Fools talking it up around some sides, but it's only like having a comedian making a few rude jokes, isn't it? Why has anyone ever taken that stuff seriously?'

'Here we are!' called Lucas from the cab at last. 'Let the band get started first, then go for it on the signal. And remember – you go out dancing! What do you say?'

'Rats!' the boys shouted, so loudly that they almost deafened Derek Alton. He came in late, only managed to mouth the word a beat behind the others, and felt ashamed that he had missed the cue. He swore that he'd get everything else right from now on.

As soon as the van doors open and he clambered out after the others, Alton recognized the church, and realized they were in Tintwistle. Then it dawned on him why there was a crowd of spectators to greet them.

'Oh my God. It's the blessing of the wells. There's the Rural Dean and the church choir, and the whole of the women's institute, and … Oh Lord, what are they going to do?'

ALTHOUGH IT HADN'T been used by its owner for two years, the Audi was fully taxed. The disc inside the windscreen showed that its road fund licence didn't run out until March 2004. Fry was willing to bet that its insurance cover had been renewed by the Renshaws, too. Everything was ready for the moment Emma returned. Or was it?

'So you must have had it MoT'd,' she said.

'Sorry?'

One look at Sarah Renshaw's face made it obvious that the question hadn't even occurred to her. But every vehicle had to go through an annual MoT test, once it was three years old.

Fry looked at Howard. His expression was impassive, and she found she couldn't read anything into his manner. But whatever the reason for his pretence, he was fully aware of the age of the car.

Howard turned towards his wife, touching her arm gently.

'I had that done a few months ago,' he said.

'Yes. Thank you.' But Sarah still looked as if she didn't understand.

Fry opened the driver's door of the Audi. From inside the car wafted a strong scent she didn't recognize at first. It seemed to rise from the carpet and seep out of the upholstery of the seats, a warm, woody smell. She realized she was inhaling the lingering traces of Emma Renshaw's favourite fragrance, trapped inside her car for more than two years. Its emotional significance hit Fry powerfully. It was as if she had just found Emma herself sitting in the driving seat, laughing and flicking back her hair, and spraying Rive Gauche behind her ears.

Fry straightened and looked round at the Renshaws. She hadn't been the only one to catch the scent, and for the

Renshaws the effect of its release on the trapped air in the car had been devastating. Sarah's face was suffused and contorted as tears flooded down her cheeks. Howard stared at Fry in despair as his wife buried herself in his Arran sweater.

Fry pictured Mrs Renshaw, watching out of the window all day long for her daughter to come home. The daughter she was expecting was not only alive and well, but still nineteen, and still wearing the same clothes as the day she went missing, ready to finish the picture she'd been painting or take her Audi for a run.

When young people went missing, they would always be remembered exactly as they had been on the day they disappeared. Perhaps that was the real secret of eternal youth – an early death.

'Mr Renshaw, have you used this car recently?'

'No, of course not,' he said.

'Has it been borrowed by anybody?'

'No. We wouldn't do that. It's Emma's car.'

Fry looked at Sarah, who seemed to be gradually shrinking away from her husband.

'Mrs Renshaw, do *you* know whether this vehicle has left the garage recently?'

Sarah Renshaw glanced at her husband, who seemed to become aware of her silence. He turned away from the car to stare at her in astonishment.

'It was only for a few hours,' she said. 'And I knew Emma wouldn't mind. In fact, it seemed quite appropriate at the time.'

'Sarah, what on earth are you talking about?' said Howard.

'I did think about what Emma would say, if she were here. And I knew she'd say "yes". So I let him take the car. It was while you were away at that conference in London.'

'Mrs Renshaw –' said Fry.

'I was sure it wouldn't do any harm. It was a kind of connection. For a while, I was able to imagine that they'd gone out together and he'd bring Emma back with him when he returned the car.'

'I can't believe this,' said Howard, smacking the wing of the car. 'You did this while my back was turned. Why didn't you tell me?'

'I thought you might be angry. I thought you wouldn't see it the same way.'

'Mrs Renshaw,' said Fry, 'who did you allow to use this car?'

'It was Alex,' she said. 'I let Alex Dearden borrow it.'

GAIL DEARDEN STOOD in her kitchen at Shepley Head Lodge and stared at her husband. Suddenly, the kitchen didn't seem to be hers any more. It had been made unfamiliar by an object that lay on the table.

'Where did the shotgun come from?' she said.

'Somebody left it in the pick-up,' said Michael.

'What? Just like that?'

'Yes.'

'I don't believe you.'

He shrugged. 'It's up to you.'

Gail thought she recognized where the lie came from. It was the answer given by a defendant in a court case a few years ago – a farmer who had been sent to prison after shooting a burglar in his house. Michael had cut out the newspaper report, and it was still in a drawer somewhere. She'd noticed it only recently.

'I think you bought the gun from someone when you went to Manchester at the weekend,' said Gail. 'I knew you were up to something.'

Dearden shrugged. 'It doesn't matter.'

'And what exactly are you planning to do with it, Michael?'

He didn't look at her, but stared out of the window as he spoke. 'If they come again tonight, I'll be ready for them.'

'Don't talk stupid.'

But Gail could see that his hand was shaking slightly where he clutched the stock of the shotgun. He was wound up to a pitch where he might actually do something stupid.

'I hope to God there are no bullets in it.'

'Cartridges,' he said. 'They're called cartridges.'

The phone in the hallway began to ring. Michael placed the shotgun casually on the kitchen chair before he went to answer the call. Gail looked at the gun, seeing it properly for the first time, examining it as an actual working implement rather than some anonymous symbol of violence. She had never seen a shotgun before, except in films, wielded by ancient red-faced aristocrats as they blasted away at innocent birds, or a sawn-off version carried over the shoulder of Vinnie Jones. She wondered how it opened to put the bullets in. No, the cartridges. She had a vague picture of something bigger than a bullet, with a thick metal casing and a section that burst open when it was fired. Were these cartridges packed with lead shot, or something like that? Of course they were – that's why it was called a shotgun.

She had bought a couple of wild duck once from a butcher in Glossop, and she had wondered what the small black pieces of grit were that had almost chipped her teeth as she chewed the meat. She had mentioned it to the butcher next time she had gone into the shop, and he had laughed at her and told her it was the shot. She had been embarrassed to feel that she had shown her ignorance, and she hadn't asked any more. But she had realized that was the way they shot wildfowl: with shotguns. Those small black pellets caught the bird in a lethal hail, piercing its flesh and lodging themselves in its muscles and internal organs, maybe in its brain. She shuddered. She supposed it was a quick death, for a bird or a small animal. But what would the effect be on a human being?

Gail looked at the shotgun again. It seemed quite old, and almost had the look of an antique. Even she could see that it was a well-made piece of equipment, the stock made of good wood with an attractive grain, well polished. In fact, the wood looked so attractive and smooth that she wanted to touch it. Her fingers were halfway towards a caress before she drew her hand back, feeling almost as if she had dipped it in something slimy. Beyond the stock, the barrel and the mechanism were dark and covered in a sheen of oil. Now she realized she could smell the gun, that in fact she had been smelling it for several minutes. Its odour was a mixture of oil and metal and varnished wood, dark and sharp and tangy. The smell was part of what had given a new, unsafe feeling to the kitchen. It clashed with the scent of the herbs on the pine dresser and the warm aroma from the Aga. Yet somehow it was at home with those smells, too.

She looked a little more closely at the gun, her nostrils flexing at the smell. She had a feeling that a shotgun opened halfway along, that it sort of broke in half, with a hinge just behind the barrels. But she couldn't see a lever or a switch that she might be able to press to open the hinge. In fact, she flinched at the thought of even trying to open it. No, she wouldn't dare to touch the shotgun, in case it was loaded, after all. She was sure to touch the wrong thing, and it would go off in her hands. She would fire it into the wall, or through the window. Probably the lead shot would shred the pair of thrushes pecking about on the bird table. She almost laughed. It would be one way of establishing whether the gun was loaded or not.

Most of all, she wished that Michael would come back and take the shotgun away, out of her sight, and out of her kitchen. But at the same time she hoped that he would never touch it again. She wondered fleetingly whether she could hide it before he came back, in the hope that he might then forget it had ever existed.

And who would leave the gun in the pick-up truck? A neighbour? What neighbours did they have? No one that would give them the time of day. Someone who knew the problems they were having? Or was Michael really lying to her about where he had got it? She didn't think so. She could usually recognize when he was telling the truth.

He didn't have the wit to make up a story like that. His imagination would fail at the effort. And she didn't think he would know how to go about buying a shotgun for himself, either. As far as she was aware, he was almost as ignorant as she was herself about guns.

That was the only thought that gave her any reassurance. He surely wouldn't know how to use the shotgun.

MICHAEL DEARDEN TOOK the shotgun from the chair and held it in front of him like a shield. The position felt wrong. He tried to remember the way he had seen the shooters carrying their guns when they went up after the grouse. He thought they carried them in the crook of their arm, with the barrels pointing downwards for safety. He tried that, but it still didn't feel right. If the gun were to go off accidentally while he was walking with it, he would shoot his foot off, surely.

Dearden settled for holding the shotgun clutched across his chest at an awkward angle, with the barrels pointing upwards. An accidental shot would now go through the ceiling of the kitchen into the bedroom above. He thought of Gail lying in bed immediately above him, and he put the gun down hastily. But then he remembered that the gun wasn't even loaded, and he felt ridiculous and useless.

What sort of a man was he that he had no idea how to hold a gun? Boys were supposed to pick it up by instinct, turning any handy bit of wood into an imaginary rifle to play at shooting people. He hoped it was just a matter of getting used to the thing. Maybe he ought to practise firing it. Dearden glanced up at the ceiling again. Perhaps when Gail was out.

BEN COOPER WAITED in by his phone that night. He was nervous about the call he was expecting from Angie Fry. He had decided what he was going to say to Angie, but couldn't quite settle on the words he would use.

He poured himself a beer while he waited, sat down in an armchair, got up again, turned on the TV and used the remote to reduce the volume. Randy put his head round the door from the kitchen, hoping that Cooper might be in a suitable position for settling down with for the evening. But the cat seemed to sniff the air suspiciously, turned away and went back towards the conservatory to sleep by the central-heating boiler instead.

When the phone rang, Cooper jumped as if it had been completely unexpected. He grabbed for the remote, remembered the volume was already down, and reluctantly picked up the receiver.

'What have you decided?' said Angie's voice.

'I'm not going to do it.'

She let out a long breath that sighed intimately down the phone into his ear. 'Ben, don't you care about what happens to Diane?'

'Yes, I do. And that's the reason I won't do it. You've picked the wrong person, Angie.'

'There wasn't anyone else,' she said. And Cooper thought she could barely keep the disdain from her voice, hardly disguise the unspoken inference that she would rather have been dealing with anybody in the world but

Ben Cooper. 'There was no one else I could find who might be called her friend.'

'I can't help that.'

'The only people back in the West Midlands she keeps in touch with are our old foster parents in Warley, and I can hardly go and talk to them.'

'It would be a bit of a shock for them,' said Cooper.

'Diane hasn't kept in contact with any of her old colleagues in the West Midlands. I can't understand it.'

'Maybe she just wanted to put that part of her life behind her,' said Cooper. And he listened to the silence at the other end of the phone, picturing Angie Fry screwing her face, figuring out how she should respond.

'I'm going to have to come and see you again,' she replied.

'No.'

'I have to, Ben.'

'I don't want you coming here again. I'm serious. You know I can cause trouble if I have to.'

Angie sighed. 'Where then? Name a time and place, so I can talk to you properly.'

'I'm busy this weekend. It'll have to be Monday, when I'm off duty.'

For a few seconds, the sound of her breathing went away from the phone. Cooper pictured Angie silently consulting someone, and wondered if his conversation was being listened in to.

'And not here in Edendale,' he said. 'I'm not having you at my home again. Or anywhere where I'm known.'

'OK,' she said. 'But where, then?'

'If you come out of Sheffield on the A616 past Stocksbridge, there's a village called Midhopestones. You can catch a bus.'

'Right.'

Cooper almost laughed. No doubt she had no intention of catching a bus, but would be getting a lift in the dark blue BMW.

'There's a pub at Midhopestones called the Pepper Pot,' he said. 'I'll pick you up there at two o'clock, and we can go somewhere quiet to talk.'

'Ben, you're not planning to do anything silly, are you? It would be a mistake, you know.'

'It's entirely up to you,' he said. 'Don't come if you don't want to. I'm not really bothered.'

'All right, all right. I'll be there. No problem.'

Cooper put the phone down and shook his head sadly. It seemed that Angie Fry hadn't changed her low opinion of him, even now.

Chapter Thirty-Four

SATURDAY

TOMMY WAS KILLED by eleven-thirty on Saturday morning, which was a little later than planned. But on the Edendale Day of Dance, nothing ever got done on time.

Tommy died in the Market Square, just outside the Wheatsheaf Inn, with the sweet smell of Bank's Best Bitter drifting from the doorway of the pub, and the setts underneath him still damp from the morning's showers. He lay curled in a foetal position, with his arms clutched across his chest and his legs pulled up into his stomach.

The small crowd that had gathered on the pavement stood and stared at him for a while. They had been attracted by the noise, but had been expecting more excitement, perhaps a little more blood. When nothing else interesting happened, they gradually began to drift away, hoping to find something to look at in the shop windows in Nick i' th' Tor and Nimble John's Gate.

As always when he was dead, Tommy went into his method-acting mode. You could practically see his limbs stiffening with rigor mortis and the blood draining into the parts of his body that were in contact with the ground. He was so convincing that a few flies were beginning to gather. Some of them landed on his sleeve, sniffing with interest at the beer stains and a lingering trace of chicken biryani. In a moment, they would be clustering in his available orifices, eager to lay their eggs while he was still warm.

'Where's the chuffin' Doctor?' he muttered through clenched teeth.

'Get up,' said one of his friends standing nearby.

'I can't. I'm dead.'

'Get up.'

'Not until the Doctor's cured me.'

'The Doctor isn't here.'

'He has to cure me with the virgin, and all that.'

'He isn't here. We think he's in the pub.'

'Is he looking for a virgin?'

'No. Just getting pissed.'

'Bastard.'

The morris dancer playing Tommy in the mummers' play rolled over and sat up stiffly. The flies buzzed off him angrily.

'It's coming to something when you can't trust the Doctor,' he said.

'That's the NHS for you. Maybe you should go private.'

'These cobbles get harder every time.'

A mummer helped him up off the street.

'I could have died for real down there, and nobody would have noticed,' he said.

'We had quite a good crowd, but they've buggered off now.'

'Did anybody get round with the hat for the money?'

'No, we didn't have a chance.'

'Bastard.'

DIANE FRY STOOD quite still as the beast came towards her. Its progress was unsteady, and there was no way of knowing which direction she should dodge to avoid it. It veered from side to side as it stumbled across the cobbles, lowering its head and snapping its jaws. Red and yellow ribbons fluttered from its neck. It lunged towards a small girl, who flinched away with her hand covering her eyes. When the beast was within a couple of feet, it darted towards Fry, its mouth gaping and red.

Fry put out a hand and tapped on its muzzle. It sounded hollow, and wooden. A pair of eyes peered up at her through the jaws. Fry saw a glint of sweat on a forehead and caught a blast of beery breath.

'Excuse me,' she said. 'We're looking for the Border Rats.'

The voice that answered her was muffled, because it came from somewhere deep inside the canvas frame.

'Piss off,' it said. 'Can't you see I'm busy?'

'What time do you finish, then?'

'When these prancing buggers get tired.'

The beast staggered away, roared half-heartedly at some teenage girls, and veered back towards the team of morris dancers.

'I don't suppose you've ever seen Mr Fox?' said Gavin Murfin.

Diane Fry stared at the retreating hobbyhorse.

'Who?'

'They're a group from Langsett, just over the hills from Withens. I saw them about two years ago.'

'Two years? Is that real time or Renshaw time?' said Fry, who wasn't really listening.

'They all dress up in hooded cloaks and fox masks, and they only perform at night, by torchlight,' said Murfin. 'And when I say torchlight, I don't mean things powered by Ever Ready batteries, I mean flaming torches. You never quite know where they'll turn up.'

'Fox masks? If they turn up here, I'll set the hunt on them.'

'Isn't fox hunting illegal yet?'

'I don't care whether it is or not.'

A group called Betty Lupton's Ladle Laikers were taking their turn to perform in the market square, while dancers from the Norwich Shitwitches looked on. Outside the Red Lion, Fry could see yet more ribbons and bells, where Boggart's Breakfast and Treacle Eater were taking a beer break.

'When we were young, our dad used to tell us that morris dancers were to blame for the spread of VD,' said Murfin.

'Why?' said Fry.

'Oh, we never thought it was right. We knew it was to do with not taking precautions when you had it off with a bird, like. You know, you could catch it if your johnny burst or something. We could never quite see where bells and hankies came into it.'

'How old were you at this time, Gavin? Thirty-two?'

'Give over. I was very mature for my age. I had my first proper girlfriend when I was fourteen.'

'I don't think I want to know any more.'

'Sharon was two years older than me. She worked on the checkout at Tesco's, so she had strong fingers. She got free food, too – stuff that was going to be chucked out because it was past its sell-by date. But the trouble was, she wouldn't go all the way. She was scared to death of getting pregnant, the way some of her mates at school had done.'

'I didn't know there was a Tesco's in Edendale,' said Fry.

'Not any more. *They* had to pull out, too,' said Murfin gloomily.

They had parked the car partly on the pavement, nudging a yellow 'no parking' cone out of the way. Edendale town centre was solid with vehicles today.

'Anyway, it was the sort of thing Dad said to us,' said Murfin. 'I reckon it was his way of saying morris dancers were a set of soft jessies. These days, he reckons they're responsible for AIDS.'

Fry locked the car and looked back at him. 'Are you coming, or are you happy just reminiscing about your vanished childhood?'

'These morris dancers,' said Murfin. 'I don't suppose they're actually gay. Most of them have beards, don't they?'

'I've no idea.'

A little bit of sun was out. That meant people would be crowding the garden centres and nurseries, buying up bedding plants that would be killed by frost within a week. In the car park behind the market square, a girl in a converted Bedford van was selling ice cream.

'Don't think I'm obsessed or anything,' said Murfin. 'It's just that Mr Hitchens had me helping with those enquiries into the gay community when he found out about Neil Granger. I think it might have turned me a bit funny, like.'

The venues chosen for the dance groups were all within a couple of minutes' walk of each other. As a result, it was possible to hear several different kinds of music at once, all coming from different directions. Over there, towards the river, was a country and western line-dancing tune coming from a portable speaker. Behind the shops, in one of the cobbled courtyards, someone was playing 'Zorba's Dance' on a CD, and probably just getting to the stage where they all tried to dance too fast and trod on each other's feet.

From the market square came the sound of melodeons and a banjo, where one of the border morris teams was performing. That was definitely live. Fry could almost smell the sweat.

There were extra officers on duty in Edendale today, too – not to control the morris dancers, but because Stoke City football fans were in town, passing through on their way to Sheffield for a match. Traditionally, they called at Bakewell, on the A6, to tank up on beer in the local pubs, which they always left wrecked. But last year, the pub landlords in Bakewell had shut their doors for an hour or two until the Stoke contingent had moved on. This year, the fans had chosen to come to Edendale instead. And their arrival had coincided with the Day of Dance.

Fry found a grey-haired morris dancer taking a rest on a bench. He was dressed in white shirt and trousers in the Cotswold style, with ribbons tied to his wrists and ankles and a colourful baldrick across his chest. He was using his handkerchief to wipe some of the sweat from his face.

'The Border Rats? They're down in that little court-yard by the river, I think,' he said. 'What have they done?'

'Nothing. We just want to talk to them,' said Fry.

'Well, it's no use talking to the Squire. He's an Oxley. You might as well talk to that lamp post.'

'Have you got a better idea?'

'Aye, their Bagman. He's the one that has the brain cell.'

'Bagman?'

'Secretary, if you like. The organizer, the admin man. He has to make sure everyone gets to the right place at the right time and knows what they're supposed to be doing. That's no mean task with that lot, I can tell you. I'd rather try to herd a pack of wild dogs.'

'And what's this Bagman's name?'

'Neil Granger. You might have a bit of luck there, I suppose.'

'I'm afraid Neil Granger's dead, sir.'

'Is he? Well, I didn't know him so well. I just remember him from last year. The Border Rats raided one of our sets.'

'Thanks a lot, sir. You've been very helpful.'

'Well, don't tell anybody that. I'll get kicked out.'

BEN COOPER HAD already found the right place by following the noise. The courtyard was a new development enclosed by shops and paved to match the original setts. The design amplified the sound of the Border Rats band, which included a melodeon, concertina, drum, recorder and fiddle. Cooper didn't recognize any of the musicians, even allowing for the costumes and make-up. Presumably, these were some of the Hey Bridge contingent. But Scott and Ryan Oxley were there, with their rag coats, top hats and blacked-up faces, along with Sean and Glen, and even little Jake, blacked up and with his own stick, almost as tall as himself.

There was no sign of Lucas Oxley. But the old man, Eric, stepped forward from the band and addressed the crowd to introduce the group and the first performance.

Then the music began – melodeon and concertina playing in a minor key, with the drum beating time for the striking of the sticks. Six of the dancers stood up straight, crossed over once, then twice, turned and clashed their stick together. A double clash, then another turn and they advanced again, with the sun flashing off their mirrored sunglasses and the black make-up on their faces glistening with sweat.

Instinctively, the audience began to draw back, shuffling their feet uneasily as the dancers moved towards them. The Border Rats marched proudly, almost swaggered, their sticks over their shoulders and heads held high, confident that no one would get in their way. In contrast, their spectators began to resemble a small flock of sheep, huddling closer together and shying nervously as they clutched at their hot dogs and cameras. One small child seemed momentarily paralysed. His fingers lost their grip, and his ice cream landed on the flags with a crunch and a splatter of white.

The dancers did an about-turn and advanced towards the crowd on the far side. Then they spun through ninety degrees and did the same to left and right, with the crowd backing away from them each time, until they had cleared sufficient space in the middle.

The music paused, then started again, much faster. The dancers had established their territory, and now they were going to perform their ritual.

In the enclosed courtyard, the simultaneous clash of the sticks was so loud and at such a pitch that it was painful on the ears. The Border Rats were building up a head of steam and really going for it in a dance called Much Wenlock. Then Eric Oxley announced that the next was a fighting dance. This turned out to involve charging, screaming and clashing. Some of the tourists in the audience were starting to look a bit scared. They were backed up against the shop windows and had no escape route when the sticks started flying and the boots came trampling near their sandals and trainers.

A dance called Brimfield looked positively obscene, with the dancers holding their sticks thrust into their groins as blatant phallic symbols. But then they started throwing the sticks instead. They passed high overhead, but were caught each time before they landed among the audience. Cooper wondered whether their public liability insurance was up to date.

Cooper spotted his new neighbour, Peggy Check, across the crowd, and he worked his way round to speak to her. She gave the impression of being a small oasis of good humour and normality in a widening desert of irrationality, and that was what he needed at the moment.

'So what happened to the coffee?' she said when he reached her.

'Sorry?'

She smiled. 'You invited me round for coffee the night before last, and when I called you weren't in. Or you didn't answer the door anyway. Did I get the time wrong?'

'Oh God, I'm sorry.'

'You forgot.'

'Well …'

'I was hoping you got called away on urgent police business or something exciting.'

'Well, it was something like that.'

'You're not very convincing, Ben.'

'I'm really sorry.'

'And now you're blushing.'

'Look, can we make it Monday instead? I'm off duty then. Or maybe we can have lunch?'

'OK, that would be great.'

To Cooper's relief, she seemed to put it out of her mind then, and turned to watch the dancers. They had begun a chant. The words seemed to be something about darkness and light, death and renewal.

Peggy had an expensive-looking digital camera with an LCD display on the back panel. Cooper watched her try to focus on the performance over the shoulders of the crowd.

'Why digital?' he said.

'I'm going to e-mail some shots to my mom in Chicago,' said Peggy. 'She can't wait to see what Edendale is like now.'

'I see.'

'Also, I have a personal website. I'm going to put up a report of my trip when I get back.'

Before Cooper could say more, an ominous drum roll preceded the next dance. The dancers lined up in two rows of four, shouldering their sticks and steadying their breathing. The drum stopped, and there was a tense pause. Then, from a passage between the shops, the rat ran out into the courtyard.

Cooper knew that when the Border Rats talked about their beast, they didn't mean what everyone else might mean. 'Beast' could be used by a cattle farmer to refer to one of his animals. It was also prison slang for the despised sex offenders, particularly paedophiles. But when the Border Rats referred to their 'beast', they meant the man in the rat costume.

Lots of dance teams had a beast – it was traditional, like the Betty and Tommy in the mummers' plays.

Most beasts were a hobbyhorse, or something like that.
But it might as well be a rat. So the rat was the beast. And
Lucas Oxley was its operator, the man called the Beast
Master.

The costume consisted of grey painted canvas stretched
over a wire frame that concealed Lucas's body. The large
head was complete with eyes, ears and mouth, and there
were even whiskers around a sharp-pointed nose. A long
tail dragged on the floor behind Lucas. Cooper couldn't
see what it was made of, or how the right impression of
scaliness had been achieved. The overall result ought to
have been absurd, but it was more than countered by
Lucas Oxley's jerky, scurrying movements, the spasmodic
clutching of his wiry fingers, and the scrape of the tail on
the paving stones. The audience drew back and hung on
to their children, as if they might be snatched away by the
rat. Some of the adults looked distinctly nervous, too –
especially when the dancers suddenly surrounded Lucas.
That was when the screaming began.

The dance itself involved little springs in the air while
clashing the stick on the ground, like monkeys in a display of aggression. The dancers moved around the circle,
banging their sticks on the ground, narrowly missing
the feet of the rat caught in the middle. They built up the
rhythm steadily, and there was no mistaking the threatening message. They were hunters who had caught their
prey and were building themselves up for the finishing
stroke.

They rapped their sticks on the ground, crouching and splaying their arms to keep their balance.

Beneath the pounding of their sticks was the sound of their boots scraping on the flags and the rustling of their rag coats. They struck so hard and so fast that it seemed certain they would splinter their sticks. But gradually they were moving forward, step by step, cracking their sticks and grinning from their black faces.

And in the middle of it all Lucas darted backwards and forwards in his rat costume, screaming the high-pitched scream that Cooper had heard him practising at the Quiet Shepherd. It was certainly realistic. Somewhere nearby in the crowds, Cooper could hear dogs starting to bark. A terrier of some kind was working itself into a frenzy.

Some of the Border Rats' sticks were taking a hammering now. Fragments of bark were flying off, and splinters of the pale wood were flaking away. The dancers put so much energy into the dance that bits of their rag coats fell off, too, and occasionally a flower from their hats. When they'd finished, sweat was pouring from their temples and streaking their black make-up.

'So what is it supposed to represent?' said Peggy Check. 'Do you know, Ben? I bet you do.'

'Well, as it happens, I do.'

'I knew I'd picked the right person.'

'The tradition started in the nineteenth century,' said Cooper, 'when workmen were building some railway tunnels a few miles north of here. The site was infested with rats, and the dance represents the workmen killing the rats with sticks.'

'Mmm.' Peggy sounded doubtful.

'They call themselves the Border Rats. Border is the old working men's dance tradition, with the sticks and blacked-up faces, like mummers. And the rats bit is obvious.'

'It looked like more than that to me,' said Peggy. 'I studied a bit of folklore as an undergraduate. And this looked like a classic resurrection ritual. They were always performed around this time of year. They represent the death of winter and the arrival of spring, the growth of new crops.'

'But the rat –'

'*Someone* is being symbolically killed. I think the rat is a symbol. Of course, the blacking of faces is just a disguise.'

'Nathan Pidcock,' said Cooper.

'Excuse me?'

'A killing. But not symbolic. A real one.'

Cooper looked across the courtyard to where Eric Oxley stood next to the musicians watching the dance. Eric had said there were foreigners in the pub the night that Neil Granger was killed. What foreigners? Did he mean lorry drivers? But they parked their lorries in the lay-bys on the A628, and they wouldn't want to walk all the way down into Withens. Or were the foreigners walkers on Euroroute E8? Perhaps. But surely Eric Oxley wouldn't be bothered by a few hikers passing through the village, even if they did have foreign accents? It was possible that by 'foreigners' he might mean people from the other side of the hill, in Yorkshire. Attitudes like that still survived in the more isolated valleys of the North of England. In Longdendale, Cooper himself was a foreigner.

A FEW MINUTES later, Cooper reached his car and began the battle to get out of Edendale through the tourist traffic and the diversions. He found he was passing the cricket ground, where the first match of the season was getting under way. Because of a stoppage ahead of him, he had to sit in his car watching the players moving slowly around the pitch.

From a distance, the cricketers in their white flannels bore a striking resemblance to the Cotswold morris dancers. Some of the players wore hats, and the batsmen were padded up and carried the bats over their shoulders. Many of the players even had beards and beer guts. As Cooper watched, they took their places in the field and began the first innings. After only a couple of deliveries, the entire field seemed to leap into the air and give a cry of 'howzat!' The bowler took out a hankie and mopped his brow. After six balls, they all changed places.

To an untrained eye, there weren't all that many differences. The ritual was pretty much the same. Their square had been carefully prepared and marked out – what had the Reverend Alton called that sacred space? The temenos. Cooper had no doubt the cricketers would consider their square sacred, something to be worshipped and protected, preserved for their weekly ritual. And the first match on the sacred ground marked the end of the winter and the start of spring, the rebirth of their hopes for a successful season. Later on, perhaps, there would be a harvest of trophies and winners' medals. Or maybe not, in Edendale's case.

Cooper glanced at the sky. It was starting to look like rain.

LUCAS OXLEY WAS still in his rat costume. But Diane Fry peered into the mouth and saw his face was bright red and glistening.

'Mr Oxley?' she said.

'Who are you?'

'Detective Sergeant Fry. Would you like to take the costume off, sir, so I can talk to you properly?'

'I can't.'

'Sorry?'

'I can't be seen out of character by the public. It ruins the illusion. I have to put it on and take it off in the van.'

'Nobody's looking. They've all gone off to watch something else.'

'Besides, I'm not wearing any clothes under here. It gets too hot.'

'Right.'

Fry glared at Gavin Murfin, who was beginning to snigger. He was standing near a coil of the rat's tail, as if he might be about to stamp on it.

'I need a beer anyway,' said Lucas. 'What the hell do you want?'

'There was an incident yesterday at Hey Bridge, sir. We had some complaints of damage and intimidation.'

'Oh, that. We were just practising. We call it a raid – we turn up somewhere we're not expected. It's traditional.'

'Why did you take Mr Alton with you?' said Fry.

'The vicar? He wanted to come. He's been desperate to get in with the Border Rats ever since he arrived. He comes and watches the rehearsals, and practises the moves and the words to himself in that church of his. He loves every minute of it.'

'It seems strange for him to have taken part in this escapade with you just at that time.'

'Eh? Oh, skeletons in the churchyard. Well, I suppose it helped take his mind off it.'

Fry could see moisture gathering in the lower folds of the rat costume and soaking through the canvas. It must be really hot in there.

'Mr Oxley, when was the churchyard last cleared? Was it before Mr Alton came to the village?'

'Yes, it would be.'

'Was it cleared after the last incumbent left?'

'The old chap? I don't know. Can't remember.'

'Who used to do the work?'

'There were a few folk chipped in. Look, I'm fed up of this. I'm going for that beer now.'

Lucas Oxley tried to walk away past Diane Fry, but found himself brought to a halt near her shoulder.

'I'm afraid my colleague appears to be standing on your tail,' said Fry.

'Tell him to get off.'

'I'm sure he'll be gentle. He's an animal lover.'

'Some of us went up to the church to help sometimes. Me, Dad. Scott did a bit. Marion nagged us to do it, because she's a churchwarden. Is that what you wanted to know?'

'That's very helpful, sir. But why did Mrs Oxley stop nagging?'

'Things got hard. We had to go looking for work more. We didn't have time.'

'No time to clear some weeds from the churchyard?'

'No.'

'Are you telling me the truth?'

'If your bloody ape doesn't get off my tail, I'm going to make a complaint.'

'By all means,' said Fry. 'The RSPCA is round the corner.'

Now THE BORDER Rats were on a high. With their performance over, they were left almost delirious from the physical exertion, the noise and the sound of the music, the response of the crowd and the different level they seemed to be lifted to when people performed in harmony. It was what they had put so much time and effort into practising for, week after week. Their legs ached and their hands and wrists tingled from the repeated impact of their sticks. One of the Hey Bridge men had taken a blow on the shoulder from Scott's stick, and he would have a terrific bruise in the morning. But he didn't care.

It would take a while for them to come down again. And relaxing properly involved beer. Lucas seemed to be busy, so the dancers left the musicians to pack up their instruments and count the money, and they edged away towards the Wheatsheaf, each with the same thought in mind. Scott told them he knew a short cut, so they followed him.

They had to pass through a narrow alleyway between tall buildings. The moment they stepped out of the square and into the shadows of the alley, they began to feel cold. The sun never reached here, and the dampness from the river beneath them was rising through the setts. Their sweat began to dry uncomfortably on their skin. But they were still laughing and joking as they emerged at the top of a flight of stone steps that led down into the lane off Bargate, where the Wheatsheaf stood. The Rats had kept their sticks with them, ready for another set after the beer break. Unconsciously, they were still moving almost in step, with the rhythm of the drum still sounding in their ears. In a few minutes, they would be shouting at each other to be heard above the noise of the pub, and the rhythm would gradually subside in their minds.

But there was shouting already in the lane beneath them. Scott and Melvyn were in front, and they halted on the top step, with the others crowding behind them. They lowered their sticks from their shoulders.

In front of the pub, a group of youths had knocked a Cotswold morris dancer to the ground. He was on his knees, and his white shirt and trousers were covered in dirt, and his baldrick was torn and flapping loose. He put his hand to the side of his head, where a stream of blood was running into his beard. One of the youths put his boot to the dancer's backside and pushed him over, making the bells on his legs jingle. The rest of the youths cheered, and gathered round the fallen morris man.

'What's going on here?' said Melvyn.

At first, they thought it was an impromptu performance being staged by one of the Cotswold sides. It was strange that there was no music, and they didn't recognize the dance. In fact, there seemed to be no pattern to it, and the dancers kept falling over a bit too often, even for hanky men. And how come the audience seemed to be joining in, and doing less falling over than the dancers?

'Fight,' said Scott, with a note of admiration in his voice. He never knew that hanky dancers were fighters.

'They're getting a pasting, aren't they?'

And in fact, it was clear through the slight haze of alcohol that two white-outfitted Cotswold morris men were being given a kicking by a group of football supporters. No doubt the row had started with some sarcastic comment. But it didn't usually descend to this level of violence.

Then one of the group looked up and nudged the youth next to him.

'Hey, look,' he said. 'What the hell's that?'

The youths turned towards the steps and looked at the Border Rats. They saw figures dressed all in black, with blackened faces and mirrored sunglasses, and heavy sticks in their hands.

'Hey, mate, you need a wash!' shouted one youth. 'Have you been up a chimney?'

'Well, there's no need to give me a black look. Ha!'

Scott and Melvyn could hear the other Rats breathing excitedly behind them, and were conscious of their strength as a group. They looked at each other briefly, though they couldn't see each other's eyes because of the mirrored sunglasses. They took a firmer grip on their sticks and leaned forward, balancing their weight on their toes. Renewed energy flowed through their limbs. At a silent count of three, they leaped into the alley. Their screams reverberated off the stone walls as their sticks swung through the air. And then they attacked.

Chapter Thirty-Five

ALEX DEARDEN WAS going to upset Gavin Murfin again. His silence was wasting tape. And not just one tape, but triplicate tapes, all turning slowly in the West Street interview room. With a solicitor sitting alongside him, Dearden was saying nothing.

'Would you care to tell us why you needed to borrow the Audi car from the Renshaws?' said Diane Fry. 'You have a car of your own, don't you? A Mercedes, I understand.'

'My client accepts that he asked Mr and Mrs Renshaw for the loan of a vehicle when his own had mechanical problems,' said the solicitor. 'He also agrees that he has a vehicle of his own, which is a Mercedes. Beyond that, he declines to answer any questions.'

'The car in question is an Audi, which was seen in the Southwoods area, near Southwoods Grange. Would you tell us why you were near Southwoods Grange on the night you borrowed this car?'

Dearden was wearing black jeans again, but a different T-shirt. His goatee beard was neatly trimmed, and almost as dark as the T-shirt.

'We've made enquiries at Eden Valley Software Solutions, Mr Dearden, and it seems you've bought yourself a partnership in the subsidiary company that will develop uses of the software you were telling us about the other day. That must have been the chance of a lifetime, from what you were saying. It could bring you a fortune. At such a young age, too.'

Alex Dearden smiled a little. His solicitor began to smile too, but resumed his professional seriousness when he found Gavin Murfin glowering at him.

'You must have needed a large amount of money quickly, so as not to miss that opportunity. How much do you earn, Mr Dearden?'

The solicitor leaned over and whispered.

'My client is prepared to produce his salary details. He's quite well paid, and has very few commitments.'

'Really? But stolen antiques are much more lucrative, I imagine. Large quantities shipped to the right buyers. But I can't see you as a burglar, so what was your role? Are you the man with the right contacts?'

Dearden could have been quite good-looking. He had good bone structure, and he was well groomed. If he made an effort to be pleasant and courteous, it would be no surprise that Sarah Renshaw had a soft spot for him. Besides, he was a link to Emma.

'DC Murfin here has been talking to some of your contacts,' said Fry.

He frowned for the first time then. His hands, which had been quite still, moved a little on the table.

Murfin looked at his notebook. 'You've been to the USA quite a bit in the last couple of years,' he said. 'I've never had the chance to go myself. But they tell me they're very hospitable, the Americans. And very keen on British heritage, stuff like that. Not having much history themselves, like.'

Fry watched Dearden carefully. If anything could break his complacency, Gavin Murfin could. He certainly did it to her every time.

'Some of the blokes on the list were very interesting to talk to,' said Murfin. 'This one here, in California – he said he thought my accent was "awesome". He says I can take my family over and stay at his beach house in Malibu any time I like. That's brilliant.'

'Er, Detective Sergeant …' said the solicitor.

'And he was happy to talk about you, Mr Dearden. He knows you very well. What's this Silicon Valley place? Is it where they make breast implants?'

'Get on with it,' said Alex Dearden impatiently.

'I told your friend about this bronze bust we found. Lucius Verrus, it is. And do you know, he has something very similar. We had quite a long chat. Next time he comes over, I'm going to show him round Chatsworth House. I just hope he realized I was joking when I said I was the Duke of Devonshire's nephew.'

'Do we have to put up with this?' Dearden said to his solicitor. 'I've had enough.'

Murfin turned over a page. 'And you've been to Japan, too!' he said. 'I bet your address book is interesting.'

The two pouches at the sides of Dearden's mouth were quivering a little. The angry hamster could be about to make an appearance.

'Do you have any more sensible questions, Sergeant?' asked the solicitor.

'Yes. I'd like to invite your client to tell us who his associates are in the stolen antiques business.'

'You know we aren't going to answer questions like that.'

'And where are the antiques kept prior to shipping? They don't seem to be at your house, Mr Dearden. Where are they?'

'That's a no comment,' said the solicitor. 'Really –'

'And why did you fall out with Neil Granger, Mr Dearden? Did he want a bigger cut? It's usually money that's the problem, isn't it?'

Dearden began to shake his head vigorously, until the solicitor put a hand on his arm to steady him. Fry remembered the project Dearden was working on at the software company. Technology designed to prevent human error. But Alex Dearden wasn't a computer; he was as human as anyone else. And sooner or later, he would make an error.

IT HAD BEEN a bad day for Chief Superintendent Colin Jepson, commander of Derbyshire Constabulary E Division. Edendale had attracted all kinds of people this weekend, and his officers were stretched to the limit dealing with all the crime and disorder that followed crowds of people around like horseflies.

DI Hitchens and the CID team were almost the only people Jepson could find in the station at West Street. They were still laboriously following up on calls from the public about missing persons who might possibly have turned up in a shallow grave in Withens churchyard, no matter how far from their homes it was, or how recently they had gone missing. Officers were explaining patiently to distraught mothers that it was impossible for somebody who had been missing for only twenty-four hours to have been reduced to a skeleton in that time, no matter how badly they'd been eating recently.

'And then,' said Chief Superintendent Jepson wearily. 'And then, after everything else that's happened to me today, I come back to my own police station, expecting to finally get a bit of peace and quiet in a civilized environment. And I find the reception area full of black and white minstrels.'

He looked around the room full of officers. Some were smirking, as usual. Others looked blank, having never heard of the Black and White Minstrels because they were born in the age of political correctness.

'Who was responsible for that little idea, I wonder?' said Jepson. 'What genius turned the front desk into an audition room for *The Al Jolson Story*?'

'They're morris dancers, Chief,' said DI Hitchens. 'The town's full of them.'

'I don't need telling,' said the Chief Superintendent, 'that the town is full of them. The reason I don't need telling is that my car was stuck in a traffic jam for over an hour on the corner of Clappergate, while eighteen thousand of them paraded past me waving their bells and handkerchiefs. I know there were eighteen thousand, because I counted them. I had plenty of time.'

Jepson glared from one officer to another, daring somebody to contradict him.

'What I *do* need telling, though, is why someone took a fancy to bringing a few of them back to the station. Surely the whole point of morris dancers having bells on their trousers is so that we can hear them coming and avoid them?'

'The ones sitting in reception are waiting for their friends,' said Hitchens.

'Oh, of course. We've invited some in to give them a guided tour of the station. How silly of me not to have thought of that. Does this mean I'm going to find them jingling around in the comms room and combing their beards in the gents? I know we're trying to increase our representation of ethnic minorities in E Division. But I have to tell you, ladies and gentlemen, that I absolutely draw the line at recruiting morris dancers. Those blacked-up faces aren't going to fool the Commission for Racial Equality, you know.'

'Actually, they're waiting for the ones we have in the cells,' said Hitchens.

'Ah. And they're occupying our custody suite for what purpose exactly, Inspector?'

'Identification and interview, following arrest on suspicion of affray.'

'Affray? You do realize that when they beat each other with sticks, they're doing it for fun. It turns some people on, or so I'm told.'

'Yes, Chief.'

'Anyway, don't we have football supporters for that sort of thing? If we need to get the performance results up for violent crime, couldn't we have pulled in a few more Stoke City fans? They might not be pretty, but at least they don't jingle.'

At the lack of response, the Chief Superintendent started to go a bit red in the face, and his voice rose in volume.

'And tell the rat to take his mask off. I won't have giant rats sitting around in my police station.'

'He says he gets out of character if he takes his head off,' said Hitchens.

Jepson stared at Hitchens. The DI stared back unflinchingly, but it was impossible to tell whether he was serious, or whether he was taking the mickey.

'If he gets an identity crisis, we'll arrange for him to see a counsellor,' said Jepson.

DIANE FRY LOOKED at Howard Renshaw with barely restrained annoyance. Exactly what it would take to puncture the bubble of fantasy the Renshaws lived in, she didn't know.

'I wanted to tell you I'm sorry,' he was saying. 'I realize that I misled you by my behaviour in the churchyard, and I apologize for that. It must have put you and your colleagues to a lot of trouble. But it was a very emotional moment, you see. I'm sure you understand. Particularly for my wife –'

'But you already knew the remains weren't those of your daughter, didn't you, sir? You knew that it couldn't be Emma.'

'Well, looking back now, I suppose it should have been obvious to us that it couldn't have been Emma. I mean, how would she have ended up in Withens, let alone in the churchyard? It wasn't logical. But that's hindsight speaking. We weren't thinking logically at the time. We were both upset.'

'But maybe you didn't actually need hindsight.'

'What do you mean?'

'You didn't really believe the remains were those of your daughter.'

Howard hesitated slightly.

'I didn't,' said Sarah. 'I knew it couldn't be Emma. She's still alive, isn't she?'

'We don't know that, Mrs Renshaw.'

'All this time, Howard hasn't been believing, he's just been pretending. Emma hasn't had his belief, only mine. If she dies now, it will be my fault. I'm all she has left.'

Howard shifted uneasily in his chair, but Sarah didn't look at him. There was no exchange of meaningful glances today.

'For two years, I've thought it was something I did that made Emma go away,' said Sarah. 'I thought that if I weren't here she would come back. Then Emma would be able to get on with her life. Looking back now, it seems very silly.'

'No, I wouldn't call it that.'

'I never even liked her playing outside when she was a child. I always imagined the worst – that she would be abducted and murdered. You hear of it happening such a lot. I worried all the time when Emma was out of my sight, so I kept her where I could keep an eye on her. But at the same time, I felt guilty at not giving her any freedom. It was dangerous enough for children then. But it's worse now, isn't it?'

'Statistically, no,' said Fry. 'There are no more children being abducted or killed by strangers than there were in the 1980s.'

'But when it happens, we all hear about it, don't we? It's in the news, in the papers, on the TV. Everybody talks about it.'

'Sometimes children need to learn about risk. It's part of the process of growing up.'

'Do you think if I had let Emma take more risks when she was younger, this wouldn't have happened?'

'Nobody can say that, Mrs Renshaw.'

'I can't help wondering. I can't help thinking it was my fault. I feel guilty about the silliest things. I keep remembering them at odd moments. Like when I was breast-feeding Emma as a baby.'

Fry looked at Howard, who was staring into space through the window of the Renshaws' sitting room. He was on the leather settee, near the teddy bear, which was staring into space equally vaguely.

'You feel guilty about breast-feeding, Mrs Renshaw?'

'No, it was one little incident, when she was teething. It was only a very brief moment, no more than an instinctive physical reaction on my part. But these things can scar a child for life – especially at that age, when they're so impressionable.'

'I don't understand what you're talking about.'

'When Emma was teething, she bit my nipple. It was very painful, and it came as a real shock. So of course, I pulled away sharply – because of the pain, you know. It meant that I had rejected her at a crucial moment, when she was suckling, the time that is so important for bonding, for creating love and trust between mother and child that will last a lifetime.'

'You didn't mean to do it.'

'No, but you can't explain that to a baby. And Emma recognized that she had been rejected. She cried, and I could see it in her face. After that, if she bit me again when she was suckling, she would start crying straight away, even though I tried to bear the pain and not pull away. She was expecting to be rejected by me. Those early incidents leave a lasting impression that can never be erased. I'm sure Emma has spent the rest of her life expecting to be rejected by her mother. I need her to come home soon, so that I can explain it to her.'

Guilt was a strange, inexplicable thing. At the extreme, it became almost existential, a feeling of guilt for simply being there when others weren't. But guilt was good, in a way. The worst people were those who felt no guilt at all. Guilt could sometimes be what kept people together.

'It's the first thing I think about when I wake up, and the last thing I think about when I go to bed at night,' said Sarah. 'It's with me all the time.'

Howard finally stopped fidgeting, got up and walked out of the room. Fry watched him go, but his wife hardly seemed to notice.

Fry knew that the length of time that had passed made it much worse for the Renshaws. A few years ago, the rules for coroners had been changed to prevent the body of a murder victim being kept in cold storage for years on end, awaiting the trial of their killer. The distress caused to the victim's family had been recognized, and the need for closure acknowledged. If Emma's body had been found straight away, it would have been twenty-eight days at the most before the coroner released it for burial, even if no one had been charged with her murder. And then the Renshaws would have been free to bury Emma.

But that hadn't happened. They had been denied that closure; instead they had been allowed a glimmer of hope that they nurtured for two years, like the candle that burned in the Renshaws' window, which Sarah would never allow to go out.

The phone rang in the next room. Fry watched Sarah Renshaw look immediately at the clock, staring at its face as if to imprint on her memory that one second of the day. Fry had seen her do it before, and knew without asking that it was a ritual connected with Emma. Time was being counted down in the Renshaws' lives. Fry felt the days ticking away, too. But perhaps not towards what Sarah Renshaw expected.

'The one thing we can say is that it brought some feeling into our lives,' said Sarah.

'What do you mean?'

'Our marriage had become very cold, you see. There was very little emotion between Howard and I. Whatever is between you at the beginning of a marriage sort of fades away over the years, so that you hardly notice it going. But, when it's gone, you realize one day there's something missing. It's more of a sense of dissatisfaction.'

'I see.'

'And when this happened with Emma, it was suddenly different. It made me realize what was missing. After all that time, there was feeling again. There was emotion. And not just mine, I mean, but from Howard, too. I'd forgotten that he was capable of feeling things. But after Emma, he was a different man, the man I remembered marrying. You might not understand how comforting that was. No – more than comforting.'

'It sounds almost as though you were pleased that your daughter went missing.'

'No. That would be very shocking,' said Mrs Renshaw. 'But?'

'All I'm saying is that the past two years have brought us much closer together. There was a moment in the early days, when the police told us that they hadn't been able to find Emma. I got very upset, more at the idea that they were going to give up and stop looking for her, rather than anything else. The thing I remember most is that Howard put his arm round me and gave me a hug. I don't think he even knew he had done it, it was so natural, without any of the awkwardness I would have expected. But there was so much warmth in it, for me. I suppose that sounds trivial, doesn't it?'

'A small thing, but I suppose they can mean a lot.'

'It did in this case. Because it was the first time Howard had touched me for years.'

Fry realized she had been listening to Sarah Renshaw with a growing numbness, as if a protective shell had gradually been forming over her own emotions. She was mentally putting on the body armour, slipping on an invisible bullet-proof vest. A police officer's first priority was her own survival, unharmed. She didn't need to take on even the smallest share of Sarah Renshaw's guilt.

'You started to have doubts about your husband?'

'Yes, when the remains were found in the churchyard. Howard seemed to think it was Emma, which was ridiculous. It was then I realized Howard believed she was dead.'

Chapter Thirty-Six

DIANE FRY READ through all the Emma Renshaw files again. It was the third time she'd been through them. More than ever, the gaps in the enquiries seemed to stand out. Khadi Gupta had never been interviewed. Perhaps the other students had never mentioned her, because she hadn't been one of their social group. But she had been in the photograph with Emma that the Renshaws had given the police.

The possibility that Emma had been given a lift to the station had been raised, but only in relation to Neil Granger and Alex Dearden, and a couple of other students she had known. There had been no attempt to eliminate the other options. In particular, no one seemed to have raised their eyes from their local area and looked north for the possibilities. No one had checked on Howard Renshaw's movements that day.

Fry thought about the relationship between the Renshaws and their daughter. On Sarah's side, it was characterized by guilt. Anything that happened would be because *she* had done something wrong. At least as regards her daughter. There was nothing that Emma could have done which would not have been Sarah's fault in some way. Sarah had made sure of that, with her memory of rejecting her child at the breast. For heaven's sake. How much self-obsession and brooding had it taken for her to come up with that?

But Howard was more complicated. Or perhaps he was just more opaque. Fry recalled Gavin Murfin's verdict on Howard. He had described him as a man whose brain was ahead of his mouth. Howard never said anything he hadn't thought about first.

The Renshaws had been expecting Emma to arrive home that day. They had waited for her at Glossop railway station. But until then, had both of them been at home all day? No, Howard had said he'd been out on business.

What she'd really like would be to get Howard Renshaw in to make a statement, but without his wife present. Fry had listened to Sarah Renshaw enough.

'IT'S VERY SAD,' said Ben Cooper later. He had hardly finished following up calls from the public about potential occupants of shallow graves before Fry had raised the subject of the Renshaws. 'If there were just one of them, it might be different. But the Renshaws are encouraging each other in their fantasies.'

'Somebody's encouraging Sarah Renshaw, certainly.'

'What do you mean?' said Cooper. 'You're thinking of Howard?'

Fry nodded. 'Yes, Howard.'

'Do you think he's deliberately encouraging his wife to believe Emma isn't dead?'

'I can see that she's gone completely off the rails with this obsession. The poor bloody woman has had more than two years of it now. No wonder she doesn't know what's real and what isn't. But as for Howard – don't you think he lays it on a bit thick?'

'He handles it differently,' said Cooper cautiously.

Fry snorted. 'Differently? At one time I just thought he was sad and pathetic, like his wife. But that business with the skull was altogether too gothic and stagy. It was like something out of one of those Jacobean tragedies we had to read at school. All overblown melodrama and dead bodies lying around.'

'John Webster? *The Duchess of Malfi?*'

'Yeah, that stuff.'

'"Cover her face, mine eyes dazzle."'

'What?'

'It's a line from the play.'

'Right.'

Fry let it pass her by, as if English Literature classes had been one more interruption in her progress towards whatever goal she'd had her eye on in those days.

'But I'll tell you what, Ben,' she said. 'If it turns out Howard Renshaw killed Emma himself, I'm going to tear him apart with my bare hands.'

'I think he'd have to be a damn good actor,' said Cooper.

'OK. I'll present him with an Oscar first – and *then* I'll tear him apart with my bare hands.'

'Fair enough. But what about Sarah?'

Fry leaned back in her chair and stared at the ceiling of the CID room as she thought about Sarah.

'Sarah Renshaw isn't acting,' she said. 'Sarah Renshaw is gone from the real world.'

'Yes.'

But Cooper thought he probably had clearer recollections of reading *The Duchess of Malfi* than Fry had. The lines about covering her face had popped into his mind unbidden, thanks to an enthusiastic English teacher and a memorable reading in his sixth-form literature class.

'But that was her brother,' he said.

'What?'

'"Cover her face, mine eyes dazzle." In *The Duchess of Malfi* it's not her father who kills the duchess. It's her brother.'

But Fry just stared at Cooper as if he, too, were gone from the real world.

'Diane, I think we should take a look at Trafalgar Terrace,' he said after a moment.

'Take a look where?'

'The houses behind where the Oxleys live. There's another terrace of houses there – the same as Waterloo Terrace, but derelict. No one has lived there for years, and the houses are in quite a state. But they're not boarded up, and I'm sure the Oxleys must have access to them.'

'A great place to hide something?'

'Definitely.'

'A great place to hide a body? Or what?'

'Let's see.'

'What about a search warrant?'

'We don't need one. The property belongs to Peak Water. I've already got their permission.'

'We need it in writing, Ben.'

'No problem. I'll call Mr Venables, and we can visit him on the way there.'

Cooper folded an Ordnance Survey map over several times until he had a small rectangle showing the area of upper Longdendale he wanted.

'How do you do that?' said Fry.

'What?'

'Never mind. I guess I'm just fated to fold creases the wrong way.'

Cooper shrugged. 'If you look at the map, you'll see that we can approach Trafalgar Terrace without going past the Oxleys' houses. If we park down on this farm road here, there'll be a couple of fields to cross, and then we might have to climb over a fence or a wall. But we should be out of sight all the way, because there's a thick screen of trees.'

'OK.'

'Besides, it's such an ideal time. All of the Oxley men are still here in Edendale, being interviewed for the affray outside the Wheatsheaf. They won't be back in Withens for hours yet. We'll never have a better opportunity to take a look round without being interrupted.'

'Sounds good. But, Ben ...'

'Yeah?'

'The least sign of anything interesting, and we pull out and organize a proper search by the specialists.'

'Procedure,' said Cooper.

'It's not a dirty word, you know.'

NOW IT WAS raining properly. It was bound to, since it was bank holiday weekend and the area was full of tourists. The morris dancers would be getting wet in Edendale. Their hankies would be going limp and their bells would be rusting up. But nothing would stop them dancing.

In Withens, the dark clouds lay right on top of the village, flattening it into the valley bottom and squeezing the moors closer together, so that the rain ran out of them on to the road and down into the gardens of the brick terraces. For once, it was the black brick that seemed to blend into the landscape, while the stone houses above glinted a little too brightly as they soaked up the moisture.

'Trafalgar Terrace is up the hill there, behind the trees,' said Ben Cooper. 'Waterloo Terrace is beyond that.'

'You were right – two fields to cross.'

'Maybe we should walk around this first field, though,' said Cooper. 'We should avoid the livestock.'

'They're only cows,' said Fry. 'I do recognize the difference between bulls and cows, Ben. I'm not quite the ignorant city girl you think I am.'

'Diane –'

'Bulls have bollocks and cows have tits. See? I know all the agricultural expressions. If I wanted to, I reckon I could convince people I was a farmer and get subsidies for not growing anything. Besides, I'm not wearing anything red.'

'They're colour blind,' said Cooper.

'All the better.'

'May's a bad time to be near cows, Diane. We had an incident of a woman being savaged by a cow only the other day.'

'Come off it.'

'People get this wrong. They think cows are docile and bulls are aggressive. Young bullocks are just mischievous, and older bulls are usually too lazy even to get up. But cows in May ... if they have calves with them, they'll do anything to protect them. And they're a herd, so if you fall out with one, you fall out with the whole lot.'

To his surprise, Fry was actually listening to him. He'd had visions of her getting trampled before she was halfway across the field.

'So what do we do?'

'Walk around the outside. Avoid eye contact and walk past naturally. We'll be fine then.'

'OK.'

It worked, of course. All the cows wanted was to be left in peace in their field. Leave them alone, and they'd leave you alone. It was one of the laws of nature.

In the second field, Cooper stopped at the sound of wings fluttering against metal. He walked over to an object partly hidden in the wet grass near a wall.

'What have you found?' said Fry.

'It's a Larsen trap.'

'A what?'

'Some of the old farmers put them out to catch crows in the spring. You don't see them so much these days. They're frowned on a bit, on the grounds of cruelty to crows.'

Fry walked over to see what he'd found. 'Well, it looks as though this farmer's caught one,' she said.

'No, that's the lure bird.'

The trap consisted of a cage with two compartments. One side was hinged open, and there were three hen's eggs inside it. The other compartment contained an unhappy-looking crow, which stood among some bloody scraps of meat, splatters of its own droppings, and pools of water splashed from a small bowl. When it saw them, the bird panicked and flapped at the bars, and Cooper drew back a few steps.

'I don't understand,' said Fry.

'This bird acts as a lure. What the farmer hopes is that a passing crow will be inquisitive and think this one has found a source of food. It comes down and lands on that convenient perch there on the baited side, with its eye on a few tasty-looking eggs. Then the perch collapses under its weight, and the lid slams shut on it.'

'Which means the farmer has a cage with two crows in it.'

'Larsens are supposed to be checked every day. The lure bird has to be given food and water. And any trapped crow has to be destroyed.'

Fry shuddered. 'It does look cruel to me. I'm surprised it's allowed at all.'

'It won't be allowed for much longer, I suppose,' said Cooper. 'But some people would point out that the crows are destroyed a bit more humanely than the way they kill their own victims. They don't call them carrion crows for nothing, you know.'

'I don't want to know any more, thanks.'

They left the crow in the trap and reached a wall, where they could see the black outline of Trafalgar Terrace through the screen of chestnuts and sycamores. Water was dripping steadily from the dense canopies of leaves.

'So far, so good,' said Fry. 'Give me a hand over the wall.'

INSIDE THE FIRST house of Trafalgar Terrace, the air smelled fungal and sour, like old cider. These houses were slightly lower down the hill than the other terrace, and the damp had crept into them over the stone steps and risen up through the floors from the black peat, which soaked up water like a sponge. But beyond the dampness and the stale odour of long-abandoned carpets and ancient wallpaper, there was a more acrid smell.

The broken back door had opened on a loose hinge to let them in easily. Fry stepped over some cardboard boxes that had collapsed and begun to disintegrate in the middle of the floor. She reached the facing doorway.

'There's been a fire here,' she said.

Cooper joined her and shone a torch into the derelict kitchen. There was scorching around the sink and the window frame, and a blackened area on the wall where an electric cooker might once have stood.

'Do you think someone's been living here?' said Fry.

'It was probably just kids playing around. By all accounts, one or two of them like setting fires. Jake, for a start.'

'You think so?' She poked a pile of debris with her foot. 'Take a look at this.'

'What is it?'

'Silver paper. And half a Coke can. It looks as though some of the kids have set up a drugs den down here.'

'It's nothing, Diane. Want to try upstairs?'

She hesitated a moment. 'OK. Where are the stairs?'

Cooper could remember the layout of the houses from his visit to Fran Oxley's. Thanks to that night, he could practically find his way round in the dark. Fortunately, he had a torch this time. There would be two torches – if only Fry's didn't keep shooting up into the corners of the ceiling, lighting up hanging cobwebs.

'Not frightened of the spiders, are you, Diane?' said Cooper from the stairs.

She didn't answer, but gazed overhead like a surveyor looking for cracks in the plaster.

'Diane?'

'Oh. Carry on. I'm coming.'

Upstairs, there were some floorboards missing and ancient electric wiring exposed in the gaps. Cooper shone his torch downwards to guide his steps.

'Watch where you're walking, Diane. And don't shine your torch at the back windows, in case anybody sees the light.'

'But you said there'd be nobody in.'

'None of the men. But we don't want to frighten Mrs Wallwin at number 7. And Wendy Tagg is probably at home with the children.'

Rain was getting through the roof in several places. They could hear it dripping on the ceilings above them, like the sound of tiny footsteps. In the corner of one of the bedrooms, a stream of water glittered against the mouldy wallpaper. A rotten floorboard snapped under Fry's foot. Cooper put out a hand to steady her. When he touched her shoulder, he was surprised to find that she was trembling.

'Are you all right?'

'Fine.'

Cooper pointed the beam of his torch towards the bathroom at the end of a short passage. The porcelain toilet bowl, washbasin and bath were still in there. They gleamed in the light.

'You think we might find a stash of antiques in here, then?' he said.

'I don't know. There's a stash somewhere, that's for sure. They can't be shipping them constantly.'

Cooper stuck his head inside the door of the bathroom. 'Heck, I bet there are some big spiders living in *that* bath.'

'Where?'

'Only kidding. There's nothing up here. No attic trap door. I wonder if there's a cellar.'

'God.'

He couldn't quite see Fry's face, because she was looking back towards the stairs.

'If there is, I'll go down. You can wait by the back door.'

'I'm fine. Really.'

Cooper trod carefully back down the stairs and into the front hallway.

'If there *is* a cellar, the door will be under the stairs. Ah, yes.'

'It could just be a cupboard,' said Fry.

'I don't think so.'

The door stuck a little, but Cooper tugged at it, and a stream of cold air emptied into the hallway.

'It's probably a small keeping cellar,' he said. 'They were very handy, before the days of fridges. On the other hand, it might run under all eight houses in the terrace.'

'If we're going down, let's go,' said Fry. 'Stop talking about it.'

'All right, all right. Chill out.'

'Very funny.'

The steps were made of stone, and the little cellar felt terribly claustrophobic. Cooper could sense the hillside behind the walls, the heavy mass of peat and rock that would force its way through one day, if left to itself.

'See, there's a stone slab this side, and a chute in the top of the wall there. That will be at ground level outside. They must have delivered coal down here. What's on your side, Diane?'

'Some wooden cupboards built into the wall.'

Cooper heard the creak of a hinge as she opened one of the cupboard doors. Then there was a sudden scuttling of claws on wood and a scream that almost deafened him.

'Oh, shit!'

The light of Fry's torch swung wildly and there was a loud crash, followed by another scream, this one higher pitched and almost ear-splitting in the confined space of the cellar. Fry continued cursing.

'What the hell's going on?'

'Over here!'

'Diane, keep that torch still. I can't see a thing.'

Her beam was flickering everywhere, but illuminating nothing. Mostly, it seemed to be in Cooper's eyes. The screaming became ragged, but something was scraping repeatedly against a wooden surface.

Finally, Cooper managed to get his torch pointed in the right direction. Fry had disturbed a female rat from its nest in a pile of mouldering newspapers and shredded wool inside the cupboard. A hole had been chewed through the back corner, and the rat was trying to drag itself towards it. But Fry's panicked blow with her torch had injured it. Its back legs were trailing uselessly, and its front paws could hardly move its weight along.

'Oh God. What are we going to do with it?' said Fry.

'Hold on. Let me borrow your torch. It's heavier than mine.'

Cooper crouched to the cupboard door and manoeuvred his body between Fry and the rat, which had stopped screaming now. Gingerly, he used the end of the torch to poke the rodent into a clear area and made sure it was lying upright. Then he took aim, swung the torch and crushed the base of its skull with one blow. It lurched over on to its side and its legs kicked for a few seconds before it died.

He stood up and shut the cupboard door.

'All sorted,' he said, as he handed the torch back.

'I didn't even see what you did,' said Fry.

'No.'

She pointed her torch at the closed door. 'Thanks.'

'No problem.'

Cooper just hoped Fry hadn't seen the little heap of blind, hairless shapes squirming at the bottom of the rat's nest. There was nothing to be done about those.

BACK UP THE stairs, Fry swept her torch round the sitting room, picking out a pile of empty beer bottles, an old sweater slung over a broken chair, a used paint tin half-full of cigarette ends.

'This is wrong,' she said. 'We need to get a proper search organized. We could be contaminating evidence.'

'These houses were empty when Neil Granger lived down here, you know.'

'I do know. That's why it's wrong. I lost my witness, and I don't want to lose any forensic evidence. If there's anything in here to be found, it should be found properly. We need the task force and some SOCOs in here.'

'Diane, it could be days before we get that type of operation approved and put into action. We're here now. There's nobody to interrupt us. Besides, these houses may not even be here much longer.'

Fry began to back towards the door, treading carefully to avoid debris. 'No, Ben. I should never have let you talk me into it.'

'Talk you into it? Whenever have I been able to talk you into anything?'

'Quiet,' said Fry. 'They'll hear you across at Waterloo Terrace. It's best they don't know we've been here. Damn it, we could have screwed everything up, doing this.'

Cooper bit his lip with frustration. 'OK, Diane. Back to the cows, then. The bigger they are, the easier they are to cope with.'

Chapter Thirty-Seven

DEREK ALTON COULD see exactly where Neil Granger
had died – right there, on the scrubby grass, among the
sheep droppings and the scattered stones, with the wind
scraping across the exposed sides of Withens Moor. It
was here that his body had grown cold and his blood had
soaked into the runnels of dark water that drained from
the higher slopes. And perhaps it was on this particular
rock here that the crows had waited impatiently for his
life to be gone.

Alton had attended the opening of the inquest, and he
remembered the crows being mentioned. The pathologist
had explained why some of the injuries on the body were
not, in themselves, an indication of unlawful killing.
Firstly, the injuries to his face had occurred after death.
And secondly, they had not been of human origin.

There was still blue tape rattling in the breeze, though
one of the metal stakes the police had used had fallen

over now, the shallow covering of peat failing to provide a secure anchor for it in the ground. But Alton wasn't looking at the fluttering tape. He was watching the faint white clouds of steam drifting from the air shaft, coiling on the edge of the stones for a moment before being dispersed by the wind.

He knew he had been stupid to let himself get involved in the Border Rats' raid on the Hey Bridge well dressing. He had thought he was being accepted at last by the Oxleys – or that was what he had told himself. But it had been a mistake, and the Rural Dean had made that clear. His reputation was already damaged by a misjudgement. But that wasn't what was worrying Derek Alton most.

That afternoon, when he had looked again at the picture of St Asaph in the stained glass, he realized that the red representing the burning coals was the wrong colour. It was too pale when the sunlight caught it, too gentle in its tones – almost pink, in fact. There was nothing threatening about it, nothing that suggested a danger of scorching St Asaph's cloak.

Real fire was quite different. Real fire was a much more violent and angry red. There was no mistaking the threat from flames, the actual destructive power of them. Their red was more like what Alton saw when he held his hands up against a candle and watched the bones of his fingers become outlined in glowing crimson as flames flickered through his translucent skin. His hands looked as though they were lying in a furnace, ready to be forged like iron in an unimaginable heat. That was the colour of fire. Within his own flesh, he held the true redness of burning coals.

Sometimes, at night, it crossed his mind that the invasion of nature into his churchyard was his own fault, for having agreed to bless the well dressing. Instead of giving approval to this worship of the goddess of water and the power of the spring, perhaps he should have been evoking the word of God to exorcize the pagan powers and drive them back into the darkness. He imagined scattering the flower-dressed panels with holy water and watching the designs shrivel and burn.

But when he awoke in the morning, he knew that he was being foolish. Superstitious, even. The church was pragmatic, and it did what the people expected of it. Other churches let people bring animals to be blessed. He only blessed the water.

And it was St Asaph's patronal day, too. The first of May. The day when the villagers would once have followed the Wakes Week tradition, with a night vigil in church on the Sunday nearest the saint's day, followed by a week of celebration. Women would have baked the Wakes Cakes, based on their own traditional recipes. But no longer.

Alton didn't know how guilty he should be about his feelings towards Neil. But Philip Granger had succeeded in making it all seem extremely wrong. Since Thursday, the knowledge that had been preying on his mind was the fact that Philip had gone on from St Asaph's to Shepley Head Lodge, and not to work in Glossop, as he had said. Michael Dearden was a churchwarden.

Though Dearden hadn't spoken to Alton since then, that only made it worse. His imagination could fill in the details. He had been creating his own hell within himself, and he had to resolve it somehow.

During his walk up the hill, Derek Alton had passed through alternate bursts of clear skies and heavy showers. By the time he reached the air shaft, he was soaked. But as he turned away from the hill, it wasn't just the cold and damp that made Alton shiver and pull his coat closer around his shoulders. Dusk had descended, and it was time for him to leave.

Down below, Longdendale looked vast and mysterious in the gathering darkness. It lay like a rumpled sheet tugged into peaks and valleys by a restless sleeper, the lights of scattered villages and farms gradually appearing with the dusk.

Alton had already spent an hour on the hillside, but his vigil had brought no answers – only the chill that had numbed his fingers. He had been given no more answers here than he had in church. He had to make his own decision.

BEN COOPER AND Diane Fry both crashed into their chairs at their desks in the CID room. Cooper could see that Fry looked as tired as he felt himself. Actually, more tired. She looked exhausted and dark-eyed.

There was more paperwork on Cooper's desk, but he couldn't be bothered to look at it. He stared at the ceiling for a while and found his thoughts wandering.

'Diane,' he said.

'Yes?'

'When you went to Wolverhampton with Gavin the other day, you were back in your old home town, weren't you?'

Fry didn't respond immediately. But Cooper knew she had heard the question. He could see the telltale stiffening of her shoulders, the almost visible defensive cloak that she began to throw around herself whenever her private life was mentioned.

'Yes,' she said.

'I remember you telling me that Warley was where you grew up. You, and your sister.'

'Your memory's too good sometimes, Ben.'

'But it was important to you,' he said. 'I mean, it seemed to be important to you at the time, when you told me about it, Diane.'

'So?'

Her ability to make him feel uncomfortable was uncanny. And it came so easily to her – all it took was a very slight change in the tone of her voice to insert a little sliver of ice behind her words. She had a pretty unnerving stare, too. But this time, she hadn't even needed to look at him to let him know that his intrusion was unwelcome. There were subtle messages in every part of her body.

'I was just wondering what it meant to you now, your old home town. Did going back there make you regret leaving it? Did it still feel like home? Did it bring back memories?'

'Ben, have I ever told you that you ask too many questions?'

'I'm a detective,' said Cooper lightly. 'That's what I'm supposed to do.'

'Fine – if you were asking the right questions of the right people. But I'm not a suspect in any of your cases, of which you have plenty that you might usefully be thinking about. Perhaps we ought to talk about improving your focus some time.'

'I'll take that as a "yes",' said Cooper.

'Ben, as far as you're concerned, I've forgotten everything that I ever knew about my home town, and what happened to me there. OK?'

'But you haven't forgotten your sister,' said Cooper.

'Oh, for God's sake. Not that again.'

'Well, you haven't.'

'Yes, I have.'

'Diane, I know you haven't. Since you've been in Derbyshire, you've still been looking for her. You told me –'

'I don't care what I told you. Just because I told you something, it doesn't mean it's true.'

'Yeah, but this was true, Diane. You can't pretend it wasn't.'

She turned her tired eyes to stare at him. 'Ben, leave it alone.'

Cooper hesitated momentarily. He felt like a nervous horse lining up for the last, big fence at the Horse of the Year Show. Yet he had something riding his back that wouldn't let him shy away from the fence, but spurred him on to go for it.

'Diane,' he said, 'what would you say if I could help you find out what happened to Angie?'

Cooper wondered how much longer he could meet Diane Fry's stare. It seemed to go on for a long time, as the temperature in the room dropped and the blood began to suffuse his cheeks. Fry opened her mouth once to speak, then closed it again. Cooper hoped the waiting wouldn't last too long. It would be better to get it over with.

In the end, Fry broke the stare and stood up without speaking. She walked across the office and looked out of the window, with an expression that suggested she was seeing anything except the back of the main stand of Edendale Football Club across the road. She was trying to hold herself steady, but Cooper could see that her hands shook where they rested on the window ledge. When she did speak, there was none of the anger that he had expected. Her voice was almost a whisper.

'You're talking to me about my sister again. I told you not to.'

Cooper nodded, his throat too dry and constricted to speak. But he realized that Fry couldn't see him. He swallowed, and tried again.

'Yes, Diane.'

'So what is this? You think you could do a better job than me, even at finding my own sister?'

'No. I just thought … Well, if I could help you, I would.'

Fry's forehead sank gently against the window pane, and her eyes closed for a moment.

'I can't believe this.'

The door of the CID room opened and Gavin Murfin stepped in, carrying a paper bag which was already showing grease stains. He smiled when he saw Fry and Cooper.

'Hey, Diane,' he said, 'I've got some results on that phone enquiry. Guess who Neil Granger was making calls to the night before he was killed?'

Fry didn't even look at him. Her eyes stayed fixed on Cooper.

'Gavin, take a tea break,' she said.

Murfin's eyebrows rose dramatically. 'I've had a break already. I thought you'd want to know –'

'Just get out of here and don't come back for ten minutes. OK, Gavin?'

Murfin looked at Cooper. He screwed up his face into a snooty school-marm look and wagged his head from side to side before backing out of the room.

Fry waited until she heard the door close and Murfin's footsteps in the corridor. Then she turned away from the window to face Cooper. Her forehead was damp from the condensation on the glass and her face was pale, but at least there was a flash of anger now in her eyes, rising beyond the tiredness. Her voice rose almost to a shout.

'You have no right,' she said. 'You have no right to interfere in my life. What makes you think you can do this? You're treading on my territory now, so back off.'

Cooper began backing straight away. His chair seemed to move of its own accord on its wheels, until it hit the desk behind him.

'I was only trying to help,' he said.

'Well, don't. OK?'

As USUAL AFTER an attempt to get closer to Diane Fry, Cooper found himself covered in a sheen of sweat and pumped with adrenalin, as if he had just come through a life-threatening situation.

He wasn't even sure he was making any progress. Most people would be worn down after a while and give a little bit of themselves in return. But Fry showed no signs of doing that. He had tried the recommended body language – the non-threatening stance, the 'listening' position. Maybe he ought to have tried Father Murphy.

DEREK ALTON'S CAR was waiting for him in the lay-by on the A628, near the start of the steep footpath. The same footpath that Neil had used.

It was already nine o'clock and completely dark when Alton drove past the Quiet Shepherd in Withens. The village was almost silent, but for a couple of vehicles leaving the car park of the pub. The Old Rectory, where the Renshaws lived, was in darkness except for the flickering glow of a candle in one of the windows.

Alton continued past the county boundary sign, entering South Yorkshire. At the end of the road, he parked his car in a gateway and sat for a few minutes, staring straight ahead.

Finally, he took a deep breath and got out of the car. There was no sound around him now, but for the murmuring of water moving constantly through the landscape, and the occasional call of a sheep above him on the moor. Alton looked for a light up ahead. But for some reason, the Deardens' house was in darkness.

MICHAEL DEARDEN HAD found an old kitchen chair and positioned it among the piles of ash and charred timber in the burnt-out stable. He carefully placed the chair so that he could see straight into the yard through part of the front wall that was almost completely gone. His field of vision included the side gate, the back of the garage and fifty yards of fencing along the back field. Whichever way they came, he was sure he would see them. Without telling Gail, he had disabled the sensors that activated the security lighting at the back of the property. That way, intruders would be encouraged to approach the back of the house. And there he would be waiting for them.

Dearden practised sighting along the barrels into the night. His eyes would soon get accustomed to the darkness. True, it would be impossible to see who his intruders were before he shot at them. But unless they were up to no good, they wouldn't be in his yard at night, would they?

He moved the barrels slowly from side to side, allowing himself some satisfaction at the weight of the barrels and the hard nudge of the stock against his shoulder. He felt strong at last. Let them come now. He was ready for them.

IT WAS ONLY because his eyes were already adjusted to the darkness that Derek Alton saw the movement at all. Even then, it was far too late. The flash followed a second later. Alton would not have been able to say whether he had started to throw himself away from the direction of the discharge, or whether his body had simply rolled with the force of the blast. The impact hit him at the same time that the deafening roar filled the yard. It was a great blast of hot breath that scorched his body and burned his face, the stink filling his nostrils like a giant's belch. Alton was spun sideways by the force of the hot breath, and his shoulder and right hand were thrashed against the edge of a wall as he fell.

For Derek Alton, it was the pain that came last. And by then its dark waves barely lapped at his awareness before he floated above it and away. He experienced a surge of joy and reassurance, like a man who had made a long overdue sacrifice.

Chapter Thirty-Eight

SUNDAY

ON SUNDAY, BEN Cooper was supposed to be off duty. Instead, he found himself that morning pulling his Toyota into the car park near the Yorkshire Traction bus stop at Withens. When he got out of the car, he could hear the rumble of heavy machinery somewhere – probably the sound of a tractor on the farm next to Waterloo Terrace.

Cooper cut through a path alongside the churchyard to reach the close where the Renshaws' house was, the Old Rectory. There was some scaffolding against the side of the house, and the sound of hammering from the roof. Probably there were broken tiles to be replaced after the winter. By now, starlings and other birds would be looking for gaps in the roof so that they could get in to build their nests in a warm, insulated attic. The owners were sensible to get the repairs done.

Then Cooper realized the flat-bed lorry parked near the scaffolding looked familiar. Anonymous, but familiar.

He walked round the scaffolding until he could see one of the men working on the roof. He recognized the back of Scott Oxley's head, but couldn't see much else of him because he was hidden by some of the planks at the top of the scaffolding. He recognized Scott's voice, too, when he shouted an instruction to his mate. Another figure came into view, and an arm reached out to pass Scott a hammer. A face peered over the scaffolding and looked down at Cooper. It was Ryan.

''Morning,' said Cooper.

Ryan stared at him, still holding the hammer. Scott slithered down the roof a couple of feet and looked over his shoulder, but didn't return the greeting. Above Scott, Cooper could see a gap in the roof about four feet across.

'Replacing a few tiles?' he said.

'Is it illegal, then?'

'Depends.'

Ryan looked vaguely worried. 'What does it depend on?'

'Shut up,' said Scott. 'He's just trying to wind us up. Give me that hammer.'

'Is the householder at home?' said Cooper.

'He's gone out. And we don't know when he'll be back.'

'Pity. I might have to talk to you two for a bit, then.'

Scott began to hit a roof nail with his hammer, muttering something that sounded like 'nothing fuckin' better to do'.

But Cooper wasn't going to lose the opportunity of talking to a captive audience. The Oxleys couldn't easily get off the roof and climb down the scaffolding to reach their van. There was no easy escape route today. And the home owner wasn't even around to tell him to leave.

'Much to do, is there?' said Cooper. 'How long are you going to be on this job?'

'A day or two,' said Scott.

Ryan was slowly moving back behind the scaffolding, so that Cooper couldn't see him. How old was Ryan again? Was it fourteen or fifteen? But it was Sunday, of course, so there was no school for him to be attending.

'Just a weekend job, then?'

'Yeah.'

'Finished by Monday?'

'Yeah.'

'That's good, because they've forecast rain.'

Scott swore under the sound of the hammer. 'We've got a fuckin' tarpaulin,' he said.

'But you'll be finished by Monday anyway?'

'Yes!'

'Where do you get the tiles from?' said Cooper.

'Eh?'

'Well, they're old tiles on that roof, aren't they? It isn't easy to get a good match. Do you have a local supplier?'

'Are you thinking of going into the roofing business, or what?' said Scott.

'I'm interested. Local enterprises need our support. I might have some roof repairs I need doing myself one day.'

A mobile phone started ringing somewhere. Cooper knew it wasn't his by the sound of the ring, but he took it out of his pocket and looked at it anyway, just in case. Then he saw that Scott Oxley had taken a phone off the leather belt he wore round his jeans. Scott listened for a few minutes, grunted a couple of times, then thrust the phone back. He glowered down at Cooper.

'Bastard,' he said.

'Sorry? I was just enquiring about some work.'

'You came here to make sure we kept out of the way.'

Cooper frowned. 'What do you mean?'

But Scott was clambering down the scaffolding as fast as he could, his boots rattling on the ladder on the final descent. Ryan swung down after him, like a natural scaffolder.

Cooper took a step backwards, concerned about the change in Scott's manner. 'What's the problem?' he said. 'Why are you stopping work?'

Scott paused only for a second before he got into the cab of the lorry.

'The rain came early,' he said.

Puzzled, Cooper stood watching the Oxleys as they drove off. He looked up at the sky, then at the hole in the roof of the house. A starling flew down and landed on the tiles before hopping into the hole and disappearing. Cooper shook his head.

'I think I'll be taking my business elsewhere, after all,' he said.

As Cooper walked back towards the car park, he looked at his mobile phone again. Was there something he ought to know about? But nobody had called him, and his radio was back in the car. Besides, it was his day off, and no one would know that he was in Withens.

AS IF TO reflect the tragedy at the Deardens' house, a retaining wall had collapsed during the night. It had been holding back part of the slope behind the lodge, but now it looked as if an explosion had taken place in the hillside and burst through the wall. The dressed stones lay scattered across the yard, covered in black soil, small pebbles and plant debris. It seemed as if even the landscape had managed to force its way through their defences.

Earlier, Diane Fry had watched the ambulance bounce carefully down on to the road. Derek Alton had been alive when the paramedics got to him. But shotgun wounds were messy, and it was difficult to tell how serious his internal injuries might be. Fry couldn't believe that she might be about to lose another potential witness.

Since Shepley Head Lodge was over the border, South Yorkshire Police had been called to deal with the incident, though for once liaison had worked and news had filtered through to Fry. But with Michael Dearden holed up in the house, nobody was making a move until a firearms unit arrived.

Fry wondered where Ben Cooper was, and whether he would even pick up on news of the incident when it was a neighbouring force's operation.

'Has Dearden got any family in there?' asked the South Yorkshire inspector who had arrived to take charge.

'His wife, sir.'

'We need to get her out safely. That's the first priority.'

Fry reckoned Gail Dearden would be safe as long as she didn't do anything stupid. From what she had heard of Michael, he was reacting to a perceived threat from outside, not inside.

'Are we going to talk to him?' she said.

'The negotiator will talk to Dearden when he arrives. Perhaps he'll see sense, but it depends what his state of mind is. I'm not putting any of our officers at risk.'

'I suspect Michael Dearden didn't even know who he was shooting at,' said Fry. 'But what I'd really like to know is what the hell the vicar came up here for.'

Fry looked at the outbuildings and the back door of Shepley Head Lodge. Probably it was perfectly normal in this area to call at the back door of a house when you were visiting someone you knew. But in the dark?

'Did Mr Alton have a torch?' she said to the officers nearby. 'Anybody seen one?'

They shook their heads and shrugged. Fry turned back to the inspector.

'There are some people called Renshaw down in Withens, they're friends of the Deardens. Perhaps we should give them a call and ask them to talk to Michael Dearden.'

'Time enough for that later,' said the inspector. 'Where *is* the negotiator?'

'On his way, sir.'

BEN COOPER REACHED the Withens car park and got back into his Toyota. He sat for a few minutes listening to the messages going backwards and forwards to the control room on the radio, but there seemed to be nothing immediately pressing in his part of Derbyshire.

He had parked where he could see both Waterloo Terrace and the rest of the village. But he found that, if he looked straight ahead, he was facing the slopes of Withens Moor, where the air shafts were trailing a few wisps of steam as the cool morning air met the heat produced by the high-voltage cables.

It was strange to think that there were three abandoned railway tunnels two hundred feet below the shafts, and not far away their entrances, protected by steel gates and warning notices. Cooper found himself thinking about the navvies who had built the original tunnels back in the nineteenth century. Most of them had not been Irish immigrants, as he had always thought navvies were. Maybe he had just been prejudiced by the stereotyped image of the Irish labourer in big boots, with a handkerchief tied round his head and his backside protruding from his trousers.

But surely it was more than that. Irish migrant workers had played a major part in building England's canal and railway systems, and had later moved into other areas of the construction industry. Wasn't there one little island off the west coast of Ireland where almost all the men of working age went into tunnel building? They were all related and might even have had the same surname, too, though Cooper couldn't remember what it was.

So why were the Woodhead navvies almost exclusively English? They were from Yorkshire, a lot of them.

And Cheshire, too. But Woodhead had been in Cheshire back then. The whole of Longdendale had been in Cheshire. So really it was the Yorkshiremen who had been the foreigners in these parts.

Cooper was wondering whether he ought to call in and check there was nothing he was missing when he jerked upright, startled by a loud rap on the passenger's side window. He bumped his head on the grab handle, and rubbed at it guiltily as he peered through the window, expecting to see Diane Fry or a senior officer catching him out. He hadn't been dozing, not really. Just thinking.

But it wasn't Diane Fry, or anybody more senior. It wasn't even Gavin Murfin grinning at him through the window, pleased at having made him jump. The face he saw was Lucas Oxley's.

Cooper was so surprised that he was a bit slow to respond. He saw Oxley try the door handle, but of course the locks were on. He noticed the brim of Oxley's hat resting against the glass, turning over at the edge so that Cooper could see the man's eyes more clearly, despite the distracting reflections of his wan, startled face. Oxley rapped again, getting irritated, and gestured at him to wind the window down.

At last, Cooper pressed the button for the electric window. Well, it was pretty unbelievable. But it seemed that Lucas Oxley finally wanted to talk to him.

'IT'S NOT ME that wants to talk to you,' said Lucas Oxley. 'I hope you understand that.'

Ben Cooper had turned the radio down and invited him to sit in the car, but Oxley hadn't even condescended to acknowledge that foolish idea, and Cooper had immediately regretted it. He was on new ground here, and he had to tread carefully, take it step by step.

'Fair enough, sir.'

'It's our Ryan,' said Oxley. 'He says he wants to tell you something.'

'Sensible lad.'

'But I've got to be there when he does.'

'Certainly, sir. I would have insisted on it anyway. Ryan is a juvenile.'

'He's fifteen.'

'Yes.'

'I've tried to talk him out of it, of course,' said Oxley. 'I don't even know what it is he wants to tell you – he won't say. And God knows we've got enough on just now. But the lad's stubborn. Stubborn like –'

'His dad?'

Cooper was rewarded with something that was almost a smile. Oxley's mouth slipped out of shape, but he sniffed and managed to correct himself.

'Our Ryan's not a bad lad,' he said. 'But he's not like the others. He does have this stubborn streak.'

'I understand.'

Oxley peered at Cooper a bit more closely. 'None of my sons are bad lads, you know. There are some kids you see who spend their whole lives indoors with their computer games and the internet. They grow up as fat as slugs and as pale as tripe. But these here are good lads. Despite what folks round here might have told you.'

Cooper kept silent. Also what the police and court records might tell him, he thought. Not to mention the schools and social services. But no kids were ever bad, as far as their parents were concerned. They were all little misunderstood angels. Their parents shouted their love for them in court, even as they were taken down from the dock on a life sentence for murdering an old lady and cutting out her heart to eat it and drink her blood.

But the Oxleys weren't exactly vampire killers. They were just kids who didn't fit in.

Cooper was vaguely aware that a voice on his radio was muttering about a major incident, but it seemed to involve the neighbouring South Yorkshire force, and he filtered it out.

'Where would you like to do this, Mr Oxley?' he said.

Oxley thought about it for a few moments. Cooper could see that an inner struggle was taking place. It had cost the man quite an effort to walk over the road and approach Cooper's car. But this was crossing a boundary. It was a big decision for him to make.

'I suppose,' he said, 'you'd better come into the house.'

BEN COOPER HAD followed Lucas Oxley as far as the entrance to Waterloo Terrace before he began to have doubts. The noise of heavy machinery hadn't been coming from the farm, but had gradually grown louder as they approached the terraces. Above the rumble of diesel engines, he could hear the whine of chainsaws. But they seemed to be operating in the sycamores and chestnuts nearer the road.

'What's going on?' said Cooper.

Lucas stopped. 'They came,' he said. 'That's all.'

'Who?'

Cooper peered downhill through the tree screen. Now he could make out bright yellow machinery – a bulldozer and a JCB excavator with huge steel jaws. There were other vehicles, too, gathering in the field adjacent to Trafalgar Terrace – the same field he and Fry had walked through the previous day.

'Our landlords are moving in to start demolition,' said Lucas. 'Don't tell me you're surprised.'

'Surprised? I can't believe it.'

Cooper pulled out his mobile phone and dialled the number for Peak Water in Glossop, then remembered it was a Sunday. There was no way J. P. Venables would be working on his day off. But he had Mr Venables' home number, too.

'Mr Venables, why didn't you tell me it was today you were moving into Withens to start demolishing the empty houses?'

'Ah, well, we have to be circumspect about these things,' said Venables.

'Damn circumspect,' said Cooper.

'Really. It wouldn't have helped the situation if the residents of Waterloo Terrace had been given too much prior warning. We couldn't predict what attitude they might take.'

'You could have told *me*. We might have had time to organize a proper search.'

'You?' said Venables, with an audible smirk. 'The friend of the Oxleys?'

LUCAS OXLEY HAD been waiting patiently while Cooper made the call. His expression was sardonic, a tilt of an eyebrow that said a lot.

'Search?' he said.

'Routine,' said Cooper. 'But, well … It's too late now.'

Lucas walked slowly towards the gateway. The houses of Waterloo Terrace looked blacker than ever beyond the trees. For now, the sound of the chainsaws had stopped. He tried to make out the figures that he knew must be somewhere in the undergrowth around the trees. But all he could see was little Jake, lurking behind the wall of one of the outside privies.

For a moment, Cooper considered the possibility that the Oxleys might take the opportunity to hold him hostage. He had no idea what they might be planning, or how they would behave when they were driven into a corner.

'Are you coming, or not?' said Lucas.

'Yes.'

As he came nearer, Cooper could smell the wet leaves of the sycamores and the sharp scent of the sap leaking from their flesh where the chainsaws had ripped into them. Beyond that, from the houses, he could smell cooking. Onions were frying, despite the time of day. But even that was obscured by the stronger, more incongruous aroma of sun-dried tomatoes. Cooper guessed the Oxleys must be burning some of the old car tyres in their yard. Smouldering tyres released similar sulphur-containing chemicals, which produced that distinctive smell.

For many weeks afterwards, whenever he thought of Withens, Cooper would still smell the wet sycamores and the sun-dried tomatoes, and still hear the roar of the chainsaws.

He took the last few steps towards the terrace of houses, passing under the trees. Then a petrol motor roared, and a branch cracked. There was a shout from somewhere above him, in the branches. And a fine rain fell on his face, warm as blood.

GAIL DEARDEN STARED at her husband, trembling at the sight of the shotgun still in his hands. He was dirty and dishevelled, and had a distracted look in his eyes. Michael was frightened. And she knew frightened men were dangerous.

'Who did I shoot?' said Dearden.

'You don't *know*?'

'One of the Oxleys. Which one was it? They were coming to see what else they could find. Did I injure one of them?'

'The police are out there,' said Gail.

'Who called the police? The Oxleys?'

'No, Michael. I did.'

Dearden finally put the shotgun down. He laughed quietly, but seemed to be on the verge of tears, too, when he looked at his wife.

'They came, then?' he said. 'For once, they actually came.'

Chapter Thirty-Nine

LUCAS OXLEY STOOD throughout Cooper's visit. In fact, he stood near the door, which Cooper wasn't terribly comfortable with. It meant he had already broken the first rule and lost control of his immediate environment, if a threat to his safety should develop. But Lucas didn't look threatening, not at the moment. He had his back to the door, but more as if to stop anyone else entering than to prevent Cooper leaving. His manner was defensive, not aggressive.

'Is Scott all right?' said Cooper.

'He'll be fine. Daft bugger. I've told him to be more careful with that thing.'

'No harm done.'

Cooper wiped a hand across his face and looked at the streaks of oil on his palm. The spray had hit his face from the spinning blade of the chainsaw just before it fell towards him from the tree. Scott Oxley's face had stared down at him, shocked and white, as the branch he'd been working on snapped unexpectedly, loosening his grip on the handles. A few feet in front of Cooper, the chainsaw had dug itself into the dirt track in a spurt of mud.

'He'd just oiled it,' said Lucas. 'He got oil all over the handles and didn't bother wiping it off. He's lucky he didn't break his silly neck or chop his hand off.'

'Or someone else's,' said Cooper.

The interior of 1 Waterloo Terrace came as a surprise. It was remarkably clean and neat, with two Laura Ashley-patterned sofas crammed into the little sitting room, matching curtains, and even a mock goatskin rug in front of the fireplace. It had a distinctly feminine feel, and suddenly both Lucas and Eric Oxley looked awkward and out of place. Eric was wearing worn brown slippers, while Lucas had removed his boots on the doorstep to reveal woollen socks bunched uncomfortably at the toes.

'You've been all along this terrace asking questions,' said Lucas. It was a plain statement of fact, a preliminary laying out of the ground.

'Yes, I've made no secret of it,' said Cooper. 'I'm conducting enquiries in connection with a murder investigation, as I'm sure you know, Mr Oxley. The murder of your own nephew, Neil Granger.'

'He was my wife's brother's lad.'

'I know.'

'But nobody here knows anything about that. You've been asking your questions in the wrong place, if that's really what you're up to.'

'Why should I be up to anything else?'

'I don't know,' said Oxley. 'That's for you to tell us.'

'I've just explained it.'

There were no handshakes at Waterloo Terrace. And there were very few rural Derbyshire homes where Cooper would not have been offered at least a cup of tea by now, unless he had actually come to arrest a suspect. But the Oxleys seemed to think that they were automatic suspects, and they were behaving accordingly. Perhaps, Cooper thought, he *should* be regarding them as automatic suspects. But he'd always had a contrary instinct. If everyone else thought the Oxleys must be guilty of something, he'd find himself looking for their good side. With the Oxleys, though, he might have to look very hard.

The old man, Eric Oxley, wore striped braces beneath a knitted cardigan, but over his shirt. They weren't the brightly coloured braces once favoured by city whizzkids of the 1980s. These braces dated from an earlier fashion, and their colours had faded with age. Besides, they weren't for show at all – their function was to support the baggy trousers.

Eric's body was almost swallowed by the worn armchair he sat in. The chair didn't match the rest of the furniture in the Oxleys' sitting room. It was much older, and wasn't at all the right colour to match the Laura Ashley patterns or even the mock goatskin. Eric and his armchair looked like an island surrounded by a sea of encroaching modern frippery.

Cooper wondered how many battles there had been over the armchair when the new furniture had arrived, and whether the old man had clung to its arms with his thick fingernails as his family tried to prise him loose. There was a space two or three feet further towards the centre of the room where the armchair would have fit more neatly with the arrangement of the furniture. He could picture Marion Oxley moving the armchair into that spot every night after the old man had gone to bed, perhaps pushing it on its casters with the toe of her carpet slipper, rather than touch its grease-darkened upholstery. Equally clearly, he could see Eric sucking his false teeth as he heaved his chair back to its place by the fireside every morning. Territory was important, even if it consisted of an old armchair by a fire.

'You know they want us out?' said Lucas.

'I understand it's the empty houses they're demolishing,' said Cooper. 'They must be dangerous. A health hazard, at least.'

Lucas curled his lip. 'It's the first step. It's us they want out, so they can sell this place and make a nice bit of money. They think we're dirty. Our homes are unsightly. *We* are unsightly. We don't fit into this world today.'

'Aye, they want to get shut of us,' said Eric. 'I just hope I pop my clogs first.'

Lucas nodded. 'They think we're mucking up the water for folks in Manchester – all the water that comes off these hills and goes through the aqueduct down the valley. It seems funny, doesn't it, when it was our folk who were killed by the cholera that came from the filthy water they were given to drink? We might as well run over the hill and throw ourselves in the reservoir, like a lot of lemmings. That would solve everybody's problems.'

'I was assured by Mr Venables at Peak Water that these houses aren't a problem for the catchment area.'

Lucas Oxley's expression said merely that it was Cooper's own fault if he allowed himself to be fooled by people like J. P. Venables.

'When they come to try to move us out, I suppose it'll be your lot behind 'em putting the boot in, making sure us little folk don't get in the way of progress. I don't suppose our homes look much to you, do they? Got a nice, modern detached house back in Edendale, have you?'

'Well, not exactly.'

'If we didn't have our homes in Withens, where would we go? People like us can't afford to buy anywhere. And what chance is there of finding somewhere we can all live close together? They'd split us up and put us on council estates. It would be the end of this family.'

Through a doorway, Cooper watched Marion Oxley fussing around in the kitchen, slamming cupboards, peeping under the lids of saucepans as if some secret lurked inside that she could never share with anyone, and glaring suspiciously at the windows. Her disapproval filled the moments of silence like a bad smell.

The glimpses of her reminded him of his own mother, as she had been in her best days at Bridge End Farm. Though she seemed to be busy, she was watching. Always watching.

The picture of family life he was gathering from the Oxleys was completely unlike what he had been used to, yet they were as close as the Cooper family, in their own way. The comparisons he saw all around him made

Cooper uneasy. He was trying to concentrate on the job in hand, but his memory kept unpacking old recollections of his childhood at Bridge End Farm. Time and again, he had pushed the remembered images back into their boxes. But as soon as his mind was distracted by a phrase or a gesture, the memories came tumbling out again, unfolding their carefully packed shapes, falling open like the petals of pale flowers, too long untouched by the sun.

'Did they tell you at the water company that somebody wants to buy this land?' said Lucas.

'Yes, I know there's a developer interested.'

'But I don't suppose they told you who's working for that developer locally.'

'No. Who?'

'Dearden.'

'Michael Dearden?'

'Aye, at Shepley Head Lodge. The people with the money are in London, but they pay him to do the negotiating locally. He's a surveyor of some kind.'

'How do you feel about that?' said Cooper.

'It doesn't surprise me. I've had the odd set-to with Dearden.'

'You had an argument with Mr Dearden?'

'Aye. You might say so. A disagreement.'

'What about?'

'The road. That road up there. It runs all the way down to their place, Shepley Head. We never could agree on who ought to keep it in order. He's always chunterin' about it, silly bugger. He goes on about how the potholes are damaging that car of his. I wasn't standing for that. So I gave him what for.'

'How did he take it?'

'I thought he was going to burst into tears. What a mard-arse. I've never come across anyone so mardy in my life. But I knew what he was on about really. He blamed the road for the time he hit our Jake and smashed his leg. He blamed everything and everybody but himself.'

Cooper recalled the glimpse of Michael Dearden sitting in his car, terrified at the sight of Jake and the other boys in the road outside Waterloo Terrace.

'Are you sure, Mr Oxley?' he said quietly.

Oxley gazed at him for a moment, waiting for an explanation.

'You might not realize this,' said Cooper, 'but Michael Dearden has been obsessed with the idea that members of your family are persecuting him, ever since the incident with Jake. He imagines Oxleys in the darkness around his house every night. He even avoids driving through Withens because he has to pass the spot where he ran over Jake. I think Mr Dearden is consumed with guilt, but he won't ever admit it to you.'

'Happen you're right, then,' said Oxley.

Then Cooper smiled. It had occurred to him that, after the incident in the Oxleys' yard on Wednesday, he might be imagining Oxleys in the darkness at night for a little while himself.

'Take a look at these –' said Lucas, gesturing at a couple of black box files on a table. 'They go back years. Years and years of getting nowhere. Years of people not listening to us. We don't fit into their computer systems, so they don't know what to do about us, apart from getting rid of us. Read some of them – they keep repeating a lot of jargon that doesn't mean anything. Whatever we say, it comes up against a blank wall. The bureaucracy machine just rolls on. One day, it's going to roll over us.'

Cooper picked up some of the letters.

'Did you know,' he said, 'that one of these is an eviction notice?'

Lucas shrugged. 'It's not the first.'

'You do realize that if nobody does anything about it, your family is in danger of being evicted from Waterloo Terrace?'

'Yes, I know.'

'Have you talked to anyone. Got proper advice?'

'There's no one we can trust.'

'There must be *someone*.'

'Everyone we've ever dealt with has let us down, or outright lied. It's too late now. But we can dig in; we're ready for a fight.'

'That won't do any good at all, Mr Oxley.'

'It'll keep our pride.'

Exasperated, Cooper looked at the old man, Eric Oxley. In a strange way, he was the one member of the Oxley family who made most sense to him. Eric made him think of a Border collie that had lived with the Coopers at Bridge End Farm when he and Matt were children. The collie had been called Sam, and he had first arrived as a puppy, bounding with energy. But he'd lived to be a grey-muzzled old dog who spent his life panting painfully in the heat of the sun, endlessly circling and circling until he could find a comfortable place to sleep. Eric was like that old collie, grey and tired, seeking only a place to settle down and rest. Yet a glimpse of the strong young man that he had once been was still visible now and again, as if it lingered in his shadow.

In another way, Eric reminded him of his great-uncle, whom he had known as a child, and had been fascinated by. He still clearly remembered the smell of his great-uncle's clothes and the feel of his trousers as he clutched the fabric tightly between his fingers and pushed his face shyly into his leg. He had loved his great-uncle when he was a small boy. But he had died when Ben was seven or eight years old.

And then there was Lucas. Surely Lucas Oxley was nothing like his own father. Nothing like him at all.

'We don't reckon much to you as a policeman,' Lucas was saying. 'But you're a sight better than most of the buggers we're expected to deal with. If that's what we have to put up with, you'll have to do.'

'Thanks,' said Cooper.

Eric stirred in his chair. 'Though happen you ought to be looking elsewhere, instead of bothering the likes of us.'

'What do you mean, sir?'

'Look for the foreigners.'

'Foreigners?'

'You've been around here asking about last Friday night, before Neil got himself killed?'

'Yes, of course.'

'Well, look for the foreigners. There were foreigners in the pub that night.'

'What foreigners?'

'That's up to you to find out.'

Ryan had come into the room, and Cooper could see straight away that he was nervous. But the boy looked from his father to his grandfather, and he seemed to take reassurance from their presence.

Cooper remembered from the files that Ryan's date of birth was 26 June, so he had entered the world just after the 1987 General Election, when Margaret Thatcher won a landslide victory and became Prime Minister for the third time. In fact, anyone between thirteen and twenty-three had been born in the 1980s, that decade of marginalization and social exclusion, when some parts of society were making more money than they had ever dreamed of. All of the Oxley boys had been born into that time, except Jake.

And the reason Cooper could remember Ryan's birthday was that it was almost the same date as his own, though a different year. They were fellow Cancerians. They were known for clinging to their shells.

Emma Renshaw had been born in the 1980s, too – some time in the spring of 1982, around the time of the Falklands War. Cooper was willing to bet that Howard Renshaw had done well in the 1980s – the companies he carried out work for had no doubt benefited from the boom in the construction business. So was Howard worth a lot of money? Did he have a nice nest egg of capital stashed away that he had managed to protect from the decline in the stock market?

Money was such an obvious motive for every kind of crime. Cooper made a mental note to ask Fry if she knew where Howard stood financially.

'What was it you wanted to tell me, Ryan?' he said.

Ryan swallowed before he spoke. Cooper was expecting something about minor offences – the damage to the church vestry, perhaps. But what Ryan wanted to say was nothing like that.

'It's about Barry,' he said.

Cooper had to re-focus his thoughts quickly. There was only one person he'd heard of by that name recently.

'Barry? Barry Cully?'

He noticed Lucas and Eric had suddenly gone very still. Maybe this hadn't been what *they* expected, either. There was a silence in the room that allowed the croaking of the rooks to penetrate from outside.

'Fran's bloke,' said Ryan.

'I know who you mean. But I've never seen him. He's away, isn't he?'

'Yes.'

Lucas Oxley cleared his throat. It was one of those signals that ought to mean something to his family. A warning perhaps. But Ryan refused to look at his dad now. He was staring fixedly at Cooper as if clinging to something he had finally managed to grasp.

'He knocked Fran about a lot,' said Ryan. 'She never said anything, but some of us knew about it. We could tell when we went round there. The door is never locked, and sometimes we'd go in when she wasn't expecting us. We worked it out all right.'

'Did Fran ever make a complaint?'

'No.'

'I'm going to have to talk to her. When is Cully due back?'

Then Lucas interrupted. 'We don't know,' he said.

'Can you give me a phone number where I can contact him? Or tell me what company he's working for?'

'To be honest, he's left,' said Lucas.

'For good?'

'We hope so. We don't know how to get in touch with him.'

Cooper looked at Ryan. The boy's stare was so fixed that his eyes were becoming glassy, and he was pale with some painful internal effort.

'It was Craig who used to get most upset about it,' said Ryan. 'He used to get really, really angry.'

Lucas took a couple of steps forward and stood over his son. There were veins standing out on his neck, and his fists were clenched.

'We don't –' he began. But whatever he was going to say seemed to stick in his throat when he saw the boy's expression. It was fear. But not a fear of his father.

Ryan looked past Lucas at Cooper, like a trapped animal seeking the smallest escape route.

'Craig got *really* angry,' he repeated desperately.

'But Craig is dead,' said Cooper. 'I can't ask him about it.'

There was a message here that Cooper knew he wasn't picking up. His brain felt really slow, as if his thoughts had been blunted by the days of frustration and lack of communication.

The Oxleys were watching him almost pityingly, in the way they might watch a dumb animal trying to figure out what was happening as it blundered blindly from its pen to be slaughtered. The old man had a particularly disturbing stare. It had begun to feel like something physical, a sensation on Cooper's skin, as if a spider had landed on him and was crawling across his neck. Cooper wondered what was going on in the old man's mind that made his thoughts so uncomfortable.

Then Cooper realized there was an important question he should be asking. But nobody here had been cautioned, and he couldn't invite them to incriminate themselves.

'Tell me something about Barry Cully,' he said, looking now at Lucas.

'What do you want to know?'

'For a start,' said Cooper, 'does he have a finger missing on his left hand?'

'HOLD ON, WHAT'S happening now?' said the South Yorkshire inspector, pacing the yard at Shepley Head Lodge.

'He's coming out, sir.'

'Everybody move back.'

'He doesn't seem to be armed.'

'Thank God.'

Michael Dearden walked across the yard with his hands in the air and tears running down his face. His wife appeared in the doorway behind him, shielding her eyes against the glare of the lights.

Four officers moved quickly in on Dearden from different directions, shouting instructions at him. Within a few seconds, he was handcuffed and had been searched for weapons. One of the officers gave a thumbs-up sign.

'It's all over,' said the inspector with undisguised relief.

But it didn't feel over to Fry. There was a smell in the air that was too strong to be the lingering reek of a discharged shotgun. It was a smell that carried a meaning and presence as powerfully as the scent of Rive Gauche from Emma Renshaw's car. She turned away from the house and swung her binoculars upwards.

'Smoke,' she said.

'What? Not another damn moorland fire!' said the inspector. 'If you ask me, those kids from Manchester should be shot and roasted over the flames.'

'No,' said Fry. 'This smoke isn't coming from the moors. It's coming from Withens.'

Chapter Forty

BEN COOPER HAD asked to use the loo, when he heard Marion Oxley begin to shout. He'd really wanted to take a look upstairs, where he found a door had been knocked through the wall from number 1 into number 2, providing access to the bedrooms in both houses without having to go outside and back in again. He thought this was probably one of the unauthorized structural alterations that J. P. Venables had complained about.

He had also been looking for a chance to use his mobile phone without the Oxleys overhearing. Under cover of the noise of the toilet flushing and water running into the hand basin, he called Diane Fry.

'Ben,' she said, 'I was just going to call you. I'm on my way down to Waterloo Terrace. You might want to get there as soon as you can.'

'Er, Diane, that's where I am already.'

'You *what*?'

'I'm at number 1, Lucas Oxley's house.'

'Ben –'

'Listen, that skeleton in the churchyard – it looks as though it might turn out to be Barry Cully, Fran Oxley's bloke.'

'Ben, haven't you *noticed* the fire?'

'The what?'

'Fire. Smoke, flames. You must be right in the middle of it. Get everybody out, for God's sake.'

Cooper turned off the running tap and pulled back the lace curtain to peer out of the tiny bathroom window. It looked out on to the back yard, with its mountains of scaffolding poles and wooden pallets, and towards the front doors of the derelict houses of Trafalgar Terrace.

'Oh shit,' he said. 'That's more than just smouldering tyres.'

Now he could hear what Marion Oxley was shouting in the kitchen downstairs. It came to him clearly above the increasing noise of crackling flames and the barking of the normally silent Alsatian dog.

'Where's Jake?' she was shouting. 'Has anybody seen Jake?'

BY THE TIME Diane Fry reached Withens, the derelict houses of Trafalgar Terrace were well ablaze. Coming over the hill from Shepley Head Lodge, she could see the smoke billowing out of the upstairs windows, thick and black. There was an acrid stench in the air, as if the houses themselves had been full of old tyres that were now burning. The upper floor must already be smoke-logged. The windows had been shattered by the heat, and the smoke was pouring out of them in waves. The smoke was so thick that only the occasional tongue of flame could be seen in the midst of them.

Fry found PC Tracy Udall and a colleague parking their Vauxhall across the road to stop any traffic going further than the car park.

'Where the hell's the fire service?' said Fry.

'According to Control, some of the local crews are still up on Withens Moor damping down. The nearest appliance is coming from New Mills.'

'Is there anyone inside?'

'We don't know. We've looked in the ground-floor rooms at this end of the row, as far as we could. But the fire seems to have started at the other end, and the smoke is too bad to get near. The fire crew might find anybody who's in there, if they get here soon. But if there was anyone upstairs, then I reckon they've had it by now. No one could breathe in that smoke.'

'And what about the people in the other terrace?'

'Mrs Wallwin is over there, from number 7. She's perfectly OK.'

'And her neighbours? The Oxleys?'

'She doesn't know. She's a bit stressed and confused.'

'They all have to come out. There are hundreds of railway sleepers and wooden pallets stacked in the yard at the back. A couple of vehicles, too. If all that stuff catches fire, their homes will go up like a bomb.'

'There are some demolition contractors down there in the field with a JCB and a bulldozer,' said Udall. 'They say they've been sent in by the landlords. They were due to start work on knocking down those empty houses, but someone has got to them first.'

'So I see.'

'The contractors have created an access through the fence at the bottom of the field. The trouble is, we can't get to Waterloo Terrace.'

'Why?'

'Because they've dropped a couple of trees across the entrance, using chainsaws.'

They jogged through the farmyard and down the field to where the contractors' machinery stood uselessly by.

Now Fry could see the pigeons circling Trafalgar Terrace. Their pale grey shapes were passing in and out of the smoke like tiny ghosts. At the far end of the terrace, the roof slates were glowing red from the heat of the burning rafters beneath them. But the pigeons kept trying to land on the ridge of the roofs, despite the heat and the flames, which were now licking through the slates. After making repeated attempts to land on the roof, one of the birds was finally caught by a burst of flame that erupted from a gap in the tiles. Its pinion feathers flared and blackened immediately, and its feet curled and shrivelled as the tendons burned. The pigeon tumbled on to the roof, where it writhed and flopped desperately as it roasted in the intense heat from the slates. But finally it gave up the struggle, slid down the roof and disappeared into the smoke. Oblivious to its fate, the other birds continued to attempt to land.

'We did see people moving around earlier on,' said Udall. 'One of them was carrying something. No – two of them were. Long, heavy objects. But we couldn't quite see –'

'Were they armed? We know they have air rifles, at least.'

'I'm not sure. Not air rifles anyway. Maybe just chainsaws.'

Fry tried Cooper's number again, but there was no answer.

'Tracy, ask the contractors if I can borrow a hard hat and one of those yellow jackets.'

'Why?'

'I've got to go in. I'll use the access they've made through the fence here, and see if I can work my way through the yard before the flames get to those pallets.'

'Diane, you can't.'

Fry pushed her phone back into her pocket. 'Ben Cooper's in there somewhere,' she said.

Udall nodded. 'I'll come with you, then.'

THE MOMENT HE heard what Marion Oxley was shouting, Ben Cooper ran back down the stairs and through the house to the kitchen. Marion was gazing in horror at the smoke, which was starting to drift across the yard, obscuring the top of the highest piles of pallets and seeping through the mesh of the chain-link fence.

'I don't know where Jake is,' she said.

'When did you see him last?' said Cooper.

'About half an hour ago, when you came in with Lucas. He should be here, but he went off somewhere.'

'He'll come home when he sees the fire, won't he?'

Marion stared at him. 'You don't understand. Jake likes starting fires. When he gets upset, that's what he does. Normally, one of the other boys keeps an eye on him, but nobody is with him.' She pointed out of the window. 'That's where he'll be.'

Cooper found Lucas Oxley already in the brick passage, trying to calm the barking dog.

'It's all right, you're safe,' he said.

'We've got to find Jake. The wind is blowing in this direction, so we might only have one chance before the fire spreads.'

As soon as he was outside, Cooper could feel the heat from the blaze. Every breath he took drew in the acrid stink of the black smoke. There seemed to be a lot more smoke than ought to be possible for the amount of visible flame. But he remembered how damp it had been inside 8 Trafalgar Terrace, and the rain that had fallen since. If all the houses in the row were the same, the flames might not get hold so quickly.

The yard was a maze, and Cooper despaired of finding a quick way through the stacks of tyres and scaffolding. Somewhere near here was the spot he had met some of the Border Rats in the dark the other night. In a few minutes, it would be as dark as it had been that night, because the smoke was sinking into the yard, as if borne down by its own weight.

Then Lucas tapped him on the shoulder and jerked a hand. 'This way. There's a gate at the back of the garage.'

'I'll follow you.'

They skirted the corner of some pallets and reached the doors of the garage. They stood open, revealing the bonnet of the pick-up. Alongside stood the flat-bed lorry.

'Somebody should move these out of the way,' said Cooper. 'They're potential bombs.'

'Scott could do it, but I don't know where the bugger is.'

Lucas began coughing as the smoke reached his lungs. He reached into the back of the flat-bed and found a cloth rag, which he tore in half. He pushed one half at Cooper and wrapped the other over his mouth and nose.

'Jake'll be in either number 1 or 2,' said Lucas, almost having to shout now through the rag and above the noise of cracking roof tiles and burning timbers. 'They're both easy to get into. It's where the lads go sometimes. I think that's where he'll have gone. It's where – Well, you try number 1, and I'll try 2.'

Cooper paused a moment, trying to listen for the sirens of approaching fire appliances, but they were still too far away.

'OK,' he said. 'But let's do it *now*.'

And together, Ben Cooper and Lucas Oxley ran towards the houses of Trafalgar Terrace, vanishing into the smoke like the doomed wood pigeons that had no more sense than to return to their burning roosts.

DIANE FRY COULD hear the dog, but she couldn't see it. Her view was blocked by the contents of the yard and the smoke that was beginning to drift in little swirls between the stacks, touching the pallets and roof tiles as if testing them for their potential to burn.

'I think it's usually chained up,' said Tracy Udall close to her ear. 'And from what Ben said, if you can hear it barking, you're safe.'

But it wasn't the dog that had made Fry pause. It was the sight of the flames licking from the windows of the houses, just visible through the haze. It was the sound of the slates cracking and the growing roar of the flames consuming the houses room by room, damp floorboards followed by abandoned furniture, window frames catching light from doors. It was the smell of the burning wallpaper, the scorched and blistering paint, the black bricks baking so hot that they were oozing moisture that bubbled and steamed.

She could have stood nailed to the spot for ever, matching the tongues of flame to the picture in her mind, watching for the burning figures leaping and dancing in the light of the blaze. But it was Tracy Udall who broke the spell, running forward to catch hold of a figure she had spotted through the smoke. It was Marion Oxley, standing at the side of the fence, still calling desperately towards the blazing houses. She was calling for Lucas. But also for Jake.

Udall spoke to her, then urged her away through the passage to the front of Waterloo Terrace, where support should be arriving now. At long last, Fry could hear the sirens coming over the hill. She looked at the flames leaping from windows to roof, and prayed that assistance wouldn't be too late.

BEN COOPER CROUCHED opposite Lucas Oxley in the cellar of 1 Trafalgar Terrace. The body of Jake Oxley lay on its back on the stone floor between them. The cellar smelled of death – that ripe, sweet, intimate smell.

Cooper filled his lungs with air, bent forward over Jake and breathed into his mouth, watched the boy's chest rise with the breath, then sat back on his heels. He looked at Lucas, but could barely see more than his eyes, white above the rag that covered his face.

'What the hell has been happening in here?' he said. 'It stinks.'

And it wasn't just the smell of death. There was a strong smell of petrol here, too, and singed cloth and paper. It seemed as though Jake had come down the steps to set another fire, but there hadn't been enough oxygen in the tiny cellar.

Lucas didn't reply to the question. 'Is he going to be all right?' he said.

'We need to get him into the air. Help me carry him up the steps.'

Cooper was glad he couldn't see the cellar clearly. He was sure there would be old bloodstains and worse on the walls and floor. They might have been there weeks or months, but the distinctive smell of them hadn't faded in the enclosed, airless space. It was a perfect environment for a forensic team to salvage evidence from, but it wasn't going to last long enough for them to reach it.

He took Jake's shoulders, and Lucas took his feet. They had left the door open at the top of the steps for air, but they could hear the flames coming steadily closer. When Cooper reached the top of the cellar steps, he could see that the floorboards of the hallway and the treads of the stairway were smouldering. But the route to the broken front door was still reasonably clear.

When they got out of the house, they made progress, staggering away from Trafalgar Terrace towards the rutted track and damp trees near the Oxleys' homes.

'OK, stop,' said Cooper breathlessly.

Finally, he could see up towards the road. And he realized Scott Oxley had organized the other boys to clear the trees they had felled only a short time before, and were waving wildly at a fire appliance approaching the entrance. Cooper stooped to look at Jake. He was breathing, though raggedly.

Now the air was full of the sound of sirens. Cooper imagined the convoy coming up the road – fire appliances, police vehicles, ambulances, a whole parade, like the arrival of a besieging army. Maybe they didn't quite have catapults and ballistas, but the firemen would have axes and heavy cutting gear, and he was willing to bet there would be a police van with a battering ram or two. Maybe it was time for him to choose sides.

Together, Ben Cooper and Lucas Oxley waited, listening to the sound of the sirens dipping and soaring as the emergency vehicles crested one hill after another on the road into Withens.

DIANE FRY WAITED for the ambulance to move off. She had been standing watching Ben Cooper for several minutes while Jake Oxley was lifted on to a stretcher and loaded into the ambulance by the paramedics, accompanied by his father.

Finally, Cooper looked up and saw her. Fry saw the expression of surprise on his face, and remembered that she was still wearing the hard hat she'd borrowed from one of the contractors. She must look almost as bad as he did, with his face and hands blackened by smoke, like one of the Border Rats made up for a performance.

'Ben,' she said, 'how often have I told you – no heroics.'

HALF AN HOUR later, DC Gavin Murfin arrived in Withens with the latest contingent of emergency services. Ben Cooper had been sent off to hospital with orders to get himself checked over. And after Murfin enquired about casualties, he had some news for Diane Fry.

'That missing teddy bear turned up,' he said.

'Emma Renshaw's golden plush?'

'Yep. Guess where?'

'I've no idea, Gavin. Did Alex Dearden have it? Have we traced where the antiques are stored?'

'No such luck. It was in the car.'

'Which car?'

'*Her* car – Emma's. It was in the boot.'

'So the Renshaws had it all the time, and didn't know.'

'Looks like it. Bit odd, that.'

'Yes.'

'Oh, and the hospital say the verdict is hopeful on the vicar. He was lucky – the wall of the building he was standing next to took some of the blast, and most of the shotgun pellets that hit him went into his arm and leg down the right side. Good job someone got to him quick, though – the doctors say he might have bled to death otherwise.'

'Is he feeling well enough to talk yet?'

'Nope. He's had most of the pellets dug out of him, but he's still in dreamland from the painkillers.'

'Pity.'

Murfin looked at her.

'You're sure everybody's all right, Diane?'

'Yes,' said Fry. 'Everybody's fine.'

Murfin turned towards where some uniformed officers were trying to restore order among the residents of Withens. 'I'll see what's going on over there, then,' he said.

'Gavin …'

'Yeah?'

'Weren't you supposed to be checking on what calls Neil Granger had been making on his mobile the night he was killed?'

'I did. I told you.'

'No, you didn't,' said Fry.

'Well, I tried to anyway. But you were talking to Ben at the time. You were having some kind of heart to heart, like.'

'Tell me again, Gavin.'

'Neil Granger made several calls to a number in Glossop. The number was in his phone's memory, so it was easy to find out who it was.'

Fry stared at him. 'You should have told me this, Gavin. If I was busy, you should have told me later. This is important.'

'Not really,' said Murfin defensively. 'It was only who you might have expected him to be phoning.'

'Hey!'

Diane Fry turned at the shout. A man in a yellow fluorescent jacket and a hard hat was standing behind her, holding a roll of blue plastic sheeting.

'What do you want? Are you one of the contractors? I'm afraid you'll have to wait. There'll be no work on this site today.'

'No, I work for the National Grid. Tunnel maintenance.'

'I'm sorry, but whatever it is you want, you're in the wrong place. You'll have to move away.'

'Well, I'm only doing what I was told. And it was one of your blokes that told me to do it.'

The man seemed to be about to offer Fry the roll of plastic he was carrying. She backed away.

'Sorry? What are you talking about? *Who* did you say you are?'

'My name's Norton. Sandy Norton.' He clutched the plastic sheeting to his chest again and inclined his head sideways. '*He* knows me. That one over there.'

Fry followed his gesture. 'Gavin! There's a gentleman here says he knows you. Deal with him, will you?'

'Hey up, mate,' said Murfin, walking back across the road. 'How's it going down in Tunnel Town? What have you got there?'

'It's what I found.'

'Found?'

'In the middle tunnel. Under the air shaft. We had a look, like your mate told us we should. This is what we found. I thought you'd want to see it. But say so if you're not bothered, and I'll burn it.'

'Let's see.'

Norton began to unwrap the plastic. There were several layers, and Fry was beginning to think there was nothing inside it at all, when the contents finally appeared.

'A stick,' she said. 'Gavin, it looks like one of those sticks the Border Rats use.'

'You're right.'

Norton pointed with a grubby finger. 'And look, at this end –'

'Don't touch it!' said Fry. 'Have you touched it?'

'I was wearing gloves in the tunnel,' said Norton defensively. 'And as soon as I saw this, I wrapped it up. Was that the right thing to do?'

'It'll do fine, thank you.'

'Well, I'm glad about that. It's blood, isn't it?'

'It looks like it.'

'It was the other bloke that told me to look, you know. But I couldn't find him to give it to him. Was he right, then?'

Fry looked over her shoulder at the black terrace and the smouldering buildings behind it. The grey shapes of a few wood pigeons still flapped in and out of the clouds of smoke. They would have to look for a new home soon.

'Yes, he was right,' she said.

Chapter Forty-One

MONDAY

BY THE BANK holiday Monday, Withens didn't feel quite
so isolated. In fact, the entire world was rushing by only
yards away, and it seemed to be coming nearer.

There were visitors in the village to see the well
dressing, and the Quiet Shepherd was doing good
trade. But Ben Cooper felt the world was intruding
in other ways, too, perhaps more subtly. Walkers following Euroroute E8 all the way from Turkey were
ending up in Longdendale. Lorries on trans-Pennine
journeys often turned off the A628 to park overnight
by the side of the road above Withens, gradually creating their own lay-by by churning up the grass and
compacting the ground. Those lorries were from all
over the world. Even the acid rain destroying the
peat moors might be from anywhere, too – not just
Manchester.

Sitting in his car with his mobile phone pressed to his ear, Cooper reflected that if he drew everything on to a map, it would show the village surrounded, though still isolated. It was cut off by the traffic roaring by to the south, and by the power cables of the National Grid and the proposed new trans-Pennine expresses in the tunnels to the west. Together, they formed a net that Withens would never escape. Perhaps the water company would want to clear the whole valley to preserve the purity of its water. The land might be needed for a lorry park or maintenance sheds for the new rail link. And when that happened what would become of people like the Oxleys?

'I don't believe it was Craig Oxley alone who killed Barry Cully,' said Cooper into his phone. 'Do you? It's too convenient.'

Diane Fry's voice sounded distant. Not only was she miles away in Edendale, but her mind would be on other things, preparing for an important interview. She was always meticulous about planning interviews, making notes on the areas she wanted to make sure she covered with her questions. Nothing was to be missed out.

'There's no evidence otherwise, Ben,' she said. 'The rest of the Oxleys are saying nothing at all.'

'And they won't, no matter how often they're interviewed. I think Ryan only spoke up because he's been terrified by the Anti-Social Behaviour Order. He knew that if anyone else got into trouble, the whole family would be out of Waterloo Terrace. So he decided it was safer to break ranks and blame Craig, who is safely dead and out of the way already. But I'm convinced the Oxleys do things together, not alone.'

'And that's your theory, Ben?'

'And the story is right here, in the collective memory of the Oxleys, and it always will be. We just have no way of getting access to it. Not in a way that we could present to a judge and jury.'

Cooper watched a group of people passing along the road in their black rag coats and their hats and sunglasses. They were some of the dancers and musicians arriving from Hey Bridge for the May Day performance of the Border Rats.

'You mean all that Border Rats nonsense?' said Fry. 'The Crown Prosecution Service would love us if we presented them with that lot as key witnesses.'

Because of the crowds and the displays in the village, Cooper had been obliged to park his car on the roadside below the village, on the other side of the church. Somebody driving too fast into Withens had hit a carrion crow that had been feeding on the squashed remains of a rabbit. Its tattered black shape lay half in a pothole on the verge.

Cooper stared at the remains of the crow, its pinions fluttering in the slipstream of a passing car.

'Nature turned out not to be on their side, didn't it?' he said.

'Who?'

'The Oxleys.'

'Don't talk rubbish, Ben,' said Fry.

Cooper didn't bother to defend himself. He was watching the movement of the loose scree on the opposite slope as it slid a little bit nearer to Withens. It might take time, but nature never did give up the war.

'I was thinking about Craig Oxley on the way here,' he said. 'I'm not sure what the point is of sending young people into custody. Not in the present system. They just come out worse at the end of it.'

'I know.'

'If there's one group in the prison system who could actually be helped, surely it's young people. If anybody really cared about them, their lives could be turned round at that age. They could be given education, at least. I mean proper education – not training for a future as a car thief or a mobile-phone bandit.'

'There aren't all that many cases like his, Ben.'

'No. The system probably considers Craig Oxley to be one of its successes. He won't be clogging up the courts again, will he? He won't be taking up valuable police time any more.'

'There's no point in talking to you when you're in this mood, Ben,' said Fry. 'Go home and get some sleep, see if you can get a dose of reality. Or a sense of proportion at least. You'll have got over it in the morning. And don't forget, we've got a meeting to re-schedule. We still need to have that talk about your future.'

'You're kidding.'

'Not at all.'

'Give me a break, Diane.'

'We can't keep putting it off.'

'But you'll be busy.'

'Not too busy for you, Ben.'

There was a pause while Cooper tried to picture the expression on her face. Sometimes phones just weren't good enough for communication.

'You said you'd be in Withens later on?' said Fry. 'You want to see this Border Rats thing through to the end, don't you?'

'That's right. You're still coming, aren't you?'

'Unfortunately. I have to see the Renshaws one last time. I promised them I'd keep them informed personally about progress on the enquiry. I wish I didn't have to come to Withens ever again. It isn't going to be easy this afternoon.'

'No,' said Cooper. 'Not easy at all.'

THE PICTURE IN the Withens well dressing depicted the sainthood of St Asaph. The legend, picked out in blue hydrangea petals and buttercups, explained that 1 May was his patronal day. The makers of the well dressing had used chrysanthemums and maize, sweetcorn and rice, some of it coloured with icing-sugar dyes. Everything had to be natural.

Ben Cooper saw Eric Oxley holding a plastic watering can. He was spraying the picture with water to make sure it didn't dry out. Already, the background of the picture was starting to crumble away a little, the fluorspar trickling to the bottom of the frame, like fine gravel.

'A pity Derek Alton won't be here to bless the well dressing,' said Cooper, standing behind Eric's shoulder. 'But at least you can use the church. We've finished with the graveyard now.'

Eric turned round, sending a spray of water on to Cooper's trousers. But he was already damp from the steady drizzle, so it didn't matter.

'I'm sure you'll be pleased to hear Mr Alton will recover fully, after he's had all the shotgun pellets removed from his side. He'll be in a state of shock for a while though, I think. In fact, he had two bad shocks. I don't know which was worse.'

'Everyone knows you don't disturb that end of the graveyard,' said Eric. 'It's where the railwaymen are buried.'

'The ones who died of cholera?'

'That's right. Who would go digging up the ground there?'

'The Reverend Alton would, obviously.'

'Daft bugger.'

Cooper shook his head. 'If it hadn't been him, it would have been somebody else. A stranger. Even a foreigner.'

But Eric just stared at him. Cooper supposed this superstitious fear of 'disturbing' the cholera had somehow been inherited from the ancestors who had lived in the shanty town and had good reason to fear the disease. Where better to hide a dead body than among so many others? But the Oxleys' decision had been based on the belief that the tradition of leaving that part of the graveyard undisturbed would continue indefinitely. They hadn't seen that things were changing. They hadn't understood that change was inevitable. And that was always a mistake. Always.

'At least you've still got your traditions,' said Cooper.

'What, the Border Rats? It won't last much longer,' said Eric.

'Why?'

'Well, for one thing, these grandsons of mine won't keep it up without me and their dad to make them do it. The tradition will pass on to the folk from Hey Bridge, and other places. And they'll make of it whatever *they* want. It won't ever be the same again.'

Eric Oxley picked up his hat and his stick, and shook his head.

'Times change,' he said. 'And our time is nearly over.'

IN THE CAR park, a crowd had gathered in the rain to watch the morning performance by the Border Rats. Though the musicians from Hey Bridge were doing their best, the dancers lacked the energy and enthusiasm of their earlier display in Edendale.

Cooper could see that they were approaching the final dance, the ritual killing of the rat. Did the aggressive banging of the sticks on the ground really represent the tunnel workers killing rats? Was it a celebration of the murder of Nathan Pidcock? Was there any difference?

The men who began the ritual might have known its meaning, but by the third, fourth and fifth generation, the story had changed. It meant whatever it had to mean for those performing it.

His neighbour, Peggy Check, had made a good point. Somebody was being symbolically killed in this ritual. It might be Nathan Pidcock, the carrier who had caused the cholera outbreak through his greed. But the target of the sticks might also be more recent, the victim of a murder committed by a close-knit group who would never talk. And no witnesses except, perhaps, for one frightened boy. The postmortem on the skeletalized remains found in the churchyard had revealed several broken bones. Barry Cully had been beaten to death and his body concealed in a shallow grave among the other dead of Withens. The scene of his murder had burned to ashes.

The Border Rats' performance might be an old tradition. But the story they told could be much more recent. Could it be the story of Barry Cully's murder?

He waited, listening to the chant and the screaming, watching the dancers approach the climax of their performance. The rat fell and was symbolically beaten with the sticks. Then he got up, and the Border Rats took the sporadic applause from the damp crowd.

Was he any the wiser? No. But it had been a nice theory.

Cooper began to walk back across the road, passing in front of the church. He didn't give a second glance to Ruby Wallwin, who had been asked by Marion Oxley to put the finishing touches to the Withens well dressing. She was clutching a handful of the most delicate petals of all, which she had collected only that morning. She had shuffled down to the bank of the stream in her bedroom slippers, her joints still stiff because she had only just got out of bed, but knowing that the petals had to be perfectly fresh. They were white dog roses, pure and gleaming, still damp from the rainfall overnight.

Mrs Wallwin had never got a chance to talk to the vicar, and it was too late now. But she thought it was probably for the best anyway that she hadn't said anything. The Oxleys were starting to accept her now, and it wouldn't do for them to think she was passing on the things she overheard them shouting at each other when they forgot she was there.

Ruby Wallwin bent to the bottom corner of the picture, where a group of black figures had been created from tiny alder cones and roasted coffee beans. She wasn't sure of the meaning of the picture. But she knew that the white rose petals she lay at the feet of the black figures looked very much like bones.

DIANE FRY WAS sitting in an interview room at West Street with DI Paul Hitchens. She stared at the man across the table, hoping they weren't going to have a repeat of the silence she had endured during the last interview she'd conducted here.

'The stick that was found in the railway tunnel has Neil Granger's blood on it,' she said. 'Not to mention traces of his cerebrospinal fluid, and fragments of bone embedded in the wood.'

She looked up, but got no reaction.

'At the other end of the stick, we have some fingerprints. As it happens, these are prints that we already had on record.'

'That was lucky, wasn't it?' said Hitchens, with a smile. 'Sometimes, we do get a bit of luck.'

Fry nodded. 'Detective Inspector Hitchens is right. We collected these particular fingerprints very recently.'

There was no response, but she hadn't asked a question yet. Fry stared at the man opposite her, and he met her gaze calmly. She was a little unnerved by his appearance – his paleness, the blackness of his hair and the dark stubble on his cheeks.

'We took these prints for elimination purposes,' she said. 'The same prints were on the bronze bust we found, and on a small brass box.'

He actually nodded then, as if encouraging her to continue.

'They were also elsewhere in your brother's house,' she said.

And Philip Granger smiled at the mention of his brother.

Chapter Forty-Two

DRIVING ON THE A628 towards the Flouch crossroads, Ben Cooper found the treacly expanses of Black Hill and Withens Moor opening up all around him. When he looked down into the valley, he could see the rain drifting across the face of the hills in sheets, like mist.

He had already passed the sites of two of the villages that had been on this road, the communities that Tracy Udall had said were removed by the water companies. Woodhead and Crowden at least had a few isolated houses left to show where they had been. But now the map said that he was approaching Saltersbrook.

Cooper looked down the hill from the road. There was a stony track leading down into a small valley, where a brook fed into the River Etherow and on down to the reservoirs. At the bottom of the track, he could see a tiny stone bridge over the stream. It looked like a packhorse bridge – presumably for the traders who had once brought salt on their packhorses from Cheshire to the cities in Yorkshire. This must have been the original salters' way, which the village of Saltersbrook had been named after. But now, there was nothing here.

Deep banks of bracken grew on the slopes at the sides of the brook, masking some of the ground where Saltersbrook had once stood. All that remained of the village were the foundations of a few houses and the ruins of the village inn. Fireplaces were still visible in collapsed rooms where the inn had stood on rising ground beyond the bridge. The climb to it from the bridge was very steep, and the track had been cobbled to provide a secure grip for the hoofs of the packhorses. The fallen stones of the inn were overgrown now with nettles and rough grass. At the moment, they were being grazed by a few sheep.

Apart from the traffic on the A628, there was nothing else human in the landscape, except for the turbines of the wind farm to the north-east. He noticed that two of the turbines were motionless. And when he turned a bend, he suddenly had a clear view across the expanse of moor to the wind farm. There were several vehicles parked there.

Cooper pulled into the side of the road, careful not to drive too far on to the soft verge, where his wheels would surely sink into the peat. Clustered at the base of the turbines, he could see a couple of Land Rovers, a minibus, even a small mobile crane. There were people working at the wind farm, presumably a maintenance crew. How long had they been working there, without him being aware of them? Who might they have seen going to and from Withens from their unique vantage point?

Cooper looked at his watch. He was early yet. He had plenty of time to pay them a visit.

PHILIP GRANGER HAD decided to ignore the advice of the duty solicitor and explain himself. He did it with the same smile, as if he were helping his interviewers to get their ideas straight.

'You have this all wrong,' he said. 'I didn't intend to kill Neil. Why would I do that? He was my brother.'

'We know that Neil was going to help the Reverend Alton dig up the graveyard. You knew he would find the remains of Barry Cully. All of your family knew that. And somebody had to stop him. We think the obvious person to do that was you, Mr Granger.'

Philip Granger looked paler than ever. He didn't seem to have shaved for several days, and his clothes didn't smell too clean either. He had deteriorated noticeably during the last week, and someone ought to have noticed.

'Yes, yes. But I didn't mean to kill him,' he said. 'I meant to break Neil's arm, that was all – not to kill him.'

'But you *did* kill him, Mr Granger.'

He shook his head. 'It was an accident. He moved at the wrong moment. He hit his head on the stones at the bottom of the air shaft. You *know* that's what happened. It was an accident.'

'A broken arm wouldn't have kept him out of action for ever,' said Hitchens. 'Besides, you should have known Mr Alton would carry on clearing the graveyard on his own, which is what he did. Did you really hope that the remains of Barry Cully would never be found?'

'We hoped Alton would leave. We hoped the church would be closed.'

'We?'

'The family were behind me,' said Granger.

'But the vicar put a spanner in the works.'

'He was a bit obsessed about that graveyard. I don't know why it was so important to him.'

'The damage to the vestry?' said Hitchens. 'The theft? The vandalism to his car?'

'We didn't have anything against him, really. But nothing seemed to take his attention away from that bloody graveyard. He should have left things well alone.'

Fry consulted the notes she had made before starting the interview. One of the first things she'd noted was the record of Neil Granger's calls from his mobile phone the night he was killed. They were calls to a number in Glossop – his brother's number.

'Well, there you go, then,' said Philip, when she asked him about the calls. He glanced at his solicitor with a little triumphant smile, but the solicitor didn't respond. 'Would Neil have phoned me to arrange to meet, if he thought I would do anything to him?'

'The fact that Neil didn't expect you to attack him doesn't cast any light on your intentions,' said Fry.

'I didn't mean to kill him. I mean, why would I?'

'You tell me.'

'Look, he pestered me to go up there. He had an idea about some ceremony at dawn on May Day, and he wanted to rehearse it. I think he'd had a row about it with Uncle Lucas and the others. So he had a point to prove. He was a bit like that, Neil – pig-headed. But it was no good to him doing it on his own, because he needed somebody to prove his point to. That's why he thought of me. I had my uses, even for my little brother. Hell, do you think I wanted to go up the hill to that air shaft in the middle of the night? He pestered me until I said "yes". I don't know why I agreed to it.'

'Perhaps you suddenly realized what a convenient opportunity you'd been presented with.'

'I don't know what you mean,' said Philip, shaking his head.

Hitchens folded his hands together on the table as he took a turn to let Fry prepare her next question.

'How did you actually get up to the air shaft to meet Neil?' he said. 'We've interviewed lorry drivers on the A628, and no one saw any cars parked in the lay-by, except your brother's.'

'I don't have a car. I ride a motorbike. I parked it behind Neil's car, where no one would see it from the road.'

'And you walked up to the air shaft from the lay-by?'

'It isn't that far. If Neil could walk it, why shouldn't I?' Philip grimaced. 'I was a bit shattered by the time I got there, to be honest. I'm not quite so clean living as good old Neil. That was another way he always made me feel second best.'

'You could have ridden up on the bike,' said Hitchens.

'I'm not totally stupid. There would be tracks.'

'You were worried about leaving tracks, yet you say you didn't intend to kill your brother?'

Philip opened his mouth, then stopped and looked at his solicitor, who shook his head sadly.

'That's a "no comment".'

Fry looked at Hitchens, who sat back, content. Time for a change of tack. If Granger thought he could get off lightly, he was going to be mistaken.

'Mr Granger,' said Fry, 'according to the postmortem report on your brother, some of the cerebrospinal fluid from his head injury was transferred to his hand while he was dying. That could only have been done by you. Do you agree?'

Granger looked a little sick. If he could have gone any paler, he would have done. His voice was a little quieter when he spoke.

'It was still quite dark, but I remember the sound,' he said. 'It was a sort of thud and crunch, like somebody had dropped a packet of biscuits in the street. I could see that Neil wasn't dead. He was still moving a bit, and making noises like an animal. But I couldn't hit him again. I couldn't hit someone who was injured, it's not the same.' He looked up at Fry for some understanding. She found she couldn't look away.

'I was always like that,' he said. 'I could never understand how uncle Lucas and some of my cousins could kill injured animals. Lucas always said it was putting them out of their misery, that it was a kindness. But I could never bring myself to do it like he could, not killing an injured thing in cold blood, no matter how badly hurt it was.'

'So what did you do?'

'I held Neil's hand and waited with him, until he died.'

'Do you expect us to believe that?' said Hitchens.

Granger dropped his head. 'He took a long time to die. But time always passes, doesn't it?'

Fry looked at Hitchens. They both knew that Philip Granger's account didn't quite tally with the postmortem report on his brother's injuries.

They allowed Granger a moment to recover. But Fry had a lot of important questions she still wanted to ask him.

'And now, Mr Granger, we come to the subject of Emma Renshaw.'

THE MAINTENANCE CREW at the wind farm turned out to be Danish. They said they were employed by the turbine manufacturers, a specialist wind-power company in Denmark. The wind farm looked quite different at close quarters. The towers were elegantly tapered, but the massive blades of the turbines looked like propellers from an aircraft of unimaginable size. When six of the turbines were lined up, they reminded Cooper of that Hindu goddess with too many arms. Their eighteen blades rotated hypnotically, like white scimitars carving the Pennine air.

When Cooper drove into the parking area near the sub-station building, he noticed that the towers were numbered on their sides. At the moment, numbers five and eight were motionless, the ends of their blades turned back like claws. Small doors set into each tower were reminiscent of bulkheads in a submarine. Built on concrete bases, the towers hardly seemed to vibrate, despite the weight and the movement of the blades.

'You should get plenty of wind up here,' said Cooper to the foreman of the maintenance crew. 'Too much, perhaps.'

'Yes, sometimes. But there are aerodynamic stalls on the blade tips to prevent damage to the gearbox and generator, and hydraulic disc brakes to lock the turbines.'

'You know what looks a bit frightening about these things?'

'Frightening? What's that?'

'These blades are so big. They're out of proportion. They look too big for the tower to support.'

'Yes, the rotors are over 120 feet in diameter,' said the foreman. 'The towers are 114 feet.'

'So they *are* wider than the tower is high. It seems wrong.'

The foreman smiled at him. 'It's perfectly safe.'

The noise of the wind was in Cooper's ears up here. But it couldn't disguise the sound of the turbines, that steady whoosh-whoosh, like a giant washing machine on its rinse cycle. No – a whole laundrette full of giant washing machines. Closer to number one tower, Cooper could hear the hum of the motor inside the base and the occasional metallic clunk of a switch. But there was an eerie whistling somewhere, too – a high-pitched keening from the blades as they sliced through the air. It was like a ghostly voice singing on the wind. And since the turbines ran constantly, all day and all night, that uncanny whistling and thudding must never cease.

It might be a little scary to come upon the wind farm unexpectedly in the dark, and to have your car headlights catch the movement of those vast white arms as they turned against the night sky.

Cooper turned his back on the towers to look out over Longdendale. Viewed from this height, the valleys were like deep wounds in the moors, and it seemed amazing that there were people living down there. To the west, the sky was so dark and heavy that it seemed more solid than the land.

Sometimes visitors looked over a vista of peat moors like Withens and Black Hill and admired what they thought was entirely natural scenery. They thought the view had nothing man-made in it – no houses or roads, no walls or telegraph poles, nor even electricity pylons.

But they were wrong, of course – the entire landscape here was man-made. Longdendale had been primeval forest once. There had been wild boar here, along with deer, wolves, bears and even wild bulls. Now the only signs left of their presence were in the place names – Wildboar Clough, Swineshaw and Deer Knowl. The monks who had been given control of the valley had cleared the woodland for their sheep, and the Industrial Revolution had begun to produce the acid rain that had fallen on the Dark Peak for centuries, destroying the vegetation and eroding the peat. What visitors admired now was the devastation left by thousands of years of destruction by man.

'We offered to help down in the village, you know,' said the maintenance foreman, coming to stand by him.

'Down in Withens?'

'Yes. It's our policy to have good relations with the local community. So we offered our services on some projects. But some of the local people there are not very friendly.'

'I think you must be talking about the Oxleys.'

'You know them?'

'We've met.'

People like the Oxleys knew perfectly well that this wasn't an unchanging landscape but a dynamic one. They were like the hefted flocks of sheep on the hillsides, who were so crucial to the balance of the ecology. For those flocks, their grazing territories had become inherited knowledge, passed on from one generation to the next. To farm the vast, unfenced areas of moorland, shepherds had to make use of the sheep's natural behaviour patterns. After centuries of hefting, they became practically wild animals, relying on the strong territorial instinct that went with their feral nature.

Down on the Withens road, Cooper could see PC Udall's Vauxhall Astra. He recognized it by the identification number on the roof. In this kind of landscape, those numbers weren't only for the use of the air support unit's helicopter crew.

'It's a shame about Withens.' The foreman shook his head sadly. 'We were thinking of offering to clear the graveyard at the church. It's very badly overgrown, you know.'

'Not any more,' said Cooper, thinking of the task force officers who had spent the past few days painstakingly removing the tangled vegetation and sifting through sinewy roots looking for clues to the identity of the skeleton and the manner of the victim's death.

'We even went into the pub a few times, but they didn't like us being there, we could tell that.'

'Ah. Foreigners in the pub,' said Cooper.

'Excuse me?'

'Nothing important.'

Despite his vantage point, all Cooper could see of Withens was the tower of St Asaph's church. But he was surprised to find that he could also see the roof of Shepley Head Lodge, out beyond the village to the north, apparently isolated and inaccessible.

The Reverend Derek Alton had created an involuntary link between the two. Early this morning, the vicar had finally been well enough to talk. Among other things that he had needed to get off his chest, he had revealed that Neil Granger had discovered his brother Philip was involved with the spate of antiques thefts in the area. A stolen bronze bust had been the conclusive evidence, he said. And Neil had gone to Alton to ask for his advice about what he should do.

'And what did you advise him?' the vicar had been asked.

'To face him. To tell the truth.'

PHILIP GRANGER LAUGHED then. He seemed to throw off the mantle of guilt too easily now that the subject had moved away from the death of his brother.

'Emma? Emma was mad about Neil. How stupid was that? She pursued him for months. I remember she was so thrilled when he moved to Bearwood to stay in the house with her and the other students. But he was gay. I told you, didn't I, that he was gay?'

'Yes, sir, you did.'

'But why did nobody tell Emma? Why didn't Neil tell her? It would have made it so much easier. Things would have turned out differently. But I had to tell her myself, and she didn't believe me.'

'*You* wanted Emma for yourself?'

'Yes. I used to e-mail her a lot, because it wasn't easy to go up to her house to see her. But she always ignored me in favour of Neil. I'm only the brother, you know. Why should he always have got the best? Why did everybody always like him more?'

'Did you pick Emma up from Bearwood that day?'

'I waited outside the house until I saw Neil go.'

'But you only have a motorbike.'

'I *can* drive, you know,' he said. 'What do you think I am? I borrowed a mate's car, so there was no chance of Neil recognizing it. I pulled up to the kerb when Emma was on the way to the bus stop. She was surprised to see me, but I told her I was in the area looking for work, and she didn't think anything of it. It was starting to rain then, and the trains would have been packed. I said I was just on the way home, so she got in the car.'

'She would have mentioned it to Neil afterwards, if –'

'Yeah. But I only wanted to talk to her, you know. It wouldn't have mattered, except – Well, it went all right for a while. We chatted about all kinds of things, and I thought we were getting on really well, until she started to talk about Neil. Do you know what she wanted? She wanted me to speak to Neil for her, to tell him how much she liked him. How pathetic is that?'

'How far on the way home did you get?' said Fry coldly, picturing the quiet road where Emma's mobile phone had been found.

'I don't really know. We argued a lot. I turned off the A6 somewhere when she started to get really upset. She got her mobile phone out and was going to phone her parents, but I grabbed it off her and threw it out of the window.'

'We found that,' said Fry. 'What I want to know is where you killed her.'

'I don't know. I really don't know where it was. She started calling me all kinds of things and comparing me to Neil, so I lost my temper and hit her. Then she started screaming and got out of the car, so I went after her and hit her again. I hit her a few times, until she stopped screaming.'

Fry paused. Not for Granger to recover this time, but for herself. Now, finally, she could picture Emma Renshaw – but it was as Emma had been at the moment of her death, not as she had been in life.

As soon as she was finished here, Fry had to visit the Renshaws. She had made them a promise that she would keep them up to date personally on the enquiry. But explaining the facts of the case against Philip Granger to them would not be easy.

'This must have been a very quiet spot, Mr Granger,' she said.

'I parked on a grass verge somewhere. All I remember were some stone walls and a gate into a field.'

'What did you do with Emma?'

'I dragged her into the field and hid her behind the wall. No cars came past all the time we were there. So I was lucky, too, I suppose.'

'Yes, you were.'

'Mr Granger, we're going to ask you to look at some maps and show us the area where you think you were at the time,' said Hitchens.

'I was lost,' said Granger. 'I can't tell you the exact place.'

'Nevertheless, we'll want to narrow it down as much as possible, so that we can do our best to find Emma. Are you willing to co-operate in that, sir?'

Granger shrugged. 'OK. But you have to realize it was all my brother's fault.'

'I don't think so,' said Fry.

'Oh, yes, it was,' he said. 'It was his fault. My dear little brother.'

BEN COOPER WATCHED through his rearview mirror as a bus pulled up near the Pepper Pot Inn in the village of Midhopestones. Only three people got off the bus. Two of them looked at the threatening sky and went into the pub. The third one waited until the bus had set off again and began to walk slowly up the road.

Cooper hadn't felt the need to tell Angie Fry what sort of car he drove. She probably knew that already, along with its registration number. And maybe his date of birth, his mother's maiden name and his National Insurance number.

As Angie got into the Toyota, he continued looking at his mirror, expecting to see a car turning into the road or manoeuvring to leave the pub car park. But there was nothing. He started the engine.

'Where are we going?' said Angie.

'Somewhere quiet.'

'Embarrassed to be seen with me, Ben?'

Cooper didn't answer, but continued to drive back towards the Flouch crossroads. They passed through Langsett, and soon the surrounding landscape began to look suitably remote. He felt confident that Angie would not be familiar with this area and would have no idea where they were heading.

'Angie, I take it you know what happened to Diane there before she transferred to Derbyshire?' he said.

'Yes.'

'In fact, you're remarkably well informed for someone who hasn't been in touch with her sister for so long.'

Angie hesitated. 'There are ways of finding these things out.'

'I'm sure there are. Especially with the help of your friend who drives the dark blue BMW with a blocked registration.'

'Blocked registration?' she repeated, dumbly seizing on the part of his sentence she didn't understand.

'What is he? National Crime Squad? Special Branch? Who are you working with who doesn't want some long-lost sister blundering on to his pitch?'

'Ben, you don't understand the situation.'

'No, I don't,' said Cooper.

And for the first time he began to feel angry about the way he had been treated. He had known from the start that he was being lied to. There was no way that Angie Fry could have obtained the information that she had without inside help, without someone with exactly the right contacts and the means of asking. Being lied to was bad enough. But it was the underlying contempt that really angered him, the assumption that he was just some stupid bumpkin copper who would go along with anything he was asked to do.

Cooper had no idea what bigger cause he was expected to become a minor sacrifice for. Probably an undercover operation against major drug dealers, or some other large-scale organized crime. For himself, he didn't really care. But Diane was expected to be an unwitting sacrifice, too.

And worst of all was the fact that the whole plan seemed to have been put together with such casual arrogance. He was appalled and infuriated by the utter cynicism of the idea that he would willingly be the means of destroying someone's hope – someone who apparently considered him a friend.

'Angie, you should tell your friend that he ought to have trained you to lie better,' he said, and put his foot down to drive a little faster as he hit the A628.

Angie slumped back against the headrest of her seat. 'I'm sure there's a way out of this situation,' she said.

'Yes, there is.'

She rolled her head wearily and looked at him sideways.

'What do you suggest?'

'There's always a way out of situations like this,' said Cooper. 'It takes a bit of courage, but it's the only way.'

'I've a feeling it might be something I don't want to hear about.'

As the white turbines of the wind farm appeared to the north and the air shaft for the railway tunnels came into view on the face of the opposite hill, Cooper began to feel more and more in control of the situation. It was the first time he'd felt in control since he'd visited Withens.

'This way involves telling the truth,' he said.

Angie sighed. 'That's what I was afraid you'd say.'

Chapter Forty-Three

MOST OF THE visitors to Withens were carrying umbrellas or wearing nylon cagoules with hoods turned up against the gentle rain. At least Eric Oxley wouldn't have to water the well dressing much today.

Ben Cooper had taken up a position on the edge of the small crowd surrounding the well dressing. The sight of the tourists had just reminded him that he'd made another date with Peggy Check for this afternoon, and he had let her down again. He hoped she would understand. There was already too much in his life that was going to be hard to explain.

Cooper didn't have to wait long before Diane Fry came to stand at his side.

'So how were the Renshaws?' he said.

Fry hunched her shoulders in a characteristically tense gesture. 'Sarah Renshaw forced me to watch a video of Emma. A selection of memories, specially edited.

One sequence showed Emma in black make-up, playing the recorder for the Border Rats.'

'I'm sorry.'

'Funnily enough, Neil Granger was in it, too.'

Cooper hadn't brought an umbrella, or a waterproof. He could feel drops of the Withens rain starting to trickle down his collar.

'What's the progress on Philip Granger?' he said.

'We think he's pretty well tied down for the killing of his brother. It'll be up to the lawyers whether they go for a murder charge or manslaughter. We can't prove his intention.'

'Did any of the Oxleys know that it was Philip who killed his brother?'

'They say not. And do you know, Ben, I think I actually believe them.'

'Maybe it just wouldn't occur to them – he was a member of the family, after all.'

'We can all be wrong about our family.'

'Yes.'

'But there isn't enough evidence to charge Philip Granger with the murder of Emma Renshaw. Not unless Emma's body turns up. We did trace the phone thief through his prints – they were all over it, but they were left in the blood after it had dried. He was picked up at Matlock, and he's told us where he found the phone.'

'It *was* Emma's blood?'

'They matched the DNA.'

'So he picked up the phone, found it didn't work, and dumped it. Or noticed the blood and panicked.'

'Yes.'

Cooper began to move away, but Fry held him back by putting her hand on his arm. He wished she wouldn't touch him. The way it made him feel didn't help him to be sure in his own mind that he was doing the right thing. He could only hope that she wasn't going to ruin it completely and be nice to him.

'And while we're on the subject, Ben, asking the National Grid maintenance man to check the tunnel under the air shaft was a very good thought.'

'Thanks.'

'It's a pity you completely forgot to mention it to me.'

'Right. Sorry.'

They began to walk across the road together towards their cars. Gradually, the crowd of people began to thin out in front of them.

'Anyway, I'm sure we'll find Emma's body soon,' said Fry. 'Granger says he hid it behind a wall, but he was in such a panic that he can't remember where it was, or even what road he was on. He was genuinely lost. But the search teams are working their way through all the likely areas.'

'I suppose it's only a matter of time.'

'Let's hope to God it's soon. The Renshaws can't stand this much longer. It will overturn their lives completely. But nobody can go for ever without knowing the truth.'

'That's what I think,' said Cooper.

Fry stopped suddenly in the middle of the road, oblivious to the mud that splashed on to her shoes from a puddle. Cooper walked on, bending his head into the rain. He was moving towards the sound of the water that streamed through Withens, washing away the ash and eroding the surfaces down to the bedrock.

For a moment, he had seen two figures that were so alike they could have been mirror images distorted by the rain. They both looked lonely and isolated, and both stood with their shoulders stiff with tension and readiness for a fight. From twenty feet apart, they stared at each other. But the moment couldn't last.

Cooper couldn't bear to wait to see what would happen; he knew it was something he shouldn't be observing. It wasn't his business. All he wanted to do was reach his car and get out of the rain. Get out of Withens.

But while he was still within earshot, he heard someone speak. He wasn't sure whose voice he heard, and it was only one short word.

'Sis?'

THE TOUGH BLACK plastic that Ivan Matley's silage bales were wrapped in was practically indestructible. No biodegradable rubbish. It could be pierced by the steel spike on his tractor, but not by much else. So Matley was puzzled by the holes in the bag he had just lifted from the stack that afternoon. Rats? Foxes? Vandals? But the bag didn't really look as though it had been bitten or ripped. It looked more as if acid had eaten through the plastic, rotting it into small, ragged holes and causing discoloured streaks in the shiny black surface.

Matley climbed down from the cab of his tractor to take a closer look, in case the inner bag had been punctured and the silage inside had rotted. It had been standing here for years, and he wouldn't ever have expected to use it if the weather hadn't been so bad earlier on.

You could always tell good silage by the smell. But when he sniffed, he thought there was something about this bag that wasn't right. Perhaps air had got in through the holes and ruined it. Ivan Matley had smelled silage that had gone off before, and this was certainly foul enough.

The rest of the bales were lined up against the drystone wall, stacked three high. From this side, they looked in perfectly good condition – their outer bags nice and shiny, and tight. That was why he had never noticed anything wrong, though he had driven past them in the field many times. But the damage on the bale he had lifted seemed to have been at the back.

'Damn fly-tippers,' he said.

Matley felt sure that people using the track on the other side of the wall must have thrown something into his field. And to have damaged the plastic like that, it would have to have been something pretty toxic. Battery acid was his guess. If he looked down the back of the silage stack, between the bales and the wall, he reckoned he would find at least one old car battery that somebody had dumped because they couldn't be bothered to dispose of it properly. It wouldn't have mattered a bit to them if there had been livestock in the field, either. Cows were inquisitive – they might have licked at an abandoned battery and burned themselves on the spilled acid.

Matley walked round the end of the stack and tried to see behind it, but found the gap between the bales and the wall was too narrow for him to squeeze into. Now that he had passed fifty, he wasn't quite as slim as he used to be – as his wife kept reminding him.

But he could see more small, ragged holes in the black plastic near the centre of the bottom row. Yes, he was sure it was battery acid. What else would be corrosive enough to eat through his silage bags like that? And what else would smell quite so bad?

Puffing a bit, Matley climbed on to the top of the wall and balanced precariously on the toppings. It was the sort of trick he would have played hell about, if he had caught anyone else doing it. Once the toppings had been dislodged by people climbing over them, the rest of the wall would lose its stability and soon fall down. Then motorists would be complaining to the police because his cows were out on the lane again. He couldn't win.

'Why do I waste my bloody time?' he said.

But there was no one on the track this morning to hear him. He could see wheel ruts on the verge the other side of the wall, where someone had backed a car or van in from the lane. He wondered what else they might have fly-tipped. But he couldn't see anything in the grass or in the deep banks of whinberry between the wall and the track. Why should they bother dumping stuff on the track when they could chuck it over his wall? Out of sight, out of mind. And leave the poor old farmer to clear up the mess, as usual.

Matley edged gingerly along the wall, supporting himself on the stack of bales. The smooth surface of the bags felt cold and slightly damp to the touch. But beneath the plastic, the silage itself gave a little under the pressure of his hands and released a surge of warmth. His fingers left indentations in the plastic as he pushed himself along to a position where he could see what had been thrown over his wall. Rank grass was growing in the narrow space, but it didn't get much sun behind the silage stack, and it looked pale and sickly.

'And what the bloody hell's *that*?' he said.

IN THE OLD Rectory, the Renshaws' phone rang. Sarah Renshaw looked up at the clock in her sitting room. It was 3.45 p.m. precisely.

About the Author

STEPHEN BOOTH was born in the Lancashire mill town of Burnley and has remained rooted to the Pennines during his career as a newspaper journalist. He is well known as a breeder of Toggenburg goats and includes among his other interests folkore, the Internet, and walking in the hills of the Peak District, in which his crime novels are set. He lives with his wife, Lesley, in a former Georgian dower house in Nottinghamshire.

www.stephen-booth.com

Visit www.AuthorTracker.com for exclusive information on your favorite HarperCollins authors.